The One Who Got Away

L.A. Detwiler

OneMoreChapter

One More Chapter
an imprint of
HarperCollins*Publishers*
The News Building
1 London Bridge Street
London SE1 9GF

www.harpercollins.co.uk

This paperback edition 2020

First published in Great Britain in ebook format by
HarperCollins*Publishers* 2020

A catalogue record for this book
is available from the British Library

ISBN: 9780008324667

Set in Birka by Palimpsest Book Production Ltd, Falkirk
Stirlingshire

Printed and bound in Great Britain by
CPI Group (UK) Ltd, Croydon CR0 4YY

L.A. Detwiler is the *US Today* bestselling author of *The Widow Next Door* and a high school English teacher from Hollidaysburg, Pennsylvania. During her final year at Mount Aloysius College, she started writing her first fiction novel, which was published in 2015. She has also written articles that have appeared in several women's publications and websites. L.A. Detwiler lives in her hometown with her husband, Chad. They have five cats and a mastiff named Henry.

@ladetwiler1
@ladetwiler
/ladetwiler
www.ladetwiler.com

To my grandfather, Paul J. Frederick

'I became insane, with long intervals of horrible sanity'
– Edgar Allan Poe

Prologue

West Green, Crawley, West Sussex, UK
Smith Creek Manor Nursing Home
2019

Clutching the chilled silver edges of the picture frame, my shaking hands rattle the loose glass shards that rest on the photograph. The peeling wallpaper of my room is marked with a mystic yet clear warning. I smooth my thumb over the ridges of the familiar texture on the frame, looking down at the unassuming, smiling faces in the photograph. They had no idea that years later, they'd be pawns in this sick and twisted game. How could they, after all?

Claire brought me the photograph only a couple of days ago to replace the last one. Has it really only been a couple of days? So much has changed. I can't even keep track of the days, the hours, the minutes. Tears splash onto the glass shards, swirling in small, delicate puddles over our faces. I can feel my heart constricting, tightening, and I wonder if this is where it all ends.

'Charles, what is this? What *is* this?' I whisper into the room, my breathing laboured as the glow from my lamp dances over the message on the faded, sickly wallpaper. I shake my head, trying to work out what to do. I could push the call button over and over until one of them comes. I could wait for a nurse to get here. They would have to believe this, wouldn't they? They would have to see that I'm not mad, that this is real. They wouldn't be able to feed me lines about my warped perceptions of reality or this disease that is degrading my mind.

They'd *have* to see it.

Then again, who knows anymore. No one seems to believe me at all. Sometimes I don't even know if I can believe myself. I stand from my bed, setting the crushed picture frame down and leaning heavily on the tiny wooden bedside table. I pull my hand back, looking down to see blood dripping from where a piece of glass has sliced into me. The burning sensation as the redness cascades down my flesh makes my stomach churn.

What's happening to me?

I need to solve this, but I know I'm running out of precious time. He's made it clear through the message on the wallpaper that this is all coming to a devastating conclusion – and soon. I don't know when this story will end or exactly how. But this tower is ready to topple, crashing down and obliterating me in the process. I can't let that happen without uncovering the truth. I can't leave this place as the raving lunatic they all think I am. I have to stay strong and sort this out. Charles would want me to uncover this debauchery. They all need me to work this out, even if they don't realise it.

And most of all, I need to die satisfied that all has been set right, that injustices have been paid for. I can't leave this world with all the murky questions swirling in my mind, and with all the old guilts rattling about. Someone needs to pay for the sins of the past – and I don't think it should just be me.

I take a step towards the wall, my bones aching with the effort. I am careful not to slip, a few loose shards and specks of blood dancing on the floor in intoxicating patterns. I focus my gaze back on the words that taunt me.

I lean my forehead against the wall, not caring that the oozing liquid will be in my hair, on my face. I inhale the rusty scent of the dripping note in the corner of the room.

You're mine.

It trickles down, the blood an oddly blackish hue on the tired wallpaper of Room 316. I lift a trembling hand to the phrase, my finger hesitantly touching the 'Y'. Its tackiness makes me shudder. It's *real*. I'm not imagining it. I'm certain that it's all real. Taking a step back again, I slink down onto my bed, my cut hand throbbing with pain as I apply pressure to it. My fingers automatically pick at the fluff balls on the scratchy blanket. I should probably push the call button. I should get help, get bandaged. I can't force myself to move, though. I tremble and cry, leaning back against my bed.

I don't understand. There's so much I don't understand.

I rock myself gently, my back quietly thudding against the headboard. I think about all the horrors I've endured here and about how no one believes me. Like so many others, I'm stuck in an unfamiliar place without an escape. Unlike Alice, my wonderland is a nightmarish hell, a swirling phantasm of both mysticism and reality – and there are no friendly faces left at all to help me find my way home.

The babbling resident down the hall warned me. She did. On my first night here, she told me I wouldn't make it out alive. Now, her words are settling in with a certainty that chills my core. True, it wasn't the most revolutionary prophecy. No one comes to a nursing home expecting to get out alive, not really. Most of us realise that this place is a one-way ticket, a final stop. It's why they are so depressing, after all. It's why our children, our grandchildren, our friends are all suddenly busy when the prospect of visiting comes up in conversation. No one wants to come to this death chamber. No one wants to look reality in the face; the harsh, sickening reality of ageing, of decaying, of fading away.

Still, staring at the warning scrawled in blood on my wall, I know that maybe the woman down the hall meant something very different with her words. I'm going to die here, but not in the peaceful way most people imagine. I'm going to pay first. I'm going to suffer.

But why me? And why now, after so many years have passed since those horrific incidents of my past?

I don't know who to trust anymore. I don't know if I can trust myself. My mind is troubled, and my bones are weary. Maybe the nurses are right. It's all nothing more than this disease gnawing away at me.

But as I look one more time at the blood trickling on the wall, I shake my head. No. I'm not that far gone. I may be old, frail, and incapable of surviving on my own, but I haven't gone mad yet. I know what's real and what's not. And I'm certain this is demonically, insidiously real. Someone here wants to make me pay. Someone here has made it their mission to torment me, to toy with me. Someone here at the Smith Creek Manor Nursing Home wants to kill me. In fact, someone here has killed already.

My hands still shaking, I appreciate the truth no one else can see – it's just a matter of time until they do it again.

I lie back on the bed, the pieces of glass and the blood cradling me. Maybe, in truth, I resign myself to the fact that I'm helpless, that I'm at a mysterious Mad Hatter's mercy in this ghoulish game of roulette. I stare at the ceiling, the hairline crack beckoning my eyes to follow it. I lie for a long time, wondering what will happen next, debating what new torture awaits, and trying to predict what the final checkmate will be in this sickly game.

After all, no one gets out of here alive. Even the walls know that.

Chapter 1

Smith Creek Manor Nursing Home
2019: One month earlier

The first thing I notice as I'm led into Smith Creek Manor Nursing Home is that the creeping ivy vines strangle the windows. Up, up, up, the vines twist and turn, suffocating the glass panes, choking out any hope of the sun shining into the unsettling, old building. They are a prominent scar on the stone front of the building, marking it as forgotten and dilapidated. It's a violent disparity with the clean, modern look in the pamphlets they gave to us months ago.

'Charming, isn't it?' Claire beams as she squeezes my arm too tightly, leading me through the creaking front door of the majestic yet decaying building. As I cross the threshold into the draughty building, reality settles in.

There's no turning back. I live here now. People will walk by on their way to work or to restaurants or the shops, oblivious to me. They won't think about me or the others here as they try to shield themselves from the stone presence that is a blatant reminder of their own fate. I'll be the one no one's thinking about, abandoned in a place called home but feeling like nothing of the sort. The familiar, terrifying twinge in my chest aches, and I clutch at my heart. I squeeze my eyes shut, pausing inside the building as I gasp for air. It hurts to breathe, and the panic doesn't help. As my heart constricts, the familiar fear usurps me – this time, it will be too much to take. This time, the throbbing won't stop, and it will all end here, right now.

'Mum, are you all right?' Claire asks, patting my shoulder with a concern a mother should express for her child, not the other way around. The order of things is so warped during the ageing process. It takes a moment for me to respond. I try to catch my breath, leaning on the wall, my fingers resting on the scratchy, chilled stone. It's happening again. Why does this always happen?

After a long moment where I wonder if my lungs are going to keep working, the feeling passes. I open my eyes to look at my daughter, her face contorted with fear. This is why I'm here. This is what put me here, I know. I probably *do* need to be here, but that doesn't make it any easier.

I take another deep breath, nodding at my daughter in assurance. She stares for a moment, probably deciding what to do. But I'm here now, and this is the best place for me – or so everyone says. Thus, she leads me forward, and we methodically trudge further and further into the cave that is Smith Creek Manor. Claire bubbles on about how lovely the statue is inside the door and how bright and airy the entrance is. I nod silently, knowing why she's raving about architectural features. She wants this to work out. No – correction – she *needs* this to work out. As a fifty-two-year-old divorcee, she's got more pressing matters to worry about than her daft old mother who is incapable of living on her own. She needs to get back to her job, the life she's created for herself here in Crawley. She wants me to be happy here to quell her rising guilt. I understand. I don't blame her. But it doesn't mean I find Smith Creek Manor charming or likeable or anything of the sort. I don't want to be here, even if my thudding chest and exhausted mind tell me I probably need to be.

It's true, I'm being unfair. Any place but 14 Quail Avenue would be a disappointment to me right now. I miss my familiar house in Harlow. I miss Charles. I miss my marriage, my life and the place I called home for so long. This isn't home. Crawley hasn't been home for decades, not for me at least. I suppose in many ways, even all those years ago when I lived here during my teenage years, it never was home. In fact, for many years, it was a dark stain in my life, a reminder of all that can go wrong in the world. And for so many years, I've thought all of this was in my past – buried deep, deep in the past.

I know it's pointless to get nostalgic or angry. It's all done. It's over now. The *for sale* sign in front of our house in Harlow was changed to *sold*. My few belongings were packed, the finances and paperwork were taken care of. I'm here. There's no turning back.

It pains me to think about 14 Quail Avenue having new tenants. I hate the thought of some new couple dancing underneath the kitchen arch where Charles used to kiss me on the cheek before leaving for work. I loathe the thought of some frilly woman redoing the wallpaper that I loved so much in the sitting room or modernising the charming fireplace that Charles built by hand. Pain throbs in my chest at the thought of the new couple's children or grandchildren playing with toy cars and dolls in the spot of the sitting room where my dear Charles fell over, dead, one year ago. I hate them. I hate this place. I hate it all.

'Ms Evans, welcome. So lovely to see you. Welcome to Smith Creek Manor. What a lovely choice for your new home,' a woman in shiny way-too-high heels offers. She shakes Claire's hand before rubbing my shoulder. Thus, the patronising gestures begin. I shrug it off. I know I'm just sensitive today.

'Now, let me show you to your residence. You're so lucky, a third-floor room. You've got one of the best views here,' the chipper woman announces as her bone-coloured shoes clack on the floor, her feet landing close together with each step as her hips sway with confidence. She acts as if she's on a fashion runway instead of in a cold, damp corridor in a home for the dying that reeks of medicine and hospital. She leads us down the corridor and through a doorway that has a code on it. Above the code box is a bright coloured painting. It's as if they're trying to disguise the fact that this is only one step above incarceration.

Claire and the lady – has she told me her name? I've forgotten – chatter on about meal timetables and activities and all sorts of things, both trying to convince themselves that this is a perfectly acceptable arrangement and that I'm not coming here to die. Once inside the locked door, we wait for the lift to take me to my new view. I peruse the open area. The smell of this place matches the depressing sights. All around, people in various states of decay clutter the common room, some sitting stooped over in chairs, some sleeping. A few traipse about, dragging their feet on the carpet and muttering incoherently. Only a handful look conscious, reading a book or staring at a telly that looks like the first set Charles ever bought for our house.

The word *death* floats above these people, tainting the air with a musk of disintegration mixed with rubbing alcohol. That smell. How does one describe it? A sterile crispness infiltrated with what one would suppose melancholy smells like if it had a describable stench. It assaults my nose as the lift dings and the doors drag open, the fluorescent lights blinding me as I creep into the metal box. The doors screech closed, a grating noise that makes me anxious. I can't help but feel like I've been enshrouded in my funeral clothes as the doors shut and we float up, up, up, the lift clunking and sputtering like a death trap. My heart pounds as I lean on the wall, my armpits getting profusely sweaty at the claustrophobic feeling. The lift grinds and creaks, and I may be imagining it, but it feels wobbly.

The ride seems to take forever, and, at a point, I wonder if it's broken. When it slams to a stop, the doors take an interminable amount of time to creak open. Finally I see the bright lights of the corridor and I'm thankful, shoving my way out to escape the metal box of death. If I never have to get in the thing again, it would be too soon.

'The lift's just a bit slow. But I think it's a good thing,' the tour-guide woman announces as she and Claire follow me out.

I don't understand how anything about the lift is a good thing. It's just another reminder that this place isn't anything like we thought it would be. My heart races as I consider the possibility of riding in that box again, the slowness of its heavenly ascent jarring.

My heartbeat steadies, and I take a few breaths. It wouldn't do to let the lift ride get me worked up. After all, the doctor is always chattering incessantly about my heart troubles, palpitations, and stroke risks. He's always trying to help us prepare for what to expect with the dementia as well. He *reassures* me with the promise of lucid days and moments amidst the days of confusion, as if that's a true comfort to the soul to know that even though my mind is failing, there will be moments everything is clear.

Sometimes, I'm convinced he just likes to use medical

jargon to sound important. Sometimes, though, I think maybe I'm actually falling apart, especially on days when the familiar pain resurfaces and I can't catch my breath. Regardless, his warnings worked because eventually, it convinced Claire that living at home alone wasn't suitable for me anymore. She'd ensured me that it would be safer for me to be in a *residence* like this, as she called it. My heart problems mixed with the early onset of dementia are a dangerous concoction, it would seem.

Claire's busy, too. Her job in marketing keeps her floating around from place to place, which is perhaps how old what's-his-name she was married to escaped with his flighty heart. With her travelling so often for work, it would be impossible for me to live with her – not that I'd want to impose on her life like that. Thus, she'd pleaded and begged for me to move somewhere more suitable and somewhere closer to her so she could spend time with me when she was home.

I hadn't wanted to give up my home in Harlow, of course. True, most days the place felt like a mausoleum or a shrine dedicated to a life I could no longer live. There wasn't much left for me on Quail Avenue except struggles and uncertainties. Getting around was exceedingly more difficult, and keeping up with the empty, chilled house was no longer easy. Then, of course, there were the incidents the neighbours were quick to report to Claire – like they've never forgotten anything before. Things were never the same on Quail Avenue since Charles passed, but at least there, I had memories and familiarity. I had some remnants of my dignity and privacy. I had a sense of home.

I'd fought Claire for months about moving out, insisting I could handle myself. In truth, I suppose I wasn't afraid of going out in the same house Charles did. Perhaps a piece of me thought that if we were connected in our manner of death, it would be a good omen for the next life – something I try not to think too much about. However, months of Claire's nagging coupled with a few scary moments on my own finally managed to free me of my devotion to living alone. Perhaps it was also the fact I was so tired. It had all become way too much.

Nonetheless, coming back to Crawley, well, that hadn't been easy. The heart palpitations seemed to worsen at the idea, an old fear resurfacing at the thought of stepping onto this haunted ground. I found myself evaluating what I was doing. Why had I even considered coming?

Claire, of course. To be near my daughter. I was willing to risk anything, to face any fears, to make her happy – and maybe I felt the need to protect her.

I'd always hated that Claire had settled down here, an area where I had lived in my late teen years. It had been one of the darkest periods of my life, a time I would do well to forget. Sometimes life is full of surprises, and not always in a good way.

After Charles died and Claire, in the middle of starting her life over again after her marriage fell apart, announced her move to Crawley, I almost collapsed.

'What do you mean, Crawley?' I had asked, my heart fluttering.

'I just need a change, Mum. I need somewhere peaceful that's still easy to commute from. I've found a lovely little flat in Langley Green in Crawley.'

I felt as though my heart was lodged in my throat. I'd protected Claire from the past for so many years. Charles and I didn't talk about it. We'd moved on from Crawley and never, ever looked back. But to hear my adult daughter talking about those places – it was too much.

'I don't understand,' I murmured, trying to maintain my composure.

Claire sighed, turning the cup of tea in her hands across the table from me. 'Mum, don't get angry. I know you and Dad don't like to talk about those years in Crawley. I know it was complicated. But a few weeks before Dad died, I don't know, I just got curious. I'm in my fifties, and I don't know that much about you two, in truth. I never knew my grandparents. I know you didn't like to talk about them, but it's like the both of you wiped away your past. It was a hidden secret hanging over us. I got curious. Dad told me about Langley Green and how much he loved it there. He told me about how you two met, about how he would travel to West Green to visit you. He told me how much he loved you from the beginning. I don't know, I guess after he died, I just felt like it was a sign. Maybe that's where I'm meant to be. It seems like a good place to start over.'

Vomit rose in my throat. I tried not to cry. *How could you, Charles? After so many years, you planted this idea in her head?* Searing anguish I thought had died decades ago had risen in my chest.

'What else did he say?' I asked tentatively. Fears rose. But there are things even Charles didn't know. There were secrets even Charles couldn't tell.

'The same thing you two always said when I asked you. "It was complicated." Mum, I know Crawley was a dark place in those years. But I don't know, I think I could be happy there. I think it would be nice to be somewhere strange yet familiar in a weird way. You lived in West Green, close to where I'll be. Dad lived there. My grandparents, whom I never got to meet, lived there.'

That conversation haunted me for weeks. I was angry at Charles. I was terrified for Claire as old fears surfaced. But eventually, I'd talked myself down.

Decades and decades had passed. It wasn't the same place anymore. Heck, most of the people I once knew were probably long since gone, moved on in one way or another.

Still, I didn't understand why Charles would open such wounds. After trying to escape from Crawley's clutches for all of those years, to have my daughter reconnect me with it – it was the thing of nightmares, enough to drive me truly bonkers if I'd let it.

Yet, even after insisting to Claire I'd never go back, no matter how much she begged – here I am. Back in Crawley's hands, back in West Green more specifically.

It was all so long ago, I remind myself. It doesn't matter anymore. But I know that in truth, it always matters. It will always matter. I shudder at the thought, tension rising as I try to shove it back down.

As I follow the woman and Claire down the corridor, peeking in at the faces I will be seeing too much of from now on, I sigh. Now that I'm here, facing the prospect of a life staring at these sterile walls, I'm having regrets. Maybe I should've fought a little harder. Maybe this was a bad choice. This place rattles me, strangling me like the vines creeping up the stone walls outside.

Or perhaps I'm just being paranoid. Of course Smith Creek Manor wouldn't feel like home yet. How could it? I just need to give it a chance. I'm tired from mulling it all over incessantly, my brain throbbing already. In a few days, I'll adjust to the atmosphere, and it won't seem so terrible. I just need time.

I peek in at the rooms of my neighbours as we parade down the corridor to my own. A man sits on the single chair in his room, staring at the telly. In another room on the right, a woman rocks what appears to be a baby doll, singing a lullaby. I pause at the opening to another living space, perusing the scene with fascination and horror. A woman stands, lopsided in the centre of her space, half of her face distorted. She is completely naked, and she walks in tiny circles by her bed, singing the words to some unrecognisable song. She laughs in between choruses, over and over, her sagging skin marked with burns and scars.

I want to peel my eyes away, but I can't. The storm that is this woman is on full display. How long has she been stuck in this merry-go-round of terror? Why isn't anyone stopping her? It's unbelievable that a human being would behave this way – or be allowed to behave this way in such a place. What is this? What is this, indeed. I peel my eyes away, feeling embarrassed for witnessing her in this state.

I continue on down the corridor, room after room presenting new views. It's like I'm wandering about a zoo, staring in at the exhibits of various species. Some mad, some sane, some essentially gone. All of the doors are open, wide open, except one. When we get to Room 312, I notice that the door is closed. For some reason, it's like the door calls to me. I think about reaching out and touching that knob, curious what the door could be hiding. Inside, I hear a cough, weighty and raspy. It startles me. I don't know what or who is behind the door to 312, but there's something unnerving about the space. A chill rattles my body and I shiver, a darkness surrounding the room even from the corridor.

But it's also unsettling to see so many doors wide open, patients in all state of dress and activity out in the open. Is there no privacy here? Has everyone truly lost their sense of dignity that they'll let everyone peer into their lives in their tiny little rooms? Will I lose mine as well? Will I even be me here? I shudder involuntarily as I plod towards the new 'home' that awaits me.

The woman in heels leads us down the corridor on the third floor, down, down to the very end. She stops at the room on the left, which is next to a staircase. There is, of course, a locked door at the staircase, the tiny code box beside it reminding me that I'm not free anymore. I suppose escaping isn't something they look favourably on around here.

'Here we are, dear. Room 316. Your new home. Welcome. I do hope we've managed to arrange the things your daughter sent over correctly. If not, we'll be happy to help you set things up just as you wish. Come on, let's get settled in and meet your roommate.'

I stop at the threshold of 316, staring in at what has become my whole world. My home with Charles was never a castle. It was a modest house, tiny to most. But compared to this space, it was a palace.

I step inside, willing myself not to cry. Claire is here, after all. I can't break down. She needs me to be strong. I can't be more of a burden than I have been already. I peer about the room that is more hospital than home, and my stomach plummets. This is it. This is where I'll reside for the rest of my days, the icy, bog-standard room surrounding me with its monotonous bleakness. I shake my head at the prospect, my hand reaching up to tug at my long, stringy hair.

'Ms Evans, I'd like to introduce you to your roommate, Ms Rose Wright. All right, Rose?' The woman prances over to the other side of the conjoined room, a curtain that presumably divides our halves pulled to one side so I have a full view of my new companion. I hate that I have a roommate here. Certainly, Claire told me I'd have my own room, didn't she? Most facilities do, after all, offer individual rooms. Why is this place different? I shudder at the realisation that already, my new home isn't meeting my expectations.

I glance over to the woman on the other side of the dividing curtain, trying to move beyond the fact that I won't be alone. She is sitting up in bed, leant against a pillow, her mouth partially open. Drool drips visibly down her chin, and she's wearing a transparent blue nightshirt. She stares, deadpan, straight ahead at what, I can't determine. Her breathing is raspy, every single inhalation rattling something in her chest. On her bedside table, a statue of what seems to be a religious figure perches. I can't tell exactly what it's supposed to be. It's chipped and warped. Its demeanour is more ghoulish than holy. Angled, it appears to watch her, its unseemly eyes bulging out. I don't like it. I wonder if she hates it too.

Behind the statue is a noticeboard, just like I have on my side of the room. A child's drawing of what appears to be a rose is pinned there, centred on the board. At least I will be able to recall her name, I realise. Rose, just like the picture. I lock it into my mind. Wouldn't do to forget my roommate's name, after all.

Our fearless tour guide and master of ceremonies plods forward, walking to Rose's side to stroke her thin, dishevelled hair. The woman doesn't move. I blink, turning to Claire. I don't know why, but I recoil at the sight of this Rose woman, more dead than alive, who fights for every breath. Her delicateness irks me, stirring an uneasiness I can't explain. It makes me feel guilty for thinking these things about a suffering woman. Nonetheless, the woman doesn't offer any reaction to my presence. Our tour guide looks back to us, smiling gently.

'Rose won't be much of a bother to you, I suppose,' she reassures, and although the words sound harsh, her eyes are kind. I nod slightly, offering a smile to the woman who isn't even looking at me. I trudge over to the window, needing to get some air in this stifling room. I wrap my arms around myself, trying to counter the rising panic in my chest. I can sense the tour-guide woman and Claire exchanging some kind of look or communication behind me. The woman is probably trying to soothe the rising guilt in Claire for leaving me in a place that feels so suffocating. I look out into the morning, taking in the view of the courtyard, the U-shape of the building offering me a look at the inside-back wall of Smith Creek Manor. Another resident's window sits across from me. I stare, the outline of a person – a man, perhaps? – standing in the window. Someone else is looking out into the courtyard as well. I should find it comforting, I suppose, that I'm not alone, that someone else is lost in thought at this place. My mind is numb, though. There are too many things to absorb, and I'm not ready to take it all in just yet.

'Isn't it a lovely view? I told you the view up here is just grand,' the woman says. I hate that she's trying to sell me on this place. I'm already here. Plus, there would be no selling me on this place. The view is claustrophobic, if you ask me. I can't see the outside world, not really – just the grass, the air between the wings of Smith Creek Manor. It's like I'm trapped by the stone building, the rooms of patients my only view.

I look out, training my eyes on the roof, on the sky, on the great beyond. I wonder if I'm staring in the direction of Quail Avenue. My mind conjures up an image of the tiny house squeezed between the neighbours. I can picture that alabaster colour, those tiny shutters Charles painted in a stunning yellow. I yearn to feel the front door, my hand shakily touching the cold, harsh glass of the window instead.

I peer down now, staring at the gazebo that rests in the courtyard way, way below. When my eyes catch sight of the ground, absolute terror seizes me, grappling with my heart like a clutching, clawing fist. What I see when I look out the window convinces me of one thing I've been fearing: I can't do this. Not here. I'm not going to be safe here at all.

Missing West Green Girl Found; Corpse Shows Distressing Signs of Tampering
West Green, Crawley, West Sussex
13 June 1959

The West Sussex Constabulary has reported the discovery of the body of Miss Elizabeth McKinley of Greenville Avenue, West Green, around dawn yesterday, 12 June 1959. The body of Miss McKinley was uncovered in a skip at the current construction site for the new Crawley Hospital. A worker found what appeared to be a large trunk in the skip that seemed out of place. Upon opening the trunk and discovering what appeared to be limbs, the police were called to the scene to investigate. Detectives later arrived, and a chief detective is currently on the case.

Several other trunks included the remains of what was determined to be Elizabeth McKinley after further investigation. Investigators also revealed the presence of bite marks on various limbs and pieces of the dismembered corpse. It seems that the bite marks were made post-mortem.

The deceased, Elizabeth McKinley, 19, daughter of Mr and Mrs Jonathan McKinley, disappeared from her home 26 May. Mr and Mrs McKinley had left to attend a dinner in Brighton. Miss McKinley had stayed behind due to illness. Upon returning home, Mr and Mrs McKinley found signs of a break-in, although no valuables were removed. Miss McKinley had not been heard from since 26 May by any family or friends.

Searches have turned up few clues, the constabulary notes. West Green has been on edge since the disappearance of the girl that neighbours called 'godly, sweet, and kind.' Elizabeth McKinley was engaged to be married to Paul Hazenstab, also of West Green. Their wedding was to be announced in the coming weeks.

Police are calling the death 'a brutal homicide of the darkest kind', in reference to the disturbing bite marks found on her thigh, chest, and left arm. The dismemberment of her body has also raised concerns that this was an act of revenge or hostility. Several West Green residents interviewed mentioned fears that a deranged killer is on the loose, but Chief Constable Warren of the West Sussex Constabulary wishes to reassure the residents of Crawley that there is not enough evidence at this time to establish a motive or to stir such fears.

'We will be investigating,' Chief Constable Warren noted, 'and we will not stop until we find the savage murderer who took this sweet girl's life in such a sinister way. We ask the people of Crawley to be vigilant and to report any strange occurrences.'

Arrangements for the funeral of the deceased have not yet been announced as the investigation is still underway.

The pencil between my teeth, I gnaw and gnash, closing my eyes and thinking about how it all transpired. A surge of warmth flashes through me as I recall the supple flesh between my teeth. I recall how my tongue danced at its surface. The gnashing of my teeth against her flesh quenched, if only for a quick moment, the primal urge within me. The suppleness of her arm, her chest, her inner thigh – all so satisfying yet also stirring of a deeper hunger.

I'd known that first kill would be delectable – but I hadn't realised just how so.

I sit back in my chair, my fingers finding the tip of the pencil as my teeth incessantly chomp down, almost as if of their own volition.

I've done it.

I've accomplished the first.

I'd always imagined the first to be the hardest when I'd gone over my plans. The logistics of it, sure. But also the feel of the life exiting a body. It had excited me, the mere thought of it driving me to a place of utter joy rarely known in all of my years of living. I'd worried, though, if it would meet my expectations. What if the taste of death wasn't enough?

It was a fear I've always battled with, a question that often held me back. But there was no more holding me down. I'd finally risen up. I'd finally done what I'd always needed to do, what I'd always been capable of doing.

I'd found myself, my strength. A grin paints itself on my face. Brilliant. There is no other word for it. I'm finally brilliant.

Bloody brilliant.

I've done it, after all. I've finally achieved it. I carried it out, succeeded in the first step of the master plan. I finally feel a surge of life pulsing in my blood. It's as if her death has incited a new energy, a new sense of life within me. It's a foreign feeling, yet it's one that I feel like I've always been craving. All of those years of being lost, of searching. I found it. It's paradoxical yet it completely makes sense. I finally feel excited about something. Dazzled by the feel of death, I now know I can be the one to wield so much power. I can choose when and how they leave this world. And I get to be there in the final moments, to see them beg, to hear their desperate pleas for another day. My lips curve into a crooked grin.

I'm the one in control. Who would've ever expected it?

They wouldn't have. It's always the quietest sheep, the ones on the outskirts, that surprise you the most. Aren't you surprised now? *I think, my mind flashing over her stoic face. She would be so surprised now. My hand rubs my forehead, leaving the pencil.*

I had been patient, my plan reviewed over and over for

months before claiming the first one on the list. I'm no fool. I'm not. I'm sensible and smart. I'm capable. I'd taken my time after picking the girls. I have my list of chosen ones. I know the order, the plan. I won't ruin it or rush it. I'll be successful. I'm no quitter. I'll do it right.

I'd been observant for months. It isn't hard to learn about others if you just pay attention. Few people pay attention, I've come to realise. But I do. I always do. I watch. I study. I learn routines and entrances. I examine the possible entry routes and the escapes. I peruse timetables and plans to find just the right time. It has to be exact.

I'd determined Elizabeth would be first because she was the least exciting. She was a quiet, submissive girl. I knew she wouldn't resist much. Which I knew wouldn't be as satisfying – but it would be less risky.

Still, she wasn't as gratifying as the final one will be. I know this already. I've thought ahead, you see. I'm saving the exciting one, the wily one, for last. Oh, yes, that last one will be a masterpiece of a kill. I'll work hard and perfect my craft. I'll master the rules of the game before I tackle the final one.

Patience is a virtue. That's what I always learned. Patience. Patience. Patience.

She's special, that last one. Even before I allowed myself to recognise the thirst in me and welcomed it to the top of my consciousness, I'd perhaps known it would be her. She's always drawn me in. Why? I don't know what it is. Maybe it's her spirit, that zestful way she walks and talks. Maybe it's the fire in her eyes that reminds me of her. *I don't know.*

It's hard to pinpoint. But when you know, you know, whether it's love, lust, or some other form of the two. For three years, she's drawn me in, a moth circling the flickering light but never getting close enough to get zapped.

Soon enough, she'll be the moth, entangled and entranced by me. I'll be the one wielding the light and then snatching her wings before she can get away. It'll be me. All me.

I shake my head, taking the pencil from between my teeth and tossing it across the room. Dammit. I'm getting ahead of myself now. Bloody hell, it doesn't do to get ahead. The plan is carefully laid. It's why I spent so much time plotting it out. It needs to be perfect. One misstep, and that glorious, final moment of power won't come.

I must be patient, stay calm. The task has started. I can't lose my mind now. I've got to keep with it, to be careful. It won't do to get caught now. It'll ruin everything.

I tap my fingers on the edge of the table, calming my mind, lasering it in on Elizabeth. Recall the details. Think about it all. You need to perfect this. You need to master your craft. Do a good job.

Elizabeth. My mind trains itself on her, and I think back to the tale I've written, the ending to her story that began with my meticulous, godlike planning.

Once I'd learned of the dinner invitation, I knew my opportunity would arise. I'd overheard Elizabeth talking about the evening with some friends in the town centre, complaining about all the fuss her parents would make her go through when she'd rather just stay home and spend time with her fiancé. She made a plan to feign illness, and I knew my time had come.

The night of the dinner would be the perfect time to strike, I'd decided quickly. I knew how girls like her worked. I just had to be calm and collected. I had to be sure. I'd do some watching and waiting, just to ensure I was correct and that she didn't back out of her plan. And then, once all was set, I had to make it fast. No luxuriating in the actual kill this time. The first would have to be efficient. This would not be a pleasure kill, not completely. I told myself I would not afford myself that bonus. It would be all about the craft, the tactic, the mastering of the art.

There would be time enough to feed my fancies and to bask in the excitement of it all.

Taking her life had been the easy part, much simpler than I'd once imagined. I am strong, and she was so weak. Females are all so, so delicate. It makes them beautiful, but so easy to kill. Moving her to another location to handle her body, to leave my mark – that had been more challenging. But I know all the alleys in town. I know the most inconspicuous routes. I know a lot about West Green that so many overlook.

And I'm also always up for a challenge.

I fold the newspaper article and tuck it into the wooden box underneath the unopened post. I close the box shut with a grin, wiping my hands on my stiff trousers. I've done it. And they have no clue it was me. The fools have no clue.

'Deranged killer'. They think it's the work of a 'deranged killer'!

I laugh at the thought. They think they know. They think

they have it all figured out. But they have no idea. They don't know my master plan.

And I can't wait to show it to them, one by beautiful one.

Chapter 2

West Green, Crawley, West Sussex
13 June 1959

'Adeline Walker, you aren't going, so I don't know why you bothered taking all that time to get ready,' my mother spits. I gawk at her as she twirls the pearl earrings in her lobes. I think about how her red lips and eyeshadow are way too much, even for a woman like her. Hand on her hip, she stands at the other side of our dining room table, her eyes lasering into me as if she can cause me to spontaneously combust.

I stare vehemently back. 'For Christ's sake, Mum, I'm nineteen. You can't keep me hostage forever, especially if you're so damn worried about me being a spinster.'

'Adeline Walker, you will not speak to me like that in my house.'

'Then maybe I'll scurry on out of *Dad's* house,' I spew back, putting the emphasis on *Dad*. She hates that I'm a daddy's girl. I think it makes her jealous that he gives me more attention than her.

'Enough. Now look. I know you have these lovely plans, but I'm sorry. With no updates from the police on Elizabeth's killer, it's not safe.'

I raise an eyebrow. 'Weren't you the one who swore up and down that moving to West Green would be just lovely when you pulled me out of school three years ago to come to this beastly town?'

'That's enough, Adeline. I hope someday you realise what you have here. Two parents who love you, a father with a good job. Honestly. What more could you want?'

'To go on my date with Charles and have a little fun.'

'Fun is what got you into trouble in the last town, if you recall. I won't have you ruining your reputation again. It's been three years, Adeline. Three years since we had to move away. You were lucky we could run away from it all last time. I won't have you ruining yourself now.'

I roll my eyes, anger flaring at the mention of what happened. I was young. I was a little reckless, yes. But I was a girl who followed her heart.

'You act like I murdered someone,' I spew.

'It could've been worse. If we'd stayed, you'd have actually ended up pregnant at sixteen. And then what?'

'We're not talking about this,' I argue. I hate when she brings up the past. I shudder at her words, thinking about all that she doesn't know. All that's happened since we moved to West Green. All that's happened in the past few months.

I return my focus to the conversation at hand. 'Well, you should be chuffed then, *Mother*, that I'm getting serious. I'm nineteen, and I'm in a serious, steady relationship. After all, isn't that what you want? You did mention that West Green could provide me with a "suitable man", didn't you?'

Mother rolls her eyes, sighing. 'A factory worker isn't exactly what I had in mind.'

I sneer at her blatant disdain towards Charles Evans, who hails from Langley Green and not money. This infuriates my mother to no end. When she meant we could find me a "suitable man" here in West Green, I believe she was hoping we'd find one from a wealthy family who was naive about my somewhat lacklustre background. A man like Oliver, whom mother still thinks I have a chance of reconciling with. If only she knew the truth.

Instead, to her dismay, I'd met Charles Evans at the train station in Northgate. I suppose at first she thought he was a phase, a rebound after Oliver. But three months later, I think she knows better. I think she sees what I've known since that first night – Charles is the one I love. And she couldn't be more peeved at the thought of her daughter marrying a working-class man with no social standing. If I'm being honest, this only makes Charles even more appealing to me.

'All the more reason for me to go out tonight. Besides, what's the worst that could happen?' I ask, fiddling with my nails.

'You could end up dead. Aren't you a little bit afraid? Elizabeth lived a few streets over. I'm quite alarmed. The killer's still out there. He's probably just waiting for his next victim. I won't have my only daughter be one of his tallies.' She crosses her arms in a defiant, dramatic gesture. Of course, she would make Elizabeth's murder about us. It always has to be about us.

'Better to be murdered than courting some factory boy, huh?' I ask defiantly, awaiting the tumultuous explosion that is certain to come.

'Don't be dim. You barely even know this bloke. With a girl dead in town – *murdered* –you can't be too careful.'

'Mum, are you really suggesting that Charles had something to do with Elizabeth?' I shake my head, incredulous. This is ridiculous, even by Nora Walker standards.

'I'm just saying you barely know him.' She tosses her hands up as if she's truly innocent.

I roll my eyes. 'So because you deem him too poor for our standards, you toss murder accusations around? You're off your trolley.'

'And you're making some bloody awful choices,' she stabs back, her words harsh and angry.

'I don't care what you say. I'm going. Charles will be with me. We're just going for a quick stroll, after all. We won't be gone long. Besides, with all the roaming patrols around, the killer would be a fool to strike again. And I'm no Elizabeth, anyway. The girl always was a bit of a muggins, if you ask me.'

'Adeline, how dare you speak of the dead that way. Where are your manners?' Mum uncrosses her arms, leaning on the chair nearby. I avert my eyes to the ground. I always go too far. I always take it way too far.

'Sorry, Mum. You're right,' I admit, sighing, fiddling with my hands. 'It's awful what happened. She didn't deserve that, no matter what.' My words are sombre, my guilt real.

Not that I'd ever admit it to my mother, but I do feel a bit anxious about the whole thing. It's not every day you hear about someone from your town being murdered and chopped up, her body dumped in some skip like a discarded sandwich. I shiver at the thought, imagining Elizabeth's sweet face, her long brown hair, as she was hacked into pieces and shoved in a trunk. What did she feel in those last moments? When did she know it was all over? Did she suffer? I take a deep breath, disturbed by the thought of it all. In my opinion, she was too goody two-shoes for her own good. But she didn't deserve to die. Not like that.

I think about what Mum said. She's probably right. The psycho is probably still out there, lurking in a corner, waiting for someone else to add to his tally. Elizabeth had no enemies. None. Everyone thought of her as sweeter than sweet, and there was no one who would want revenge. Plus, only a true psychopath would do that to a body. Bite marks? That's bloody terrifying.

For a moment, I think that maybe I should stay home. Maybe I should tell Charles I can't make it out. Then again,

I miss him. I want to spend time with him away from mother's scowl and her scrutinising gaze. You can't live your life in fear, I suppose. Besides, with Charles Evans, I know I'm safe. He'll protect me.

'Does this mean you're staying home?' Mother asks, the *I-win* look painting itself on her face. Her ruby red lips widen as she prepares for my confession of defeat.

I raise my gaze to meet hers. 'Don't be ridiculous,' I snap.

She groans. 'Adeline Walker, honestly,' she bellows, but I march to the front door to grab a light pullover from the hook.

'Goodnight, Mum. Be sure to lock the door. Wouldn't want you to go missing, would we?' I tuck myself into the pullover, yank open the door, and offer her a little wave as she gapes at me.

And before Mum can chase after me, I dash out the door to wait for Charles. He is the escape from my house I desperately need.

*

'Surprised your mother let you leave the house,' Charles says a few minutes later when he finds me outside of a house just down the street, near the church. He slides to a stop on his bicycle, propping it against the wall after he dismounts.

I sit on the wall near the hedges, staring up at the sky, my feet kicking against the stones as I wait for him to come over to me. He helps me off the wall, wrapping his arms around me as he kisses me boldly on the lips. I giggle when he pulls away, happy to see him.

'She's probably got the whole town out looking for me by now,' I say as I turn to look at him, his hand in mine as we walk on. His dark hair is slicked back and his steel-blue eyes shimmer in the sunlight.

'Well, Addy, you can't blame her, can you? It's all the town's been talking about since Elizabeth went missing. All the investigations, all the questions. Just has everyone on edge. And now with the body found and the bloody bastard on the loose, well, I understand why she's worried, you know? You need to be careful.'

Charles wraps his arms around me, pulling me in for another kiss as we pause in the middle of the walkway. I like how his rough, manly hands wrap around my waist, how his lips feel on mine. I'm consumed by him, by us. He is nothing like Oliver Parsons, the mistake I dated before Charles. No, Charles is different, a working man, a strong man. A kind man. With him, I feel safe, even with a potential homicidal lunatic on the loose.

'Usual route?' he asks as we walk down the path, past the rows of houses and the few construction sites around. I shudder when we pass a skip, thinking about Elizabeth.

'Absolutely,' I reply, smiling as we walk under the blue sky towards our destination.

We stroll on, gallivanting towards the town centre, neighbours waving as they scatter about. Charles and I are a common sight these days, him calling on me whenever his relief from work at the factory allows it, to my mother's true agitation.

Charles tells me about his workday as I listen, interested in the other side of his life I can't begin to understand. Mum thinks it's improper for a girl like me to work. After all, she reminds me, Dad's job is good enough that neither of us need even dream of working. She thinks that's fortunate. A part of me thinks that's a shame. It would be interesting to get out of the house and to have somewhere to be.

When we reach the town centre, I glance around at the neighbours wandering around, caught up in their own activities. The shops are bustling with activity today. In our travels, though, we see several constables patrolling, reminding us that a lot has changed. I shove aside thoughts of Elizabeth once more as we take a seat on a bench outside of the post office, stopping to people watch and to catch up.

'Addy, hello,' a voice says, and I turn to see my best friend, Phyllis Barnes, skipping over. She waves, her mum by her side. Her mum offers a smile, but I notice she studies Charles with interest. Phyllis' mother and mine are close friends, so I'm sure she's heard quite a bit about how inappropriate of a match Charles is for me. I brush the thought aside.

'What are you two doing?' Phyllis asks, sliding over beside me as I budge up to make room. Charles nods at her politely.

'Just escaping from the clutches of Mum,' I reply honestly. Phyllis groans, knowing what my mum is really like. Phyllis knows a lot of things about me, things no one else does. I lean on her shoulder, happy to see her.

'Lucky you. Wish I could find a bloke of my own. Charles, have any mates in the factory?' she asks.

'Got a few looking for someone to be sweet on. I'll check with them. One commutes to work with me.'

'You do know there are some jobs opening up in Manor Royal, don't you?' she asks. 'Would be good if you're thinking of settling down, you know?' Phyllis winks at me, and I shake my head. She's been obsessed with asking if Charles is going to propose. I assure her over and over we're not at that stage yet, but secretly, I can't help hoping, wondering where it will all go, if we'll settle in Crawley. Although being close to my mother would be an annoyance at times, it would be enjoyable to perhaps see her discomfort at her precious daughter marrying a 'commoner' – although even with Dad's advertising job, we're far from the royalty she so believes. You'd think we're descendants of the Queen herself.

'So,' I reply, trying to change the subject.

'Terrible thing, that story about Elizabeth, huh? Such a sweet girl. Honestly. Who would do something so awful to her? I overheard my dad talking to Mum about it. Said the bite marks were deep and bloody and all over the girl. Even on her unmentionables. Disgraceful, isn't it? Can you imagine? And to chop her up and put her in the skip like rubbish. I don't even understand. It all just makes me ill,' Phyllis says.

My stomach churns at the thought. Phyllis' dad is one of the constables, so she gets all sorts of inside information. Today's, though, sends a shiver through me. I find my eyes darting around, as if at any moment, the killer could jump out and strangle me. Suddenly, the town that once felt dull feels lethal.

'They have any leads? Any motives?' I prod, squeezing Charles' hand for comfort. He squeezes it back, a gesture I've come to love in our few months together.

Phyllis shakes her head. 'That's the truly scary part. They've got nothing. Nothing at all. Whoever did it has covered his tracks well. I don't know if anyone has any idea. But golly, isn't it just terrifying? The killer out on the loose? Do you think he'll strike again?'

I touch Phyllis' hand, mostly to comfort myself. 'I'm sure it will be okay. There's no reason to believe it will happen again. Who knows, maybe Elizabeth was mixing in the wrong crowd, you know?'

Phyllis raises an eyebrow. 'You know you don't believe that.'

I sigh, admitting she's right. There's no one in the world let alone West Green who could believe that saintly girl – too saintly for my liking, sometimes – would have any enemies.

After some small talk about cheerier topics, Phyllis parts

ways with us, heading off to catch up to her mother near the front of the market. Charles and I stay put, me leaning on his shoulder, taking in the sights of the town beside him. As always, I search for that disgusting face. It's been a few weeks since I've encountered Oliver's rage, mercifully, and he's never been bold enough to harass me in public. For that, at least, I can be thankful. Still, it's always in the back of my mind that someday, that all might change. It wouldn't do at all to have him around Charles. It doesn't do to have him lurking about me, either.

Eventually, we rise from the bench, and I stretch in the rays of the sun. Charles and I pass the hour hand in hand, walking and talking, kissing and revelling in each other. When he drops me off later, tipping his hat to Mum, she simply glares, not even extending a dinner invitation as would be proper. No matter. Charles kisses me on the cheek, promises to call on me again as soon as he can, and heads to the church to retrieve his bicycle and ride home.

Dad returns home well after dark, as usual, and Mum expresses her fears to him about my gallivanting about with a murderer on the loose. As always, Dad manages to calm Mum, winking at me over her head as he hugs her and soothes her. At least one of my parents is somewhat likeable.

Later, when I head to bed, sitting at my desk by the window to peer out onto our street, my mind wanders to what Phyllis told me about the murder. Bite marks in all sorts of places – disturbing. Haunting. Who would do such a thing? To think it happened here, in West Green, this laid-back, lacklustre town.

I lean against the window, staring out into the drizzly night when suddenly, I clutch my chest. Squinting, I lean closer to the murky glass, the hazy rain and darkness making it difficult to see, even with the streetlight. Still, as my heart beats wildly and I peer into the darkness, I'm certain that I'm not mistaken.

Across the street, a shadowy figure stands on the walkway, studying the McConnel house. It's too dark to make out who it is or what the person is doing, but even from here I'm certain it's a male figure due to the bulk of his stature. A lump forms in my throat as the figure turns, as if peering up at me. I shudder, trying to make out the face but unable to as suddenly, the person turns and walks casually away.

What was that? Who was it? I wonder, tears forming as panic rises. Is it – no, it can't be. He must have calmed down by now. It's been a few weeks since I've seen him. Time has dulled his resolve to get retribution, hasn't it? But could the figure be someone else with even more sinister intent than Oliver? After all, Oliver's a monster in his own right. But even he wouldn't stoop to such horrific levels as the maniac who killed Elizabeth – would he? It's a terrifying prospect, thinking that anyone in this town would be capable of such an atrocity. I think of Elizabeth's mangled body tossed in the skip like rubbish, her face contorted. I shudder. I think about waking up my parents, to tell them what I've seen. But what have I seen? A person in the street? Nothing criminal, of course. I'm sure it's just my weary brain panicking due to all the paranoia in town. That's all. Who wouldn't be bothered by the thought of Elizabeth in pieces? We're all on edge. And when one's on edge, the mind doesn't hesitate to play warped tricks.

I crawl into bed, talking myself down. I take a deep breath and count, one, two, three, just like Mum always told me to do when I was nervous. As a child, I was often panicky, my heart racing at odd moments. She always taught me to count to three and to let it all go with the exhale of breath.

When I close my eyes, I reassure myself. No sense in getting my parents worked up over nothing. It was just a person in the street. Gosh, it was probably a constable patrolling, after all. Elizabeth was an unfortunate tragedy, but nothing more. It will all be fine. West Green is a safe place to live. But as I drift off to sleep that night thinking about Charles, I know the dreams that come will be more like nightmares as the terror from recent events settles into my chest, my bones, and my heart.

Chapter 3

Smith Creek Manor Nursing Home 2019

It feels so far below. The little pathway, the ground. It's *too* far. My breathing is rapid as I study the ground. I thought I could do it, but I can't. I can't be up here. I turn now, looking back to Claire and the woman who are standing in the doorway.

'It's so far up,' I say shakily. Claire steps forward.

'It's going to be fine, Mum,' she consoles.

My head shakes, my heart racing as panic rises. I'm so far up here. *One, two, three*, I count in my head, just like my mum taught me so long ago. Over and over I count to three, the magic number. I need to calm down, but I can't.

'It's too far up. If there's a fire ... you know I can't be this far up,' I say, my voice croaking out the words.

Claire reaches for my hands now. 'Mum, listen. You know it's okay. It's very safe here, right Ms Martin?'

'Oh, yes. State-of-the-art fire alarms and sprinklers. All will be okay, darling. No need to worry. For now, this is our only open room. Maybe in the future we could move you, but for now ...'

My breathing picks up as I can feel the flames on my hands, licking up my body, scorching my face. I will burn here. It's too far up. Why did they put me on this floor? My mind flashes to indistinguishable, panicked faces as the fire consumes them. It shows me a blip of my own face as I scream in agony, the smoke choking me as I claw at the window. I bury the thought, squeezing my eyes shut. So many years, but it never gets any easier, and my fears only seem to get stronger.

'Mum, listen. You need to calm down. This isn't good for you. You know you're safe here. That's why we picked this place. Safe. Sound.' She leads me to the tiny bed, and I sit down. I breathe in and out. It's okay. I'm going to be okay. Claire's right. I'm fine. This fear isn't anything new. I'm going to be fine.

I glance over to the bedside table where the staff has propped up some of the photographs Claire had sent over from my house. A photo of Charles and me sits by the lamp, another of Claire as a child right beside it. I smile at the memories, at the happy times. I think about how when I was in Charles' arms, I could battle these fears from long ago. But he's not here. And soon, Claire will be gone. I need to tackle my demons on my own. I'm on my own now, even though I'm surrounded by people. I've never felt more alone.

'Here, dear. A glass of water will soothe you until we can get some tea up here,' our tour guide says, handing me a tepid glass. I look up at her.

My heartbeat seems to calm as I sip the water. It's bitter, chalky almost. It coats my throat in a peculiar film. I force down the chemical taste before holding up the glass, the water inside tinged and imperfect. I set the glass on the wooden table nearby, abandoning it. A moment of silence goes by. Finally, I look up to Ms— Her name. I don't remember her name. I shake my head in frustration. I hate when this happens.

'Well, I think I'm okay now. Thank you,' I say to her, giving her the hint that she can leave. I'm tired. I need some time alone. I don't want her hovering. There will be time enough for that.

'Okay, well, if you need anything, there's a call button right here,' she says, showing me the button by the bed. 'Or you can wander out to the nurse's station. It's the whole way down the hall and to the right, though. Kind of a long walk. No need to trouble yourself, dear. Just push the button, okay? The common area is down that way as well, in addition to a reading area, a community room, and some activity rooms. Oh, and the dining room. We can't forget that. But I'm sure the staff will be happy to show you around when you're ready.'

'Thank you,' I reply, knowing for sure I'm not really up to the common area just yet. Maybe I'll never be ready for it. Maybe I'll just pass the days here, staring out the window, or watching some mindless programmes on the tiny telly that's in the corner of the room. Or maybe in a few days, I'll be like my roommate, impassively staring at another world, gone from this one in all ways but my breathing. It's hard to tell, and I'd rather not think too much on it.

Claire stays for a bit, chattering on and on about the activities and painting classes offered here and some dog that comes to visit the residents. I smile and nod, only half listening. I'm tired and numb, but my eyes are also peeled the whole way open, my heart racing as I take in the reality of this place. In truth, I don't know what I am anymore. Smith Creek Manor has already stripped me of so many things – and it's only been an hour or so. How much more will it take as the days tick by? I shudder as I consider it all.

'Well, love, no use staying here all day. I'm sure you have plenty to do,' I proclaim after a while, Claire holding my hand as she sits beside me on the bed.

'Oh, nonsense, Mum. I took the day off. Wanted to get you all settled.' Her smile is warm, her glossy lips turning up in the familiar gesture. Such a pretty, sweet girl, that daughter of mine. My miracle child. I squeeze her hand, thinking about how lucky I am in that department. I didn't deserve a girl so beautiful after everything that happened.

'Well, settled I am. Look, love. I have everything I need. Thank you. I'll be just fine. And maybe I'll do one of those ... those ... oh, what's the word? Activities. That's it. I'll do one of those.'

Claire looks at me hesitantly, wondering if she should really go. I know this isn't completely easy for her, either.

None of this has been easy. She lost Charles, too, at the same time she lost that husband of hers. Good for nothing man, in my opinion. I knew it from the beginning. Her life has been in a state of upheaval like mine. And now she's got my burdens to carry. I need to make things easy for her. I need to make Smith Creek Manor work – or at least make her feel like it is. My life is determined, the best days over, but hers isn't. She still has some years left to enjoy and adventures to chase. And now more than ever, I understand how important that is.

'Go on, now. Get yourself home. I know you've got plenty waiting for you there to keep you busy. I'm fine. You can ring me tomorrow, check in about that painting class and hear about all my excitements here. As you said, it's a lovely place. I feel right at home.'

It's a lie, and I think Claire knows it. But it works because she wants to believe it. We will believe almost anything when we need to, I realise.

'All right, Mum. If you're sure. But I'll be back soon, okay?'

I smile, knowing her words are genuine. That daughter of mine has a good heart. Charles and I got that part right, at least.

'I know, darling,' I reply as she squeezes my frail hand.

'Promise you'll ring if you need anything?'

'Cross my heart,' I reply, smiling as she leans down to kiss my cheek before leaving. I take a breath once she's gone, knowing I will do no such thing. Claire has her own life. I know she wants me here so I could be close, to make things easier. I obliged. But I don't expect her to spend her waking hours here in this depressing place. She has things to tend to. She has a busy marketing career taking her all over the place. I will not tie her here.

I decide to walk back to the window, sitting down in the beige chair that's near it as I stare out into the day. A bird flies by, landing in a tree. My eyes follow it, watching it flitter about for a while before I focus on another sight – the window across the way, the room on the same floor but on the other side of the U-shape. The figure is still there, a man staring out into the courtyard as well. He hasn't moved, and suddenly my stomach lurches because it feels like he is staring right at me. I shake my head, steadying my gaze back on the trees, trying not to think about how far up I am.

So much upheaval in one day, so many changes. Still, there's a familiarity here in this town as I remember where I am. I'd thought I'd never see Crawley again. I thought I'd never wander through West Green or Northgate, especially after I promised Charles all those years ago to leave this place in the past. Yet, now, here I am, and I don't like it one bit. It's been so long. So much has changed. But there's still one thing that hasn't – the feeling that Crawley won't quite let me go, even after all this time. *What were you thinking, Charles, telling our girl about this place? After the promises we made to leave it in the past – how could you do this?*

I squeeze my eyes shut, looking away from the window. It wouldn't do to get upset now. I open my eyes again and glance at the clock. Lunch isn't for an hour or so, I think.

What time did that woman say? I don't know. It doesn't matter. I'm sure I'm not very hungry anyway. Perhaps it would do me some good to take a walk.

I stand from the chair, my knees cracking with the effort. When did I get so old? I wander out to the corridor, but I stop at the threshold and glance at my roommate. What's her name? Shoot. My eyes land, however, on the notice-board near her bed and see the drawing of the rose. Is that it? Rose? I think so. My eyes fall back on the woman. She hasn't moved, still sitting and staring at the centre of the room. I study her for a moment. Her eyes shift, her head moving almost imperceptibly.

I think for a moment she might talk, her lips flapping slightly, her hands curled in on themselves in her lap. She moves one hand up and down, slowly, carefully. It bangs on her legs, tucked in underneath the white blanket wrapped around her.

She emits a moan from her lips. She's trying to speak, her eyes desperately locked on mine. She blinks over and over and over, a rapid succession of movement from her that I haven't yet seen. My heart flutters as I walk across the room.

'Rose? What is it?' I ask, reaching for her hand. She jumps as I touch her, the groan intensifying.

I can't understand her. I stare into her drooping face, but no answers come. The poor thing is lost and confused. Is she even really in there, mentally? Does she understand what's going on around her? I'm not sure.

'There, there, Rose. It's okay. I'm going to go for a walk,

okay? You take a rest.' I pat her hand, her skin cold and clammy like she's already in the grave. In many ways, I suppose she is.

I smile once more, turning to leave. She emits a screeching whimper, desperation clinging to every piece of the sound. It spreads like a plague in my chest, drowning me in uncertainty. Although sorrow for Rose certainly builds within, another emotion pools beneath it: terror. How am I going to survive this? How can I endure a place where death and devastation are in my face every single moment? I know I should be glad that even with my health problems, I still have mobility and my wits about me. I have a lot in Smith Creek Manor terms. But there's something about the home that just seems to remind me of all I have to lose. I can already sense a harsh reality few want to uncover; this place divests a person until they're nothing but a pile of bones under a blanket, mumbling incoherently as saddened onlookers try their best to unsee the realities. I don't want to face Rose's fate. I don't. It feels like there's a contagion in this place, and the closer you get to someone like Rose, the more likely it is you'll fall prey to the unseemly loss of all you hold dear.

So I do what so many do in these kinds of homes. I turn my head, leaving Rose alone, as I step further away and into the corridor. The staircase is adjacent to the left, that door guarding it. A code box hangs beside it on the wall, the cool metal of it taunting me as the fluorescent light glides over it. Instantly, my heart starts to beat faster and faster until it's racing wildly. A sensation rises, a familiar paranoia I try so hard to suppress.

I'm trapped. I'm trapped *here*. I can't escape. Even the stairs have a code, one that I don't know. My breathing increases. I count to three. I need to calm down. I reach for the wall to steady myself, tears forming.

'Dear, is everything okay?' a voice says as footsteps echo on the floor. I turn to my right to see a young nurse with brown hair and a reassuring smile. She quickly marches towards me.

'I'm fine,' I offer weakly, but my face must say otherwise because the woman quickens her pace. She clutches my arm gently, and I let myself lean on her.

'There, there. I know. All such a change. I'm Grace. Come on, now. Let's get you to a chair. Looks like you've seen a ghost or something.'

I don't argue, letting her lead me back into my room, towards the chair I just left. I avert my eyes from Rose, willing myself not to look over there. My heart beats frantically, which causes my panic to rise. I know I have to stay calm. I can't let this happen, not again.

'Now, come on. What shall I get you? Fancy a cuppa?' Grace asks, her melodious voice wrapping itself around me as I settle by the window once more.

'The code,' I spat at her, without any thought.

'What code?' she asks, stooping down to look into my face.

'The stairs. I need the code for the stairs.' My fingers viciously cling to the velvety feel of the chair's armrest.

She studies me, her smile pitying. 'You won't need the code for the stairs. After all, who wants to use them when there's a perfectly good lift?' Her smile is warm. I might like her in other circumstances. But thinking of that lift, I shudder. I wouldn't describe it as perfectly good, or even safe. I think about the creakiness, about the jolting noises.

I persist, hoping she'll give in. 'I need the code. If there's a fire. I need to know it. And that lift is so terrifying. I hate the lift,' I demand, shaking my head, frustration building. She doesn't understand. She just doesn't know.

'You'll get used to the lift, love. It's just a bit old, but it's completely safe, I promise. And there hasn't been a fire at Smith Creek Manor, ever. If there were, we'll be right here in a jiffy. No need to panic, truly. Now why don't you come with me? I'll show you the common room down the hall. Do you some good to meet some friendly faces. There are some sweet women down there who love knitting and gossip. And tea. They love their tea, of course. Now how about that cuppa?'

I stare at her, blinking. My mind hurts. I don't know why I'm so – what am I? Goodness, this is all just confusing. I don't know how to feel.

So, I say the only thing I can. 'Fine.' I let her lead me down the sterile corridor, the lights still blinding as the nurse waffles about this resident and that, as if I'm starting a new school instead of the first day of the end of my life.

Chapter 4

'Listen, trust me. This floor isn't so bad. Sure, we got a few who are a bit crackers up here. It's true. And a couple that just, well, between you and me, give me the absolute creeps and all, some creepy ones. But overall, it's okay up here. Fewer nurses to bother you, and there are even a few sane residents here on Floor Three. But then again, the nurses don't mind us much up here. We're sort of the forgotten floor, you know?'

The woman knitting beside me at the table chatters on and on. Dorothy, I think she said her name was. I don't remember her surname. I clutch the tea that the nurse gave me, my hands warming on the Styrofoam cup. No fine china here, I suppose.

A game show blares in the community room area nearby, and a few patients – residents, I stand corrected – gape mindlessly at it. One woman is parked in a wheelchair in the corner, touching the wall, repeating the name *Philip* with such angst, it makes my heart ache. Her whimpers rise above the announcer on the show, mixing in a strange cacophony of joy and agony, symbolic of what this place holds.

Dorothy sits, knitting some crooked, scratchy blanket. The nurse sat me at this table, told me I'd make quick friends with this woman. I don't know. But, looking around, she seems to be one of the few who can hold a conversation. These people are just so – old. So old. So gone. Or maybe this place just does that to a person.

I sigh. 'Doesn't sound like a good thing to be forgotten.'

'It all depends, Adeline. It's Adeline, right? Did you say Adeline?'

I nod. 'Friends call me Addy.'

'I'll go with Adeline for now, then, if it's all the same to you. Too soon to tell if we're going to be friends or not.'

I nod again. I can respect that.

'Regardless, as I was saying, being forgotten here is not a terrible thing. Fewer nurses means less poking and prodding. It means more peace and quiet. And if I'm going to leave this world soon, I could use some peace and quiet. Of course, I suppose there are downfalls to being forgotten. That woman in 306 found out the hard way a while back.'

I look up from my tea now, staring at Dorothy. 'What happened to her?' My curiosity is piqued, but I suppose in a place where magazines, knitting, and some weak tea are the only excitement, it doesn't take much.

Dorothy shrugs. 'Murder, or at least that's what rumour has it. Staff of course claim it was a bad fall. But I've never seen someone turn a hue of purple like that from a simple trip, you know?'

I blink, waiting for her to crack a smile, some sadistic joke. She doesn't laugh, though. She stops knitting and looks at me.

'Who did it?' I ask, needing to know but afraid all the same.

Dorothy shrugs. 'Some say the staff were in there to sedate her with something right before she was found dead. Apparently, she had been raving about some odd occurrences, had been seeing some strange stuff.'

'The staff?' I ask, making sure I've heard her correctly.

Dorothy looks up at me, peeks left and right as if to see if anyone is listening. Then, she leans in. 'Did the whole tour guide bit fool you? Gets the best of most of us. But shall we say this place isn't quite what it seems to be from the little pamphlets they give you? Sure, they give you plenty of tea. But it's not as cosy as they want you to believe. In fact, from some of the things I've seen, it's downright dangerous here if you're not careful.'

My stomach churns. This is not what I wanted to hear. Suddenly, a wave of fear slaps into me. Regrets flood over me, a feeling that's all too familiar. Suddenly, returning to Crawley seems like the worst idea I've ever had, this eerie building in an even eerier section of town stirring a sense of foreboding in me.

'Dear, don't worry too much, though. If you play it smart and wind your neck in, it'll be okay. As I said, Floor Three is the perfect place to blend in. Just don't stir any trouble, stay unnoticed, and you'll be fine. And that Grace on our floor, she's a true gem. Really. Besides, the talk about the woman in 306 – who really knows what happened, right? – could just be Chinese whispers, truly. Or it could've been one of the patients who lived here at the time. Some smarmy fellows have come through here, if you ask me.'

I study her face, trying to decide if she's telling the truth now or if she's just trying to calm me. I don't know. But in my gut, something tells me that Crawley's dark past is still haunting these grounds – and now I'm back in its clutches.

Regardless of what happened in 306, this is all a bit frightening. I already feel lost in this place – but now, I realise there's so much I don't know. This certainly is some unwelcome news, and not the kind of excitement I was hoping for.

'Oh, my apologies. My late husband always said I had a penchant for ruining the mood. There, there. Nothing much to worry about. It was a couple of years ago, after all. Who knows what happened? No trouble since then. Smith Creek Manor isn't perfect, mind you, but it could be worse. It could always be worse. Besides, few last long in this place anyway. New people all the time. Except me, I suppose. I've been one of the few to outlast Smith Creek, at least so far.'

I stir in my seat, readjusting to try to get comfortable. I don't know if I can. Murder isn't the sort of thing I'd envisioned in a place like this. True, when I came here, I knew it was a final stop. I just hadn't imagined going out like that. I close my eyes, thinking about the strangling ivy on the stone walls. It's almost like I can feel it all constrict a little more, like the air is going out of this place. The all too familiar feeling of being trapped resurfaces from long ago. It's a claustrophobic feeling I don't welcome.

'Anyway, enough about me. Tell me about you. First day's always tough. Have you chatted with anyone yet?'

'My roommate doesn't talk, don't think she can. And then just you. Not much to tell, I suppose. I'm simply trying to sort everything out.'

'Not much to it. Everyone essentially keeps to themselves. But I will say, there are a few fit ones here if you're searching for that sort of excitement.' She winks, causing me to smile.

'I've been there before. Not sure that's really what I need right now.' I grin.

'Oh, I do. And when you see the few gentlemen Floor Three has to offer, well, maybe you'll change your mind. Room 313 has quite the smouldering eyes. I imagine he was a good catch in his day. Oh, and I think it's 310, the priest, he's got some nice features, too. I'm not picky, after all – religious or not, he's quite a feast for the eyes. But you do have to look out for him. Temper on that one. Nice to look at, but that's about it. Still, got to get our fun where we can.'

'What room are you in?' I ask, letting my guard down. She seems nice enough.

'305, dear. On the other side of the nurse's station and down the hall a bit. Stop down anytime. I keep a lovely stash of digestives and Jaffa Cakes. The food is depressing around here. So start stocking up any time family comes. Stash all the sweets you can. Trust me. Insider tip.'

I nod, taking a sip of my tea. It's weak, but not terrible. Better than the water, I suppose.

'Oh, and one more thing.'

My head turns as I look at Dorothy, who continues her knitting. Her face is serious now, her gaze hardened.

'Be careful not to ask for anything at night if you can help it. The night nurse who takes care of your end, well, he's one you want to avoid.' Her warning is quiet but stern. I know there's no joke there.

'Why?' I ask, my head aching from so much new information.

'Let's just say he's not the kindest man. Gives me the downright creeps, if I'm being honest. His name's Jones. Seems to have a strong fancy for the female nurse on the second floor, which is all right by me. It means he's not up here when he should be sometimes. But, well, trust me – when he's up here, be careful. Other than that, it's all great here on Floor Three. Yep. Absolutely perfect.'

I take another sip of tea, turning in my seat to look out into the common area. The Philip Woman has drifted off to sleep, her head lolling at an awkward angle. I wait for someone to come and fix it, but no one does. Her hair is lurched forward, a tangled mop of grey curls covering her face. She looks like an abandoned, mangy sheep dog. I guess Dorothy's right. The nurses here are few and far between. It looks like we may just be on our own around here in more ways than one.

*

I jump up in a cold sweat, my heart racing as I clutch my chest. The moonlight shines through the window onto my bed. But this isn't my bed. Where am I? I don't understand. What's happening? I don't know where I—

'You'll die here. You will. Get out now. Get out while you can. You'll die here,' a bewildered voice pleads as a wrinkled hand clutches my arm. I startle. There is a figure standing over me, muttering over and over, repeating the phrases that send true terror to my heart. I yank back, but the person seems to climb towards me, closer and closer. I flinch, trying to pull away, ready to scream. My lips tremble and my breathing is ragged. I open my mouth, but no sounds come out. What's happening? My mind wildly flails about, trying to settle on one interpretation of the scene.

'You'll die here. You will. I'm telling you, lady. Get out now. Get out.' The words spew faster and faster, and spit lands on me. The figure is close enough that I can make out her short, curly hair, her feminine jawline. She is frothing at the mouth as she yanks at my arm and claws at me. She shreds the shoulder of my nightshirt with one hand as the other vehemently digs into my arm. Saliva leaks from her lips as she repeats the lines endlessly in a racing fury. I move my arms about, trying to startle her away, but she doesn't flinch. Her fingers are crusty with what, I don't know. Her nails, long and sharp, scratch into my arm painfully, and I'm afraid to look at the damage she's causing. A warm, sickly feeling oozes down my arm. I think I must be bleeding. I struggle away, shifting on the bed, trying to back up. The call button. I need to push the call button.

I reach around the figure, my eyes adjusting. I grab for the button, my sanctuary. I push it over and over and over. No one comes. I push it again as the woman paws and mauls me, scratching and clawing incessantly as she repeats her mantra. I look up at her, trying to calm her, pleading with her to stop. Her eyes are glazed over and white. They look like they're oozing in a supernatural way. Her gaze is blank, marred by the milky white haze of cataracts.

I'm ready to shout out, to scream, when suddenly, a cackle rises from her slimy lips as the hand lets go of my arm. The woman turns and slowly trudges out of the room, the deranged laugh bellowing as she does. Tears drip from my eyes. I push the button again. And again. But the person is gone. All quiets down, and I wonder why no one is coming. A few minutes pass as my heart beats wildly. I pant and wrap my arms around myself. Tears trickle down my face. I stare at the doorway, wondering if she'll come back, trying to assess the situation. I'm too afraid to look down and see what sort of condition I'm in.

After a few more moments pass by, I reach for the cord of the lamp. I turn on the light and take stock of my arm, of the room. My arm is bleeding, scratches up and down it like a rabid animal has mauled me. In some ways, I suppose it's true. The curtain that separates Rose's area of the room from mine is pulled across, so I can't see her, but I hear a raspy gurgle from her side, a sputtering inhale that does nothing to calm my frayed nerves. I touch the blanket on the bed, rubbing the threadbare material between my thumb and forefinger. It's real. All of this is real. It's not a nightmare. It's happening. I'm not home. I'm not at Quail Avenue. I'm here. *That's right.* I'm here now.

What was that? Who was that? I don't know. Grogginess lifted, I slink out of bed, stand, and slowly stretch my stiff legs. After a long moment of staring out the window, a voice bellows into the room.

'What is it?'

I startle, jumping out of my skin. I turn around to see a man in a nurse's uniform, standing back from the doorway. He is bald, but his dark moustache curls up on his lip, giving him a sneering look. Or maybe he is sneering.

'Th-there was ... someone was here ... I saw someone.' I want to ask why he didn't come sooner, but something stops me from uttering the words.

The man crosses the room in three quick strides. 'Get back to bed,' he orders gruffly, not waiting for me to explain.

'Sorry, there was someone—'

'Come on, old woman. There's no one here. Get in bed.' He grabs my arm, the same one the person – there was a person, wasn't there? – was grabbing. He roughly hurries me towards my bed, ignoring the scratches and blood dripping on my arm. My skin burns at his touch, the flesh still raw. I fall a little before he forces me into bed and roughly adjusts the blanket around me. He cocoons me in as if the blanket will keep me hostage in the bed and he won't have to deal with me again.

'I won't be having any more trouble, will I?' he asks, raising an eyebrow. He leans in now, closer and closer. He is centimetres from my face.

'No, sir,' I whisper, a new fear gripping my heart.

'Goddamn right, I won't,' he whispers harshly into the space between us, and I shudder at the way he looks at me. It's a threatening glance, one that challenges me to defy him. I don't dare consider it.

He backs up, looking at me for an uncomfortably long moment, before pulling the lamp cord. But before he does, I notice a nametag. I see the familiar name.

Jones.

Why do I know that name? Why is it ringing a bell? I search in my mind for the answer. Was it the knitting lady? Did she say something about him?

My head throbs as I try to sort all of it out – the mysterious figure, the nurse, the name. Jones curses again under his breath, the darkness plummeting about me, as he leaves the room. When he's gone, I begin to wonder if there's more to worry about on Floor Three than I could have ever imagined.

Chapter 5

A hand startles me awake, and I sit up, gasping. It takes a moment for me to recognise where I am, the sunlight now streaming through the windows and illuminating the room. I stare at the pink wallpaper, faded to a dusky, decaying rose colour. The floral pattern is so muted and miniscule that it looks like scratches on the wallpaper instead of the ornate design the decorator probably intended. My eyes absorb the depressing sight of the room, my home now, as I take another deep breath. Exhaustion pounds in my skull, crackling against my brain. I didn't sleep well, not at all, and my neck is stiff from the tension.

'Mrs Evans, it's breakfast time. Are you going to the dining room to eat with the others, or shall I bring your morning meal to you?' I peer up at the nurse standing above me. Her red hair is pulled tight into a bun, the pasty skin on her face stretching back so tautly her cheek bones look like they might rupture through. Her face is placid, stoic, as she says my name with tart condescension mirrored in her eyes. I'm not sure if she's just got a permanent poker face or if her hairstyle prohibits any expression from showing through. My head spins and aches. It craves to be plopped back down on the pillow and to let sleep wash away all of last night's calamities.

'Can I just take my meal here today?' I ask.

'Fine. I'll bring it back around when I get to it.'

With that, the harsh-looking woman is off to jostle Rose, who doesn't have a choice in the matter since she can't speak up. The woman flings back the curtain, the only semblance of privacy in our room now foiled. Rose coughs and sputters, squealing at the sight of the nurse. As the serious woman rousts Rose up from the bed, my frail roommate stares at one thing – me. Her arm, trembling from the effort, rises just a bit. I notice her hand, curled into a fist, is shaking violently. Is she shaking it at me? I don't have time to decide because harsh woman is complaining about the mess Rose has made and how she'll need to tend to that before breakfast. I sigh in my bed, transferring my gaze to the window. There's so much wrong in this place, but I feel a little guilty. It could be worse. Rose has it harder than me, for sure. I suppose I should be grateful that at least I can choose where to eat my breakfast. At least there's still that.

When the nurse has gotten Rose into the wheelchair with the assistance of some brute of a man, she wheels her out of the room. Rose's head is cocked towards me, shaking to the side. She mumbles as they wheel her away.

I feel terrible, but I am gloriously thankful when they are gone and the room is quiet again. I settle back into bed, but I find that sleep doesn't return. I blink, lying on my side as I peer out the window into the dismal greyness of the day. What day of the week is it? I don't much know anymore. It seems time in here is a whirling enigma. Truthfully, I guess it doesn't matter much anymore what day it is. They are all the same, and I have nowhere I need to be. No one is expecting me anywhere, and no one is remembering me, in honesty. That's a lonely thought. I decide to push it aside.

I blink a few times, thinking about last night, about the arm on my hand. I think about Jones and his reaction. I think about the blood-curdling feeling that all is not well on Floor Three, that this place isn't quite what it seems. The faux homey appearance they try to create with the dusty, dried bouquets of flowers sitting on archaic stands in the hallways. The cheery-coloured paint in the common room, the bird cage with tiny finches near the lift. It's all a façade to make us feel at home. But this isn't home. And something tells me I might not want it to be.

Whoever was in my room last night had a warning, clear and painfully frightening. It's not safe here. I shake my head and squeeze my eyes shut so tightly that I see specks in the forced blackness. It's nonsense. It must be. What real danger could there be in a place like this? Who would come here to carry out malicious plots? What would be the point, after all?

The harsh nurse drops off a tray a few moments later with a spot of tea, some eggs, beans, and what I suppose is meant to imitate breakfast ham. It looks rubbery and grey, an oozing film coating it in an unnatural, unappetising way. After wrestling with the thought of tucking myself back under the blanket and making this whole place disappear with sleep, I decide there's no use. There will be no serene sleep today, my nerves battling my mind's need to rest. I sit up wearily, gently folding the scratchy blanket back from my legs.

After plodding to the loo, I gather my strength to get dressed. I'm supposed to push a button to ask for help to change. I find that insulting. I have a heart condition and some forgetfulness that comes and goes. I am not a child. I slowly, painfully pick out an outfit from the chest of drawers, tucking myself into a plain grey pullover and some comfortable trousers. I don't dare look into the mirror. Goodness knows I don't need to be any more depressed than I already am.

I snatch the tea from the tray and I wander out of my room, glancing first towards the staircase. It still irks me that it's locked. I take a breath, though, knowing it's pointless to worry about it now. I need to focus my mind on other things. Thus, I turn to the right and set out for the common area, deciding that some exploring may do me good.

I plod onward, peeking into rooms here and there, the doors all flung open. When I get to Room 312, though, I notice the door is still shut. *Odd*, I think. I stop for a moment to catch my breath and wonder what curiosity the room holds. I'm tempted to reach out and touch the door knob, to peek in. I don't, though. Wouldn't do to make enemies here by intruding. Still, there's something unnerving about Room 312, a murky horror that evades all reasoning. I don't know what it is, but something about the door both lures me in and repels me with all its might.

I keep walking, passing a man in a wheelchair, his head slumped slightly backwards, his throat exposed. He rolls gently back and forth. His eyes pierce into mine, and I shudder, feeling like there's something he wants to say but can't. Agony drips from his watery eyes. It seems like tears want to fall from them but can't. Slowly, methodically, careful not to trip, I march on until I finally reach the common room.

'There you are. We thought you escaped already,' Dorothy announces, cackling over a cup of tea. Another lady sits beside her in a wheelchair, but she just stares up at me and grins. She's missing an eye. I tell myself not to stare at the gaping socket, not to be rude. I sit down in an empty chair beside her, my tea in hand.

'You look like you didn't sleep a wink. Rough night?' Dorothy asks.

I shrug, biting my lip. I wonder if I should tell her. I don't know her yet. I don't want people to think I'm – what? What would they think? I did nothing wrong.

'Yes,' I admit. 'Some crazy things happened.'

'Crazy in a good way?' Dorothy asks.

'Crazy in the way that someone was standing over my bed last night.' I tuck a long, grey strand of my greasy hair behind my ear.

Dorothy shakes her head. 'Babbling Barbara.'

'What?'

'Babbling Barbara,' Dorothy repeats, slowly this time. 'I could almost bet my life it was her. She's the floor's lunatic. She's madder than mad. Been here since before me. I think she's too bonkers to die, you know? She wanders this place like a vagabond. Not even sure the staff know where her room is anymore. She gets lost all the time, even at night. One time I caught her sleeping in my bed while I was in it. Frightening but harmless. Nothing to worry about, dear. Nothing at all. She's truly not capable of hurting anyone, although her crazy babbling is enough to send even the sanest of us to the loony bin.'

'She hurt me, and it was pretty frightening. Look what she did,' I reply, rolling up my sleeve to show Dorothy my wounds.

'Oh my goodness,' Dorothy gasps as she shakes her head. She leans in to examine my arm more closely. 'Barbara did this?'

I sigh. 'I suppose, if it was truly her. Yes. It was awful. She mauled me and wouldn't stop.'

Dorothy shakes her head. 'She's never done anything like this. It's peculiar. She truly has been harmless. But goodness, that's terrible.'

Dorothy's gaze lifts from my arm, and as she stares into my eyes, I get the sense she's telling the complete truth. She shakes her head again before sighing and moving on with the conversation. I want to shove the worrisome event aside, to pretend it didn't happen. Still, as Dorothy blabs on about some of the soap operas she watches and her grandchildren, I stare into my tea, thinking about Barbara's words.

You'll die here. You will. Get out now. Get out while you can.

For a mad woman, they sure were coherent phrases. Why did she choose those words? Does she say them to everyone? And above all, if what Dorothy said is true, why am I the only one who has been attacked by her? It's too frightening to think about. I try to forget the worries, but they sink their teeth into me, gnashing and grinding conspicuously in the recesses of my memory to be rustled out later.

'It's a shame you missed breakfast, you know? I would've introduced you to some of Floor Three's finer residents. But don't worry. There's still time, of course. We've got plenty of time. Hopefully.'

The woman beside Dorothy chuckles at that, like it's the funniest joke. I do not.

After a long while, I stand from the table. 'I think I'll go ring my daughter,' I announce, suddenly feeling confined in this room. There's too much furniture here. I don't like how everyone is just sitting around. I need to be alone. I suddenly, mercilessly thirst for solitude.

'Are you sure? I think the painting class starts in two hours. Be certain to come. It's really fun. And the university boy they bring in is a real dream. If I were just a tad younger, I'd have a go at him. Give him something really special to paint.' Dorothy winks before readjusting her glasses to underscore her point.

'Okay,' I reply, turning with my almost-empty Styrofoam cup, slightly surprised by Dorothy's forward promiscuity. My fingers crunch the cup until a piece falls in on itself.

But before I even turn the whole way around and pointing in the correct direction, I startle, dropping the cup.

'Get out while you can. Get out,' she gurgles, her craggy face scrunched up as her finger wags in my line of sight. Her milky eyes are crusty today, the bright whiteness of them alarming in a foreign way in the light. The words strangle in my throat, and I'm suddenly sputtering and coughing, clasping my chest as I back up, almost upsetting the table.

'Barbara, dear, you're scaring Adeline. Stop it,' Dorothy orders, standing from her chair.

Barbara clenches my arms, though, aggravating the fresh scratches she left last night. She leans in close, her musty breath careening into my face. Her milky eyes laser into mine, sending a shiver through me. It's as if she can see straight through me, even though common sense tells me she can't. Her fingers are sticky.

'You'll die here. You will,' she whispers, and tears form in my eyes as a creeping, crawling feeling reverberates through me. Before I can respond, though, she hoots, smiling, and releases my arm. She clunks off down the corridor in the other direction, slightly leaning to the right and mumbling about daisies and the red rain.

I stand for a moment, staring down at the cup on the floor. It's crunched up and broken, the few drops of tea that lurked in the bottom spattered about it.

'There, there, dear. Here you go,' a nurse says, stooping down to pick up the cup. 'I've got it, Mrs Evans. It's fine.'

I look into the brown eyes of the nurse. Tightening my face in confusion, I grab my head. 'Who are you? I don't know you,' I say, needing this woman to back up, to give me space.

'I'm Grace, dear. Remember, we met yesterday?'

I stare at the woman, so desperately needing to know her. I will myself to place her. But I just can't. Fear bubbles inside, and I place a hand on my chest.

'It's okay. No problem. You had a hectic day yesterday. Come on, let me take you to your room. This way now,' her voice reassures. I'm still stressed, but her voice is kind and her eyes reassure me. I follow her.

'I'll check in with you later, Adeline,' a voice calls. I turn around to see the woman at the table, knitting. Dottie? Dorothy? I think it's Dorothy. I'm pretty sure. But then again ...

I hate it when this happens. I hate it when I can't remember. I hate it when I forget simple things. I hate it when I feel out of control, like I'm not even in charge of my own self. The forgetfulness comes and goes, some days better than others. The doctors say it is to be expected with this disease, but they don't understand how frustrating it is. From day to day, from moment to moment, my mind warps and twists so quickly. Some moments, everything is as clear as a crystal. And others, a murky fog settles in, threatening to obliterate every basic memory and thought and rendering me incapable of the smallest task. How helpless can one be? My hands ball into trembling fists, and every joint screams in pain.

The nurse leads me back to my room, and I unfurl my fists, giving my fingers a chance to relax. I reach up to the wall outside of my room and let my fingers trace the black numbers. 316. I live here in 316.

'Need anything? More tea?' the nurse asks.

I shake my head, staring at the tray of cold breakfast foods beside my chair. I inhale, but before the nurse can leave, I reach out and touch her arm.

'Wait. My daughter. I want to talk to my daughter,' I assert.

'Certainly. Do you know the number?'

I look at the phone sitting on the nightstand as I cross the room slowly, my feet shuffling along. When I finally get to it, my hands reach for the phone. Do I remember? Can I do this? I'm so afraid I won't remember. However, I know I need to get a hold of myself. I'm not a quitter. I don't back down.

'Yes,' I say confidently, even though I don't quite believe it. My fingers slowly reach towards the numbers, and I pause, wondering if they'll be able to accomplish the feat. I sigh when they methodically dial the familiar numbers. They remember even when I don't. All isn't lost, I realise, assurance surging through me as I hear Claire's voice on the line.

'Mum, everything okay?'

'Yes, Claire. Lovely. All is lovely. Just having some tea and thinking of you,' I say, looking to the nurse to smile and thank her. But she is gone. Too much to do I suppose. Too much to do in a world where so many of us have nothing left at all. How cruel life can be.

'Do you want me to come over?' Claire asks.

I do. I so desperately do.

'No, no. It's all fine. I just wanted to talk to you,' I lie.

We continue our conversation, Claire filling me in about the new client she's working with at the advertising agency. She talks about things I don't understand, but I don't much care. It's just nice to hear a warm, friendly voice I know. It's so cold here.

While I'm chatting, there's a knock on the threshold. I turn to see a man stooped at my door. His eyes are dark, his eyebrows unruly. He's got a strong jawline, I notice, but it's like his nose is too small for his face, like his head has swallowed it up.

And then there's the scar, a bubbling, blatant scar along the top of his forehead, a line that's parallel with the floor. I try not to startle. Wouldn't do to be rude. All the patients around here tend to wear clothes that look like pyjamas, but not him. He's wearing a button-up shirt and some brown trousers that seem like they've never been taken off. They're ripped and worn, a stark contrast to the nice-looking shirt.

I leave the phone up at my ear. The man smirks, offering a little wave. The smile comes off as a crooked sneer, the few teeth peeking through tarnished brown.

'Menu,' he whispers, holding up a piece of paper. He limps into my room to the noticeboard on the wall closest to the door. His eyes flit about, as if he's taking in the sight of my room but also terrified to encroach on my space. His movements are dramatic, as if he has to show me he's only hanging something on the noticeboard and nothing else. I like that. I like that he's respectful of my space. See, you can't judge a book by its cover. I feel rude now, judging him for some ailments and disfigurements. As if to make up for it, I nod and smile overly wide, Claire still talking about some new initiative at work, as he tacks up a pink paper on my board.

I think about telling Claire to hold so I can thank him, but he's too fast. He's out of the room before I can blink, the limp no longer seeming to ail him. I wonder who he is. Is he one of the men that knitting woman was talking about, but which one? He looks somewhat familiar, but I've passed so many people, it's hard to tell or to place him. I suppose I have time to figure it out. In some ways, I have nothing but time.

When Claire and I are finished talking, I hang up the phone. Standing from my bed, I decide to venture back out. No use being cooped up in here the whole time. I meander around, peering in rooms but trying not to get caught. I don't want people thinking I'm snooping.

The day goes surprisingly fast. Later on, the nurses eventually find me to take me down to Floor One where the medical rooms are. I shudder as they lead me into the shaky lift. As the metal doors screech to a close and the metal box sputters, I want nothing more than to climb right back out. The ride is jumpy and creaky. It takes so long to get to the bottom floor that I convince myself it's definitely broken, that we'll be trapped in the box of death for hours. My heart races, and just as I'm ready to start clawing my way out, the doors mercifully creak halfway open, pause, and then open the whole way. It's like the indecisive doors are thinking about staying shut. I scuttle out and pray I won't have to use it too often in the coming months.

I have a few check-ups on the first floor with some doctors who seem to want to talk way too much about my heart, giving nosy nurses too much information about my medical history and telling them what to look out for like I'm not even in the room. When I return from their poking and prodding, I spend most of the afternoon sitting with the knitting woman, wandering about, and eventually taking a seat in the little lending library at the other end of Floor Three. I enjoy the peacefulness of the reading area so much, I return after dinner instead of joining in some activity downstairs later that night. I doze off, and when I startle awake, the nursing home is quiet except for a few characteristic moans from Floor Three. I rise from my seat, deciding it's time to return to my room.

But when I get to the corridor, I'm disoriented. It's been too long. Where am I? Where is my room? What room am I in? I look to the left. There are a few rooms that way. I look to the right. There's a long corridor around the corner. Where do I go? I don't know. I take a breath, going right. I walk looking in rooms, peering at numbers. What number do I need? How don't I know? I don't understand.

'This way, Adeline,' a voice barks. I look to see the harsh woman from this morning ushering me down the hallway. Is she still here? What a long day for her.

I nod, following her to my room, relieved she was there despite her glower and her angry mutterings about imbecilic residents. I ignore her icy, squeezing fingers on my arm that dig into my flesh as she yanks me forward. I was going the right way, I realise. This soothes me. Still, when I get to the room, my fingers trace the numbers again. I need to lock them into my mind. 316. I live in 316.

She doesn't offer to help me change out of my clothes, instead shoving me into bed with a quick movement that jars me.

'Don't be wandering, you hear? We have enough to do without chasing down lost rubbish,' she spits at me. I blink, staring up at the woman, feeling so powerless. Once she's gone, I exhale out the day's stresses, trying to think about all that's happened. My eyes are heavy with exhaustion, and I know I'll soon be asleep – even with Rose's gurgling. Still, I know there's something I must do.

My mind is wavering, whether I like it or not. But I must stay sharp. I need to stay with it. If the knitting lady is right and this place isn't as safe as it seems, I need to be careful not to slip up. I lean over to the stand beside my bed and yank on the lamp cord. I slowly pull open the drawer and find a Bible and a notebook. I pluck a sheet of paper from the pad, locate the pen in the drawer, and lean onto the hard surface of the stand to jot down notes.

316: my room.

Knitting lady … Dorothy? Deborah?

Code to the stairwell?

I look at the list of reminders to myself. Not very impressive, but I haven't been here long. At least this will help me keep track of information. Maybe it will nudge me tomorrow to remember what I need to find out. I need to keep my wits about me. That's the one thing I'm certain of.

I tuck the paper in the back of the Bible, out of sight. I don't need Claire or the home discounting me as mad. I don't need them having more ammunition to write me off as nothing more than a disintegrating pile of flesh. I tug on the lamp cord, settle back into bed, and close my eyes. Rose's gurgles continue to rattle in the background, but I'm so exhausted, it doesn't matter. Drowsiness settles in, and I almost forget about everything that happened the night before.

But a while after I fall asleep, with the blackness of

the night enveloping me, I hear something that sends pure terror through me. It's a startling sound I just can't ignore.

Second Body Discovered in West Green; Citizens on High Alert as Threat Spreads

West Green, Crawley, West Sussex
28 June 1959

Citizens of West Green are on high alert as a second body this month has been uncovered in Ifield Pond Saturday morning, 27 June 1959, after a thorough investigation.

The body of Mrs Helen Deeley was found in Ifield Pond after a shoe was discovered by a Crawley resident at the edge of the water. Questioning of Mr John Deeley led investigators to believe that the shoe belonged to the missing Helen Deeley, and a search ensued. The body of the deceased was removed from the pond, and detectives are still conducting a search for more evidence in this case.

Mrs Deeley was not at their residence when Mr John Deeley returned home from work on 22 June, which was unusual for the housewife. When Mrs Deeley failed to return by the next morning, an extensive search ensued in West Green, but there was no sign of the woman.

Mrs Helen Deeley's death comes only a couple of weeks after the body of Elizabeth McKinley was discovered in a skip in West Green. With two murders in less than a month, residents of the typically peaceful neighbourhood are on high alert. The West Sussex Constabulary will not offer speculation as to whether the two murders are related despite the unarguable similarities regarding the bite marks on the bodies.

However, Mr Deeley was questioned in his wife's disappearance after detectives exposed that he was involved in an extramarital affair. The West Sussex Constabulary notes that John Deeley is considered a prime suspect in his wife's murder. Constables and detectives on the case offered no comment at this time, but sources have told reporters that dental records of Mr Deeley are being compared to the bite marks on both victims.

Despite the rise in violence in recent weeks, residents of the town are no stranger to horrific crimes. Many have expressed concern that this may be the work of a copycat of John Haigh, the Acid Bath Murderer. Haigh was executed on 10 August 1949 after being convicted of six terrifying murders. Haigh was notorious for his use of concentrated sulphuric acid to dispose of the bodies of his victims.

'We are shocked and scared. Who would do something like this to a woman as sweet as Helen?' Mrs Christopher Eades noted. 'Helen was always such a giving woman. Always volunteering and active in the church. I just don't understand.'

Detectives are still investigating the area at Ifield to search for any other clues. The person who discovered the shoe that led to the uncovering of Helen Deeley's body remains anonymous but is being thoroughly questioned at this time.

Women are delicate and weak creatures who are delicious to prey upon. But they aren't imbecilic, not by a longshot. And a woman always has a way of knowing when something is terribly wrong with the one she climbs into bed with. At least that is what I've come to believe.

Helen Deeley was no exception. Sweet and godly like the newspaper article says. She didn't deserve to be cheated on by her scoundrel of a husband. And she knew it.

They always know it, subconsciously at least.

Mr Deeley deserves to die for his disgusting behaviour. But I won't deviate from my plan. I won't abandon the list. I will stay focused because I'm in the middle of it now. I've selected my chosen ones. Everyone else would just be a distraction. I can't afford to be distracted.

Besides, I can't be too livid with the bloke because his digressions left the perfect opening. When a woman is riddled with doubt, she'll do anything to get to the bottom of it and set her perfect view of her life right again.

A letter strategically sent. A meeting place when John was going to be 'late at work'. The perfect, secluded spot at Ifield – and an easy place to rid the world of the evidence. After I made my mark, of course. And after I'd planted the shoe. After all, it wouldn't be any fun if she was never found, and those moronic bobbies are so incapable. The newspaper uses words like investigation *and* thorough, *but I know the truth. They'll never figure it out. They're too easily distracted, so very easily thrown off the case. Bloody hell, I had to lead them to the body. Yet they think they'll catch me? They have no idea. Wrapped up in dental records of the husband, the affair, of course, not painting him in a good light. They'll be focused on him for so long that they'll forget there is even another possibility.*

I shake my head, smiling at their idiocy. It's made the game easier, certainly. But sometimes I think it would all be so much more fun if they were actually smart – if it were actually challenging. What it must be like to kill in a place with real risk of being discovered …

But that's not what this is about. This is so much, dare I say, more intricately beautiful? This dance between strong and weak.

Sickly boy. Frail boy. Weak boy.

Not anymore. I'm not that boy anymore. No, I'm not. I chuckle. No one has any idea, do they?

I tuck the piece of the newspaper between my front teeth, closing my eyes as I bite down. So thin, so delicate. My teeth click over it, creasing it. But I'm careful not to taint the actual words of the article. I need to preserve it, my trophy added to the collection.

Oh, Helen. Did you regret your mistakes? Did you think about everything that led you to me?

Helen hadn't the slightest clue. The look of shock on her face when she saw me instead of the secret informant she was hoping for, the one to confirm her husband's affair, to give her the proof that would shatter her world. But I shattered her first. Oh, did I shatter her.

It was laughable, really, the look on her face. They're always so surprised. Someone they've seen countless times in town. Someone they've overlooked over and over. To them, I'm just the means to a necessary duty. I'm just a servant, in some ways. I'm just a nobody in West Green like I was all those years before.

But this nobody is certainly gaining infamy, even if it isn't by name.

Helen was a little old for my taste, really. I usually like them younger, fresher. The skin is just better. Soft and supple between the teeth – it's inviting. I savour the taste of vibrancy that seems to emanate from their skin. In truth, I'm not quite sure why Helen ended up on my list. I'd studied the women in West Green for weeks, thinking and pondering. Making the plan. Maybe it was the sadness in her eyes day in and day out. Maybe it was the fact she just seemed so lonely. Was she a pity kill? I don't know. I'd like to think it was more than that. I'd like to think there was something more there, calling to me.

But she was the second. And not the last. There are many more steps on my path to the end. It's a lot of work, really.

Exhausting if it weren't so energising. And, when I ask if it's all worth it, despite the intoxicating warmth that pulses in my blood, I know she *will make it worth it.*

The finale. The last one. The beautiful, wily one who will be the denouement to this masterfully executed plan. I've already found myself lurking, watching, peering at her through the darkness. I know I should wait. I've got the next one to worry about. I've got the next one to carry out. But she's just so beautiful. And her spark is something magnetising.

It's okay, though. I'm not jealous. Because I know I'll be the last one to appreciate her. And I'll get to put that beauty on full display soon enough.

But not yet. It's just not time yet.

I take the article reluctantly from between my teeth. I blow on the wetness, staring at the intricate pattern before I tuck away the mementos with the others and close the lid of the box.

Chapter 6

West Green, Crawley, West Sussex
28 June 1959

I glance out my window into the darkness and smile at the sight. He's here. Time to go.

I wait a moment to ensure that the house remains enshrouded in darkness. When a few minutes pass and I detect no stirring from Mum or Dad, I carefully nudge my bedroom door open, the stillness of the house reassuring me as I creep towards the stairs. I inch my way downwards, careful not to step on the squeaky ones. Every step feels painful and dangerous, but in a way, it thrills me. Maybe it's the knowledge that I'm sneaking out, or maybe it's the fact that in a few moments, I'll be with Charles.

I finally reach the front door and cautiously pull it open. Every millimetre seems to take an eternity, my cautious movements making me feel like I'm tearing apart a bomb that could explode at any moment. When the door is finally open, the muggy air oozes into my lungs. I turn and let myself look at Charles, grinning at the sight of him.

'Careful,' Charles whispers as I pull the door shut, gingerly clicking it behind me. My heart palpitates as I cross over to him, knowing the risk of all of this is worth it. Charles is worth it. Ever since I met the factory worker from Langley Green a few months ago when I was at the train station for a rare trip to the city, my heart hasn't been quite mine. Sitting beside Phyllis on that bench waiting for the train, I had seen the man who would change everything. He came into my life at a time when I didn't think life could be changed. We were headed to the city for a small trip, Phyllis knowing I needed a boost and inviting me along. It was when we were sitting there that Charles walked over, buying a ticket and standing nearby. He caught my eye, and I was entranced.

I don't know if it was his messy hair in a sea of boys with perfectly placed locks or if it was that he had the hands of a man's man, his factory job gruelling in ways boys of what my mother deems our 'social status' don't have. Maybe it was the way he introduced himself, or the way he seemed to drink me in with his eyes. Whatever it was, Charles Evans from Langley Green claimed me that day over three months ago. He possessed me at a time when I was certain I'd never open my heart again, when I was at a point in life when I was feeling like all was lost. In truth, it was a time when all *was* lost. He changed my mind, and I knew I'd spend my life wanting to thank him for that.

So here we are, months later, Mum still bashing Charles at every corner, trying to match me up with men from Dad's office. Here we are, me slipping out to go for a walk with the only man who understands me, who can lay claim to me once more.

Without another thought, I toss myself into his arms, relieved to be free of the imprisonment of the house. We pause in the grass for a moment, listening to make sure Mum and Dad aren't stirring. We watch the windows, waiting for a light to pop on. It doesn't, miraculously. Mum and Dad are apparently snoring away, blissfully oblivious to the disappearance of their only daughter who had been forbidden to leave the house after dark. With a second woman dead in West Green, Mum had incarcerated me a prisoner of my own home until the mass murderer – she is certain it is a mass murderer at work – is caught. So, at this rate, I'll be imprisoned in our quaint West Green home for the rest of my life.

Charles pulls me in tightly, his oaky scent entrancing me as it always does. He kisses my cheek. 'Come on, let's go.'

I follow him, his hand wrapped around mine, as he pulls me down the pavement, the streetlights illuminating our path. We wander along, me relishing the feel of his hand in mine, as we chatter incessantly about his job, about Mum, about all sorts of things.

We talk about Helen Deeley and the case. We talk about how long it will take for Mum to come around to liking Charles. We talk about the future Charles has promised me, once he gets enough money saved and can properly make an honest woman out of me.

We wander West Green, stroll into Ifield, and meander back towards my house. It wouldn't do to push things, although a part of me feels like I'm nineteen and Mum really has no say over the whims of my heart. I'm a grown woman, not a child. Still, as we mosey back, I freeze as we get about halfway down the street. Coming down the pavement is a figure, hands in his pockets, staring right at us. He is stopped a few paces ahead of my house. My heart skips, my blood curdling. I would know that arrogant pose anywhere. It's been a miracle that I've managed to keep him away from Charles this long, that their paths haven't crossed. But all of that is about to change, I realise with a chill. Everything could change.

'Who is that?' Charles whispers, gripping my hand tighter. Even if we won't admit it, the occurrences of the past few weeks have everyone on edge.

I almost utter that I don't know, but as we walk on carefully and the figure gets closer, my heart shreds. Why is he here? It's been a while since I've seen him around or sensed his presence. What is he doing here right now? And what are the chances we would see him?

'Evening, Addy,' he says, tipping his hat at me. 'What are you two doing out and about at this hour?'

We stop, the three of us on the pavement, the June sky hazy around us. A lump grows in my throat. The air is thick and weighty, choking my lungs with its humidity. I haven't seen him in a couple of weeks. I thought maybe, just maybe, he'd moved on, that he'd gotten over it all. But now, looking at that familiar glint in his eye, I know he's not done yet. He'll never be done. How could he be?

I don't know what to say as my horrific past comes crashing into my present and my potential future. This is what I've feared all along – Oliver's harshness looming like a dark cloud over my future happiness.

'Didn't catch your name,' Charles answers, puffing his chest as he clings to me.

Oliver extends a hand. 'Oliver Parsons. I can't believe Addy hasn't talked about me.'

Charles doesn't accept his hand. 'Why would she?' he asks, turning to look at me.

I feel my face turn a pathetic white, my whole life flashing before me. Seeing Oliver brings back so many intense feelings. Every single time I see him, a wave of what happened comes slamming into me. A wave of terror is always rippling closely behind. I want to cry. I want to vomit. I want to stab him in a violent storm of vengeance for the things he said to me, for what he's done to me. I want to make him pay.

Instead, I stand meekly, hating myself for bowing to him.

'Oh, didn't she tell you? You see, Addy and I were going steady for quite some time. Would you say a year, Addy?

Yes, we had so much planned out. But, shall we say, plans changed?'

I look up to see the smirk on his face, and it sickens me. There is a blustering hate in those steely eyes. I can't let go of what I've done, but seeing him, the hate glimmering, I know that Phyllis was right all those months ago.

'I suggest you get on home and leave us alone,' Charles says, stepping between us. I love him for it, but I hate him for it, too. I hate that Oliver will see what he means to me – because that simply assures Oliver will try his damnedest to ruin this. I can't let him.

'Cheerio, then,' Oliver says, tipping his hat, brushing past me as he walks on, whistling to himself. Shaking, I fall into Charles' arms.

'What was that all about?' Charles asks.

I can't speak, disturbed by what Charles and I running into Oliver could mean. Why now? It's been months. I've managed to keep Charles away from him for three months. Oliver has made his appearances here and there, always lurking nearby. He's always made his anger, his presence, known, and in truth, he's kept my fear alive. I know what he's capable of. Nevertheless, Oliver's never shown any real interest in interacting with Charles. He prefers to sneak about in the background of my life, dictating the rules from behind the scenes. Now, though, he's brazenly announced himself. What will this mean? I thought I could keep him at bay, could keep the two parts of my life separate. I thought I could hide my past in the background and keep Charles in the forefront. I believed that in a few months, things could be different – Charles and I with a new start, and Oliver fading out of my life for good.

Now, I'm not so sure. Oliver's a jealous man, and he's also an angry man. It makes for a deadly combination. Ever since that night in my room, I've been terrified about what he could possibly do. He thirsts for power in any form. With Charles in my life, Oliver must believe his power over me will diminish. The question is: what is he willing to do to latch onto what control he has left? What will he do to retain it?

After all, he has the one ace in his back pocket, the dangling thread between us that could ruin everything ...

Will I ever really be free from him? When I made that life-altering decision, I naively thought I'd severed all ties. Now, I realise Oliver will always have something to flaunt in front of me, something to own me with. I'm still his in so many ways. Vomit threatens to spill over at the mere thought of it all.

I could tell Charles the truth. I think he really does love me. I think maybe he could understand. But there are no guarantees, especially when I'm not sure if I understand myself.

Tears well in my eyes. Life is too complicated.

Charles leads me home, comforting me, assuring me all is okay, but the way he looks back down the street, I can't be so sure. I know he's nervous, and that only intensifies my anxiety and underscores the lingering guilt within me.

I sneak through the front door, careful to avoid the noisy steps. Back in my room, I sit for a long time, dazed and terrified about Oliver Parsons and what his appearance here, now, will mean. I glance out the window and see Charles, standing on the pavement, hands in his pockets. He is watching, waiting to make sure I'm safe. I love him for that. But you can't always protect someone, no matter how badly you want to.

*

'I was just in town, and guess what I've heard?' Dad utters as he hurries through the front door the next afternoon. Mum and I are baking a tart as Mum chatters about the latest fashions she saw in the catalogue.

'What is it, dear?' Mum asks as I stop rolling out the pastry, my head groggy from getting so little sleep last night. Every sound startled me, every broken dream a flash of Oliver Parsons.

'I was talking to Joseph,' he says. Joseph is Dad's closest thing to a friend in town. He is a constable, albeit it not a very good one, if rumours are to be believed.

'What did he say?' Mum prods.

'Well, although they aren't releasing this publicly, apparently the body was found thanks to that bloke you courted, Addy. Oliver.'

My stomach drops. Did he just say *Oliver*? Certainly, I heard wrong.

'Oliver Parsons? Now that was a mighty fine bloke, wouldn't you say?' Mum asks, making even the discovery of a dead body about my love life. I mentally bat her comment away.

'O-O-Oliver found the body?' I ask, needing confirmation that I haven't misheard.

Dad shrugs. 'He found a shoe by the pond and thought it was peculiar. That's what I've heard. Odd for him to be wandering out by the pond, but apparently, he was. I guess he was out for a stroll, said he was blowing off steam about something, when he came across a woman's shoe. He thought it suspicious and notified the police. One thing led to another, and they found poor Helen. Looks like your old chap's a hero.'

I steady myself on the table, squeezing my eyes shut. Oliver Parsons. He found Helen's shoe, which led police to the body? Bizarre. Strange. Peculiar. Horrifying.

My mind whirls with possibilities. Could he—? I don't even dare finish the thought. This is madness. Sure, Oliver turned out to be nothing like I thought he was. He showed his true side as our relationship continued. He proved to me that being a good husband wasn't in the realm of possibility. He scared me, especially after what I did all those months ago. But just how deep do those angry tendencies go? How far will he go to execute his temper, his strength? I sink into the kitchen chair, fears spinning about in my mind. It can't be. He wouldn't. *He couldn't …*

Perhaps I'm not the only one with a secret to harbour.

Chapter 7

Smith Creek Manor Nursing Home
2019

'What are you doing out here?' a male voice shouts behind me.

I turn from the door to the staircase to see a man I haven't seen before walking down the corridor, rushing towards me. He's wearing night clothes and his face is worn and tired. He wears thick spectacles with dark frames that make his eyes look tiny. Still, he seems to move about confidently, unlike most of us in this place. I shake my head, realising my hands are touching a cold, metal door. I turn back to see it's the door that shields the stairwell. What am I doing here? How did I get here? My bare feet are cold on the linoleum of the corridor.

The man roughly grabs my arm, pulling me towards my room, the door wide open as always.

'Come on, now. You're in here.' His words are gruff and

unapologetic. The icy tone coincides with the chill of the floor.

I look up at him, his steely eyes serene and beautiful but mysterious, too, behind the thick spectacles he wears. There's a strangeness to them, an unfamiliar familiarity that bleeds into me. It's too much to take in. My head hurts.

He walks with me inside the threshold of 316. My room, I remind myself. Yes, 316 is my room.

'You okay?' His voice is a hushed whisper, barely audible but also defining in the stark silence of the night-time hours.

'I – I don't know,' I admit, holding my aching forehead as I walk to my bed. The familiar gurgles of Rose echo in the room.

'Why were you over there?' he interrogates as he stands beside my bed, arms crossed. Rose emits a soft moan, but I don't glance over.

'I-I-I don't know,' I repeat. And it's true. I'm just as confused as he. Why was I at the stairs? Why was I touching the door? Did I have a dream?

Think, Adeline. Think. Like a sputtering car, my mind churns out possibilities, touches upon shifted memories from yesterday, from the night, from a few moments ago. What's real and what's fiction? What happened today and what is a snippet of a memory from long ago? My head pounds as I will it to sort through things, to put everything in order. I count to three in my head, thinking about it all. Processing. I wring the fingers on my left hand, squeezing and focusing and thinking.

And finally, as I feel the fog lift and the dust settle, my

mind does its job. It wasn't a dream, I realise after a few moments of silence. And I wasn't sleepwalking. I remember now, bits and pieces. Banging. I heard banging.

'I think I heard banging in the stairwell,' I announce as if to solidify my own memory.

'Impossible. The stairs are blocked off except to staff. Maybe one of them was on the stairs, but I doubt you heard it. Why would they be banging?' Rose's gurgles intensify, becoming moans of an eerie variety.

'Check the stairwell. I'm sure someone was in there.' My resolve strengthens. The banging in the stairwell happened, and it was strong and steady like a beating drum. I know what I heard. I know what I was desperate to investigate. *I know.*

He sighs gently as he takes the spectacles from his head, wiping the lenses on the fabric of his sleeve. 'I'm sure you just imagined it. Maybe you were just dreaming.' His words burn, and I exhale as I sink onto the bed. There is no banging now. Whatever I heard is gone, long gone. The only sound is Rose, snorting and sputtering. She's louder than I've ever heard her.

'How did you find me? Did I wake you?' I ask, my thoughts travelling to new territory now.

He stands over me, readjusting his dressing gown. 'Sometimes I wander at night. Easy up here to get away with it, after all. I like to check up on everyone up here, keep an eye on them. I was making my rounds when I saw you standing there,' he replies. He looks at me stoically, his face grim. Maybe it's the time of night, or maybe it's the thought of him wandering about aimlessly night after night. Regardless, he looks – frustrated. The way his forehead crinkles, the way his eyes watch me, I can tell he's not thrilled at finding me during his watch.

'Thank you,' I reply, smiling weakly, practically shouting to be heard over Rose. Why is she so agitated?

He stares at me for a moment too long before he nods and trudges out of the room. Despite the frustration in his eyes, there's a somewhat detectable kindness in his face, in his voice. It reminds me of how Charles used to look out for me. I like that familiarity. I like the incongruency between his eyes and who he seems to be.

When he's gone, Rose mercifully quiets down. I only hear the characteristic gurgles now and again that I'm used to already. I lie down, tucking myself in underneath the scratchy blanket. I drift off to sleep peacefully as I try to remember if the man told me his name. I can't remember. I just can't remember. Nonetheless, I don't wake up until morning, and for that, I'm glad.

Chapter 8

'Talk-like-a-what day?' I ask as Dorothy, the knitting woman, smirks at me. I've confirmed she's Dorothy, the other residents calling out to her as we came in. I must write it down in my notes when I get back to my room so I don't forget. I hate when I forget.

A strange hat, flimsy and black, perches on Dorothy's head. It looks like the kind a child would make in primary school. Dorothy readjusts it, as if my thoughts are discernible. I follow her into a corner room, off the common room, where several of Floor Three's residents are gathered.

'Talk-like-a-pirate day. It's quite fun. The staff all dress up, we get all types of savoury foods they disguise as pirate foods, and we play games,' Dorothy announces as I glance around the room. It's decorated with sea creatures, fake gold coins, and what appears to be a foam sword in the middle of the table.

I shake my head, not sure what to think about this super 'fun' day the staff has on the activity timetable. But

Dorothy insisted I come with her to the first activity, which is some kind of ridiculous charades game. How we're going to play charades when half the residents here can't even stand up or speak is beyond me. What's the alternative, though? Claire is out of town on a marketing trip. She'll be gone for a few days, and phone calls will be few and far between. There's nothing else here to keep my attention. So talk like a pirate or a buffoon or whatever else they have planned it is.

I spend the morning with Dorothy as we get to know the residents of Floor Three. I see the man who brought the paper for my noticeboard yesterday. He grins at me from the corner of the room, the scar on his forehead gleaming in the sunlight that cascades in. The man with the thick spectacles who helped me last night is also here, sitting with a woman who Dorothy says lives beside her. The woman is wearing a bright red dress that looks a bit too fancy for the occasion. She stares at me, and I think at one point she mocks me. I turn away, trying not to worry myself too much with it. There's enough to worry about as it is.

I'm starting to feel better, despite last night. I manage to laugh a few times. We finish the charades game, and our team wins. I take it as a good sign. I decide that maybe I can make the best out of being stuck here.

After lunch, I decide to take a nap while Dorothy goes to therapy on the first floor. I'm taking off my pullover, hot from all the activities, when my eyes land on something on my noticeboard. After I look at it once, twice, three times, I blink. It's still there. It's real, posted to the right of the pink menu that's tacked up.

Shaking my head, I back up and plant myself on my bed, wondering how I could've been so wrong. This place is nothing like it seemed.

Nothing.

Investigation Underway With West Green Killer On the Loose

West Green, Crawley, West Sussex
1 July 1959

Citizens of West Green and surrounding areas remain on high alert as investigators continue to search for confirmation of the killer responsible for two slain women in recent weeks.

Bite marks on the bodies of the two women, Elizabeth McKinley and Helen Deeley, seem to suggest a connection between their murders as well as the brutal disposal of their bodies. The proximity of their residences and the discovery of their bodies has also led to many questions for detectives.

Mr John Deeley, husband of the second victim, was initially a prime suspect in the case. However, several people have come forward to clear his name, providing an alibi. Detectives have not released results of a comparison of the dental records of the suspect and the bite marks on the victims. However, investigators are currently questioning those in surrounding areas and seem to be expanding their search to areas outside of West Green.

The only evidence garnished from either scene

was a shoe at Ifield Pond. No signs of struggle were apparent at either the McKinley or Deeley residences. Sources have told reporters that the constabulary in West Green has brought in special investigators to continue to search for clues and conduct interrogations of suspects. However, the constabulary is not revealing the names of any other suspects at this time, leading many to believe they are stumped on the trail of this maniacal killer.

Additionally, fears are running rampant as a third woman has been reported missing. Doreen Thompson was reported missing on 29 June, just 48 hours after Helen Deeley's body was retrieved from Ifield Pond. Although constables are not verifying a connection between her disappearance and the other murders, residents of West Green are quickly connecting the dots.

'We don't feel safe, and we don't feel like investigators are getting anywhere. They don't seem to be close to finding the killer, which is terrifying,' a resident who wishes to remain anonymous has stated.

'We have no proof at this time that the killer is a West Green resident. We could be dealing with an outsider coming into town for a few quick kills. Heck, the train station is so close. It could be anyone,' Paul Browning, a local florist shop owner, told reporters. Many residents concur with Browning, making this case truly terrifying.

With a skilled killer clearly at work and few pieces of evidence left behind at the scenes, investigators will certainly have their hands full. Currently, the strongest leads have led to dead ends, according to an anonymous source close the case. The constabulary continues to plead with anyone who may have information to come forward and continues to seek out suspects in the case.

'Perhaps the bite marks will be his undoing,' Joseph Greyson, head schoolmaster in Horsham, noted. Greyson, a former resident of West Green, has been writing a book on the John Haigh murders and is no stranger to the works of homicidal killers – his own mother was murdered fifteen years ago in the same town.

Certainly, word is spreading quickly about the mass murderer on the loose in Crawley, and residents in neighbouring areas are growing concerned that this may be just the beginning.

I've thought about slowing down a bit. Perhaps I'm gathering too much attention too quickly. It doesn't do to rush.

Gnawing on the edge of the fork, my teeth clinking the metal, my nerves are grated. Maybe I did it too fast. Dammit. I'm patient. I shouldn't be doing this so quickly. I need to be patient.

But I saw her again this weekend. That hair flowing down her back, those slender legs practically inviting me to take a taste. My insides churn with longing when I see her, wanting so badly to taste her flesh, to feel that cold skin between my teeth as I bite down, as I mark her. I long to feel the power of usurping the life from her body, of adding her lifeforce to my own.

Weak boy. Sickly boy.

Not me. Not anymore.

Does she even know me? Does she see me? Sure, she's passed me enough times in the past few weeks. She's even brushed against me now and again in the past few days. She's looked into my eyes as I stare back at her, trying to supress the smirk.

But does she really see me? Or am I just the bloke she thinks she knows? She's got me all wrong. All wrong indeed. But that's okay. Her day will come, and so will mine.

I look at the article again. I need to be careful. I need to stay collected. It will get harder and harder with each one. But I'm patient, and I'm no fool. I've prepared for this. I can win this game. They can't. They'll never win, not this time.

I used to be upset about being invisible, about fading into the background. But now, it's an advantage, you see. The one they always overlooked is rising up right underneath them – and they have no idea.

Oh, how glorious it would feel for them to know. I smile at the thought, at the look on their faces. They don't know what I'm capable of. They never did.

I'm doing it now, though. I'm really doing it. Would it have made a difference? I think about all those times I stared in the mirror, wondering what it would take. Now I know – and it's electrifying. Power is addictive, especially when it comes from the ultimate price.

Stay calm. Stay smart, *I remind myself. They're searching harder now. But search away. Because they have no idea. No idea at all. And the next one is going to be even better, even more beautiful. I'm getting better. I'm getting stronger. And they'll never guess what happens next.*

I fold the paper carefully. I need to keep the souvenirs from the masterpiece I'm creating. I need to keep the proof for myself, always just for me. Because that's what this is for, no matter what I thought in the beginning.

It started for her, but it's for me now. It's all for me. Every glorious one of them.

I carefully place it on top of the letter from Doreen. A simple letter, one that comes every month from her cousin up in Yorkshire. Nothing exciting. Just babbling about the weather and shopping and the new market down the street. A mundane letter. Those are always my favourite. They remind me that even on the simplest of days, everything can be snatched.

Even her. Even she could be plucked away in the simplest of moments. That's where the rush comes from. I crave that feeling, that control. Does God feel like this, sitting up high, waiting to twist and turn the paths of life? I grin, shaking my head.

Silly boy. Weak boy. All mighty and powerful man.

I like that no one is ever expecting it – the letter, the moment, the blood leaking from their bodies as they stare into my eyes and wordlessly ask, why?

Chapter 9

Smith Creek Manor Nursing Home
2019

I'll be watching you.

After finding the strength to stand from my bed, I pull the note down from the noticeboard for a closer look. I hold the crumpled piece of lined paper in my hands, shaking. The scrawled letters taunt me as I trace them with my gaze, analysing every loop, every curve, the dot in the 'I'. What does this mean? Who did this? And when? The questions swirl in my blood like a plague I can't get rid of. I squeeze my hand into a fist, a frigidness throbbing in my veins. My mind races, trying to place the note, the meaning, the person who did it. Why? Across the room, a gurgling sound reminds me that I'm not alone, not ever. Rose is more vocal than usual.

The curtain to her side of the room is open, and I look over. Rose sits, wide-eyed, her chest heaving as she gasps for breath. Her eyes fall on the note in my hand, and her lips begin to move, bloody mucus dribbling from her mouth.

'Rose? What is it?' I ask, certain now that the woman wants, no *needs*, to tell me something. She stares, babbling incoherently, as her hand shakes violently. It seems to take every effort for her to lift her arm, the stilted movement taking so long that my heart has time to race again.

'Rose? Talk to me. Tell me,' I coax, my fingers squeezing the paper between my fingers tightly, as if I'm afraid it will disappear if I loosen my grip.

Her hand whips wildly as she balls all her fingers on her left hand into a fist – all but her pointer finger, which is crooked but still somewhat outstretched. I think for a moment she is pointing at me, but instead, her finger carefully lines up with the note at my side.

Her lips move, her eyes frantic. I wish I could read her mind. She knows something. She does.

'Rose, what is it?' I ask, desperate for the answer I know I won't get. *Think, Addy. Think. She knows something. You need to figure it out.* Maybe if I could get her paper ... could she write? If I helped? If I could only ...

'What's going on in here?' a voice asks. I turn to see Jones in the threshold. What's he doing here? It isn't night time, is it?

'She just seems upset,' I say, hiding the note instinctively. Wouldn't do for him to see it. That is one thing I do know.

'Of course she is. She's a bloody vegetable,' Jones spews,

rolling his eyes as he storms over. 'What are you doing over here? Get out. Go to your activity or something.'

'Don't you usually work nights?' I ask, trying to shield the note from view as I slink back to my side of the room, distracting him with what I hope will be a simple question.

'That's none of your business,' he retorts, his jaw clenching.

He retrieves Rose's wheelchair from the corner of the room. Her arm is still out, stiff and straight, pointing, her eyes wildly flipping about. I bite my lip, not sure how to resolve the issue, still thinking about the secret paper in my hand.

'Where is she going?' I ask, curious.

Jones stops, scowling across the room at me. 'Why do you care? Wind your neck in, you daft cow.'

I sigh. *What to do? What to do?*

'Well, it's just, you see, I'm a bit worried. It seems as though Rose was trying to tell me something. I think she saw something ... troublesome.'

'Oh, did she now? Bloody amazing, I'll tell you. A mute and barmy woman is now telling you secret messages. It's especially amazing considering this old hag doesn't even have a tongue.'

I freeze at the words, considering them carefully.

Jones shakes his head, rolling his eyes. 'Honestly. I don't even know anymore,' he spews. 'Now get out. Rose here is headed to see the doctor. Apparently, her meds are a bit off. She's been more agitated lately, according to the day nurse.' There is an eerie look in his eyes that causes me to pause. The way he discusses her meds chills me a bit, especially because of how he beams. Something just irks me about the way he looks at me.

I study Rose as he lifts her into the wheelchair like she's a sack of items from the market – but perhaps with even less care. As he's lifting her, some of Rose's blood-tinged drool lands on the front of Jones' shirt.

'Jesus Christ, bloody disgusting!' he screams, revulsion painted on his face. He glances around the room, finding one of Rose's shirts on the bedside table. He grabs the shirt, wipes off the spit like he's wiping off remnants of the Black Plague, and flings the shirt into the centre of the room. Muttering expletives under his breath, he wheels Rose past, and I gape at her. She doesn't turn her head. I look to see that even in the chair, her hands are still shaking. She murmurs and whines as he wheels her out, and a tear falls down my cheek.

I glance back at the note, my mind whirring with fear and confusion. Who would do something like this? Who is watching me, and why?

And then my mind flashes back to that second night and the man with the thick spectacles. He told me he likes to wander, that he likes to keep an eye on everyone here. Could this be his doing? I shiver at the prospect.

And then I shiver again as I think about dear Rose. What was she trying to tell me? What does she know? And more importantly, how can I find out?

*

I try to quell my nerves, but the chaotic atmosphere downstairs isn't helping. They've ushered all who are willing and able down to Floor One, a seemingly rare visit. It looks like Floor Three, of course, but there's something about being on a lower level that makes me feel slightly better. It's like the air down here is more breathable, even though the smell is still the same.

The patients I presume live on Floor One look angrily at the residents from the other floors, as if we're invaders. A few nurses at the front of the large room try to demand quiet as the forty or so patients gathered argue, grumble, and just generally make noise. I settle into my seat beside Dorothy, happy to have a friendly face nearby. Our bingo cards sit in front of us on the table as we wait for the game to begin. It seems like a lot of hassle for the staff to gather us all just for a game of bingo, but I suppose we've got nothing better to do. Plus, it's done me some good to get away from that room, from Rose, and from everything that's happened up there.

I peruse the room, looking for the man with the spectacles. He lives close to me, in 313. I saw him go in there, and I wrote it in my notes. Was it really him that left that note on my board, or could it be someone else here?

'You look like you're a million miles away,' Dorothy sputters, interrupting my thoughts. 'Not that I can blame you. This game seems like a terrible idea. I should've stayed in my room. *Cranford* was playing, and I do love that one, you know?'

I bite my lip, glancing around at some familiar faces and some unfamiliar. The priest from down my hallway, I think 310, sits at a table nearby. He taps his foot incessantly, his head ticking to the side as he does. He is murmuring something indiscernible, and he presses his eyes shut. I look over at the seat beside him, Babbling Barbara chattering away as well. There are a few more residents from Floor Three down here, including the man with the scar who brought the menu for the noticeboard and a woman from Dorothy's side of the floor.

I sigh, returning my attention to Dorothy. 'I found a note in my room yesterday,' I whisper to Dorothy, leaning in so as not to have anyone else hear. I don't know why, but this just feels like the sort of thing I should keep to myself.

'Love note? Got a secret admirer?' she asks, winking and shimmying her shoulders.

'No,' I reply, stone-faced. 'A quite frightening note, actually. I think someone is, well, it seems someone is watching me. Like someone here is after me. I'm feeling quite anxious about it.'

'That's silly. You just got here. Who could possibly be upset with you already?' she asks.

'Well, I had an interaction with the man from 313, the one with the thick spectacles, on the second night. He said he wanders about, keeps an eye on everyone. I don't know, there was just something weird about the way he looked at me.'

'The man with the spectacles? Oh, you mean the handsome one?'

I shrug noncommittally.

'It couldn't be him. He's such a nice guy. Gorgeous, but also just nice. And I've never even seen him wandering about, so that can't be right.'

I shake my head, wondering if I have it all wrong. Have I mixed things up again? I will have to look in my notes when I return to my room. But I must have it right. He is the one who found me. Isn't he?

'Well, you know, maybe it was Barbara. She has a habit of wandering around nonsensically, as you know. Probably just her being a bit off her trolley again.' Dorothy fiddles with her bingo card.

'Perhaps,' I say. I've thought about the possibility, it's true. Barbara does make her way around. Still, the woman is blind. How would she write those words with such perfect penmanship? Could someone have written it for her and used her as the delivery person? Or could it just be an unusual occurrence that has no evil intent behind it? Could it just be me overreacting? Both Claire and Charles used to say I tended to do that sometimes. There's no reason to believe the note was actually a warning, after all. I haven't done anything. I just moved in. I barely know anyone here, in truth. Who would be after me, and why?

'Okay, ladies and gents, bingo is about to begin! Get ready, and eyes down,' an overly chipper male staff member says from the front of the room. He's young and jolly, not someone I've ever seen on our floor. He must be a

Floor-One nurse or brand-new. I look down at my card. The room quietens as he prepares to call the first number.

'What do we win in this game?' I ask, glad to have my mind occupied with a task, even if it is just bingo.

'Some boxes of digestives or sweets, I think. Don't get too excited. Stakes are low. Still, you have to watch out. Some of these scoundrels try to cheat, and some get downright mad about winning. Watch your card closely,' she orders, focusing on the numbered paper in front of her, concentrating like the veteran she apparently is. I lean on my hand, not able to focus on the numbers but not wanting to think about everything else.

'Double five, fifty-five,' the caller yells, and the room is abuzz with lukewarm excitement as residents mark their cards. Some ask for repeats, and a few just stare off into the distance, unsure of how bingo even works. But from the table beside us, someone lets loose, the game clearly too much.

'Dammit!' a voice shrieks from the table nearby, a fist smashing on the table violently. I turn and see that it's the priest with green eyes. He shoves his chair back, kicking at the table.

'I bloody hate that number! Why would you call that? Why? Unreal. *Unreal*,' he shouts, shaking and frothing with rage as he clears the cards off his table, almost hitting Babbling Barbara with his fist in the process. Some nurses cross the floor quickly, trying to calm him, but he boils with outrage. He spews and sputters, stammering about numbers and blasted nurses and all sorts of injustices. Barbara, still beside him, claps and giggles at the spectacle. As the nurses lead him out of the room, I stare up at him.

'Don't look at me, you sinner,' he spits, glaring right at me with a venomous rage. He glowers at me as he passes, and my heart pounds. What was that all about? I don't even know him. Never even spoke to him. But the way he looks at me, I wince. The vehemence, the insidious glare – it says a lot. He hates me. I don't even know why. Could he be the one who left the note? Could he be the one I need to watch out for? I don't know.

'Don't worry about him,' Dorothy says, reaching out to touch my hand. I startle. 'That one just spent too much time in the good book. Made him a bit of a nutter, if you ask me. I guess going without sex for that long would do that to a person, you know? He's pretty far gone, wrapped up in his religious fury.'

'Oh,' I reply, not sure what to say.

'Okay, everyone, back to the game. Who is ready for a new number?' the still-jovial young man up front asks, trying to salvage things.

'What did I miss?' a voice asks from behind me as the young nurse calls the next number and the residents settle down, most forgetting about the priest's outburst in favour of winning a bag of crisps. I jump at the sound.

'Sorry, Addy. Didn't mean to startle you. Can I sit here?' I glance over to see the man with the thick spectacles who found me by the stairwell. What did he say his name was?

Did he say his name? Too many names to remember. I need to check my notes when I get back.

My words catch in my throat, my heart racing at the sight of him. I stare at him with suspicion, not sure if I can trust him after the note on my noticeboard. It just seems too coincidental, and even though I trust Dorothy, I don't think she's right about him. He might be good-looking, but something tells me he isn't harmless. I stare at the empty seat beside me, beckoning him forward. He sits down as I wordlessly study him.

'Oh, just Father Patrick losing his cool again. They should know better than to bring him down here,' Dorothy says. 'Good-looking fellow, but wow, that temper.'

'He does this all the time?' I ask, curious about the man down the hall from me, Father Patrick apparently, and what his frenzies could mean. Could his outburst be a sign that he's trouble? Could he somehow be connected to the mystery note on my noticeboard? I need to write this down so I don't forget.

'All the time. Crazy temper on that one. Nutty, isn't it? I suppose a life of celibacy has a way of catching up to you. I don't know what his life was like before this place, but goodness, I hope he was milder mannered in his glory days. That man explodes every day. The only time he seems calm is when he's got a Bible in his hand. They used to let him lead prayer services in the community room, but then he got a bit overzealous. They don't let him do it anymore, and ever since then, his temper has gotten worse.

You ask me, I think they should just let him lead a fully fledged church service every single day, all day.'

I jiggle my foot, glancing over at the man beside me as he leans back in his chair. The numbers continue on and on in the game, but I barely pay attention.

A voice from the table to our right chimes in. 'So, clinging to the new girl, huh? What, she have something on you?' a woman hollers. I turn to see a woman with very bright red lipstick and a royal-blue dress glaring at our table. If it weren't for the fact she was missing an arm and looked rather worn out, I wouldn't know she was a resident. Her outfit is too put-together for this place, unlike the joggers and pyjamas most wear. She looks like she could be going out for dinner or to a gala, not to bingo.

'Piss off, Vivienne, he's with me,' Dorothy says, rolling her eyes. 'He can sit wherever he wants.'

'What's that about?' I ask, Vivienne still glaring at me.

'Nothing,' the man beside me says. I should ask his name, but I feel silly doing that now. 'Vivienne just likes to think I'm her property.'

'That woman acts entitled. Thinks everyone here should bow down to her. Like she's something special.' Dorothy shakes her head, underlining the conflict between the two. I can tell already that Vivienne thinks she's the queen of the floor. It's obvious she feels the need to assert herself.

Life in Smith Creek Manor seems so complicated. I thought my days here would be monotonous and simple. I never expected so much drama. The bingo game moves forward, and Vivienne continues to stare, making snide comments about me and my outfit. The man beside me just shakes his head.

'Angry woman,' he mumbles, staring at me. I'm not sure if he's talking about Vivienne or something else. His eyes glare with an unclear motive.

'I hope she's not angry with me. I'd hate to make enemies here already,' I admit.

The man with the spectacles peers at me. 'You're worried about making enemies?' he asks, smirking as if it's a joke. It's so strange, his mannerisms, his expression.

'Apparently I'm doing a wonderful job at it,' I answer, not sure what to say. He stays silent, shaking his head slowly.

We finish the game, and I win a bag of crisps. I give them to Dorothy, who exclaims gleefully it's our table's first win in a while. I must be lucky, she proclaims. I beg to differ. When I'm walking towards the lift with the man with the thick spectacles, Vivienne stops in front of me.

'Better watch yourself, Evans. Don't think you can come to Smith Creek Manor and take over. You're nothing special,' she says, spitting towards me as I shake my head. Unbelievable. She stumbles off to the lift, making sure she's first in line. I remain behind with the man and Dorothy. Babbling Barbara is stooped over next to us.

'Women,' the man says through gritted teeth as Vivienne glowers at me again.

I look up at his eyes, and something flits through me.

There's something about him that feels soothing, that feels homey. But there's also something else, something I can't explain. Something that makes me feel quite uncomfortable, uneasy. It's like I can't sit still near him for fear of – what? What is it that could possibly bother me about him? I don't know why, but I feel like he's a refuge here in this chaotic whirl of confusion, but I also feel like he's a whirling confusion in what's supposed to be my refuge. Despite the sinking sensation in my gut when I'm around him, I feel like I know him. None of it makes sense. Then again, very few things do make sense anymore. I sigh in frustration at all that's slipping away, at all of the chaos that plagues me every single moment.

When the four of us finally get our turn in the rickety lift and return to Floor Three, we walk together, saying goodbye to Dorothy who is off to take a nap. We pass the nurse's station where a nurse is snoring away at the desk. We trudge forward until we get to Room 313.

'Well, it's my stop. Goodnight, Addy. Be careful.' And with that, the man in the thick spectacles is inside his room, off to the corner to lie down.

I continue towards my room, my head hurting. I don't understand what it is. It's been an emotional day, from the note, to Rose, to the priest's outburst, to Vivienne. But that's not what's bothering me. It's something else. As I stop near the threshold to my door, tracing the familiar numbers outside my room as has become habit, I pause as the realisation slaps into me.

He called me Addy. Only my closest friends and family call me Addy. No one calls me that here. It's just so – familiar. That's it. He feels familiar because the nickname is familiar.

I walk into my room, troubled at the prospect. What could it mean? What could it mean indeed? But I don't have time to ponder it too long because when I get into my room, I gasp at the horrific sight before me that reminds me of the truth: no one is safe here. No one.

Chapter 10

Purple. Her face is a ghoulish, faded shade of purple. If this were an Easter celebration, the hue of her face would complement the dull pink of the dusky wallpaper in our room. Her eyes wide open, staring ahead like she's done so many times, she's frozen in place as if she just needs a good thaw. My chest aches, screeching in an agony I can't label. I need to calm down, but how do you breathe through the sight of death?

There are no gurgling sounds, her lips parted and drooping as if she's desperate to say something but silenced. I cradle myself, shaking my head as if I can will this all away. The longer I stand, cemented in place, the more certain I am that she'll inhale any second.

I cross the room cautiously, tears flowing, but I know before I get to her bed, before my hand touches her waxy skin, the fingernails already white, that she's been gone, long gone for a while. How many hours had she been sputtering for air? How long has she been here in this bed, staring up at the ceiling, waiting for a saviour who never came? Death does not look peaceful on her. Death looks mangled and twisted, a macabre reminder that the scythe always strikes when we're fighting to breathe once more.

Why did I go to bingo? If I had stayed put, maybe I could've saved her. Maybe I could've helped her. I'd like to think she's at peace, but staring at the horror marring her eyes, I'm not sure. She didn't slip away. She didn't drift off to the quiet unknown.

She was ripped from this world, clawing to a life that was no longer hers but was life, nonetheless.

I rush to the side of her bed, slamming my thumb into the call button over and over. After a long time, a nurse comes by, the brown-haired nurse. She gasps when she walks in, seeing me standing over the body.

'Oh, dear. Come on, Adeline. Come on. It's okay,' she says, ushering me out as she reaches for the phone by Rose's bed, calling for help. I cower in the corridor, fearful I'm going to go out too right now, my heart thrashing. I need to sit down. I need to get to the doctor. This is too much, but I can't look away. I'm drawn to the body, mesmerised by the scene. I keep gawking in at the purple-skinned, white-haired woman I barely know yet can't help but mourn for. She was here this morning. She was *here*. Who noticed her slip away? Who will notice her absence? Who will grieve for her silent descent into the great darkness? It pains me to think that maybe no one at all.

I lean my head against the wall, tears falling, as I think

about earlier. She was anxious to tell me something, fighting to make her lips form the words. And now she's gone. I can't help but wonder if it's connected. If it is, I realise as a team of nurses and professionals storms into our room, Rose's decaying body no longer alone, I'm in more trouble than I thought.

It's not safe here. The realisation slams into me like a train pummelling down the rails. None of us are safe – yet, somehow, I can't help but think a darker version of danger lurks about my room specifically. The note this morning, and now Rose. It can't be a coincidence, can it? But what does it mean? My mind wanders to frightening memories from long ago, a familiar sense of foreboding bubbling in my chest.

No. It's been so long. It can't possibly have anything to do with any of that. It just doesn't make sense. After all this time? That chapter has long since been closed and all but forgotten. Hasn't it?

Still, coming back to Crawley, all sorts of ominous visions blur my mind. Chaotic memories and anxiety spin together, confusing me. It's not safe here – but why? Are we all in danger, or is something more specific, more *planned*, at work?

My chest heaves as I think about the possibility. Staring into the room as the professionals race about and I hear questions exchanged about how they'll possibly explain this one, my mind dances with questions of my own. Who will be the next one claimed by Smith Creek Manor? How long until I, too, am desperately clawing my way up for air while no one notices a thing? The nurses flitter about, shouting orders. No one spots the tiny, crouching old woman at the edge of the room who is on the brink of disaster herself. There is no one to save me. I need to calm myself.

'You okay?' a voice asks as a hand touches my shoulder, startling me.

I turn to see the man from 313 standing behind me, his dressing gown open over his clothes as he readjusts the thick spectacles.

'Heard a commotion and figured I'd see what was going on.' His sinuous voice is deep and warm, despite the cracking of it from age. I hang onto his words, rubbing my clammy palms together. He is warm. He is inviting.

I look up into his face, those steel eyes shining down on me. I study the wrinkles, the stubble growing on his chin. His hair is slicked to the side, grey and stiff. Still, those eyes ... I'm certain now. I *know* that he's familiar. I'd know those eyes anywhere. I don't understand how I missed it. It all makes so much more sense. Yes, I realise as it dawns on me. Everything makes sense.

At first, the understanding is a warm, smooth stone unearthed and treasured. My mind isn't completely gone. It hasn't failed entirely. I've sorted it through. I know him. I do. But, as he continues peering down at me, my mind dancing about through memories and past moments, a darker realisation takes hold.

Instead of comforting me, the understanding that, yes, I do know him, only affirms my deepest, cagiest fears. This man, this memorable man, is here at a time when I don't know who I can trust, at a time when my roommate has died and I don't know why. He's standing here, ready to catch me when I fall – or so it would seem to the unassuming.

However, as I look into the eyes of the man from my past, I know one thing for sure: decades ago, he was not a man who would catch me and save me from slamming into the ground. In fact, at several points in my life, he was a man who would willingly trip me, let me crash into the cement and fracture into a thousand pieces. In many ways, he did shatter me over and over until I was one crack shy of oblivion. And in many ways, I'm certain that even this much time couldn't heal the wounds and the desire for vengeance.

I take a step back, wondering how and why, questions spinning round and round as I count to three.

Third Missing Woman's Body Discovered; Police Still Searching for Killer and Motive West Green, Crawley, West Sussex 5 July 1959

In a new development in the string of missing women from West Green, Crawley, a third body has been uncovered. Miss Doreen Thompson of 15 West Street, West Green, was reported missing 29 June, less than forty-eight hours after the body of Helen Deeley was uncovered in Ifield Pond. Doreen Thompson's remains were uncovered in Langley Green, Crawley, around 6.00 p.m. on 4 July 1959.

Miss Thompson was reported missing by her parents on the night of 29 June when she failed to return home from an outing to a friend's house. The friend, Linda Jennings, reported later that Doreen, 17, never appeared at her home. Investigators are uncertain of where Thompson went instead or if she was potentially snatched by the killer on her walk down the street. No witnesses have reported seeing Thompson walking.

Police were called on 4 July after a resident of Langley Green reported finding a dismembered body in several bags in a wooded area near the Langley Green pub. Detectives noted that the body of Thompson had bite marks that appeared to be created by a human, similar to Elizabeth McKinley's body uncovered in a skip in June. Several stab wounds were also found. Detectives are currently considering the fact that the three women from West Green are the work of a mass killer due to the proximity of the sites of their discoveries and the rapid occurrences of their deaths. Investigators are not sharing any leads they have at this time, but Chief Constable Warren did reveal that investigators are currently widening their search for the suspect, considering the bodies are being found in various parts of Crawley.

Citizens of West Green and Langley Green are on high alert. Police are asking residents to be on the lookout for odd behaviours and to be cautious when travelling alone, especially females. Anyone with information is asked to contact West Sussex Constabulary at this time.

Funeral arrangements are being made for Doreen Thompson, who was an active member of the West Green Choir.

Sweat pours from my head as the hot water laps over me. I haven't got much time. I need to be ready, and it's already been a busy day.

The vigil is tonight, a town gathered for prayer in the midst of tragedy. I chuckle aloud, my laughter mixing with the water dripping. Am I the only one who knows how pointless prayer is? They'll all be asking why and how, but only I know. Prayers are pointless, and hopes are drowned in a pool of blood. Doreen Thompson's blood.

Why do the people of this town make it so easy? Words like mass killer *popping about, yet the youth of the town insisted on rebelling, even in the face of danger. It was so easy to snatch Doreen from the darkened street, the girl climbing out the window of her house. I'd almost considered waiting. Did it count if it was such an easy kill? Especially when the idiot girl had taken the back way to the Jennings' home? It was like the heavens were aligning for me to carry out my plan. It was too easy.*

But I knew I had to keep the plan moving. It has to keep

going, and although Doreen was one I was excited about, she isn't the *one. Her black hair cascading down her neck, her olive-coloured skin – these things thrilled me. But not as much as the finale will. Not as much as Adeline.*

I've still been keeping an eye on her, the final one on my list. There's another example for you, that final one – despite all the warnings, she's sneaking about foolishly. I've thought about how easy it would be to snuff her out early, the itch in my veins almost prompting me to do something rash. But I don't want to deal with that bloke. I don't want the bastard to be any part of her end. I need to be with her, alone, for it to count. That's when the satisfying thrill of it all sinks in. Watching in desperation as I alone observe their exit into the next world.

When I was in school, I remember learning about Charon, the ferryman to Hades. Even as a boy, I thought about what that job must be like. To have such power. To be the one driving the souls to the underworld. A lonely job, but an exciting one, I thought. The other kids dreamt of being the gods, but I knew that real power came from the darker work.

Now, I am my own form of Charon, and I take my payment from the women before they die. I ferry them off, out of this world, and help them crossover into the murky waters of the next. If only they could see me now, all those people who thought I'd never be someone.

Weak boy. Troubled boy. Bad boy.

Not anymore. No, not anymore.

I lift a hand easily out of the water of my bath, slicking back my hair as I stare up at the ceiling. I close my eyes, sinking into the feeling of the water surrounding me and of the feelings of success that envelop me.

I'm doing it. I'm really doing it. And no one suspects a thing.

Sometimes it's hard to accept that I'm invisible. Sometimes I just want to shout from the rooftops that it's me, that I'm the brilliant one. I want to share this glory with someone, with everyone. But there is no one. It's just me. It's always just me.

I want to talk about how easy it was to pull the letter opener from my pocket, to stab Doreen over and over in the alleyway, her screams silenced by my hand as I felt her body grow limp.

I want to tell them how brilliantly I dragged her away, how perfectly I marked her as mine, that final touch on the masterpiece, the seal on the letter, the checkmark on the list. I'm getting better now. I'm learning. Even when I was in trouble, the headmaster always said I was a good learner. I was skilled at memorising details. I was. No matter how many times I was chided, they couldn't deny I was good at learning.

But now, I'm an even better learner. The town is my classroom, and the bodies are my practice sculptures for the epic finale. It will be grand, for sure, because I'm truly becoming a master I never even expected I could be.

I was made for this. I was bloody made for this.

It's a shame, though, that I must keep calm. At least tonight will be a little different. I will be there amongst them, and they won't have a clue. But I will. I will know that I'm winning at this game, the entire town oblivious in grief and naivety and in ignorance. No one suspects me. I'm so good at what I do.

Most of all, the next one on the list doesn't have any idea – and I've already started. I've already studied her, watched her, and prepared.

The next strike will be soon. It must be.

But that's a concern for another night. I sit up, draining the tub and thinking about how tonight, I'll simply bask in the glory of my sinister secrets, wearing two hats – the one I wear in public, and the one that I'll keep hidden.

Chapter 11

West Green, Crawley, West Sussex
7 July 1959

'Surprised they're still having this get together with Doreen's death and all,' Phyllis says, sitting next to me at the long table, plopping her tea and digestives down beside us.

'Yeah, it feels – wrong,' I reply before taking a sip of my tea.

'Well, apparently Doreen's family wanted the church to go on with the youth gathering tonight. Thought Doreen would want it that way. I think they're still in shock,' Anne says, a girl from a few streets over who has always been closer to Phyllis than to me. She sits across from me. Dozens of other teenagers stand in the queue at the table where some stony-faced adults serve tea and digestives in the church basement at Crawley Community Church.

The youth gathering has been a regular occurrence for

the past couple of years but still, we were all surprised when it was going ahead in spite of circumstances. With Doreen dead and the town in an uproar about the killer on the loose – everyone certain it's a mass killer now – I thought for certain this whole evening would be cancelled. There are several constables placed at each door as a precaution. All our parents are upstairs in the church, holding a vigil for Doreen. Such an uncanny night in the community. Everyone is bewildered by the tragedy and unsure of how to act, to talk, to just be.

'Crazy, isn't it? To think Doreen is gone?' Anne asks, playing with a digestive and dunking it into her tea. We all nod, lost for a moment in the thought. I knew Doreen. She'd been a nice enough girl, someone I talked to from time to time when I saw her around the neighbourhood.

'Can't imagine what Linda's going through,' Phyllis adds. 'I wish they had found her alive.'

We all warm our hands on our cups, a table of rowdy boys behind us laughing as they make crude jokes. We all avoid the reality we don't want to admit aloud. Doreen's probably not the last one. Anyone could be next.

'Where's your bloke tonight?' Phyllis asks, seemingly eager to change the subject.

'Charles is working,' I offer.

'Guess you're left with just us then,' she says, and I lean against her shoulder.

'Could be worse,' I reply, grinning.

The night continues with games for the teenagers, letting

us forget about the harsh realities of the town. At one point, Phyllis and I decide to wander upstairs, our awkward age of nineteen letting us hover between the youth and the adults, not quite fitting in either world. But, Phyllis wants to pay her respects, to say a few prayers for Doreen. Who am I to stop her?

We stagger up and find a pew in the back of the church. As the pastor leads the congregation in prayer, I glance around. It seems like our whole town is here. I see the owners of the pub, the café, the florist shop, and the market stalls scattered about, all offering their prayers. The town barber is parked in the front row, tears falling shamelessly from his eyes. A few pews back, the postman bows his head, sitting alone on an end seat. He shakes his head as if in disbelief, as we all are. One of our school teachers sits in the second pew, tears falling as he clutches his hat to his chest as if it will give him comfort. Everyone is just seeking anything to bring them comfort. The butcher, our choir leader, businessmen and homemakers from West Green all gather – so many people here to pray for Doreen and grieve for another girl who died too young.

A few other teens make their way upstairs, perhaps feeling guilty for having fun while Doreen is cold and decaying.

Looking around, I'm unexpectedly soothed by the warm presence of the town gathered in solidarity. For a moment, I forget that West Green is on the verge of disaster, that someone is tearing this community apart. For a while, I think about the serene connectedness here, how everyone pulls together. I glance around the church, taking in the gathered, concerned community members.

And then I see him. Oliver.

He runs a hand through his hair as he catches my eye. I turn away, but not before I notice him glaring at me. Everyone else sits in a reverent way, painted with grief. But not Oliver. Instead, he is poised and calm, his jaw clenched. He taints this aura of beautiful connectedness in the midst of tragedy with a cockiness that verges on excitement. What's wrong with him?

The service wraps up and families cautiously prepare to make their very closely monitored walk home. Oliver approaches me as I'm getting ready to leave.

'Adeline, lovely to see you,' he murmurs through gritted teeth. I notice his fingers are tapping on the top of the pew nearby, a pattern that is hard and fast.

'Oliver,' I reply so as not to draw unwanted attention.

'I see you aren't being escorted tonight. Alone, are we?' he asks, grinning.

'I'm with my parents. I must be going,' I answer, heading over to Mum who is talking to some of the other women in the church. As I'm passing by, all of the town enraptured by their individual conversations, I feel Oliver's familiarly strong fingers wrap around my wrist. He pulls me back, and I involuntarily shudder.

'Be careful, Adeline. Bad things happen when girls are

out alone around here. Wouldn't want you to ruin your reputation sneaking around. Or worse.'

My chest rises as I suck in air, trying to stay calm. I can feel his eyes lasering into the back of my head, can picture the sickening way he's looking at me.

'Let me go,' I demand. His fingers wrap around me tighter.

I feel his breath against the back of my head. 'I'll never let you go, Adeline. Never. Remember that when you're out galivanting around with that scum from Langley Green. You're still mine. I haven't let you go. Anytime I want, I can claim you as mine. Don't forget it.'

'Adeline?' Mum says from a few pews away. She looks over just as Oliver is letting go of my wrist, raising his hand to wave and exchange pleasantries. I realise my hands are shaking as I shove them into my pockets.

'Come on, Addy. Let's get home,' Mum says as she pushes past a few stragglers in the pew near me. I turn to see that Oliver has crossed the church, marching to the side exit. He turns around and catches my eye, grinning sadistically. I whirl back around, smiling at my mum, relieved she is here. I try to shove Oliver's threats aside. They're just empty threats. Aren't they? He wouldn't do anything ...

'Stay close,' Mum demands as Dad finds his way over to us and we head out the door. I don't argue for once. I'm glad to have Mum and Dad flanking me. What is this town coming to? Is anyone safe? The murders seem to be getting closer and closer to home, each kill seemingly a street nearer. Who is next? And when?

I shudder at the thought, reaching up to touch the locket around my neck. Charles gave it to me. I always find myself clutching it when I'm anxious, and today, I'm certainly a bundle of nerves. The streetlights illuminating our walk, the hordes of West Green residents making their way to their seemingly vulnerable homes, I stop in my tracks.

'What is it?' Mum asks. I frantically feel around my chest, my pockets with no luck. It's gone.

'My locket. I think I lost it in the church. We need to go back. It's my favourite,' I announce, panicked.

Dad grabs my arm as I'm turning. 'We'll get it tomorrow. We don't want to be wandering about with all that's going on. We can find it tomorrow, okay?'

I open my mouth to argue, but Dad yanks me forward. I know there's no use arguing with him. He isn't Mum. He can't be won over. I silently trudge forward, feeling naked and empty without my locket. Tomorrow. Tomorrow is another day.

But that's more than we can say for Doreen. More than we can promise for anyone, I realise as I climb the stairs and trudge to my bedroom once we're home, ready to sleep away the depressing day and fall prey to the glorious blackness of night.

*

'I didn't get a chance to thank you,' I murmur to Phyllis a couple of days later when we're at Doreen's official funeral, the wails of her family sending jolts of melancholy through my body.

'Thank me for what?' she whispers back, our heads bowed as we stand in the pouring rain at the back of the service.

My fingers automatically travel to the smooth silver. I do wish Charles was here. But he had to work again, and I understand that if we are to be together someday, he needs to keep his job secure.

'For returning my locket,' I reply. I turn to eye Phyllis, whose face is quizzical.

'I didn't, though,' she says. 'What are you talking about?'

'Peculiar,' I reply, shrugging. 'I lost it on the night of the youth gathering, when we had the prayer service. It came through the letterbox yesterday with a note. I thought it was from you.'

'Well, I'm glad whoever found it returned it,' she says. We bow our heads, the service continuing, the bleakness of death enshrouding us and the entire community.

We hear the pastor talk about youth and the fragility of life. I touch the locket again, thinking about the note, the scrawling handwriting that looked hurried and sloppy.

Saw you drop this. I'll be seeing you soon. – P

If the P wasn't for Phyllis, then who? Who else would have seen the locket, would've known it was mine? Goosebumps on my arms spread, the thoughts racing in my mind.

Stop it, Addy. It's nothing. There are so many people in this town with the initial 'P'. It could've been anyone, for goodness sake. The florist, the tavern owner. Who knew? And what does it matter? They returned the locket. Clearly there was no foul play there. And clearly there are bigger problems to worry about.

But as the service continues and my fingers rub the smooth silver over and over, I can't help but wonder who was watching so closely that they saw me drop the necklace – and who would go to those lengths to return it without showing their face. I can't help but shake a little at the thought that the 'P' could stand for Parsons, and that the locket could just be a small symbol in Oliver's much larger, angrier game.

Chapter 12

Smith Creek Manor Nursing Home
2019

'I need to go,' I sputter, suddenly needing to get away from him. Those steel grey eyes tucked carefully behind those thick plastic frames. How hadn't I seen this before? Am I really that forgetful after all? Maybe I *am* losing it like everyone seems to think.

True, it's been so many years, and time has dulled the terror, the knowledge, the understanding. Nevertheless, as I stare into the eyes of Oliver Parsons, the wrinkles don't fool me any longer. It's him. I see it as clearly as if it's 1959. How long it has been, the interminable years rolling by – yet somehow it feels like no time has gone by at all.

'Addy, wait,' he demands, reaching out to grab my arm. I shudder, yanking out of his clutches.

'Oliver, I need to go.' I ball my hands into fists, trying not to let him see how they quake.

'I said wait,' he replies, his eyes glinting. Dread grows in my chest, in my heart, in my head. He leans in, his sneer unnerving me. After all these years, he still has a power over me I can't untangle myself from. Time has changed us, it's true. But despite his age and mine, there's a frightening electricity that seems to radiate from him, one that threatens to impair me with its surging voltage.

He's still dangerous, I understand as I look at him. And I've let this monster of a man near me without even realising it.

'I see you've finally come home,' he whispers, his words edgy and uneven.

Tears well in my eyes. I stare at him, wordless, as I watch his eyes dance on my face.

'Guessing this means Charles is dead? Gone? It's just you now, isn't it? What a shame.' He sneers, telling me with just a few words what I already suspected. He hasn't changed. Time hasn't improved him. In fact, perhaps it's just let the old, harsh habits boil and toughen. My lip trembles, and I bite it to keep my fear from showing. Palms sweating, I back up.

'I couldn't believe it when I saw you here. Adeline Walker, back at last. The myth, the legend, *the slag*. Back again.'

'Oliver, please. It was a long time ago. Leave me be,' I implore, a tear falling now as I reach a hand out to the wall to steady myself.

'Leave you be? Leave you *be*? After all you've done?' He

articulates each word like it's a dart being launched at a target. They pierce into me one by one.

'It was a long time ago,' I whisper again, chanting the words like a demented mantra.

'Some things, you just don't forget. Some things taint the rest of your life,' he says, his sneer melting into something much different. For an uncomfortably long, silent moment, I stare into the eyes of the man who made my life a living hell. How can he just dismiss who he was and what he did like the passage of time forgives him? How can he turn all of this on me, like he didn't play a part in the twisted drama from long ago? Does the passing of decades change who a person is at the core? And does old age equate to automatic atonement for the sins of one's youth, no matter how awful?

I want to think the answer is no, but I stop for a moment, considering what the answer could mean for me. After all, we've both done things that we shouldn't be proud of. When I look into Oliver's eyes, I know we're both guilty – but our transgressions are of different varieties. And, in truth, I don't know what other things he's done or who he's become in the years since I left.

What did his life look like after I left West Green? Did he settle into a new routine, a calm life? Did he marry, have children, and live out a life of purpose after I was gone? Clearly, he didn't stray far, his presence here verifying that. But who is Oliver Parsons now? And is he truly someone to fear in the darkness of Smith Creek Manor?

I don't know. I can't know for sure. But my hands are jittery, and as I study his face looking for the true answers to my questions, I quake. There's something about his eyes, about his face, that underlines who he used to be and the fact that he hasn't changed at all. And even more than that, he hasn't forgiven me for what I did all those years ago.

Truthfully, in ways, I haven't forgiven myself.

'Stay away from me,' I order, my words shaky and unsure. Nonetheless, I shove past him, frantic to escape from the scene. I can't handle this. My heart thuds, and I need to soothe myself. I don't want to sort through this now, all the murkiness of the past melting into the present. What's happening here? What's happening to me? I hate that I feel so lost.

I consider going to see Dorothy, but I'm not ready to talk. She's practically still a stranger. I can't divulge all of my past to her. Besides, there's too much to process, so I do the next best thing. I duck into the reading room in the nook beside the nursing desk, immersing myself in the gloominess, staring at the bookshelves, and drowning in tears for a past I don't truly understand – and a cryptic future that petrifies me.

Oliver Parsons is here, but does he still thirst for vengeance from all those years ago? I wrecked so many things back then. Now here he is, back in my life, and strange things are occurring. Notes and outbursts. A woman is dead. Is it all just coincidence, or something more horrifying at play?

Has time and age allowed Oliver's hatred to marinate, his need for revenge to warm to a point of bubbling over? I think back to all those moments when I saw his true colours, when I realised he was a beast of the vilest variety. That type of thing doesn't fade with time, does it? Can a person truly transform over the decades and lose those violent, vindictive tendencies? My shoulders sag as I squeeze my eyes shut.

'I'm sorry, Charles. Forgive me. Forgive me,' I whisper, but of course he doesn't answer. The dead can't save you from the living.

*

Time passes, but I barely notice as I lean back in the leather chair in the reading room. Mercifully, only one quiet lady from the other side of the floor joins me, but she doesn't say a word, mindlessly leafing through a novel on the sofa nearby. I don't choose a book, relishing in the quietude of the room, of the little area where I can disappear.

I try not to even think too much, my thoughts taking me down desolate roads I'm not equipped to travel. Rose, Oliver, the note – it's beyond overwhelming, and it's brought too many memories, too many terrors to the forefront of my mind. All those years that have gone by, all those fears. And yet, here I am, back in West Green, as if I'm haunting the place instead of it haunting me.

Eventually, the other woman leaves, muttering a single

word about dinner. As if on cue, my stomach grumbles, and I realise I haven't eaten today. I don't really care to go to the dining room, to gather, to see faces with quizzical looks. I don't want to answer questions about Rose. And I most definitely don't want to see Oliver.

Still, the pull for sustenance wins, and I decide to drag myself to the dining room. I can't avoid reality forever. I traipse towards the clanking of dishes and soft murmur of the residents of Floor Three as they prepare to eat. On my way, I pass the communal living space, the telly blaring. The Philip Woman is chanting in her wheelchair, rocking back and forth, repeating Philip over and over just like the last time I saw her. A nurse comes to retrieve her and take her to the dining room. She makes eye contact with me and offers a nod.

'Sorry about your roommate, Mrs Evans. Come on, now, why don't you follow Mrs Blake and me to the dining area?' the nurse says.

I wordlessly shuffle after them, pulling my pink pullover tighter around my shoulders. I walk into the room, perusing the residents until I spot Dorothy. She waves me over.

'There you are. I've been wondering where you were. I was going to come and check on you, but then they pulled me for some blasted appointment. Come, sit,' she commands, motioning to the seat beside her. I oblige, comforted by her presence.

'I heard about Rose. I'm sorry,' she says. I nod, my eyes studying the room.

Dorothy yammers on and on about Rose, telling me some story from long ago, when my gaze stops on the table a couple feet away from us.

From the table, Oliver observes me, taking me in like he's magnetised by me. I tremble at the prospect. Is it just my imagination, or is he sneering a bit? Does he relish in the fact he's making me uncomfortable? I avert my eyes, staring down at the plate in front of me, my head aching from the thought of it all.

'You all right?' Dorothy asks, touching my hand. I jump, my hand smacking against the table.

'Sorry. Yes. Just ... shaken.' I consider telling her about Oliver, but I decide against it. I'm not ready to talk about it all. Besides, how could she possibly understand? I don't even know if I understand. The staff bring in our food, and I pick at my plate, the mystery meat jiggling in the middle. It fails to incite my appetite. Dorothy changes the subject, and dinner continues without incident. I manage to choke down a few morsels of food, but I barely taste them. It's like I'm shovelling sawdust into my mouth, my lips and throat so dry. Still, I focus on the movement of my hand, on the chewing, on Dorothy's stories. I try not to look at Oliver, try to avoid making eye contact.

Halfway through the meal, Father Patrick leaps from his seat, shouts an expletive, and leaves, carrying a piece of turkey – or what is being passed as turkey – in his bare hand, squeezing it as if it's some prize. One of the staff members follows him, walking a few paces behind so as not to agitate him. Everyone here is on edge, I now understand. It's just a matter of time until someone breaks.

As I'm leaving the dinner and heading to my room, I pass Vivienne. She smirks.

'Never a good omen when your roommate dies, you know. Usually it means you're next,' she whispers, playing with the butter knife on her table with her one hand. Her forefinger runs along the edge of the knife, as if she's caressing it. She looks up at me, her sparkly blue eyes shimmering with something I can't detect. I hurriedly say goodbye to Dorothy, walk out of the dining area, and head to my room.

When I get there, I'm taken aback by the fact it doesn't seem different. Rose's side of the room has been sanitised and cleared. It looks like no one was there at all. The drawing, still tacked on the noticeboard, a child's handwriting spelling out her name above the picture, reminds me she was real. The only other remnant of her is the derelict religious statue. It's been moved in the mayhem, the distorted eyes staring at Rose's empty bed, keeping vigil for a woman who is long gone. I shudder at the thought, praying that someone comes to claim it soon. The chipped face makes it look like it's weeping. I shake my head, turning away from it.

Other than that, the room is spotless, bleached and barren. It doesn't smell of death like I'd imagined. It smells of nothing but sanitation and melancholy. I hate the smell.

I walk over to my bed, not sure if it's too early to sleep

but also not caring. I'm done with this day. I climb under the covers in my clothes, too tired to change. I lie on my side, the murmur from the telly in the community room detectable from here, the corridor lights still too bright for sleep to come. A tear drips down my cheek as I look intently at the photograph on my bedside table, wishing Charles was here to wrap me in his arms like he did so many times when we were younger. I wish he could murmur in my ear that all will be fine, that this hard day wasn't an omen. But he can't. Even if he were alive, I don't think he could make those promises.

What must be hours pass, and slowly the roar of the telly and the clattering of feet in the corridor dwindles to a dull buzz. Finally, the noise dissipates into bone-chilling quiet. A few coughs and a couple of outbursts down the hallway are the only reminders that there is some semblance of life in here, but I am so accustomed to it all now that it's hardly noticeable.

Sleep is unexpectedly hard to come by. It's just too eerily silent in my room. On the first night, Rose's disturbing noises stirred me from sleep, making it difficult to drift off. Even in the short amount of time I've been here, though, Rose's gurgles had become the white noise that helped me sleep. Without the presence of another person in the other side of the room, I feel numb. I'm alone here, the only soul in the room. I imagine the peeling statue staring at me, keeping vigil. The thought doesn't comfort me.

Despite the morose thoughts, I eventually manage to

drift off to sleep. As my mind travels away to the blackness, I think about Rose, and dreams of her mouth moving and her finger pointing at me come quickly. No matter how hard I try, I can't decide what she was trying to say. *What were you saying, Rose? And why did you leave before I could figure it all out?*

All is dark, the dreams taking me where they will, the day's hardships drowned by the exhaustion in my soul.

Chapter 14

Sleep fades away as I open my eyes, surprised to find that my room is dark. What time is it? Is it morning or night? I don't know. And how did I get to my bed? I don't remember coming to bed. My head is foggy, and my hip cries from the position I was in. I sit up, ignoring my creaking bones as I attempt to orientate myself. My gaze lands across the room at Rose's former, perfectly made-up bed, and my heart thuds as I stare at the emptiness. That's not the only thing, however, that stirs me. Groggily, I try to interpret the sight of it – the statue. It's been moved.

The peeling eyes are now keeping vigil over a new client – me. It's been turned to face my side of the room, I realise with a fright. Who moved it, and when? Someone must have been here. Oliver must have been here. Who else would do something like that? I try to calm myself, counting to three in reassurance that it's all okay.

I shuffle to the chair beside the window, staring out into the courtyard. Across the way, in the room directly across from me, I see a person also sitting in their chair. We're mirror images of each other, the fading darkness between us the only distinction. It must be early morning, a hint of brightness spreading slowly in the courtyard. The person is in the first room on the other side of the 'U'. It must be Room 300, with the evens being on the inside. Like me, their room is next to a locked staircase, I suppose, even though I've never ventured that way. Who is in 300? I wonder what they're doing up right now. Are they tortured by the same things I am? Are they wrestling with truths they also can't understand? I wish I could talk to them and share my troubles in confidence, but it's a long walk. Instead, I put a hand on the window, eyeing the figure, wondering if they're looking at me and thinking the same.

I sit and stare, my mind a blank canvas tainted over and over by the occurrences from the past few days. How could things be so complicated? What has happened, and will there be an end? I don't know what to make of this place. Sometimes, I think it's just all too much, that I've lost all semblance of reality in just the few days I've been here. It's like a warped rabbit hole and down, down, down I keep falling. My stomach knots at the mere thought.

Eventually, I must drift off again in the chair, because when I startle awake, my room is brightly illuminated with the morning sunshine. There is movement in the corridor, nurses jostling carts and waking residents with harsh voices. I stretch, glancing at the clock to see what time it is.

But before I can deem what the hour and minute hands mean, my gaze stops on the noticeboard. The menus are tacked up in their usual spot, and the day-to-day calendar that needs ripping off is where it's supposed to be. However, I squint to see what else is pinned up on the board. What could it be? I don't remember anything being there, not in that spot. No, I'm certain that part of the corkboard was always empty.

I drag myself up from my chair, crossing the room as fast as my feet will take me – which arguably isn't very fast. And that's when I get there and verify that I'm not crazy. My eyes see the scrunched up, ripped piece of paper conspicuously pinned on the board. I stare at the paper, the edges gnarled as if it were ripped from something. The letters are in red ink, a scrawling text that looks shaky and hurried.

Matthew 10:28

I look back to the table, remembering the Bible where my notes are. The Bible has sat, crisp and unmoved, for several days. I've been forgetting to write my notes in there. I will need to do a better job. Ignoring the detail in order to deal with the problem at hand, I make my way to the stand, leaning on the bed to steady my shaking legs. I open the drawer, pulling out the book. It takes my trembling fingers a while to find the page, the verse, but when I do, I sink onto the bed.

'Breakfast?' a voice murmurs from the threshold. I don't look up at the nurse, my eyes glued to the page.

I shake my head. 'Just a minute. I'll be right out,' I answer distractedly as I peruse the verse, squinting to read the tiny text. Even with my glasses, it's too small.

'Wait,' I say, changing my mind and hoping to catch the nurse before she leaves. I turn to see her stop in the doorway. 'Can you read me this verse? Matthew 10:28.'

She groans as if I'm an imposition. Still, she crosses the room and stoops down to snatch the book from me. I wait patiently as she finds the correct verse, but her face melts into a deep frown.

'Why this one?' she asks.

'Just tell me what it says, please,' I plead, my heart sinking.

She reads. 'Do not be afraid of those who kill the body but cannot kill the soul. Rather, be afraid of the One who can destroy both soul and body in hell.'

I bite my lip, shaking my head. I will myself not to cry. What does it mean? Why is it here?

'Come on. Let's go,' she orders, handing the Bible back without any further discussion.

I don't respond, the words turning over and over as I clutch the book to my chest. The ominous words rattle in my brain, the terror of the past few days all swirling around with them.

'I don't understand,' I whisper, forgetting she's there.

'Let's go, old lady. Breakfast time, and I've got other people to bring down to eat,' she says. Her words should upset me, but I'm too focused on the verse.

I think about telling her. I think about telling her that – what? What is there to tell? A few mysterious notes in a place like this? An ex-lover whom I haven't seen in decades? A woman who died – who was very sick and old? What is there to tell? I shake my head. I'm paranoid. That's it. I'm just paranoid. Charles often said I was apt to fall prey to melancholic thoughts. Of course, he understood why after all I'd been through, especially in those days in West Green. Still, my mind would often take to flights of whimsical, dark fears, often of superstitious variety. Dark rooms, mirrors in shadows, and late-night sounds often incited my mind to create fantastical, winding stories of terror. After we left West Green, there were so many things that scared me. I was always scared.

That's what's happening now, I realise. Surely that's it. My mind is warping and creating sinister tales that aren't grounded in reality. What would Charles think? He'd tell me I'm being ridiculous and that I shouldn't worry myself with such frightfully fictional stories. Yes, he is right. That must be it. I'm making way too much of a single Bible verse. I need to rein in my overactive imagination.

But as I follow the nurse to the dining area to eat breakfast, I shiver as I walk past 313. Oliver sits on his bed, peering out into the hallway as if he is waiting for me. Why? What was he hoping to see? I think about that Bible verse tacked on my noticeboard. I think about last night's encounter and all the ones before that, decades and decades ago. Could it be him? He's so close to my room. If he's still livid about everything – there's no telling what he could do. Maybe the Bible verse is just the beginning of a long string of terrors he'll unleash. It's hard to tell.

I should tell someone, I think, as I pass room 312, the door closed. Always closed. Another mystery in this cryptic enigma of a home with an unassuming name. I should tell one of the nurses so that I can protect myself. But who will believe me? Who is going to believe a woman like me? And what purpose will that serve? And am I really, truly in danger? Here? Now? It makes no sense. It just doesn't make sense. Or at least that's what I tell myself at breakfast as I sip on my orange juice, trying not to think about the ominous message.

And trying not to think about the word *kill* from the Bible verse as I go about my day, one eye always watching the corners, trying to ascertain who can really be trusted.

Chapter 15

'Newest activity timetable,' a scratchy voice hails from the doorway later that afternoon as I sit on the edge of my bed, peering into the courtyard at the drizzly day. It was so sunny this morning. I'd thought maybe I could wander outside to the gazebo that I spend so many hours staring at. It would do me some good to get a bit of warm sunshine. But of course, the clouds rolled in before I got a chance. Now, the day is a murky, oozing display of rain and biting air. The gloominess seems befitting of the day, the vacancy in the room still silently highlighting my aloofness in this place. I don't even have Rose to commiserate with anymore, the hollowness of the room, stark and ghastly.

I twist my neck to see who the voice from the doorway belongs to. It's the same man who brought the menu by when I was on the phone with Claire. It seems like a lifetime ago, even though it's only been a week at most. So much has happened. Could everything really have changed so much in such a short amount of time?

The man shuffles, his left leg dragging slightly at an odd angle. Still, his movements are confident, his gait strong and mostly quick despite his disability. He crinkles the timetable on the board, tacking it up underneath the menu. I notice with a chill that he stops and stares, looking at the Bible verse pinned up. I'd considered taking it down, but something about it made me want to leave it. Maybe I was just afraid that if I took it down, my mind would forget that it happened.

'Hmm,' he says, rubbing his chin as he studies the verse. I gawk at him, waiting for the man to say something, to ask about the note. Instead, he turns in his spot, staring back at me. His dark eyes dance over me, studying me as he did the note.

When he turns, I again notice the scar on his head, parallel with the floor. It's a long, pale scar that sinks into his face, bubbling from his skin in an inconspicuous yet daunting way. My gaze traces the scar, over and over, as he stands, almost wheezing, still staring.

'Drizzly day, huh?' I say, trying to make conversation, perhaps because I feel guilty for staring at his scar. Who am I to judge? Still, it's like my mind won't let the detail go. I can't stop looking at it, wondering what caused it. I almost ask, the question flirting with my tongue. I choke it back with a soft cough.

'Drizzly day,' he parrots, his voice still scratchy. It's a simple comment mimicking mine, but something in the way he looks at me, something in the cool collectedness of the words makes me think it was a calculated statement. As the minutes tick by and he doesn't move, I shift in my seat. I take in the sight of his mouth that hangs slightly ajar, his teeth not quite lining up in the correct way. His eyes are bulgy, too big for his face, and his nose has a crooked little tilt to it. He looks worse for the wear, and I feel bad for him. There's something just – isolating there. He's lonely. But aren't we all?

I think about asking him what room he's in, but I don't. Perhaps after all that's happened, I'm just afraid to get close to others. Perhaps it's safer to keep to myself. Or perhaps, if I'm being honest, it's the unsettling features, the way he fiddles in his pockets or the way he drags his foot on the floor. There's something eerie in his movements, in his expressions, and most of all, in his smirk. Finally, he turns to leave, his leg dragging behind him. As he goes, he does something pretty commonplace around here, a sign of age or station or something else entirely, I don't know.

He begins to whistle. The tune is familiar, but his whistle is just slightly off-key, the minor notes he hits sinking into my soul. The whistle is faint in a breathy way that just isn't quite right, that makes me want to put my hand over his mouth and snuff out the tune.

Nonetheless, despite the breathiness and the tone-deafness of the man, it's familiar. I recognise it, a song from my youth perhaps. I can't place it, but I know it's from a time that was so much simpler in many ways – but equally as frightening.

Just before I sigh in relief because of his absence, he pauses in the doorway, turning to look at me with a toothy grin. For a moment, I think I must've misunderstood him because his words just don't make sense.

'You're the one,' he murmurs, a small chuckle escaping before he recommences whistling and continues on his way to deliver activity timetables to other rooms.

Chapter 16

I'm in the community living room, sitting on a derelict tan sofa while the Philip Woman rocks in the corner when it happens.

I almost miss it, intent on earwigging on Vivienne's whingeing about how I clearly rigged the morning game of bingo – she sits on the other sofa with her cronies. I'm mentally preparing my arguments and snide retorts when a hand touches my shoulder. I jump as my heart races wildly.

'Mum, it's me. Sorry, didn't mean to scare you.'

I turn to see Claire, her dark hair pulled back in a way that emphasises her eyes. Her silky lips are stained a fabulous, subtle mauve colour that complements her complexion. I may be biased, but she is absolutely stunning in a way that is remarkable for her age. She would give women twenty years younger a run for their money. What was that ex-husband of hers thinking when he left? She's striking.

I stand, a grin painted on my face. 'Oh, how lovely. I

wasn't expecting you,' I say, noticing she's carrying a bag with her. I knew Claire was busy with her travels, and to be honest, I hadn't felt like talking to her the past day or so anyway. I was worried that my wavering voice would give it all away, and I didn't want her worrying. No, it wouldn't do for her to be worried.

'I hadn't heard from you, so when my business trip was wrapped up, I thought I'd pop in to see how you were doing. I even managed to stop and get your favourites from Sainsbury's on the way,' she beams, holding up the bag. My smile widens. How I do miss shopping there.

'I just wanted to see if you are all right. You look wonderful, Mum. Really wonderful,' she continues as I walk around the sofa to join her. I can feel Vivienne's eyes lasering into my back. Vivienne coughs at Claire's comment, and I turn and roll my eyes. That woman is a nuisance.

'I see you've made some – acquaintances?' Claire whispers as I lead her away from the community room, towards my room.

'There are some characters here,' I murmur, my eyes darting about, scanning for Oliver.

'You know, Mum, the weather's delightfully mild today. What do you say we wander out to the courtyard? There's a lovely little sitting area.'

'Perfect, dear,' I reply, glad that I won't have to show my daughter the half-empty room or divulge details of Rose's death. Wouldn't do for Claire to worry, after all.

We take the shaky lift down after I assure Claire I don't

need a pullover. I practically hold my breath as the lift clunks to a grating stop, the screeching of the doors scratching my nerves once more. Claire chatters on and on about marketing projects and new clients. I beam with pride, chuffed to see my daughter so fulfilled, so successful. It's all I ever wanted for her. It's all I want now. As she talks, I realise without a doubt she'll be okay, even after the divorce and everything she's endured. She's pieced together a new life, a new vision. She's so young in the scheme of things. She has so much time.

Thus, when we make it to the bench, the sun beaming down, I prod her with questions about herself, about the new restaurant near her house, about the latest BBC drama she's been watching. So many times, I bite back the words I ache to get off my chest – about the odd notes, about Oliver, about how something about Rose's death just doesn't sit right. I want to tell her about the hints I've seen that the staff aren't all professional. I want to tell her about Dorothy's suspicions and about how Jones seems like a truly beastly bloke. I look at Claire's beaming face, though, at her relief that she seems to believe I'm getting along just fine here – and I can't ruin it. I can't destroy the perfectly constructed painting she's made that life here at Smith Creek Manor is pleasant and calm. I can't obliterate her contented beliefs just to placate my whimsy to drop my terrors on her. I'm still her mother, after all. I need to protect her, always.

Before we part ways by the statue at the draughty entrance on the ground floor – I assure her I can make it to my room just fine – she hugs me for a long time, her vibrant, edgy perfume bold and free, just like her, wrapping around me.

'I'm chuffed you're doing so well here. You have no idea what a relief it is to see you so content,' she declares, flashing the wide, toothy grin that's reminiscent of the earlier, more childish versions of Claire seared into my memories. Feeling nostalgic, I realise how many beautiful moments I've witnessed and what a true joy it's been to see her grow up. I'm not afraid of ageing. I'm not afraid of this disease they say is eating away at my mind. But I am afraid that one day, I'll forget how lucky I am to have her as a daughter. I'm terrified that at some point, those memories of her will fade into oblivion and there will be no one left to recall what a wonderful daughter she is. I shove the thought aside, its moroseness threatening my otherwise stable mood.

I smile back at Claire, willing myself not to cry.

'I love you,' I say, glad that if nothing else, I've been able to deceive my daughter into thinking I'm fine, just fine, in this twisted place.

If she only knew what really happens here. If she only knew who was here and how our tangled pasts could mean trouble in the future, I think, as I find my way to the lift and push the button to Floor Three. *Then again, if only I knew what is really happening here and if Oliver's presence is going to spell disaster for my final days.*

*

Charles Dickens. That's it. That's the book I've been looking for, I realise as my fingers trace the spines of some weathered books on the shelves of the reading room. A sad, forgotten lamp sits on the single desk in the corner, and I squint to read the names and titles. Despite the somewhat dusty quality to the room, it's quiet and peaceful here in this forgotten locale of the floor. It's like my hideout from the harsh truths and mysteries of Floor Three.

I pull out *A Christmas Carol*, thinking about all those years that Charles would read it, chapter by chapter, to Claire every December. I can picture them tucked away on the sofa, Claire nestled into the strong frame of her father, his tired, stained hands holding the book after a long day at work. He would read to her the words she would eventually come to memorise.

Good times. Lovely memories. Now, those moments are long gone, the stale stench of loneliness taking over instead. I wander to the chair that faces the brightly lit corridor, staring out into it as I hold the book, feeling the cover. I don't want to read. Just touching the cover is enough.

I lean back, trying not to worry about what I'll find in my room when I return. I try to just remember, to go back to those moments of joy while I still can. Visions of Charles and myself from our early years, from our years raising Claire, and from our years alone together in our older age all flood back. Tears cascade down. *Why did you do this to me, Charles? Why did you leave me to face this all alone?* I can't do it anymore. I'm not strong enough or smart enough to figure out what's happening. And, maybe in truth, a big piece of me doesn't want to solve the mystery because the results could be too insidious.

My fingers trace mindless patterns on the cover of the dusty book until I drift off, away, away, into a land of sleep and harmony, where the diabolical smell of urine and age doesn't overpower all my senses. I drift off, my mind mercifully blank at last, the book still in the grip of my hands as if I'll never quite let it go.

*

When my eyes open, I try to take in my surroundings but I am confused. What time is it? Where am I? My eyes dart around, and I ascertain that I'm in the reading room. I thought the lamp was on, but it's now turned off. Someone must have pulled the string on it while I was asleep. Or did I turn it off? I can't remember. Goodness, I hate when I can't remember. Does it matter? I try to think, think, think, willing my mind back. Did I turn that lamp off before deciding to take a nap? I don't know. I don't know anything.

I give my eyes a moment to adjust before glancing around once more, calming the rising fears that I'm forgetting everything again. I look to see that there's a book on the floor near my feet. Groaning, I lean over to retrieve it from the ground. Was I reading? I can't remember. My mind is groggy. Maybe it's late. I don't know. I think I was reading.

I squint at the cover, peering through the darkness. *Crime and Punishment*. Was that the book I was reading? Really? I never liked that book much. Too dark. And even though Raskolnikov is punished in the end, there's still such hope for an evil man. There's a sense of redemption. It never seemed fair.

I shake my head to loosen the digressions, picking up the thick book to set it on the shelf. Something flutters to the ground, and I stir, glancing down to see a note cascade to the floor. I tremble, hand flying to my mouth. Part of me wants to ignore it, to walk by, to tell myself it's nothing. But I am, at times, a glutton for punishment, so I stoop down, slowly, slowly. My bones crack, my back protesting the movement. I snatch the paper from the ground. It's a page of *Crime and Punishment*, a line circled.

'A hundred suspicions don't make a proof.'

At the bottom, in red, there are scrawling letters.

I'm waiting for the right moment, Addy.

My hands tremble as a gasp escapes my lips. Oliver? Was this Oliver? When did he come in here, and what does he mean by it? I rush to the nurse's desk, but there is no one there. I glance at the clock. It's late, much later than I thought. The Jones man is on duty tonight – I saw him come in during dinner. How did he miss me for bed check? And how did he not see someone pop in here?

Unless —

No, it can't be. There's no way. Sure, Jones is a bit smarmy and edgy. But why would he have it in for me? What did I do to him? It makes no sense. It must be Oliver.

I look around, a decision to be made. There's no nurse here, no one to help. But I can handle this. I can't keep doing this frenzied dance of questioning and fear. I fold the note and put it in my pocket, proof to keep safe. I don't want someone thinking I've lost my mind. I don't want him to explain it away.

I press forward, unsure of what I'm about to do but also knowing I don't have much choice. I need to settle this. I need to take care of it. Because it's the agony, the waiting, that's making it worse. And if I don't solve this soon, I may just lose my mind for real.

Investigators Question New Suspect in West Green Killer Case
West Green, Crawley, West Sussex
10 July 1959

Crawley residents are hoping to be sleeping soundly soon as investigators narrow in on a new suspect in the West Green Killer case.

On 9 July, sources revealed that a new prime suspect was brought in for questioning in the murders of the three West Green women: Elizabeth McKinley, Helen Deeley and Doreen Thompson.

The latest suspect, Bruce Taylor, 24, is from London but has been known to frequent the Northgate station as he works in Manor Royal.

Investigators revealed that Doreen Thompson and the suspect had met three nights before her disappearance in Langley Green. Witnesses spotted the two near Langley Green Pub.

Bruce Taylor's connection to the other two victims has yet to be established, but sources note that Mr Taylor has been described as 'dodgy' and 'of an ill-manner' by previous acquaintances and neighbours. Investigators are in the process of obtaining dental records to compare to the bite marks on the three women's bodies.

'I hope we nabbed the vile murderer,' Mrs Ralph

Williams, one of Doreen's previous teachers, told reporters. 'Let's all pray they've finally got him.'

Detectives are not commenting on the suspect's interrogation or on the details of the investigation, but they have assured the public that they are getting closer to identifying the killer.

'We'll catch him, and soon. He can't outsmart us for long,' Chief Constable Warren commented in an interview.

Still, sceptical residents in Crawley fear that the case will remain open for a while.

Updates on the questioning and possible arrest of Mr Bruce Taylor will be divulged as soon as the information becomes available.

They're getting bloody desperate, if the pathetic reporters are to be believed.

A man from London who met with Doreen once? That's their best lead right now? The poor bastard was being dragged in for questioning because he met with her once? And they are wasting time on dental records?

It's outrageous, hysterical even – or it would be if the botch-job they're doing wasn't so blasted sad.

My fingers lightly trace over the ink on the page. When I picked up a newspaper on my way home from work today, I had no idea that I would get lucky again. I haven't been in the paper for a few days. I wasn't expecting an article.

It always brightens my spirits, keeps me motivated to keep the plan running smoothly.

I passed her again today. Adeline. She barely noticed me, but oh, I saw her. I always see her. Even when she doesn't know I'm seeing her. I should be focused on the next one. But I can't help it. I can't help putting in a bit extra time to observe her. She's just so beautiful, so striking. The way she walks like she doesn't belong here. I guess in many ways, she doesn't.

She came to West Green because of her reputation in another town, if rumours are to be believed. Of course, I've picked up enough bits and pieces from her conversations to know it's true. She was a bad girl in some ways, a bit immoral.

I've always been drawn to those kind. Beautiful is one thing, but beautiful and wild, that's something attractive on a whole new level. It's a challenge to tame those kind, to control them. Women are weak by nature, but at least the wild ones put up some kind of fight.

I wonder what it will be like, to feel her flesh between my teeth. To sink my teeth into her skin, to feel them piercing as I tear into the cold flesh. To have my lips draped over her shoulder, her back, her supple breasts. To feel that rush rumble deep within and release as I put that final mark of approval on her.

My teeth mark the paper, but I savour it for a bit this time. I let myself chew and chew on the article, the words running through my head.

They think it was Bruce. Like some labourer from London could handle this kind of masterful work. Like he could think this up and execute the plans so perfectly.

And the detective is just so bloody dim. He'll never catch me. Never. I'm always two steps ahead. I'm so careful. I never leave behind anything they can use.

I walk the fifteen steps to my bedroom and open the box on the table. I add the article to the stack. I think about pulling out the other letters, the other articles. I want to take a jog down memory lane. But not yet. I can't celebrate until it's all done. I need to stay focused. My eyes can't leave the target. I shut the box delicately, carefully. Wouldn't do for it to crack.

I wander to the window and stare out into the rainy day. A magpie lands in the hedge out front. Poor thing. The rain is pelting onto its back. It looks so lonely. I should remember to get some food for it on the way home from work. Wouldn't want the little thing to go hungry. My teeth chomp over and over and over, nothing between them as they sometimes do.

I wonder what the bird would taste like between my teeth, what the feathers would feel like poking into my lips as its blood oozed down, down, down my chin. A chill causes my shoulders to shudder.

I know what it would feel like.

Creepy boy. Bad boy. Don't chew on that, boy.

Too late, Mama. Way too late.

Chapter 17

Smith Creek Manor Nursing Home 2019

I count to three, wringing my hands. The moisture on my palms annoys me as my mind races, thinking of the note from the book.

I'm waiting for the right moment, Addy.

The words frantically pound in my skull, assuring me that I know what I need to do – I need to confront him. This can't go on. I need to get it under control if I'm to make any semblance of a normal life for myself here. But deep down, I'm terrified. Who knows what Oliver Parsons is capable of? It's a silly question, though. I know. I know exactly what kind of man he is. Age and time can't erase dreadful scars on the soul, not the kind Oliver once housed. They don't just fade away.

I carefully trudge down the corridor, passing a sleeping woman in a wheelchair who is parked in the middle of the floor. She snores, her tongue dangling from her mouth.

No one notices her, forgotten in the midst of Floor Three like a stale sweet you find at the bottom of an unused bag. No one cares that she's here, lost and alone. There is no one here to care. I push past her.

As soon as I'm beyond her, however, someone emerges from Room 311. I startle as Babbling Barbara chuckles, her hands flailing wildly. She's wearing a pale blue nightgown that is torn and wet. There are stains on her chest, a faded red splotch that catches the eye.

'Red rain. Have you seen the red rain?' Her voice is higher-pitched than normal, her smile wide. My heart beats wildly as she gets closer and closer. I back up until I'm against the wall, the wooden trim running down the wall carving into the skin on my back. Barbara's face moves closer to mine, her eyes crusty and milky as always. But today, there's one difference.

Splatted on her left cheek, right in the centre, is a splash of red.

'I'm going to market. Here I go. Off I go. Be careful. I need to get it.' Her voice almost trills at the end, a screeching note that threatens to shatter my eardrums. Before I can reply, she's parading down the corridor, her dripping wet nightgown clinging to her as she stumbles along. I rub the back of my neck, reminding myself that I need to stay focused. It wouldn't do to lose track of what I'm doing now.

I continue on, stopping at 313. I lean on the threshold to his room, steadying myself as I prepare to face the man who may or may not still harbour a long-simmering vendetta against me. I plod into the room, taking inventory. Oliver's roommate is fast asleep. He snores loudly as he slaps his lips. Oliver, on the other hand, sits awake in the chair by his window and stares out into the street.

'What is this?' I ask, holding up the scrunched note, carefully plucking it from the pocket of my pullover. I keep my distance. I'm close enough to the doorway to yell for help if I need it. But even if I yell, will anyone come? Jones is clearly occupied, probably on Floor Two to visit the other night nurse. There have been quite a few rumours that they have been finding the supply wardrobe on the second floor extremely – engaging. I brush the distasteful thought aside.

'Addy? What brings you here?' Oliver asks, not moving, tapping his fingers on the chair. His stoicism frightens me. I stare, resolving not to break eye contact.

'This must stop, Oliver. I know what you're doing, and you need to stop. It's all done now. It's been so long. I'm sorry for how things turned out, but I'm also not. I made my choice, and I had my reasons. You need to let it go and move on. Please let it go,' I rattle off, defiant but also imploring. I want nothing more than for this nightmare to cease. I don't want to pay for the sins of my youth in my final days. I can't.

He rises from his chair, and my heart pounds. I take a step back, and he stops, hands out.

'Really? I should just let it go? I should just let go what

you did? How you ruined me? You didn't deserve me. And now, I guess it might just finally be your time to *pay*.' He bites into the last word, spitting it at me with a vehemence that causes my blood to run cold. He doesn't deny the note, and he doesn't hide his craving for retribution, either.

I tremble. 'It was so long ago, Oliver. I can't deal with this. These notes, these threats, they've got to stop. Now.' I wave the note in the air, my hand shaking.

Oliver raises an eyebrow, seemingly confused. 'Really, Addy? You can't deal with this? Well, I guess you better get used to it. We all must pay our debts eventually.'

I study him, trying to ascertain how dangerous he really is and how bad the situation is. Slumped over, the string of his joggers hanging undone, he studies me, his jaw slightly softening now. To look at him now, he seems nothing like the Oliver Parsons I kissed behind the church so many decades ago. Or maybe he's not. Maybe, in truth, I was naive and foolish to ever believe that Oliver was anything but the manipulative, cunning monster standing right in front of me. As I stare at him, the image of the teenage boy fades – in its place falls a memory of him, in my room, my screaming pleas ringing in the air between us. The icy terror resurfaces in my veins as if we're nineteen again, and I'm afraid he's going to kill me.

Looking at the glint in those steely grey eyes, I wonder for a long moment if perhaps he's been waiting for his chance to get his revenge, to set things the way he always thought they should be. Time may have slowed him down, but it hasn't settled the mad need for power or the overarching thirst for blood. I can see that now, can feel it surging in the foreboding note, in his stance, in everything he does.

Oliver hasn't let go of what he deems as a wrong. He hasn't let go of the fact I stopped belonging to him. Perhaps he can't let go of the fact that I made a choice all those years ago.

He steps towards me now, and I hastily shove the note in my pocket and inch back as I return to the present moment. That nineteen-year-old girl is long gone, but the real threat has never died, I realise. It's why I stayed away all those years. It's why I should've never come back.

'Not another step,' I order, pointing a finger. His roommate stirs, groaning as he turns over.

Oliver takes the step, and I shout louder. 'Take another step, and I scream. I'll shriek. I'll call 999 if I have to. But you stay the hell away from me, you hear? You *hear*?' I'm trembling visibly now despite my resolve to be strong. The fingers of my free hand grab onto my hair, clutching so tight I think my bones might break. I wobble my way back, back, Oliver still staring at me. I don't turn around, walking backwards until I'm out of the room, my hands feeling behind me. They touch the wall at the end of the corridor.

Oliver peers out, and I realise I'm cornered. The staircase is to my right, but I don't have the code. *I don't have the code*. I can't make it out of here. I'm at Oliver's mercy once more.

Tears fall. 'I want to know the code,' I plead with no one in particular, my fingers still wound tightly in my stringy hair.

Oliver looks at me, then turns and heads to the nurse's station. No. I can't have Jones come and find me like this. I can't have them thinking I'm crazy. I don't want more meds. I need to stay sharp. I need to be ready, to be aware for the next time Oliver strikes. It must be him. Mustn't it? I shake, clutching my head. It just must be him.

I take a breath and count the familiar numbers – *one, two, three*. I need to stay strong. I can hear Charles telling me to pull it together. I wipe at my tears, glance at the locked staircase once more, and then make for my room, ready to tuck myself into bed. If Oliver is going to play this game, I need to be smarter. Stronger. I can't let him win. I *won't* let him win.

*

Sleep takes a while that night as I clutch the note in my hands. At one point, I startle at the sound of a banging noise in the stairwell again. I think about getting up to investigate, but there's no use. Whoever is in there, well, I can't help them. I can't escape. I'm trapped here, Floor Three holding me hostage with villains from the past and present.

*

I feel eyes watching me at breakfast the next day. So many sets of eyes, especially from the staff. Dorothy is at an appointment, so I sit silently, the Philip Lady chanting some prayer beside me as she shakily holds her orange juice. Oliver is nowhere to be found, thankfully. Still, eyes follow my every move, and one of the staff members checks on me to see if I'm okay twice during the morning meal. I tell myself it's fine, nothing's going on. I tell the staff I'm fine. But I know better. There's something off.

When I get back to my room to do some reading – Claire dropped off some magazines for me, or at least I assume it was her. I don't remember her leaving them here. Who else would it be, though? I lean against the headboard, wondering why everyone seemed to be acting so different this morning. So jumpy. What's happening? Has something happened? Did they pinpoint everything to Oliver? Do they know what he's been doing? Perhaps it's all settled. Perhaps I can breathe easier now.

A few moments later, a nurse wanders in.

'Mrs Evans? May I talk with you a minute?' she asks, but her question is more of a warning than an actual opportunity for me to decline.

I gesture towards the chair in the corner. It's not like I can say no, after all, even though I'm not up for company.

'Tea?' she asks. I shake my head. What is it about these nurses? They think their weak tea with the murky Smith Creek water will soften any blow. I close the magazine I've been mindlessly flipping through, looking up at her.

'We had some reports this morning that something troubling happened with you last night. Is there anything you want to tell us?'

I blink, looking into the eyes of the woman who is pretending to be a friend. But, is she a foe? Is she to be trusted? I decide to stay quiet, staring at her and waiting for her to go on. Her blue eyes peruse me for a long moment, as if she's about to draw a caricature of my sagging skin, my wispy hair. I watch her gaze travel over my expression, as if some mysterious answer to her question will be held there.

'Look, Mrs Evans. We all know that adjusting to Smith Creek Manor can be difficult for some. Typically, it can present challenges, especially for those residents who have relatively severe health issues. If there's anything that's making things harder or if there's anything you need, you know you can talk to us, right?'

I keep blinking, looking beyond her now at the sky outside. How I'd love to be there, anywhere but here. I don't respond, letting the silence permeate the room for a long moment. Finally, the nurse clears her throat and continues her monologue.

'Mrs Evans, Oliver Parsons claims that last night you came into his room accusing him of some awful things. He also said you had a pretty severe breakdown at the end of the corridor. Is that true? Did something upset you?'

I shake my head, disbelief rattling me. How manipulative. How cunning. How perfectly Oliver Parsons of him.

I glare at the nurse now, my hands balled into loose fists in my lap. 'Yes, something did upset me. That man has been harassing me for days. Leaving me threatening notes. All sorts of things.' My words are sharp and biting, an assault to the accusations she's sailed at me. I will not have her thinking I'm bonkers. I won't let Oliver convince the staff that I'm mad. Still, the way she looks at me, I know it's too late. Her appraisal of me is written on her face, highlighted by her dismissive look towards my words. She doesn't take me seriously.

'I see,' she replies after a careful moment. 'Mrs Evans, have you been having any difficulty lately remembering things? Have you been getting more confused?'

I look over and for the first time, I notice she's taking notes. What is she doing? What is this really about?

'Absolutely not. I'm fine. What are you doing?' I demand, gesturing to her notepad, my fists tightening now.

'We're just worried. That's all. We just want what's best for you. We want you to be safe and happy here at Smith Creek Manor. Oliver is worried too. We think maybe we need to make some adjustments to your medication to make things easier for you,' she says. Her sentences are slow and methodical, as if she's explaining something to a child.

Anger bubbles. They want to increase my medications. This is all Oliver's plotting. He's doing this. He hasn't lost his touch, and he isn't backing down.

'That's insane. He's the one who needs meds. *Look*. Look

what he's been doing.' I pull the note out of my pocket. It's crumpled and a bit torn, but as I unfurl it, I reveal the words scrawled in red ink. I hand it to her to read, hoping it will set things straight. Her soft, unmarred hand takes the note from me, her warm skin brushing against my cold, sagging hands. The nurse looks at the note, eyeing it and then me. Her face is unmoving, unemotional.

'I see,' she replies simply, folding the note again. I snatch it out of her hands. She doesn't believe me. Of course she doesn't believe me. Tears threaten to form, but I tell myself to stay strong. I sniff the tears back, clenching my jaw.

'And where was this left, Mrs Evans?' she asks, peering at me over the bridge of her too-thin nose.

I blink at her, narrowing my eyes. 'It was left when I was in the reading room down the corridor. I woke up and someone left it there.'

'Are you sure about that?' she asks.

My mind whirls, and I feel as though my head might explode. 'Of course I'm sure. I was in there yesterday. Or I think it was yesterday. Maybe the day before. But I woke up and it was there.'

'You *think* it was yesterday?' she asks pointedly.

My palms start to sweat. 'Yes, it was most definitely yesterday.' It was yesterday, wasn't it? Or was it the day before? Suddenly, the morning routines and the evenings blend together into a cacophony of catastrophic confusion. The reading room. I went there, didn't I? The one past the nurse's station – or is it past Dorothy's room? My head whirls with possibilities. Which one is right? I can't recall if it was yesterday or today. I know I was reading a book. I think I was. But where? When? I hate it when my mind does this. It's the bloody nurse's fault. It's her fault. She's confusing me. Asking too many questions. Anyone would get confused, wouldn't they?

I wonder if I wrote it down. I've been writing more down lately. I don't want to forget. I have a case to solve. I glance to the stand, thinking about getting out my notes. They're stowed in the drawer, out of sight. But I see her eyeing me suspiciously and know I can't let her see the notes.

I can't trust her. I can't trust any of them. Charles would say I'm being paranoid, but I'm not. I'm really not. Someone's out to get me, and the staff are out to get everyone. I need to be careful. *I need to tread carefully, Charles. I know I do.*

The nurse scribbles down some words as I sit silently. Finally, she speaks up.

'Mrs Evans, look. There's no harm in adjusting your meds. With your condition, it's to be expected. And we could help improve your quality of life. Help you remember more clearly and help keep you from getting so upset,' she continues on, matter-of-factly.

I glare back silently, shaking my head. Someone is leaving me threatening notes, and this is their response? To increase my medication? To put me in a medicated stupor so I'm not aware when someone is doing me harm? They want me to be a willing victim for whatever comes next? No. I can't stand for this. I dig deep, finding the fight still left within me.

'I'm fine. I don't need more medication.' My words are harsh and direct. I laser my gaze into hers now, and she shifts uncomfortably.

'Mrs Evans, this behaviour Oliver is reporting, well, it's troubling.'

'Of course it is,' I spew back. 'This is all part of his plan.'

'What plan?' she asks placatingly, and I know that no matter what I say, I won't be believed. The emphasis she puts on the word *plan* is mocking.

I now know for certain the predicament I'm in, the corner he has me trapped in. No matter what I say, no matter who I tell, he will win. He will win again. Who will believe me, after all? He is the calm, collected, charismatic older man the nurses never have an issue with. Just like his younger days, his appeal masks the shadowy truths lurking beneath the surface of his smile, of his bright eyes. I, on the other hand, am the new woman who has a history of forgetting and getting confused. I am the ragged hag who loses her mind over things like the code to the stairs. I am the decrepit old woman with a laundry list of medical ailments who is being stowed here until she passes into the night. Of course I won't be believed. *Of course not.*

'Nothing. Nothing at all. I'm fine. I promise. Last night was just a misunderstanding.' I wave her question away with my hand, as if batting away a mosquito. I inhale slowly, telling myself to stay calm, that all will be fine. They might think I've gone completely mad, but I can play at this game. Two can play. Two. And even if only one can win, I'll just have to ensure it's me.

'Okay. Well, I'm going to make a note that we keep a careful watch on everything. Just to make sure it's all right. We want Smith Creek Manor to work for you, Mrs Evans. We want you to fit in here.' Her pen loops up and down, notes scrawled down quickly. I peer at her notebook, wanting to see what she's writing, but it's angled away. Even squinting, I can't tell what story she's writing about me. Don't I have a right to see?

But she doesn't understand. How could she? How could anyone? Everyone around here is too busy or too unconcerned or too far gone to question anything that happens. It's a perfect place to fly under the radar, to commit atrocities, and to get away with them. I shudder. What will he be able to get away with next?

I want to tell the woman that being safe and happy has nothing to do with the meds and everything to do with the monster walking these halls. But how can I tell her that? I know she won't believe it – and suddenly, my heart pounds again.

'What about the code to the stairwell?' I ask.

'Excuse me?' she replies, troubled.

'You said if I need anything, I can ask. I need the code to the stairwell. If there's some kind of danger here, I'll never get out in time. I need to know the code.' *And if someone is harassing me, trying to cause me harm, at least I'll have another exit. At least I could get away.*

'Mrs Evans, you know we can't give that out. It's a safety hazard. What if you fell?'

'Someone has the code. I hear banging in the stairwell every night.'

She looks at me, clicking her pen. *Shoot. I shouldn't have offered that.* More ammunition for her case against me. I study her, waiting to see if she jots down the damning evidence in the 'Adeline is insane' file. But she doesn't. She puts the pen down. It's red, I notice for the first time.

'I'm sure it was only the staff, Mrs Evans. There's no need to worry. It's all okay. There's no danger. I promise. You're safe here. There's no reason to be panicked.'

She crosses her heart like the child she still is. I think about how satisfying it would be to cross her heart with the pen in her hand, to watch the blood stream out from the wound as her perky little smile blackens. I shake my head. Who am I? What is this place doing to me? She leaves after a few more faux pleasantries and promises to check back in with me in a few days. I remain perched in my spot, staring out the window.

I'm trapped. I'm stuck. And Oliver knows this. If I report what he's doing, what will come of it? They'll think I'm mad, the dementia completely taking over. If I tell Claire, she will worry – and then the staff will convince her that I'm mad. There's no one to turn to. No one to believe me.

Sometime later a warm voice interrupts my thoughts

asking, 'Can I come in?'. I turn to see Dorothy, leaning on her walking frame at the threshold of my room.

I smile. I have someone to tell. I have someone to trust. Maybe she'll know what to do.

Chapter 18

I lie in my bed, staring at the ceiling, shadows cast about from the brightness of the moon. I think about the days when I was young and would look up at the night sky, watching the stars and picking out constellations. Now, there are no stars in my world. Only shadows. As I look at the stark outlines on the ceiling, Dorothy's words sift through my head over and over.

'I told you about the woman in 306, didn't I? The purple skin, the extra medicine. Addy, you need to be careful. You go flinging wild accusations around this place, and the staff of Smith Creek Manor will make sure you have no capability of tossing accusations around again,' she had warned when I'd divulged the secrets I'd been harbouring. Dorothy's face had paled, her lips pursed as she'd studied me.

'They can check the cameras,' I had replied, asserting what had been rolling in my head for a while.

She'd raised an eyebrow. 'You think that Smith Creek Manor has functioning cameras? You think they'd take the time to look at them? You've been in the lift, after all. They don't even upkeep that, let alone the cameras. Maybe in the early days, the videos were there. But now? I can guarantee the cameras are just there for show if at all.'

I'd sighed, knowing I had been grasping at thin air but desperate for answers to my problems.

'I'm telling you, be careful. You're not going to win in this. They won't let you.'

'I know. 306,' I had murmured, my voice barely audible, as if the number itself were some type of prayer to be whispered silently and not shouted.

Images of my body lying on the floor, paralysed, as my mind races, as the drugs pump through my veins and stop my heart, haunt me. Tears fall. I'm trapped. I've got no staircase code. I've got no answer. And someone here wants me to pay.

I didn't tell Dorothy the *whole* story, of course. I didn't tell her about my complete history with Oliver or what I had done all those years ago to enrage him. I didn't tell her why he would have reason to be so angry. In truth, I don't know if she believes me about the notes, the Bible verse, and everything else. She's probably seen her fair share of madness around here. Heck, she sits with some of the residents who are two shakes shy of the looney bin. She probably thinks I'm no different.

I turn over in my bed, facing the door even though it's pointless. What use will it be if I see him come in? What will that prove? People wander around this place all the time. Just this afternoon, Babbling Barbara was pulled from Rose's former bed for tucking herself in and going to sleep.

Would it be worth trying the cameras? Dorothy's probably right, I realise. Smith Creek Manor might try to sell itself as legitimate and trustworthy, but after only a short amount of time here, I've come to learn how false that notion is. Additionally, could Dorothy be right in her assessment of danger, in reminding me of 306? Is it more perilous to let whoever it is keep leaving notes – or to tell the staff? Perhaps this clandestine enemy of mine isn't the true enemy. Could the real danger come from the staff, the nurses who have so much to lose if accusations start flying? I toss the possibility around in my mind until finally my eyes close. I go over the frightening evidence, as if I can will myself to remember, to think, to put it together. Babbling Barbara and the painful warning on night one. The mysterious death of the woman in 306 before my time. The note on the board warning me I'm being watched. The Bible verse that scared me. The banging in the stairwell night after night. Oliver Parsons finding me at the staircase, turning me into the staff, leaving the note in the book. Oliver's eyes that shine with some type of heat, of wrath, of anger for the past that can't be undone. And then there's Rose's death – was it an accident? Jones, who seems ready to take out his need for vengeance at any second. It's too much, all too much.

Over and over, the daunting clues pile up and circulate

in my weary mind until finally, I can't take anymore. I drift to sleep, but no peaceful dreams come. Instead, I dream of lifeless bodies, of fire, and of a staircase I can't open.

*

Footsteps in my room. There are loud, stomping footsteps in my room, I realise as my eyes dart open. The room is dark, and before my eyes adjust, a hand shakes my arm.

'You fucking slag,' he snarls in my face, spittle landing on my cheek. My groggy brain wraps itself around the image, around the face that is so close to mine.

'What are you doing, huh? Trying to cause trouble? You trying to get me fired?' Jones asks, rattling my whole body. He is still so close, I can taste his foul breath.

'N-n-no. No,' I whisper back, not moving a muscle for fear of retaliation.

Jones smirks. 'No? *No?* Is that why I got called in today about not doing a great job at keeping an eye on Floor Three? Is that why I was told by some bloody trollop of an administrator that I need to start keeping a better watch on the patients, that apparently the woman in 316 went bonkers when I wasn't around?'

'I-I-I didn't.'

'You didn't what? So help me God, you keep this up, you're going to see what cuckoo really looks like, you slag. I won't have you mess this up for me, you hear? Keep your fucking mouth shut. Or I'll shut it for you.'

I stare into the face of the man who has so much to lose. He storms out of the room, punching the threshold on the way out. I shudder. I think I've got the answer to my question. Whatever is happening on Floor Three, I need to solve it myself. Because if Oliver doesn't get me, Jones will. I'm certain of it.

I cry myself to sleep, thinking about what a mess this all has turned out to be and how I'm never going to get the harmony I so desperately wanted in my final years.

Chapter 19

But the cowardly, the unbelieving, the vile, the murderers, the sexually immoral, those who practise magic arts, the idolaters and all liars – they will be consigned to the fiery lake of burning sulphur. This is the second death.

I rock myself back and forth in the chair by the window, looking through the courtyard, the day foggy and grey. I hold the crinkled piece of paper with the familiar scrawl in my hand.

The note was tacked on the noticeboard when I came back from breakfast, and this time, it read: *Revelation 21: 8*. Another verse. Another foreboding message. Another warning, perhaps – but of what? And when was it put there? Was it there before I went to breakfast? My mind spins. *Think, Adeline*, I order myself. When did it happen? Was it there last night, before bed? Maybe it was there and I left it. I do need to take better notes. It's all too much. It's getting to be too much.

But I don't know. Regardless, it can't be a good sign.

I think about my life, about all that's transpired. I let my mind wander back, back, further back still.

How peculiar that at the end of my life, Oliver is here, reminding me of my gloomy past. As if I could've forgotten that choice, that decision, that's weighed on me over and over. The secret I harboured that became a lie I carried on – a lie I guarded with Charles, with Claire, with everyone. A lie that led to more tragedy than I could've ever anticipated. How would it have all been different if I'd have chosen another path? Or even if I'd have told the truth to Charles from day one? Or if I hadn't made that choice at all?

It's hard to tell. We can't live in regret – but sometimes, when the past comes flying back into the present, it's hard not to ponder how it could've all been avoided. Life works in mysterious ways – and so do humans, I suppose.

Guilt racks my body, and my stomach churns with nausea. For so many decades, I'd shoved the thought down, down, way into the depths of my being. I'd let that horrid scar from my past fade, let the memory dim. I'd moved on as we all must do sometimes. Charles and the life we made together made it easy to forget. It made it easy to tell myself I made the right choice that freezing winter night when I'd snuck out, got in that car with the scribbled address in my pocket, and made the decision that changed everything. But the secret I hid from everyone, even Charles, will burn its way to the surface in my final days. And maybe, just maybe, this whole situation at Smith Creek is karma. I don't know.

I stare out the window speckled with rain drops, eyeing the room across the way like I so often do. The familiar yet indistinct figure walks closer, closer to the window.

But as he presses his face up to the glass in an awkward display, I try to place him. There are still residents of Floor Three whom I don't really interact with. Which one is he? He looks back at me, and I can tell from here he's staring, studying, observing me. It chills me a bit, but then again, it doesn't. After all, I'm doing the same exact thing he is. I'm staring right back. He's the whole way over there, watching. It comforts me in an odd way, like I'm not going unnoticed. Like if something were to happen, maybe someone would witness it, someone would be there to watch me fade away.

Sometimes in life, I think that's half the battle. I think that's what we all crave – to avoid slipping away, unnoticed. Smith Creek Manor makes that wish more difficult to attain day by day.

*

'You doing all right? Any updates?' Dorothy asks as we sit at lunch later.

I study her while I sip my milk, reflecting on what's happened. I look around, trying to make sure no one's listening in. At the table beside us is the man with the forehead scar who delivers the menus and timetables. He looks at me as his lips slap together. I turn back, lean closer to Dorothy, and whisper. 'Another Bible verse. And Jones threatened me. It's a mess, Dorothy.'

She sighs. 'Be careful, I'm telling you. You need to be careful. I'm worried about you,' she utters, her eyes darting around. A piece of me wonders if she's actually concerned for me – or if she's fearful that by associating with me, she's opening herself up to some hatred as well.

I straighten my back as Oliver meanders into the dining area. He's got Vivienne trailing beside him. The two glance over at me, Vivienne glaring and shaking her head. Apparently, Oliver's filled her in. Just what I need – someone else to have an issue with me. Has Oliver told her the whole story? Does she know everything? I shudder at the thought of what secrets he could divulge.

I sink my teeth into my sandwich as Dorothy mumbles on and on about the card game on the timetable for today and the blanket she's knitting for a great-grandnephew. I try to follow along, will myself to relax, but I can't. I'm on edge, wondering what's next – and terrified to go back to my room. Oliver came strolling in late. Could he have done something in my room in the time between me leaving and him entering the dining area? It's possible. It's certainly possible.

After lunch, I edge my way down the corridor until my fingers find the familiar 316. I tiptoe inside, staring at the empty room, desolate of life. I glance around and stare at the noticeboard. Nevertheless, there is nothing alarming. I sigh in relief, but some of the tension remains because I know it will happen again. It's just a matter of when.

Before I can sit down and do a crossword or stare out the window, though, it happens.

A shriek. A scream. A woman yelling for help.

I shuffle out of my room as fast as my aching bones will carry me. Peering down the corridor, I see nurses dash into room 309, where a tiny, frail woman usually sits in her wheelchair. I don't know her name. Did anyone ever tell me her name?

'Help! Help me! He's coming. He's coming. He's coming for *me*. Call 999. Someone call 999,' she screams and cries. I follow the sounds, walking towards them to examine the commotion.

'Don't, no. I'm telling you! I'm telling you! He's coming,' she screeches. There's a group of residents gathering and looking on, terrified. Vivienne and Oliver stand near the front of the crowd.

I study the room, nurses trying to move me along. I hear the stairwell door open, another nurse racing down the hallway. When my eyes process the sight, it's too dismaying to even react to. I'm frozen in place, mouth agape, as I peruse the scene.

They hold her down as she flails about in her bed. The woman sobs in pain as tears crash down her cheeks. She's come unhinged, her body whipping about like she's twenty years younger. Her movements are so wild, she almost takes out a nurse. Her face is pale, stricken, and gaunt like she's seen death itself. I want to look away, but I can't, glued to her like some sick obsession. I need to know: what's got her so frightened?

They restrain her and beg her to calm down until finally, a black-haired nurse steps forward with a needle. At the sight of it, the woman's eyes bulge, her body manically jumping as she screeches in animalistic ways. They hold her, grabbing her arms, as the nurse attempts to stick the needle in. With her thrashing about, I fear the needle will bend or that the wrong person will get stuck. The nurse plunges the needle into the woman's arm as they inject her with something. After what feels like forever, she stops screaming, and the tension in the room dissipates. I walk on, shaken, hoping to find Dorothy in the crowd. The residents scatter, and nurses usher everyone to activities or their rooms.

'I love it when they stick 'em,' a voice murmurs behind me. It's raspy and deep, and when I turn, I realise it belongs to the man who delivers the menus, the one with the scar.

I stare up at his dark, feral eyes, his face aglow with what appears to be misplaced excitement over the scene. His words tarnish an already rusted, ugly moment. He holds my gaze for an uncomfortably long moment, and I shuffle away, shaken by the event. I find my way to the activity room and take a seat as a ballroom dance instructor tries to teach us the terminology for dancing. She even gets some of the able residents to join her in a few steps. I choose to sit in the back, though, stewing over Room 309. I'm so shaken by her outburst. How blood-curdling to be that upset but to have no one understand you. This place strips us of so much – too much.

*

My eyes blink open as my heart races. I pant for air as my lungs beg for relief. As my eyes dance over the darkness in the room, I come to, realising it must have been a nightmare.

Shaken and too afraid to fall back asleep, I reach over to the bedside table and tug on the lamp. I am getting ready to reach for my glass of water when my eyes flick over to the familiar photograph on my bedside table. I shudder, the sight of the photograph is a nightmare in its own right.

It appears that the glass has been removed, discarded somewhere, because the glossy photograph is exposed. And that's not all.

Where Charles' muscular build once was, a large black scribble violently rests. The strokes are so deep, some of the photograph has scratched away, white flakes in its place. His whole face, his whole body is scribbled out, like he doesn't exist.

And then there's me. I'm circled in red. It's not just one circle, but dozens, overlapping in a haphazard, frantic way. Stray strokes dash across my body, but the target remains apparent. I begin to sob, turning the picture over, rocking myself on the bed. I can't go on like this. I need to figure this out. I need to. It had to be Oliver, though. It had to be. He knew Charles. He hated me. This had to be him.

But why is he doing this? Does he want me to go mad, truly mad? Does he feel that would be proper retribution for what I did to him?

I don't know anymore. I just don't know. I rock on the bed, tears falling, falling, falling, as I stare at the lamplight reflected in the window. I rock until my back aches, my neck aches, everything aches because at least I can identify the source of that pain. At least I know what's causing it.

*

'I'm afraid to go to bed,' I admit to Dorothy. She looks at me with tired eyes the next night when we sit in the community room watching some crime show.

'What?'

'I'm afraid to go to my room. Every time I do, there's something awful there. I can't keep doing this.'

She sighs, shaking her head. 'This is so crazy. I do wish we could figure it out. Are you still convinced it's Oliver? Because I don't know, Addy, the way these things keep showing up, who says it isn't Jones?'

I clutch my head with a shaky hand. We've spent the last few hours discussing all the occurrences, the clues. Jones is back tonight and, after a super-fast round of distributing meds, he took the stairs down, presumably to Floor Two, to continue his nightly romp. We are, for the most part, alone, a single female nurse making rounds periodically on Dorothy's side of the floor, tending to some of the neediest patients over there.

'I don't know. I just don't know. It's so bizarre. The notes. Now the photograph. I'm not imagining it, Dorothy. I'm not,' I plead.

'I know, love,' she says, grabbing my hand. 'Have you thought about talking to Claire?'

I sigh. 'I have. But I don't want to worry her. I'm also afraid that she'll go to the staff, who will then take it out on me. Let's face it. Jones doesn't hide his disdain for us, but there aren't many nurses here who would take kindly to patients complaining. I'd be in more danger, a real target of the people in charge around here.'

'You're right,' she concurs. I nod, thinking about the situation in the room down the corridor the other day. Who's to say that a complaint won't land me in a sedation stupor, which will only put me more at risk?

Dorothy shakes her head. 'Crazy, isn't it? It's like we're in some crime show of our own. Do you want me to walk you to your room? That way, if there's something there, we can look at it together?'

I don't want to be an imposition, but I also don't think my nerves can handle one more frightening note. 'That would be perfect, if you don't mind.'

'Not at all. At least makes me feel useful. Now come on, let's go see what the oddball left behind today.'

I stand from the chair, feeling a bit better that I'm not

alone in this. At least she'll be there to steady me when I find whatever it is. Still, my stomach aches with the knowledge that there will most likely be something. There's always something.

I've thought about keeping watch, and Dorothy and I even tried it this morning. Dorothy kept an eye on the door of my room, staying in Room 315 across the corridor to chat with the woman in there – a woman who, like my old roommate, is essentially incapacitated. She stared and stared all morning, all afternoon. But nothing. It's like someone knows when we're watching. It's like someone always knows.

'Any word on the roommate situation?' Dorothy asks as we trudge down the corridor, my heartbeat rising as we get closer to my room.

I shrug. 'The day nurse said there might be some room swapping. Apparently, the Philip Lady is having issues with her roommate. Go figure.'

'Well, damn, that's not news you want to hear. There goes your quiet. Jesus Christ, you're going to go bonkers for sure with that woman in your room. Then again, maybe if you have another witness, another set of eyes, it will be more difficult for Oliver and Jones to bother with you.'

I nod.

'Too bad you can't get transferred to another floor. Aren't any of those old cronies ready to die on the lower floors?'

'Dorothy,' I chide. 'You can't express sentiments like that.'

'I just did,' she replies.

'Besides,' I add. 'I doubt that would help. Whoever is bothering with me would still find a way.'

We pass Oliver's room. I peer in. He's asleep, or so it seems. I shake my head, marching forward, until we reach my room. Just as we're peering around, looking for new clues, some loud footsteps echo down the hallway. The stride is fast and large, and as Dorothy and I turn to the threshold, we see Father Patrick in the doorway.

He's shaking his head, twitching, his hands outstretched as they also quake. Slobber falls as he froths at the mouth, spewing insults.

'You blasphemers. How dare you. Don't you dare take the Lord's name in vain. Don't even think about it,' he yells, his voice harsh and grating as he looms closer and closer.

'Sorry, we're sorry,' Dorothy shrieks, apologising, putting her hands up.

He points wildly at us. 'Don't do it again. You hear? You hear?' Father Patrick's in my face now, and I quiver under his goliath figure.

'Sorry. We're sorry,' I say, not even sure what he's talking about.

'Absolved,' he says, stoicism returning to his face as he looks at Dorothy with a raised hand.

But then he turns back to me, glowering. 'You sinner,' he barks at me, the words pointed as his eyes squint. 'You dirty sinner. I know what you did.'

My heart pounds. It can't be – it doesn't make sense. Does it?

He stares at us a long minute, turns on his heel, and walks out of the room, crossing himself as he does. Dorothy and I stand in silence for a while.

'What the hell was that?' she whispers in a hushed tone.

I shake my head. 'I don't know. I don't know at all.' But my stomach drops because maybe I do.

'Do you think it's been him? That maybe you were wrong? Maybe it wasn't Oliver?' she asks.

'It can't be. Oliver had to be behind the note in the book. The look in his eye said everything, Dorothy. I think it had to be him.' The words swirl in my mind as I try to process the notes and the new development.

But then something occurs to me, and I wander over to the bedside table and open the drawer. I pull out the notes – the one from the book, the Bible verses. I'd stashed them in the Bible with my own notes, clinging to a paper trail to remind myself I wasn't losing my mind. I spread them out on my bed, a hand moving to cover my mouth.

'Oh my,' I whisper, studying the handwriting on the different pieces of paper.

Dorothy screeches her walking frame over towards me. 'What is it?'

I sink onto the bed beside the notes, staring up at her. 'The handwriting. It doesn't match. Look,' I say, pointing towards the notes. Dorothy picks up one and then the other, squinting as she glances at them.

'No, it doesn't,' she admits, looking over at me.

Realisation swirls in my head. Oliver might have written

the note in the book, but he didn't write the Bible verses. It was the priest. Father Patrick. But why? And how?

'It's been him. The Bible verses must be him. I've been wrong,' I say aloud, the words becoming real as I utter them.

'Why would he be leaving them for you? What did you ever do to him?'

I stare out the window into the courtyard. I think about all the things I've done, but quickly brush the sins aside. Father Patrick certainly doesn't know. Does he? How could he? Did Oliver tell him? Why would he tell him? Why now?

'Listen, we need to talk to someone. You can't keep dealing with this. You shouldn't have to. It's ridiculous. What if Father Patrick had cornered us and physically assaulted us? We couldn't fight him off, and Jones is God knows where. That flighty nurse on my side of the corridor is probably out for a smoke break and, besides, she wouldn't be much help either. Someone needs to hear about this.'

I know she's right, but I also know there's no way we can turn Jones in. Even if he isn't responsible for the notes, he would certainly be out to get me. What a mess.

'I don't know what to do anymore,' I whisper, tears of frustration settling in my eyes.

'I know, Addy. I know. Life's so complicated, isn't it?'

I nod, staring out into the abysmal night, noticing the figure across the way.

'Dorothy, who lives in that room at the end of the corridor? I think it would be 300?'

Dorothy walks over to me and peeks out the window, her eyes trained on the window across the way. At the sight of her, the figure closes his blinds.

'Oh, that's the man who delivers the menus and the timetables. Sometimes they give him the post to bring around, too. Suppose he likes to stay busy, and since he's one of the few who can still get around, they don't mind the extra help. It's not like the staff care too much if we get our menus and things anyways. Don't know his name. He's been here for a while. He keeps to himself, a real loner in every sense of the word. No trouble or anything. I don't know his story. But he's not much of a looker, if you're in the market for someone, you know? Sorry to say, but it's true.'

'Oh, I've met him. When they were sedating the woman down the corridor, he made an odd comment about it. It worried me, to be honest.'

'Really?' Dorothy asks, her forehead wrinkled. 'I've never really spoken to him. He really keeps to himself. Bizarre that he approached you.'

'He's always looking out his window when I am,' I add, nonchalantly.

'Probably just lonely. Of course, these days, maybe that's a good thing. Wonder if he's seen anyone go into your room?'

I shrug. 'I doubt it. But I don't know. It may be worth a try. Perhaps I'll make a point to ask him tomorrow.'

'Can't hurt at this point. Are you going to be okay? Do

you want me to stay with you?' she asks, looking at me. I think about asking her to stay. It would be nice to have someone here. But I don't want to impose. I'm sure she wants to get back to her room.

'I'll be okay,' I reassure. 'Besides, I've got the trustworthy call button, right?' I tease.

Dorothy rolls her eyes. 'I'm convinced it's just for show at this point. All right, well, I'll be in my room if you need anything. I've got a cosy chair in the corner. You could always sleep there.'

'I may take you up on that someday,' I reply. 'A stiff neck might be better than, than ... goodness knows.'

Dorothy nods seriously before offering a cheery wave and turning to slide her walking frame out the door. I sigh as she leaves the room and the isolation settles in once again.

I ring Claire in the hopes of having a proper chinwag, but she, of course, isn't home. I leave a voicemail reassuring her that all is well and that my appointment with the cardiologist went just fine. Nothing to worry about. 'I've got plenty of life left in me,' I tell her.

When I'm in bed later, I roll onto my side, thinking about all that's occurred. Do I really have plenty of life left to live? Given the circumstances, it may be a blatant lie.

Chapter 20

'Did you hear?' Dorothy asks the next day when I wander into the dining area.

'Hear what?' I ask, taking a seat.

'The news. The floor is abuzz with the gossip. Well, okay, maybe just a few of my neighbours are talking about it. It's bad, Addy. Really bad.'

'What is it?' I ask reluctantly, not sure if I want to know but also needing to hear it.

'Someone on my end of the corridor, some woman, hurt her arm last night. She'd been pushing the call button over and over but no one came. She tried to get out of bed herself, silly woman, and broke it as she fell. When Jones finally got there – he must have been on one of his rare rounds because she couldn't reach the button to call anymore – she was in bad shape. It's hard to tell how long she was on the floor, but my guess is a long time. Jones got questioned about the whole thing, but he told the supervisors that the woman never pushed the button. He's claiming she's lost her mind.'

'You're serious?' I ask.

'Deadly. And the woman keeps insisting she pushed the button. She's one of the quiet ones, so I'm certain she's telling the truth. Jones, though, is selling some story that she didn't push the button and that she's been a real problem lately getting out of bed on her own.'

'Who are they believing?' I question, invested in the outcome for so many reasons.

'Who do you think?' Dorothy asks, looking at me pointedly. I have my answer. 'I've also heard that Jones is already furious, of course, for the woman trying to get him in trouble. All I have to say is that I'd hate to be that woman tonight when Jones is back on the floor.'

I shudder at the thought, picturing his frothing, raging face in mine. His actions just solidify what we've thought all along – we can't turn to Jones. We can't find help here because it will just end in more harm than good.

I also selfishly breathe a sigh of relief, however, knowing Jones will have a different target now. Someone else on the floor got him in trouble. Perhaps he'll be over his gripe with me.

But after I've said goodnight to Dorothy that evening and wander back to my room, I still don't feel that my torturer is done with me yet. They'll never let me rest. Never.

Chapter 21

I peel back the covers on the bed. How long has it been since they've washed the sheets? Do they ever? There's something off-putting about how they smell. Then again, perhaps the smell is just me. I'm about due for a wash. I run a hand through my hair as if to prove my point, the greasy locks sticking to my fingernails. I'll have to talk to the only kind, brown-eyed nurse, see if she could fit in some hair washing tomorrow. What's her name? Did I write it down? I can't remember. I tug on my hair, twisting it around my fingers as my mind winds tightly around the question. I yank on the strands, willing myself to remember.

I kick off my slippers, my footwear of choice these days. I'm tired, so tired. Everything that's happened has me racked with exhaustion. A part of me is terrified to go to bed because even though I've been feeling calmer, I know that I may just wake up to something dreadful. But I'm so tired, I'm not even certain if I care right now.

I pluck back the sheet. Funny. I don't remember it being tucked that way before. It doesn't matter. I strip the thin fabric back a bit more and carefully climb in, sinking down into the too firm mattress as I fluff the pillow.

But before I can get comfortable, my leg brushes against something in the sheets. It's small and cold, a weird lump of an item. Bizarre. I don't remember leaving anything in there. A chill sweeps through me. I yank my foot away from the unidentified object as my imagination runs wild. A bat. Maybe it's a bat. I've read horrifying stories before of bats getting under mattresses. Oh dear. Did it scratch me? Will I have to get vaccines?

I get back out of bed, my bones and joints protesting. I unravel the sheets the whole way back, ready for the worst. And when I see it, I gasp, backing up until I'm against the window sill, panic rendering me speechless. Inside I shriek, the dread floating through my body, as I realise without a doubt what I've been fearing all along. Things are much worse than I could imagine.

I know what must be done. I lean in to study the two mice, bloody and lifeless in my bed. Their bodies are missing patches of fur, their skin sickly blue and unnatural. Is this happening? I clutch my head, shaking it. My mind must be making things up. Stop it, stop it, stop it, I scold myself as my fingers furl into fists.

One, two, three. One, two, three. My fists constrict tighter and tighter until my bones ache. My heart races wildly, and I fear I will collapse onto the floor and be done with it all.

But instead, I find the strength to open my eyes. I reach back and pull on the lamp cord so I can get a better look. I crumple against the bedside table once I do, certain now that I'm not crazy.

The mice have bite marks chewed into their flesh; human bite marks.

I'm not crazy. This is real. I remind myself over and over, an eerie chant in the lonely room.

This is real.

This is real.

This. Is. Real.

With shaking hands, I snatch the creatures from my bed, thinking about all they symbolise. I sink into the chair by the window, my legs too weary to hold me upright. I turn off the light, and stare into the blackness, stroking the poor, abused animals. My head aches under the pressure, as if it will pop. In some ways, I wish it would.

However, as I caress the dead mice and their gnarled, clammy flesh, I know that I can't escape this. I'm in too deep now, and there's so much at risk. I stroke them over and over, squeezing my eyes shut as I ask the universe, Charles, and myself the hardest question of all: *Why?*

But the only answer that reverberates through the room, through the sky, through me?

It's a dark world. A dark world, indeed.

*

Someone's sticky, cold fingers are touching my hand. I startle awake, and the crusty, milky eyes of Barbara are centimetres away from my face. I can taste her sour breath, she's so close.

'Soft,' she whispers, stroking my hand. I look down, realising I'm holding a mouse's dead body in each of my hands, my arms resting on the chair. I must've fallen asleep here.

She cackles, and before I can pull back, she's plucked one of the mice from my right hand, rubbing her palms on it like she's going to start a fire.

'Barbara,' I whisper in a hushed voice. I shake my head, wondering why she's here. Her hair is soaking wet, but her face is still crusty.

I reach for the mouse's body, but she cackles again, stepping backwards as she does the unthinkable.

She puts the mouse's floppy body in her mouth, her teeth sinking into the fur. I gasp, shocked and horrified.

'Barbara, stop,' I demand, but she laughs louder, her teeth gnawing on the mouse as they tear it apart, bit by bit, right in front of me. Her hands are ready to catch any morsels that fall.

Terror seizes me, and I stay put, watching as Barbara gnaws on the corpse.

'Red rain, red rain,' she sings, her mouth full and muffling the words. She turns and leaves the room, her midnight snack still between her teeth.

I sit, cradling the remaining body, wondering how everything could go so terribly, terribly wrong.

Chapter 22

I claim my usual seat at breakfast the next day, my nerves a wreck and my mind exhausted. I find it strange that Dorothy isn't in her typical chair – she almost always beats me to meal times. A few moments later, though, I hear the familiar screeching of her walking frame. Pale-faced and out of breath, she plops herself into the chair beside me and leans in.

'Listen to me,' she whispers, her breath still coming out in huffs. 'I have something important to tell you.'

'Okay,' I respond, staring at Dorothy. She doesn't look at me, though, her eyes darting around as if she's afraid of who might be here. Her hands tremble slightly as she reaches for her glass of water.

'Dorothy, you're scaring me,' I whisper. She leans in close, staring at me and grabbing my hand.

'It's serious, Adeline. Really serious.'

'So just tell me,' I order.

She shakes her head as she looks about again, her gaze dancing over the room. 'There are too many prying ears.

I can't let him know what I know. It's too dangerous for us all if he knows,' she murmurs in a hushed voice.

My heart leaps at her terror. I can't imagine what she could possibly need to tell me.

'Who? Who are you talking about?' I ask, my voice shaky.

Dorothy just shakes her head, her gaze darting about the room.

'I've discovered some things that might just tell us what's going on. I've uncovered some pieces that I think are vital to solving this whole situation.'

'Please, just tell me,' I say, my heart unable to take it any longer.

She is adamant, though, her lips sealed and her head shaking. 'As I said, it's too dangerous. We'll talk later. Meet me in the reading room around 7.00 p.m. tonight. It's private there, and the night nurses will be on duty. There won't be so many nosy ears listening in. Until then, we need to act normal. Act natural. It's important that no one suspects a thing, Adeline.'

'7.00. I'll be there,' I reply, repeating in my head. But how will I wait that long? How will I be able to just pass the time knowing that Dorothy has information that could change everything? I tap my fingers on the tablecloth. I need to write it down. 7.00 p.m. I chant it over and over.

'So, dear, tell me, did you watch another episode of *Cranford* this afternoon?' Dorothy asks loudly, her cheer clearly feigned. I paint on a crooked smile and play along, my eyes dancing around the room periodically, trying to figure out what she could possibly have to tell me – and what could be so dangerous that we must take part in this elaborate dance once more. When we say goodbye after eating, Dorothy leans in again. 'Be careful, Adeline. Be very careful. I don't think anyone here is what they seem.'

Before I can question her, though, she is off, her screeching walking frame leading her away, and abandoning me with my own horrendous, whirling thoughts.

I finish my breakfast, chanting *7.00 p.m.* in my mind over and over and over again. I need to remember. *Please remember.* Mind, don't fail me, please.

A few minutes later, I slowly plod down the corridor, running my hands along the wall. I pass the rooms that are so familiar now, trudging forward until my fingers find the familiar numbers. 316. I live in 316.

7.16. She said 7.16, didn't she? Is that when we're meeting? Yes. Yes, it's 7.16. 7.16.

I head to the noticeboard and jot down a note for myself so it's prominently displayed. My head aches today. I need to remember. 7.16 p.m.. Reading room. Knitting lady. Dorothy. Big secret.

My fingers massage my head. I hate it when my mind struggles. I hate it. Anger surges as I stab at the note, carving 'X's as I will myself to remember. Please, please, remember.

*

7.27 p.m.

I tap my foot, waiting for the lift desperately. I've never been so thankful to see the metal doors screech open or to climb inside the box of death.

Dorothy didn't come to lunch or dinner. It was alarming, my heart sputtering at her absence. A staff member assured me she was just feeling ill and insisted on having meals in her room. Was she ill this morning? Did she tell me she was ill? I think maybe she did say she was ill. I don't know. Or maybe it was something we ate for breakfast that made her ill. What did we eat? I can't remember that, either. It's a bad memory day.

I wring my fingers together, squeezing my hands. I'd thought about going to eat with Dorothy, to check up, but I was afraid to draw attention. I'd sat at the table in silence, a few of the other women Dorothy knows at our table mumbling about incomprehensible topics. I slurped down a few spoonfuls of soup, my eyes constantly darting about, watching for danger.

After dinner, I'd planned on returning to my room and waiting, watching the minutes tick by until 7.16, until I could find out the harrowing truth Dorothy had to tell me. I studied the note over and over, making sure I didn't miss the time. The secret. There was a secret. What was the secret?

I was getting myself ready for the long trek down the corridor when the unthinkable had happened. A nurse came to claim me at 7.05.

'Mrs Evans, we have an appointment for you downstairs.

The doctor was supposed to see you earlier, but he got held up. Come on. He just needs to check a few things.'

I looked up at her, unabashedly angry. 'No, I can't.'

The nurse sighed, exhaustion painted on her face. 'There's no choice in the matter. The sooner you cooperate, the better.'

I debated my options, ultimately deciding that heading downstairs willingly would be the fastest way to get finished and to get to Dorothy. I'd obliged, my palms sweating the entire time. I can't be late. I need to know what Dorothy discovered. The how, the why, the when – it's all driving me bonkers.

When the doors open and the nurse ushers me into the lift after my appointment, I realise I'm twisting my fingers. No use drawing unwanted attention.

We get to Floor Three after a long time, the lift's shaking and rattling still unsettling, but I hardly notice thanks to my bigger concerns. The doors barely peel back when I'm rushing out of them.

'Can you find your room?' the nurse asks, rubbing her eyes. Her shift must be about finished.

'No, I think I'll go read for a bit,' I murmur, heading towards the darkened reading room. The nurse glances at me and then shakes her head as if just remembering the reading room is even there. It's so infrequently used that it's essentially the forgotten locale of the floor.

'Right. Have a good night then,' she mumbles, heading in the opposite direction to check on patients on my side of the corridor. The nurse's station sits empty as it so frequently does up here. A few televisions play in the background, but overall, the floor is eerily silent tonight.

I shuffle towards the reading room, hoping Dorothy waited. Of course she would wait. She has to tell me. I need to know what she knows.

When I get to the room, the light is out. I carefully creep forward, trying to peer into the blackness to see if Dorothy is in the room.

'Dorothy?' I whisper, wondering if she's in the dark for a reason. What is she hiding from? What could be so terrible that she must lurk about? There is no answer. I repeat her name, but silence prevails. I feel my way over to the table with the lamp and fumble with the cord. When the room is illuminated, I turn towards the back area, looking about for Dorothy.

And that's when the floor is no longer silent, when a racking scream rattles through the room, echoing down the corridors. It's a scream that seems to have no beginning or end, the wail a wavering siren that announces that all is not well.

The scream comes from my lips, my heart racing as I take in the sight of Dorothy's bluish body crumpled on the ground, her neck at an unsettling angle.

I fall to the ground, clutching myself as a single nurse dashes into the doorway, her own yells drowning out mine. My scream fades to a whimper, then tears, and finally, a solemn silence for all that has truly been lost.

When Will the Slaughtering End? West Green Residents Wonder and Wait as Another Woman's Body Is Found

West Green, Crawley, West Sussex
20 July 1959

Residents of West Green are again on high alert after a fourth woman's body was discovered early Thursday morning behind a gardening shed at a residence on Meadlowlands Road, West Green. The body has been identified as that of Caroline Young, 20, who was reported missing 13 July 1959 after walking to the market for her family. She went missing in the early morning hours, but no eyewitnesses have come forward.

The body, discovered by Patrick Moore of 52 Meadlowlands Road, was uncovered the morning of 19 July 1959. It was intact but showed signs of trauma to the head as well as numerous abrasive marks. Bite marks were also uncovered on various parts of the victim, consistent with the other bodies discovered in the past weeks.

Caroline Young had recently called off a courtship with Paul Josephs of Northgate, who is currently being questioned as a suspect in the case. However, investigators are still warning the residents of West Green to remain on high alert, keep doors locked, and be wary of any suspicious persons.

With what appears to be a mass killer on the loose, the neighbourhood of West Green is in a frenzy. Other suspects have been cleared thanks to dental records or alibis. According to inside sources, investigators are no closer to finding the killer than they were after the first death.

'We need answers,' Miss Mary Brown, a neighbour of the Youngs, told reporters. 'It's absurd that our neighbours, our friends, our daughters are being snatched and the police have no leads. We're all terrified. Whoever is doing this needs to be caught.'

'There's a killer among us,' Reverend Hugh Morris stated. 'We must pray for swift justice for the killer, but we also know he will be at God's mercy.'

Caroline's death follows that of three other West Green women: Elizabeth McKinley found in the Crawley Hospital skip; Helen Deeley discovered in Ifield Pond; and Doreen Thompson, found behind the pub in Langley Green. All four women were residents of West Green, leading detectives to question a motive.

The West Sussex Constabulary wishes to remind anyone with information on any of the murders to come forward.

'Fucking moron, get it in check,' I murmur as I study myself in the mirror, eyeing the scratches on my cheek. I almost blew it this time. I'd been too impatient.

I was so focused on getting to the last one that I almost fucked up. Big time.

It had been early morning. I usually don't do my watching, my heavy watching, until night. Sure, there are the daily encounters with them. The inconspicuous, routine encounters that are to be expected. I glean so much information from that. You can learn a lot if you just pay attention. I'd always paid attention, even when teacher was yelling.

Pencil between my teeth, I'd bite down on the wood, quieting my chattering teeth as the kids around me laughed. I learned to bite harder, to silence them. Why did they chatter? Teacher called it nervous energy. I didn't want to be nervous. So I bit harder and harder and harder.

I liked the feel of it between my teeth.

Later, when school got more challenging because they

teased me, I bit other things to keep from exploding. Biting let me keep control. It helped. I bit lots of things.

Angry boy. Weird boy. Laugh at the boy.

But who is laughing now?

They'll be laughing again if I don't get this fucking under control. Bloody hell, after everything, I'm going to blow the game.

But I had been in a hurry. It's all her fault. I'd gotten so excited that night at the church that I'd almost fucked up. That moment when she'd dropped the necklace – well, it had thrown it all off. I'd almost blown the whole thing because suddenly, standing there on her porch, I was starving for her. I need that zany, unruly Walker girl's blood on my hands. I need to conquer her.

And I'm getting impatient.

But dammit, I'm not a fool. I'm better than that bloody moron, John Haigh, who everyone lauds. When I started this game, I set out with one thing in mind – I would beat that imbecilic man. I'd do one better than the Acid Bath Murderer who had gotten caught because he was just plain sloppy. No, I'm better than him.

The final one, though, has almost ruined it. She's almost made me lose my cool. I'm getting ahead of himself.

I'd decided a morning watch of Caroline would be okay. No one would suspect anything. I was getting a head start on my work. I could explain it away, of course. So I'd waited. I'd watched, the rain pounding down around me, the pavement pooling with water. The droplets pelted against my bare skin.

It had been a mistake. Too bold. Dammit, I'd been too bold when I grabbed her. I could've been caught. It was a fucking miracle I got away with it.

And then there had been the problem of what to do with the body in daylight. Through the murky rain, the blood from her head spattered about. Anyone could have found me. I debated whether or not I should leave the body right where I killed her. It didn't feel right. I hadn't marked her yet. And I wanted it to be a surprise. A challenge. What to do? What to do?

The Moores. They were on holiday. They wouldn't be back for at least a day or two. I regained confidence; I realised I could handle it.

I'd dragged her body the short way down Meadlowlands Road's alleyway, my eyes darting about for the first refuge from sight. The shed. The tiny shed out back.

In she went, and, with the door shut, I held her cold, lifeless body. I'd made my mark. I savoured it, knowing it was safe in there.

And then I'd left, slipping into the rainy day unnoticed, passing a few stragglers on my way back to my flat but no one gave me a second look. I am invisible in life, but that was something I was thankful for that morning.

Sometimes it's the invisible you should be watching.

Looking in the mirror now, I glance at the scratch on my cheek, beautiful Caroline's last mark in the world. It was too close. I could've been caught. I need to be more careful.

But it's okay. I'd won, in the end. Maybe it was by divine providence, or maybe it was by something unknown. Maybe this is simply the path I'm meant to take.

Regardless, I must be more careful. It needs to all work out in the end. If I don't finish the final one, it won't matter. None of it will matter.

I tuck away the unopened letter addressed to Caroline, slide the newspaper article on top, and close the box. My hand runs over the top, imagining what it will feel like to finally add Adeline's to the collection.

She is the one I'm waiting for, after all. She is the one.

Chapter 23

West Green, Crawley, West Sussex
19 July 1959

I meander down the aisle, Mum talking to Mrs Peabody about the most recent issue of their favourite catalogue and gossiping about the new family in town. I head over to the produce, eyeing up some of the apples and hoping I can convince Mum to bake an apple pie, my favourite.

'Addy, don't go too far,' she yells, pausing her conversation. I roll my eyes, feeling like an infant instead of a grown woman. I gather up a bag of apples and take them to the basket Mum holds.

'Your mother's right, you know. With all this craziness happening, you really should stay close. You can't be too careful these days,' Mrs Peabody adds. I smile politely, adding the apples to the shopping basket.

Mum and I finish the shopping, Mrs Peabody shadowing us the whole way, laughing too loudly at her own jokes. We see a few other locals in the supermarket, mostly housewives out for a stroll to plan dinner. Almost everyone seems to be using the buddy system, every woman in town in a fear frenzy at the prospect of the killer still being loose.

I'm listening to Mum and Mrs Peabody yammer on about some new recipe as we're standing in the queue to check out when a voice from behind startles me.

'Addy, is that you?'

I turn to see the familiar eyes that send a shiver through me.

'Oliver,' I murmur.

'Oh, Oliver, what a lovely surprise. I haven't seen much of you lately, which is truly a shame. We do miss seeing you about, don't we, Adeline?' My mother inserts herself into the conversation, obliviously adding to the tension. I don't say a word, staring at him as his eyes travel over my body.

'I miss you as well, Mrs Walker. I do think I'll have to come around more often, if you'll have me.'

Mother smiles. 'Why we'd love to, wouldn't we?' She nudges me, but I don't answer.

'Shouldn't you be at work today?' I ask, confused at his presence here. I never expected to see him at the supermarket at this time. This is when he's at work, far away. Too far away to come here and rattle me. This is my safe time.

'I have the day off today. Isn't that grand? Listen, I'd love to take a walk with you, catch up, if you'll be so kind to accompany me.'

'No, I'm with Mum,' I reply swiftly.

'Adeline, don't be ridiculous. Mrs Peabody will walk with me,' she replies. Mrs Peabody, on cue, waves from the front of the market.

I want to scream, to rage, to tell Oliver to get the hell away from me. I don't want to be left alone with him. Mum is worried about me walking alone, about the dangers of town. Yet, here she is, unknowingly feeding me to the lion.

'See, Adeline. It'll be just lovely. We can catch up, have a friendly chat.' His voice drips with fake sweetness and very real condescension. My mother is too enthralled by his status and his money to notice.

'What a gentleman. And I know he'll keep you safe from all this nonsense, won't you, Oliver?' Mum asks as she unloads her basket.

'Of course, Mrs Walker. You know I will.'

I keep my eyes averted, telling myself to stay calm. It's broad daylight, and we'll be out in public. There's no way Oliver can pull anything.

Then again, I know what he's capable of. I tremor at the thought. I wish Charles were here to protect me instead of working miles away. I wish I'd never given Oliver a second glance when he first started talking to me. I wish so many things, but it's no use. I'm stuck in this purgatory now, and Oliver is making sure I stay there.

After we make it through the till and Mum pays for the items, I find myself squeezing my left arm with my right hand, trying to control the rising fears in me. I rack my brain for a way to escape Oliver, for an excuse to get away. I know it's pointless, however. He's persistent. He always finds a way to win – and if he doesn't, I know I'll just pay later.

Mum waves goodbye to us as she strolls home, and Oliver offers me his arm. I squeeze my eyes shut, sighing, as he leads me towards the other route home, away from Mum.

Once we're away from the centre of town, on a quieter street, I turn to Oliver. 'What's this about, Oliver? What do you want? You know I'm with someone else. Can't you just accept that? Can't we just agree to go our own ways?'

He laughs. 'Addy, Addy. You think it's so simple, huh? You think you can just do whatever you want and there will be no consequences? You know how this works, don't you? I say when you can leave.' His hand wraps around my waist, pulling me in. I shudder at the feel of his touch. How did I once love him? How did my heart once ache for him? I can't even imagine those days anymore. Oliver's eyes darken as he stops us on the pavement, the sun beating down on us. In his eyes, I see a glimpse of that night months ago. The night that told me I wasn't safe anymore, not with Oliver on the loose. I know what he's capable of, and now, alone with him, I wonder if I'll feel his true wrath.

'Oliver, stop,' I order, fighting back tears.

We walk on, though, Oliver's hand squeezing my waist as he leads me down a desolate pavement. I can feel his arm trembling with what I presume to be rage. Having seen his temper before, felt his wrath, I shake, knowing what he could do to me. We march on to the end of the street. I glance to my left, chilling as we approach the front of Smith Creek Manor, a foreboding sight of a nursing home. I typically don't pass this building, avoiding this street at all costs. There's something unsettling about the dilapidated building with its crumbling pillars and dirty windows.

But I'm drawn away from the sight as Oliver's fingers dig into my flesh. I squeal out, my attention back on the danger right in front of me.

'Does that new bloke of yours know what a *slag* you are? Does he know what a sinner you are? Because you are, Addy. You're a *sinner*. You know that, right? You're going to hell for what you've done.' His words are barked through gritted teeth. He accents certain words, making me jump with the harshness of them.

I clutch at my chest, my palms sweaty. My heart races faster and faster. My free hand grapples with my chest, but he yanks me forward. I look around, tears now washing over my eyes. I pray to run into someone, anyone, to free me from him. But who is there to free me from Oliver Parsons? Everyone in town knows him. He's the charmer, the heartthrob, the son of the most pious, wealthy family in West Green. No one could ever believe the things he's done. Then again, no one would ever suspect the things I've done either. We all have our secrets.

He pulls me to the alley behind Smith Creek. It's empty

save for us. He's centimetres from my face, and I can feel his ragged breaths on my bare flesh. I gasp for air, tears falling freely now. What have I done? What did I see in him? And most of all, what will he do to me now?

'I'm sorry,' I squeak. And I am. I'm sorry for what Oliver and I once were. I'm sorry for what we became together. I'm sorry for the decision I had to make. The one I'd do anything to forget.

'Do you think apologies nullify what you did? Do you know what you did? You destroyed my plan for my life. I had it mapped out. I'd set the path for us, you know? But you destroyed everything. If people in this town knew what you've done, do you realise what they'd do to you? What your parents would do to you?'

'Oliver, please. I didn't destroy anything. You're okay. Your life is just fine,' I timidly offer. And it's true. Oliver's still the town's most eligible bachelor. He's from money, and his future's all perfectly set ahead of him. But it's not good enough for him. It'll never be good enough for him because it didn't go the way he wanted. He didn't get to keep control of the reins, no matter how hard he tried. I took that power from him, stripped him of the decision making. And that's what this is about.

I look up into his eyes, the stare that once made me swoon now making me cower.

'Really? You didn't destroy anything? You know what you did, Adeline. You had no right. That was my future you tainted, you annihilated. *My* future. How dare you think you can just make those decisions. You had it all with me. Didn't you see that you had it all? I gave you nothing but love and security, and that was how you thanked me?'

'Please. I'm sorry,' I whisper.

'Sorry you got caught. What, you think I don't have my ways? You don't think I have a way of keeping an eye on you at all times? I knew you couldn't be trusted, you slag. I made sure I kept an eye on you. I knew I had to. I *still* keep an eye on you.' He squeezes my wrist now, and I gasp as the bones flex under his grasp.

Standing here with him, a part of me remembers why I made that choice. This. Right here. The Oliver few know. The side of him that reared its ugly head one too many times.

It doesn't make it easy, I know that. I know I'll have to live with the pain of it forever. But as I stare into the flaming eyes of the bewildered being before me, I know that at the time, I did what I felt I had to do. I also know that Oliver doesn't see it that way. What is he going to do about it? How far will he go to make me pay, and for how long? And above all, is he the one they're looking for? Is he the one who killed those other women? They're questions I hope I don't find out the answers to anytime soon.

'Tell me, what would Charles think if he knew the whole truth? Do you think he'd still want you? Do you think he'd still find you worthy?'

'Please don't,' I mutter, hating that I'm begging but

having no choice. Because he's just articulated the fear that's been tainting the perfect love story growing between me and Charles. It's the anvil waiting to crash into us, waiting to obliterate his image of me. I love Charles. I don't want to lose him.

'Please don't,' I repeat. He squeezes harder and harder, smiling as I wince in pain.

And then, just like that, he flings my wrist away, letting me go as footsteps fall behind us.

'What the hell are you doing?' a strong voice says as a hand grabs Oliver's arm and yanks him away. I'm stunned, turning to see who could've possibly crept up on us.

'Fuck you,' Oliver shouts, arms flailing as he backs away from his assailant.

I turn to see the familiar face of the postman. He seethes and rages, his eyes burning as he studies Oliver. I could cry. I could hug him. What were the chances he'd be here to save me? A man I see so many times a week yet think so little of. He can't be much older than me, the youth showing itself in the delicate skin of his face, in his bright eyes. Still, his bulky, foreboding frame heaves as he towers over Oliver. He may only be a few years older, but his stature makes him seem much more mature. I almost smile at the ridiculous sight of Oliver, who is puffing out his chest but who clearly stands no match to the bulky man.

'I'll walk Adeline home.'

'Like hell you will. Come on, Addy. Let's get away from this psycho. What, were you following us?'

At that, the postman's arm jolts up, his fingers grabbing the collar of Oliver's shirt. Oliver pales as the postman pulls him in, and for a moment, I wonder what will happen next. I watch in silent fascination as Oliver is put in his place.

'Don't ever call me that. Do you hear? If you want to fucking see psycho, schoolboy, I'll show it to you.' His fingers squeeze, and Oliver chokes. My stomach plummets.

And then, as if he realises how surprising his actions must be, as if he knows he's proved his point, the postman lets go of Oliver, flinging him aside like a broken plaything.

'Adeline, do you want me to walk you home?' the postman asks, his voice calming as his eyes study me. Whereas his eyes were burning with something menacing a moment ago, they are now softer, almost intoxicated. I squirm under his glance.

'I'll be okay,' I assure, looking to the ground, uncomfortable holding his eyes with mine.

'I'll be watching you,' the postman spits at Oliver before walking in the other direction, the way we came from. Oliver mutters under his breath, readjusting his collar and trying to shake off the shame and surprise. He yanks me forward, but as I turn to look back, the postman stands in the middle of the pavement, staring at us, hands in his pockets. His jaw is clenched as his eyes glimmer. When we're out of earshot of my saviour, Oliver turns to me, pinching my arm.

'Don't think you'll get away with this. Don't think you can make damning choices and then run off to a happy life. You'll pay, Addy. One way or another, you'll pay. I'm just waiting for the right moment, that's all. I want to relish this,' he continues, the postman's threats having done nothing to discourage Oliver's terrorisations.

I avert my eyes to the ground, staring at his perfectly polished shoes. My palms sweat and tears fall now, but I don't dare look up. I'm too afraid to see what his eyes read, what his sneer says. I'm petrified of being here, alone, at his mercy.

The sting of his hand against my face stuns me. I reach up, trembling, to feel the flesh that he's slapped.

'Let's go, you bitch,' he barks, grabbing my wrist and yanking me forward. I fall into him, and he places my hand on his arm. 'Wouldn't want to keep your mother waiting. Wouldn't want her to worry that something happened to you, would we? After all, I promised to keep you safe. I'm a man of my word, aren't I, Addy?'

My hand shakes on his arm, his other hand squeezing my wrist. I cry out, shielding my teary eyes as we walk forward. At some point he reaches up, wiping away my tears. I cower at his touch.

'There, there, Addy. Wouldn't want people thinking you're upset. That could be dangerous, you know?'

The sun beats down on us and I will my feet to march onward, towards home. The sooner I'm home, the sooner I'm away from him, free from his grasp. At least for the time being. Because today has proved one thing – he still holds all the cards. My life is his to ruin.

Lost in these melancholic thoughts, we traipse towards my house. Oliver whistles as we near the more populated part of town, his jolly tune slicing through my bones. To think my mother is rooting for me to get back with Oliver. She doesn't know who he is. But neither did I. Neither does anyone, really. But to reveal his true self would be to reveal my secret. Mum would never forgive me, and Dad probably wouldn't either. Not after all they've been through. I don't think I can bear that pain, either.

We trudge on, down the pathway to my house and down the pathway Oliver has demanded of me. How long can I keep these lies going? How long can I shield Charles from the truth? And how long will I be stuck in limbo between the man I want and the man who won't free me? It's such a mess. I've made a true disaster of everything, just like Mum always warned I would.

We veer right, the quiet rows of houses sitting in the July sun. It's a quiet street, Meadlowlands Road, especially this time of day. I've always thought the houses here were quaint and lovely with their perfectly aligned window boxes of flowers.

But today, there's a different sight. A huge gathering of cars, of people are in front of the Moores' home. Patrick is a retired schoolteacher, and his wife volunteered as a nurse during the war. They're a sweet couple, and my heart sinks. I rush towards the chaos, wondering what could have possibly happened now. All thoughts of my own problems fade as we approach the crowd of frightened neighbours.

'What's this?' Oliver asks, stopping his cheerful whistle. He pulls me in closer, and I want to vomit at the smell of his cologne so close to my nose. I'm too concerned, however, to complain.

I find a familiar face, Mrs Wilson, a woman my mother used to invite over for tea and biscuits occasionally. Her daughter is a few years younger than me.

'What's happening?' I ask, yanking Oliver towards Mrs Wilson, who stands near the back of the crowd. He doesn't protest, and I feel safer with the presence of other witnesses.

'Another body. Patrick was working in his garden and went out to his shed to retrieve some tools. He found a body in there. Whispers are saying it's Caroline Young.'

I shake my head in disbelief. 'Did he do it? Was it Patrick?' I ask, the unthinkable question leaping from my tongue.

'I don't know. The constables are questioning him now. It's hard to say what's going on around here anymore. What is happening to our little neighbourhood? It's not safe anymore for anyone. This maniac is picking us off left, right and centre, and no one can figure out a thing. How can he be getting away with this?'

'Must be a smart bloke, that's all I have to say,' Oliver says. I turn and look at him, studying his face. He shrugs. 'I'm just saying, the constables and detectives are brilliant here. This guy must be quite the pro to be getting away with all of this.'

I manage to free my hand from his clutches. He doesn't fight, not with the crowd around us. I wrap my arms around myself, thinking about how serious the problem is. Another woman gone, another woman murdered. Suddenly, I'm freezing cold even though the sun is hot.

I stand for a moment, staring with the people I've known for the past few years, all of us suspicious and worried. When will this nightmare be over? Who else will lose their life in the process? I begin to walk back from the crowd, still studying the scene but Oliver pulls me back and leans in, close enough that his breath makes the hairs on my neck stand up.

'Better be careful, Addy. Wouldn't want you to end up in a shed like poor, sweet Caroline, would we? You better watch your step, or you could be next.'

Tears well again as he touches the bare skin on my neck, brushing my hair aside to kiss my skin with his chapped lips. 'Wouldn't do for your sweet, soft skin to be decimated, for your lifeless body to be found like a discarded rag. We wouldn't want that, now, would we?'

I bite my lip to choke back the whimpers that are forming. Oliver yanks my arm roughly.

'Time to go, Addy. A scene like this isn't for delicate women like you.'

I want to argue, but I also want to get home. I want to get away from Oliver, from this horrifying event. I leave the crowd of police and crying neighbours behind me, thinking about how shadowy the world really is.

When we're almost home, I shiver, a sense that someone is watching me rattling through my body. I glance around, studying the surroundings, but the street is empty. I stop, my heart pounding, as I look to the left. A flutter in a bush, a commotion – I take a step back, willing myself not to faint.

'Come on,' Oliver demands, leading me towards my house. I walk on but turn back, studying the bush. No one emerges. All goes quiet, and we are alone. When we reach my house, Mum rushes out, wiping her hands on a towel.

'Thank God, you two made it. Have you heard the terrible news?'

'Yes, Mrs Walker. Awful. But no need to fear. I've brought darling Addy home, safe and sound.'

I break away from him now, rushing towards my mother.

'Thanks, dear. You are such a gentleman. Would you like to come in for something to eat?' Mum asks.

I turn around, feeling emboldened by the safety of my mother's presence and by my house. 'Oliver needs to get home, Mum.'

Oliver glares, tilting his head up just a bit. 'I will be going now, but don't worry, Mrs Walker. I'm sure I'll be back. Isn't that right, Addy?'

I shudder at the way he stares at me, at the pain in my wrist, at the memory of his hand hitting my cheek. But before I can argue, he tips his hat, pivots on his foot, and strides away. I am left with just my thoughts and fears – and the knowledge that he most certainly will be back. He always, always comes back.

Now, the only thing left to ponder is what I'm going to do about it.

Chapter 24

Smith Creek Manor Nursing Home
2019

'I know Philip's here. I know it. I do,' she mutters in the corner, wheeling back and forth in her wheelchair, her eyes wide and glassy.

I've just returned to my room from lunch when I see the Philip Lady – what is her real name? I can't even remember – rolling in my old roommate's former side of the room. I glance around, noticing that the religious statue is still there, its wayward eyes staring at me. However, scattered about the side of the room are other belongings. A fake plant that is coated in dust. Photographs are tacked on the noticeboard, and a faded quilt rests on the bed. What is this? A nurse rushes past me, bringing Philip Lady a glass of the murky, polluted water on tap at Smith Manor. She is too far gone to notice that the water is disturbingly tainted.

I grumble, my new roommate still waffling about Philip

between sips. So much for peace and quiet. Just what I need right now.

I take a deep breath, the depression of the past few days only heightening with the idea that now I'll be sharing my room with a stranger. With my only true ally gone, murdered, in this place, I don't want to be around anyone at all.

Of course, *murdered* isn't the correct term, not according to the staff. *Accident* is the word being tossed around with Dorothy's death. A tragedy that she was wandering alone after dinner – she must have fallen – tripped and hurt her neck. These are the lies Smith Creek has fed to everyone. These are the lies so many choose to believe. But I know the truth. Dorothy's death was no accident. Someone was out to silence her – and silence her, they did.

I shudder to think she's gone because of the secret she harboured and because I was too late for our meeting. I am racked with guilt, and my soul, already laden with secrets from the past, is just getting darker and darker. What was the secret Dorothy died for? What did she need to tell me? My head has been swirling with questions for the past few days. *What did you need to tell me, Dorothy?* I ask her over and over, silently staring out my window, wondering who killed – and who will be coming for me.

But the dead don't answer questions, and the living are too good at hiding their secrets. I know that no one here at Smith Creek is going to be able to help. So I watch, I wait, and I tremble at the thought that my cold, lifeless body will be the next 'accident' to happen. What lies will they tell to cover for my death?

The Philip Woman keeps chanting, and I roll my eyes. I loathe her already, perhaps in fairness because I'm so exhausted. I glare at her from my side of the room, wondering if this is part of the anguish I'll endure in my final days – listening to her nonsensical chanting, my head already pounding from everything that's been happening.

Perhaps, though, I'm looking at this all wrong. Watching her, it dawns on me. Maybe Dorothy was right. With another witness, perhaps he won't be so brazen – whoever he is. Maybe Philip Lady will be just what I need to make it all stop.

'You two enjoy getting to know each other,' the nurse says in a monotone voice, traipsing out of the room. I stare at my new roommate. Unlike my last roommate, Philip Lady can speak. But I don't know if that's a good thing, I decide as I march out of the room to escape the insanity of her blubbering and the migraine she's already given me. Could things get any worse? I almost hate to ask as I head to the community room, thinking about all that's transpired and what to do next.

*

'Come on, dear. Why don't you come and see Henry?' a nurse asks in an overly chipper voice. I look up from my chair, averting my eyes from the window. How long have

I been in this chair, shielded from everyone? So many emotions have whirled about since Dorothy's death – guilt, fear, sorrow. But above all, the loneliness is getting to me. For the first time since I moved in – what? A month ago? Two? I think it's been a month, but I don't even know what month it is – I'm all alone here now. I have no ally and several enemies. It's enough to drive anyone into a hermit-like life.

'What?' I croak, my voice crackling from not being used.

'Henry, our visiting therapy dog. He's a mastiff, and the residents here just love him. He's here today. I know you've been through a lot lately. I think it would do you some good to meet him,' the brown-haired nurse offers, smiling.

I sigh. I don't feel like getting up. I don't want to go out there into the corridor. I don't want to have to watch my back. But she is insistent, even reaching for my arm to help me up.

'Fine,' I mumble, my legs stiff from not being used. I let her lead me out of the room, the Philip Woman chanting again on her side of the room. I've almost got used to it. Almost.

'Henry visits once a month, and it's always everyone's favourite day. I'm sure you'll love him,' the nurse reassures me as we walk down the corridor.

I look about to see quite a few of the Floor Three residents making their way to the Community Room. As we pass the nurse's desk and approach the room, I look down the corridor towards the room that Dorothy used to live in. At the end, the man in 300 stands, leaning on the wall outside his room, staring at me as he rubs his scar. I quickly avert my eyes, squeezing the nurse's arm a little tighter.

Twenty minutes later, I see Henry first-hand, and all I know is when he walks into the room, my stomach sinks at the size of him. He could maul someone to death in seconds.

Henry's handler gives a presentation about the benefits of therapy dogs, but I'm barely listening. Instead, I diligently peruse the people in the room. Oliver strolls into the room a few minutes late, causing my heart to race. Where was he just now? What could he have done? Did he do something? Eventually, we all get in the queue to pet Henry, and even though I'm hesitant, the handler convinces me to join the others.

'He's harmless, truly. The worst that will happen is you'll get a bit of slobber on your top,' she assures me.

I nervously stand behind Barbara. Someone stands very close behind me, so close that I can feel moist breath on my neck. I turn and almost smack into him – the man from 300. With a smile that is more of a sneer, he nods curtly at me. His breath is foul and hot in my face. He stands slumped to the side. When did he come in?

When we get close enough, I pat Henry on the head to appease the handler. I'm just getting ready to tell her that she's right, Henry's a sweet dog, when suddenly, Henry emits a low growl. I pull my hand back, my stomach dropping. I scamper back, tripping on a chair and falling to the ground. There's a commotion as the dog's handler tries to calm him, as residents shriek, and as nurses rush to my assistance.

The monstrous dog bucks and jumps, teeth bared as his hackles stand on end. I shield my face with my arms, shaking as I struggle to get to my feet. Screams and yells surround me, and a tumult ensues. The dog barks and snaps wildly, yanking the handler forward. I peer up from behind my shielding arms and realise the dog is lunging at someone behind me but not actually at me. Henry's frothing slobber flies about as he pulls his handler closer and closer to the target. The noise echoes through the room, and the nurses scream as they try to help me up. The handler shouts Henry's name, but the dog doesn't calm.

'Henry, stop,' the handler demands, but the dog is on the end of its leash, its sheer size proving to be a force that overpowers everyone. I watch as the dog lunges with its powerful jaws – but, as nurses attempt to get me up and safely away from the goliath dog's body, I turn to see the man from 300 backing up towards the wall. The dog follows him, teeth bared. Another staff member helps the handler yank Henry back, and the man from 300 edges along the wall, slinking out of the room. Only then does the dog ease up.

I gasp for breath as the handler apologises over and over to me, to the nurses, to everyone. Sitting in the corner of the room, shielded from everyone, the dog's eyes dart about the room, looking for its target. We all breathe a sigh of relief as the chaotic scene softens into something bearable.

'He never does this. He's never done this. I don't know what to say. Apologies,' the handler says, visibly distraught. It's unclear if she's talking to the nurses or to herself.

I shake my head as I hold my chest, my heart racing like it's going to explode. Arms tug me up, a wheelchair placed under my bottom as I'm rushed out. I catch my breath, thinking about the insane scene. Henry's eyes were lasered on the man behind me, the man from room 300. At the thought, a chill ruptures my resolve to stay calm.

Chapter 25

It just makes no sense, I think over and over as I sit in front of the canvas that is supposed to become a jolly beach scene. The girl attempting to instruct the class can't be more than twenty, and she just seems utterly out of place. She giggles way too much, making jokes out of our struggles. Half of the residents in the class can't even move their hands properly or drink a glass of juice on a good day, let alone paint a masterpiece. Whoever designs the activity timetable has some misguided expectations.

I sit in the second to last row in the class, alone. There's an empty seat beside me where Dorothy should be sitting. I try to shove the thought aside, but I can't. What happened to Dorothy? What really happened? And what did she need to tell me? I slap the paint brush onto the canvas, not really caring where the sand or the sky is. Instead, I mentally trace my steps that day and think about what Dorothy said. She left no clues. She left no hints. All I know is that whatever she found out, whatever she needed to tell me, it was serious.

So serious that someone murdered her for it.

I've thought over the past few days about ringing the police – but what would I say? What proof do I have? This place has death scenes down to a science. They cover their tracks. Who will believe a dementia patient with heart trouble?

And can I believe it all myself?

I've spent the past few days in and out of doubt. Maybe the doctors are right. Maybe my mind is playing tricks. Maybe I'm seeing things from a warped sense of perspective.

But no. It can't just be my fading mind playing tricks. I know what I've seen. I know the notes are real, the mice in the bed. I've been keeping the notes in my Bible. I've been scrawling down reminders of what's happened and leafing through them over and over.

It's real. It's happening. I can't be just imagining it all. Can I?

I know for sure that Dorothy is gone. Her things are gone.

And I'm pretty certain the secret she was keeping is gone.

I should be afraid, terrified actually. I should be trying harder to figure out what she discovered. But her death, well, it's hit me hard. I didn't realise how at least with Dorothy here, I had someone to trust. Now, I have no one, nothing. I'm alone, absolutely alone. Maybe I always have been.

I stare at the sky on my canvas. The instructor's is a bright blue, the kind that offers hopes and promises for a peaceful, joyous day. My own sky is tinged grey, the kind of day when one stays inside instead of venturing out. I keep painting, the darkness swirling on the canvas, the questions spinning in my head.

I paint a bird in the corner of my canvas, its gnarled feathers adding a level of eeriness to my scene.

'What are you doing up there? You do know we're painting a beach scene, right?' A voice caws behind me. I turn around to see Vivienne, perched on a chair like she's sitting on a throne, her bejewelled black dress looking even more out of place than usual.

'Suppose it is true,' she continues while I turn back to my painting. 'Suppose you have completely lost your marbles after all. With that horrid woman you called a friend dead now, it's just a matter of time until you lose it for real.'

I spin around. 'How dare you talk about her,' I reply, nostrils flaring.

'Oh, apologies. Did I bring something up uncomfortable? You ask me, I find it very suspicious. You just happened to find her in the room, dead. This place was fine until you showed up. Just fine. And now, trouble. You're trouble, Adeline. Plain and simple.'

I open my mouth to argue, but what's the point? In some ways, Vivienne's right. If it weren't for me, Dorothy could still be alive. If it weren't for me, so many things would be different here.

I spin around in my seat, returning to my canvas, and the instructor continues rambling about brush strokes. I keep painting, bird after bird in the sky, with a ferocity and swiftness that is unmatched as I mumble noncommittedly. I hate what's happened to Dorothy. I hate that I don't know the secret she was keeping. Above all else, I hate that she wasn't the only one hiding something. I hate that she never fully understood who Oliver was and about our past. It just never occurred to me to tell her, a woman from my present, about a man from my past, even with everything happening. But now, I second-guess myself. Could it have changed things if she'd have known how Oliver and I were connected? Would it have somehow fit together with the information she wanted to tell me? It's too late to change things now, and I know why I kept the secret from her. Still, as the day goes on, I become more and more convinced that the secret I'd hoped to take to my grave is about to be exposed – and that the grave is closer than I could ever imagine.

Chapter 26

I leave the community room, my melancholic painting sitting on the easel to dry. I walk alone, head in the wrong direction, and end up in a corner of the home I don't recognise. I take a deep breath and tell myself to think. I know my way around. It's okay. I look at the bouquet of dried roses covered in a layer of dust, their cheap-looking vase cracked in the front. I don't remember seeing this table, these flowers. Is this the way to my room? I look left and then right.

I'm so confused. This hasn't happened for a while. I grab my head, my brain pulsating as I try to will myself to think. Tears threaten to fall as my emotions rage. I'm lost. Where's my room? Where's Dorothy? It's all too much.

'Come on, you old bag. What the hell are you doing over here?' a voice beckons as a hand grabs my elbow, hauling me to the right.

Jones. He's shaved off the moustache, but instead of looking more put-together, he looks like a frightening man-child, arrogance now even more perceptible in the way he holds his lip.

He walks fast, so fast I can barely keep up. I almost fall a few times as he rushes me down another corridor.

'I've got better things to do than be your bloody tour guide around this place. Stay put or I'll make sure you stay put,' he barks. Tears flow now as we rush down a corridor. Finally, he flings me towards the open door. My hand catches on the wall, and my fingers trace the numbers.

316. I live in 316. 316? I thought it was 315. Or is this right?

I shake my head, so tired. It's all so exhausting.

'Get the hell in there, you blighter. I've got other shit to do,' Jones bellows before turning around and heading back towards the nurse's station. I walk into the room, and recognise the familiar comforter, the pullover I left on the chair. I smile a bit at the familiarity. I know this place. This is right. I'm okay.

But before I can settle in and relax, reassured that I haven't lost it, a voice breaks the silence and I remember something I've forgotten.

I have a new roommate.

'Philip was here. He was here. I saw him,' she rambles on and on as she stares at me from her side of the room. The sight of another woman's bluish body in the Philip Lady's bed flashes before me, rattling me. Goodness, I'd almost forgotten about her. What was her name, that roommate I once had? I rub my temples, trying to remember but also wanting so badly to forget.

'He was here. Philip,' she says again, redirecting my attention. I want to gently tell her that Philip was not here, that I don't suppose I even know who Philip is, and that she must calm down. But over and over, she chants the words. This time, though, it's different than all the other times. This time, she isn't just stating the phrase from rote memorisation. No, this time, she's looking at me as if she's seeing me – as if she's telling me something.

'When?'

'He was here. Philip was here. He was,' she repeats on and on, and I shake my head. Perhaps I'm going just as mad as the Philip Lady. Still, I can't help but notice how her eyes seem panicked, like she's seen a ghost. Maybe she has. Who am I to judge or to say what's real anymore?

My limbs throb from my fall as I wander over to my side of the room, kicking off my slippers. I could do with having a rest. The Philip Lady keeps chanting. I suppose I'll have to really learn how to block out external distractions. Perhaps I should take one of those classes on meditation next week – as long as they don't have the candles. I fluff my pillow, pausing for a moment before peeling back the sheets. There's always a bit of a pause now as I remember the mice and their damaged bodies, so cold just like Dorothy. Just like my last roommate.

Philip Woman crosses the room slowly, painfully slowly, like a caterpillar on a descent up a mountain. I stare at her, wondering what she could possibly be doing now and wondering if the harsh lady or the brown-haired lady is still around to offer her assistance. I'm beginning to understand why her past roommate was miffed. A person can only endure so much.

But she isn't heading for me, I realise, as she crosses the room, her head tilted slightly to the left, her lips crusty and peeling. Her feet shuffle forward, like a moth drawn to flame. My eyes line up with her path, and I look at what she's staring at.

I clench my fists in frustration. I knew it was too good to be true. I steady myself for a moment, squeezing my eyes shut. I will the tears to stop before they can fall. It will do no good to cry. I cross the floor, brushing past Philip Lady to the noticeboard, wondering what fresh hell awaits now. There is no Bible verse this time. Just one word, scratched over and over until it is practically carved in the paper, an engraving on a crumpled piece of cheap white lined notebook paper.

Repent.

One word to put me on edge, to make me think this is all going to end horribly. One word to remind me of the past sin I can't quite shake. One word to make me remember that this is no longer a game but potentially life or death.

'Philip was here,' she insists again, her words choppy and strained now as she takes a long pause in between each one.

'Who is Philip? Who is he?' I ask, shaking the woman.

She cries. 'Philip. It was Philip,' she bellows, her voice begging me to understand.

'Who is Philip? Answer me! Who is it?' I demand, a built-up aggression surging as I latch onto her shoulders, squeezing until my hands shake.

She shrieks and cries, the name *Philip* emitted in between gasps and screams of pain. I do not stop, though, her agitation only fuelling mine further. My fingernails dig into her flesh, the pads of my fingertips searching for bone, seeking to make her suffer the way I have. Screams resonate in the room over and over. I don't let go.

'Hey! What's going on here?' a male voice roars from the doorway. I let go of Philip Lady, snapping out of it. I try to back up, my roommate also stepping backwards, sobbing. She still chants the familiar name, but it is slower and breathier from all the turmoil.

'I said, what's going on here?' I look up to see Jones in the room, scowling. I look at him before glancing over to the board. Is this the first time he's seeing it, or is this all part of a calculated plan? Have I underestimated him, overlooked him?

I cross my arms over my chest, turning to the corner of the room as Philip Lady leaves. I feel Jones creep up behind me, his breath on my neck. 'Watch yourself, old woman. Wouldn't want anything terrible to happen to you, would we? Wouldn't want to have to make you behave.'

I quake underneath the tension he's brought into the room, an ominous cloud enveloping me with his presence.

'Do you understand?' he whispers. I nod. Gruff, strong hands spin me around, and I am centimetres from his face now.

'I said do you understand?' he spits through gritted teeth.

'Y-y-yes.'

'So you're not going to cause any problems, are you?'

I shake my head.

'All will be calm and quiet in 316. Is that right? No reports. No breakdowns. Nothing of the sort?'

I nod emphatically. I keep my arms wrapped around me.

'Good.'

I'm so cold now, so, so cold. I can feel the blood rushing out of my extremities. The blood stops in my veins, and I can feel my heart weakening.

'Yes,' I murmur, staring at his chest so I don't have to look into his eyes. I don't want to see those eyes. I don't want to see the condescension in them or the red flames of hate in them. I don't want to think about what it all means.

When Jones is gone, I crawl into bed, staring at the note on the noticeboard as I tremble.

*

'Mum, are you sure you're all right?'

'Of course, Claire. I'm fine. Just fine. A little tired is all,' I reassure, patting Claire's leg before she's off to enjoy her night. She swung by after dinner and took me for a short walk outside, dusk settling around us. There's some type of film night happening on the ground floor. Almost all the other residents are in the extra-large community room watching an animated feature. I assured Claire I didn't mind missing it.

'Ring me if you need anything,' she replies, and I paint on the familiar, fake smile a little wider. I can't let her know that behind my pale, chapped lips, fear lurks.

Once I've waved her off, I turn back around and meander to the community room for a bit. All sorts of residents sit around the projected film, my roommate sitting in the corner repeating her typical chant. Some residents are sleeping, others staring at the wrong spot in the room. A few hold hushed conversations in the back of the room with no one at all. I claim a seat in the last row of chairs, staring mindlessly at the ridiculous film as the sky darkens outside. My eyes grow heavy and my soul grows weary from the film's fake pretences. I'm not in the mood to be social, not really. I want to go back to my room, to sulk, to think. I want to keep a lookout. I want to be prepared. And maybe a part of me wants to sit and think about the past, the thing I should be letting go of but can't quite ever work out how to. After I rest my legs for a moment, I saunter out of the room, trudging past the nurse's station on the ground floor.

The lift takes an eternity to come, but I'm too tired to complain. Funny how when I first got here, I thought the lift was dangerous. Now, I've learned there are so many bigger things to fear. When the doors finally slide open, Father Patrick storms out, cursing up a storm as he marches towards the community room, a staff member accompanying him. I exhale audibly when he brushes past. Shaking my head, I get into the lift alone and take it to Floor Three. For a moment, I sink back against the wall of the lift, feeling at ease and comforted by the fact that I'm all alone in here. The four walls feel like a sanctuary, even as it screeches and the lights flicker. I'm protected from the chaos of Floor Three and the people surrounding me, if only for the amount of time it takes the lift to climb the three floors. The third floor – my home. Home in both no sense and every sense of the word.

I glance at the nurse's station, where a young man sits, doing some sort of paperwork. He looks up, studying me, and I quickly avert my eyes. Praying he doesn't cause trouble for me, I traipse down the corridor, yawning. Perhaps I'll just go to sleep for the night. So many of the rooms are empty, everyone down on the ground floor for the festivities. I amble into my dark room and head towards my bed. The stillness of the almost-empty floor soothes me. I didn't realise how much I craved silence until now.

But as soon as I'm in my room, the silence transforms into an eerie backdrop to the sight before my eyes. There's so much to take in, my eyes travelling in the darkness of the room and noticing horrors of all varieties. I will my feet to move towards the bedside table, the smashed photograph perhaps the hardest sight to absorb. I reach a shaking hand out, cutting myself as I grab the frame that is now destroyed – and along with it, any hopes that this nightmare will just pass on by.

Clutching the chilled silver edges of the picture frame, my shaking hands rattle the loose glass shards that rest on the photograph. The peeling wallpaper of my room is marked with a mystic yet clear warning. I smooth my thumb over the ridges of the familiar texture on the frame, looking down at the unassuming, smiling faces in the photograph. They had no idea that years later, they'd be pawns in this sick and twisted game. How could they, after all?

Claire brought me the photograph only a couple of days ago to replace the last one. Has it really only been a couple of days? So much has changed. I can't even keep track of the days, the hours, the minutes. Tears splash onto the glass shards, swirling in small, delicate puddles over our faces. I can feel my heart constricting, tightening, and I wonder if this is where it all ends.

'Charles, what is this? What *is* this?' I whisper into the room, my breathing laboured as the glow from my lamp dances over the message on the faded, sickly wallpaper. I shake my head, trying to work out what to do. I could push the call button over and over until one of them comes. I could wait for a nurse to get here. They would have to believe this, wouldn't they? They would have to see that

I'm not mad, that this is real. They wouldn't be able to feed me lines about my warped perceptions of reality or this disease that is degrading my mind.

They'd *have* to see it.

Then again, who knows anymore. No one seems to believe me at all. Sometimes I don't even know if I can believe myself. I stand from my bed, setting the crushed picture frame down and leaning heavily on the tiny wooden bedside table. I yank my hand back, looking down to see blood dripping from where a piece of glass has sliced into me. The burning sensation as the redness cascades down my flesh makes my stomach churn.

What's happening to me?

I need to solve this, but I know I'm running out of precious time. He's made it clear through the message on the wallpaper that this is all coming to a devastating conclusion – and soon. I don't know when this story will end or exactly how. But this tower is ready to topple, crashing down and obliterating me in the process. I can't let that happen without uncovering the truth. I can't leave this place as the raving lunatic they all think I am. I have to stay strong and sort this out. Charles would want me to uncover this debauchery. They all need me to work this out, even if they don't realise it.

And most of all, I need to die satisfied that all has been set right, that injustices have been paid for. I can't leave this world with all the murky questions swirling in my mind, and with all the old guilts rattling about. Someone needs to pay for the sins of the past – and I don't think it should just be me.

I take a step towards the wall, my bones aching with the effort. I am careful not to slip, a few loose shards and specks of blood dancing on the floor in intoxicating patterns. I focus my gaze back on the words that taunt me.

I lean my forehead against the wall, not caring that the oozing liquid will be in my hair, on my face. I inhale the rusty scent of the dripping note in the corner of the room.

You're mine.

It trickles down, the blood an oddly blackish hue on the tired wallpaper of Room 316. I lift a trembling hand to the phrase, my finger hesitantly touching the 'Y'. Its tackiness makes me shudder. It's *real*. I'm not imagining it. I'm certain that it's all real. Taking a step back again, I slink down onto my bed, my cut hand throbbing with pain as I apply pressure to it. My fingers automatically pick at the fluff balls on the scratchy blanket. I should probably push the call button. I should get help, get bandaged. I can't force myself to move, though. I tremble and cry, leaning back against my bed.

I don't understand. There's so much I don't understand.

I rock myself gently, my back quietly thudding against the headboard. I think about all the horrors I've endured here and about how no one believes me. Like so many others, I'm stuck in an unfamiliar place without an escape. Unlike Alice, my wonderland is a nightmarish hell, a swirling phantasm of both mysticism and reality – and there are no friendly faces left at all to help me find my way home.

The babbling resident down the hall warned me. She did. On my first night here, she told me I wouldn't make it out alive. Now, her words are settling in with a certainty that chills my core. True, it wasn't the most revolutionary prophecy. No one comes to a nursing home expecting to get out alive, not really. Most of us realise that this place is a one-way ticket, a final stop. It's why they are so depressing, after all. It's why our children, our grandchildren, our friends are all suddenly busy when the prospect of visiting comes up in conversation. No one wants to come to this death chamber. No one wants to look reality in the face; the harsh, sickening reality of ageing, of decaying, of fading away.

Still, staring at the warning scrawled in blood on my wall, I know that maybe the woman down the hall meant something very different with her words. I'm going to die here, but not in the peaceful way most people imagine. I'm going to pay first. I'm going to suffer.

But why me? And why now, after so many years have passed since those horrific incidents of my past?

I don't know who to trust anymore. I don't know if I can trust myself. My mind is troubled, and my bones are weary. Maybe the nurses are right. It's all nothing more than this disease gnawing away at me.

But as I look one more time at the blood trickling on the wall, I shake my head. No. I'm not that far gone. I may be old, frail, and incapable of surviving on my own, but I haven't gone mad yet. I know what's real and what's not. And I'm certain this is demonically, insidiously real. Someone here wants to make me pay. Someone here has made it their mission to torment me, to toy with me. Someone here at the Smith Creek Manor Nursing Home wants to kill me. In fact, someone here has killed already.

My hands still shaking, I appreciate the truth no one else can see – it's just a matter of time until they do it again.

I lie back on the bed, the pieces of glass and the blood cradling me. Maybe, in truth, I resign myself to the fact that I'm helpless, that I'm at a mysterious Mad Hatter's mercy in this ghoulish game of roulette. I stare at the ceiling, the hairline crack beckoning my eyes to follow it. I lie for a long time, wondering what will happen next, debating what new torture awaits, and trying to predict what the final checkmate will be in this sickly game.

After all, no one gets out of here alive. Even the walls know that.

*

I don't know how long I stay like that, blood dribbling down my arm from my glass-shredded palms. I don't feel the physical pain after a while, or maybe I just believe I deserve it. Eventually, after what must be hours, the light turns on in my room.

'Oh dear. Oh dear,' a trembling voice says. I turn to see a blonde nurse, I believe from Floor One, escorting Philip Lady to our room. The nurse abandons her charge, rushing towards me.

'Are you okay? What happened?' Her eyes inventory my body, the room and the terrors around me.

I shake my head. 'I don't know. I don't know anymore,' I mouth. The next few moments are a blur of nurses, of bandages, of cleaning up of glass. I hear murmurs of the words *meds* and *dementia*. I know they think I've done this. It's no use anymore. It's no use at all.

Finally, after a long time, they help me into bed, my arm bandaged and the walls wiped clean. The Philip Lady is mercifully snoring. I am alone once more. The nurse gives me something to help me sleep and then leaves.

I saunter over to the chair by the window once the nurses are gone, too terrified to sleep. I keep watch of the doorframe, half expecting *him* to return, half hoping he does. I need to see his face, to know for sure it was him. But instead, after a while, I find my eyes staring out the familiar window. Across the way in 300, a light is also on. The man over there stands, leaning his head against the window, peering at me. I lean my head on the chilly glass, looking out. It's hopeless. It's all hopeless. We stay like that for a moment, our eyes locked across the way. And that's when, blinking, I shake my head. I must be imagining it. I must be.

His finger taps on the glass, pointing at me, ticking like a handgun against the window pane in a manner unsettling. But that's not the most frightening part. I shake my head again. My eyes must be deceiving me, my overworked emotions and mind bowing to exhaustion. *Silly woman*, I chide myself. Silly woman indeed.

For a second, it seems like the man in 300 is saying something. It seems like his lips are moving. No, I'm not crazy. They are. His lips are *definitely* moving, but I can't make out what he's saying. What's he saying? *What's he saying?*

His lips stop moving, he leans forward, and then I see it. He drags his tongue across the window, back and forth, back and forth, his eyes locked on mine.

I blink over and over, shaking my head.

Stop it, stop it, stop it, I tell myself, banging my hand against my head over and over. *Stop playing tricks.* My mind is just playing tricks. It can't be real. It can't be.

I look back up to the window after a moment.

The light is out. The figure is gone.

Tears fall at the realisation. Perhaps the nurses are right. Perhaps I'm truly going mad. Perhaps my sense of reality is just a warped, dark sense of the truth.

I don't know anymore. I don't know, Charles. I really just don't know. I'm sorry, Charles. I should've told you. You should be here. Things should be so different.

I collapse backwards, not sure what to make of it all – perhaps too afraid to try – as sleep overpowers me.

*

'Mrs Evans? Wake up. Oh my, did you sleep here?' A hand and a ragged voice shakes me awake.

I jump, my vision hazy. My neck aches like someone's taken a hammer to it. My hand finds its way to the sore muscle, massaging it, as the brown-haired nurse helps me up.

'I must've fallen asleep,' I murmur, looking out the window and remembering with a jolt of terror what I saw last night.

When I look across the way, however, the man in 300 isn't there. I study the empty window for a moment, half expecting him to appear in my line of vision. He doesn't, though. What happened last night? Was it real? I shake my head, trying to remember. Did I write it down? I'll have to check my notes later. I'll have to see if I left myself a note to remember. My head hurts. My mind dances over clips of last night. I look up to the wall, but there is no sign of the message – what did it say? – on the wall. The only proof that something happened last night is the bandage on my arm.

The nurse helps me walk to the bathroom, my legs stiff from the awkward position of the chair. After I've taken care of morning routines, she leads me to my bed to sit.

'Mrs Evans, I heard that last night was a fairly intense evening. The night nurse from Floor One said she found some alarming things in here.'

I glance over to the table, empty now that the photograph is gone. They must've taken it away.

'Yes,' I admit, not knowing what else to say. She stoops down, eye level with me.

'It'll be all right. I promise,' she assures. Her words are kind, and I want so desperately to believe her. But how can you believe it will all be okay when it was never okay in the first place? When she sees me, she sees the Adeline Evans I am now – a weak, decrepit woman who has lost so much. She doesn't see who I was, what I've been through, or the transgressions I've committed. Most of all, she doesn't see the true terrors of Floor Three.

'It wasn't me,' I retort, seeing that tell-tale look in her eye and feeling the need to defend myself for whatever happened. Flashes of blood, of fear whir inside of me.

I've done some awful things, it's true. But not this. I didn't do this. The way she stares at me, though, placating me with her eyes, I know that she thinks it was me. She thinks I've gone completely mad, the dementia working its way through my brain and my ability to reason. The smashed photograph, the blood on the walls, the blood on my arms – she thinks I was the root of it all. They all do. It makes me livid. I'm trapped in this web of falsehoods, entombed by my own failing body and mind. Can't they see? What will it take for them to believe me? Another horrifying thought comes to mind. Claire. With all that happened, did they notify her? Did they bother Claire with this?

'Listen, it's going to be fine, Mrs Evans. It's all fine. You just take it easy today, okay?' she says.

I snatch her arm with my cold fingers, desperate for someone to believe me. 'You need to keep an eye on Oliver.

And the priest in 310. And the man in 300. It's one of them. I know it. It has to be. They're dangerous,' I plead, squeezing her arm.

For a long moment, her eyes peer into mine, piercing into me, and I think maybe it's going to be okay. Maybe I've found my ally in her kind eyes. But then her lips turn up into the familiar smile, the one that says she pities me. Tears start to fall, desperation settling in.

I continue, hoping against all odds I'll get through to her. 'The man in 300. He's dangerous. I know it. Ask him. Ask him if he saw anything. I know he would have seen.'

The nurse stands now, offering another weak smile and a pat on the arm. 'Okay, Mrs Evans. It'll be okay.'

I shake my head. I know it's a lie. Things will never be okay again. Then again, they never really were. So much of life is about false pretences, fraudulent appearances and what we convince ourselves we understand.

But as I head to breakfast, I know the cold, hard truth: I don't understand a bloody thing.

Chapter 27

I sit alone at breakfast, even Dorothy's old friends moving on to a new table. Maybe they're afraid I'm trouble or just plain bad luck. My hand shakes as my eyes dart around the room, waiting for him to come in. My nerves are so shot that I barely manage to choke down Smith Creek's weak excuse for tea.

Finally, I spot him, four tables over from me. He sits unassumingly, staring at me. The nurses serve breakfast, and I don't take my eyes off the man from 300. A flash from last night. He was in the window, staring. Wasn't he? Or was that a dream? I don't know. Think, think, think. One, two, three. Think. One. Think. Two. Think. Three.

Goodness, my head hurts. I'm weary. But yes, I remember something about the window. He was there. Pointing, wasn't he? Or was he banging? Or was that in the stairwell?

Tears fill my eyes. But I must stay strong. I know he was doing something – frightening. Looking at him as he eerily rubs the scar on his head, a shiver runs through me. Could he be the one after all? Could this have nothing to do with Oliver? Could my guilt from the past be bringing Oliver to the forefront as a prime suspect, when really I'm just overlooking the true culprit? Is he the one toying with me?

But it doesn't make sense. I don't even know him. I don't know who he is. What would he want with me? What could he possibly have against me? It doesn't make any sense at all. Nothing does.

I look at Dorothy's chair, hearing her words on our final day together. What did she say? It's in my notes – isn't it? I think I wrote it down. I need to check. I need to put it together, but it's so hard. I need help. I don't trust myself to figure it out.

Staring at the man from 300, though, a thought comes to mind. Could he have something to do with what Dorothy wanted to tell me? As I study him, his fork tracing his scar on his forehead in an odd display, I realise he's mouthing something to me now. Back and forth, back and forth, the fork traces the scar as his eyes laser into mine. And this time, I blink once, twice, three times – I'm certain I'm not imagining it. I know he's mouthing something.

And I know exactly what he's saying to me.

'Mine,' he's mouthing. 'Mine.' Repeatedly, his lips form the word.

Mine.

Mine.

Mine.

I drop the cup of tea I'm holding, the spill oozing across

the table. I don't make a move to clean it up, my muscles frozen as realisations of all types dawn on me.

'The man in 300,' I utter to myself, all by myself. 'He's the one to look out for. He's the one.'

But no one hears me. No one notices the ramblings of a woman who appears to have gone bonkers – and perhaps, I acknowledge, the madness is setting in after all. Even if I've narrowed it down, what good will it do?

I'm almost out of time. I'm certain the brown-haired nurse is going to ring Claire and tell the rest of the staff about what happened. This whole disaster is going to be out soon, and everyone will be certain I'm nothing but a paranoid lunatic. No one will believe a thing. This whole scenario may have just sealed my fate. I inhale, staring at the seat Dorothy usually occupied. She's died in vain, I realise. And so will I. If only she were here still. If only I could tell her what I've come to realise.

But just as I'm ready to lay my head on the table in despair and in surrender, there's an epiphany. It's not too late. Not yet. They haven't come for me. There's still time. There's still time to figure this out. I haven't gone mad, not yet. I can do this.

Charles, I think I can do this.

Breakfast finishes, and the man from 300 passes my table, sneering as he walks by, mouthing the word one more time.

His declaration of ownership is the final straw. It's the final motivation I need to take a chance, to take a stand.

I might go down for this. I *might* die in vain. But I shall not perish without at least understanding the truth. I owe it to Dorothy, to Charles, to Claire, and to myself. I stand from my seat, knowing what I must do.

Chapter 28

I feign confidence I don't feel as I walk into the room at the end of the corridor. Room 300. Just like my room, there's a stairwell right beside it. I wonder if it has the same code as the stairwell by me.

I inhale deeply to calm my nerves as I lead the way, jittery but aware that this must happen. All around Floor Three, the residents saunter about. A few residents have visitors today. Some are being wheeled to appointments. The day in, day out chaos occurs, all at a slow, deprecating pace. But I push forward, stepping inside the doorway.

He is in here, alone, and I notice that the other half of his room is empty. He has no roommate. He is completely by himself, the walls and the window his only company. Is that why he spends so much time looking out? I don't know. But right now, he stares out the window into the courtyard – into my room, I discern with a shudder.

'Hello?' I murmur into the cavernous room.

The bent-over man, stooped with his hands in his pockets

as he stares, stares, stares, slowly, methodically pivots. It's a surprisingly smooth move for someone with old, weary bones. When he turns, the light in the room shines off the scar, my eyes dancing over it. His dark eyes are alight at the sight of me, and he quickly steps nearer. His left leg drags behind him, and a crooked grin forms on his face.

'Adeline. What a surprise,' he croaks, his voice raspy as always. I hate that he knows my name and that he uses it. He keeps walking closer and closer, his crooked grin near enough to me now that I can smell his putrid breath.

'I need to talk to you,' I declare. I glance about, noticing that his room is devoid of personal effects. There are no photographs, no mementos. It's like a clean slate, like a blank canvas that shows no life living here. The bareness only adds to the enigma that he is.

'I need to know if you've seen anything strange happening in my room. Have you witnessed anyone going in? Anything suspicious?' I ask, not sure where to start. I want to feel the situation out. It won't do to play all my cards at once.

I stare at the man, and apprehension starts working its way down my spine. I notice that he stares at me, his dark eyes almost revolving with something I can't determine. His eyes barely blink as they drink me in again. It's like he's thirsty for the sight of me, and I can't help but be frightened by it. I take a step back. He takes a step forward.

'Oh, I've been watching all right. I've been watching and watching. I've seen all sorts of things.'

'You have?' I ask, my heart beating faster now, the methodical thud becoming a wailing drum now.

He grins a little wilder as he looms closer. 'Yes. Yes indeed. Adeline, I'm always watching you. I'm always watching,' he repeats, taking a step closer.

I bite my lip, staring back into the dark eyes, absorbing the sight of the scar. My head starts to thud, my brain shrieking as I try to connect the dots. The sight of him coming towards me, a shaky hand slowly reaching out now. The dark eyes, the way he says my name.

There's something – recognisable? Familiar? I don't know. I don't know at all. Tears build, blurring my vision as I step backwards. The man, undaunted and perhaps even encouraged by my hesitancy, steps forward again. Despite the tension in the room, his movement is slow and non-threatening. Nevertheless, as I stare into his eyes, a sinking feeling in the pit of my stomach churns. I'm not safe here. I just don't know why or how.

'Adeline,' he whispers ... and what he says next makes me certain that I'm in danger. I'm in absolute danger – and he's no longer trying to hide the fact.

When he completes his jaw-dropping statement, my face flushes and I feel my blood boiling. I need to get away. I need to retreat, to protect myself or I'm going to end up with Dorothy's fate.

Before I can turn to leave or work it all out, I'm falling backwards, the world fading to black as I hear my own guttural scream as his words sink in.

'You're the one. You're the one who got away. I killed your friend because she found out too much. Caught her snooping in my room, and that just won't do. She had to die. I couldn't risk her warning you, ruining my master plan. But soon, it'll be you. It's almost time, Adeline.'

Chapter 29

I look up at the ceiling, the hairline crack soothing in an inexplicable way. My eyes trace the line as it feathers out, the sunlight illuminating its intricacies. A few birds chirp, twittering about on the roof. All seems peaceful, cheerful even – except that I notice a nurse hovers over me.

'It's all okay, Mrs Evans. You're going to be fine.' Her voice is soft and muffled, as if she's talking to a delicate flower or an infant.

I stretch to sit up, but she pushes me back down. 'There, there. You're okay. Just stay put. You've had a bit of a fall. You're going to be okay, but you need to take it easy for a couple of days.'

'What happened?' I ask, feeling my head as the blood whooshes into it. It's thumping with pain, a stabbing sensation mixed with an outrageous amount of pressure. It's so intense that I'm happy to rest my head back on the paper-thin pillow.

'You had a bit of an accident yesterday.'

Yesterday? An accident? I try to chase the memory in my mind, but there's just an unidentifiable blankness there. It's like I'm staring at a television when the picture's not quite clear, the snowy static blotting out the blackness in repetitive yet indistinct patterns. I keep digging, trying to unearth the truth. I come up empty. Why can't I remember?

'What happened?' I ask, the brown-haired nurse leaning down closer as she adjusts the blanket around me.

'We're not exactly sure. You had some sort of accident over on the other side of Floor Three. One of the residents found you in the corridor, screaming and falling backwards. Apparently, he said you got confused and upset. We thought you were having heart issues, so when he called for a nurse, we took you to hospital. They ran some tests. Do you remember? Do you remember going to hospital?'

I stretch my mind, trying to reach into the recesses of the past. I can't. Panic sets in, a thunderous cloud fogging up all other thoughts. Why can't I remember? My pulse quickens at the prospect that a portion of my life is wiped from my memory. I hate that I can't recall so much time. What else have I forgotten?

The nurse must sense my agitation because she puts a hand on my arm. 'It's okay. You had quite a fall. It's normal for you to forget, they said. It's normal, Mrs Evans. Don't worry. The doctors said you probably had some sort of panic attack. Something must have frightened you. When it happened, you tripped and hit your head. Nevertheless, we're taking all precautions with your heart and all, so you need to call for anything you need. No getting up for a couple of days, okay?'

I think, over and over. Room 300 comes to my head, assaulting my thoughts over and over.

Room 300.

Room 300.

Yes. *Yes*. The man in 300. The man across the way. The confession about Dorothy. The familiar flash.

'Dorothy. He hurt Dorothy,' I murmur desperately, recognition of what's occurred crashing into me.

The nurse's kind smile fades a bit. 'There, there, dear. You need to rest, love. You need to rest.'

I look up at her face, squinting. It's too much to process. Why won't she answer me? She doesn't believe me. Why doesn't anyone believe me? Why can't they see? Then, my mind floats to the next pressing concern. 'What about my daughter?'

'We called her yesterday after your fall. She was away, but we left a message.'

I look up at her kind eyes. She has no idea what's really happening. Then again, do I? What happened to me? Why is the man from 300 so focused on me? And is he really behind all the madness? I rub my forehead with my thumb, inhaling deeply, those final words he muttered coming back to me. They chill me to the core.

What does he want with me? I will my mind to travel back, back, back, to sort it all out. It's no use. My pulse still races, my brain trying so hard to focus on one thought. I look over to the noticeboard, my eyes taking in some new additions.

'Oh, yes, dear. Some of the residents here were worried. They made you cards in activity time. Isn't that just sweet? Here, let me get them for you.' She crosses the room jauntily, wearing her youth in her gait. She unpins a few cards, one with a daisy on it. They were always my favourite when I was younger. Mum had a small garden patch in West Green with daisies growing.

'Here, love. Anything else you need?' she asks. I shake my head, my jittery hand grasping the cards.

She leaves after a moment, reminding me to call for help if I need anything. The Philip Woman must be out because the room is silent, no noise except my own breathing and a television game show blaring down the hallway. When I'm alone, I painstakingly take on the task of propping myself up in bed. I sweat and grunt, struggling to wiggle up as my head protests. I persevere through the agony, though. I need to sit up. I feel so vulnerable lying flat. Once I've caught my breath from the exercise, I glance to the left. I can see out the window, even from here. And even from here, I am aware of the shattering truth.

He's watching me. Even now, he's observing my every move. I squeeze my eyes shut as if by succumbing to the blackness behind my eyes, I can make this nightmare go away. What am I going to do? What does it all mean? So many confusing, whirling connections. So many possibilities. And so many threats. I will my eyes back open and look down at the cards, opening the first that was clearly made by hand.

Be careful of the red rain.

There are black scribbles all over the front of the card, whirling in an ominous display. The handwriting is clearly someone else's handiwork. I shake my head. Whoever gave Barbara crayons and thought it a good idea was clearly madder than her. I tuck it underneath, looking at the next card. This one is also handmade. There's a crooked cross on the front. I flip open the card.

Worship the LORD your God, and his blessing will be on your food and water. I will take away sickness from among you … Exodus 23:25

I take a deep breath. See? All is fine. All is okay now.

My finger traces the outline of the daisy on the last card. I've saved it for last, the white petals taking me back to a different time. I open the card. My heart jolts as I expect something horrific, something downright shocking. Inside, though, there's just a simple message:

– *I've missed you. P*

I let my fingers dance over the ink of the words, squinting. P? Who is P? Patrick? Father Patrick? Oliver, the P for Parsons? No, that seems odd for both of them to write. Who would sign their card with just a letter, though? And why does that single letter send a shiver through me, like I've seen it before? I flap the card open and shut, open and shut, as I stare out the window.

The man in 300 stands for a long while before turning his back to me. But I keep watch. I keep staring, keep willing myself to remember. If only I could remember. The mind, nonetheless, is a funny thing. I turn to shove the cards into the top drawer of my bedside table.

Once I've pulled open the tiny wooden drawer, my fingers clutching the brass knob tightly, I gasp.

Chapter 30

Psalm 127:3-5

It loops up and down the paper, up and down, up and down. Every crevice, every space, is filled with the scrawling verse. Dozens and dozens of times, it's written in an angry script. I flip the paper over, my hand shaking. In bright red ink, a line of words that command my attention, scribed with a detectible force.

Tears fall. I don't know what the Bible verse is. I don't think I can bear to look. I shake my head, staring at the paper. He was here while I was gone, hiding this for me. Does that mean he's seen all of my notes? What notes did I write for him to find? Does he know too much now? What else is he hiding for me? What does he have in mind? And why?

It's all too much. I begin to shred the paper. The pieces mix with my salty tears, my nose dripping as I rip, shred, tear. When the paper is in strips, the Bible verse numbers still recognisable, I shred each strip some more, tossing them about.

'Stop it,' I say aloud. 'Stop it, stop it, stop it,' I screech as I shred, shred, shred. My hands grow weary, and my head aches, but I keep tearing, keep shredding, keep crying, and keep repeating the words.

'Mum?' a voice says after some amount of time has gone by. I look up through watery eyes, the melancholic confetti all about me.

Claire. She's here.

'I got here as soon as I could.' She rushes across the room to my side.

The familiar scent of her perfume envelops me, but I don't move. I stare straight ahead, tears falling, the paper strewn about me. Is it night already? I thought Claire wouldn't be here until tonight. I think about that as I play with the paper around me, picking at the pieces, tossing them to and fro. I stare straight ahead. Over and over, I toss the paper, Claire rustling my shoulders and asking questions. I don't comprehend her words, though. I'm lost in a world of Bible verses and threats, of the men of Floor Three.

'It's not safe here. It's not safe here. He's going to get me. He's going to get me,' I say forlornly, still staring ahead. A moment of silence passes, Claire putting down her handbag on the chair by the window and refraining from her questions.

'Mum? What's going on?' Her voice is calm and soft,

like a spoken lullaby during a storm. Such a strange feeling to be switching roles, mother becoming child and child becoming the nurturer. I don't move, don't turn my head. My eyes fixate on the Philip Woman's empty bed. The sheets look so crisp, so fresh. Were they washed yesterday?

'He's going to kill me. I'm going to die here.' It is a statement of fact, apathetically articulated as if I'm reading the lunch menu. Roast beef with a side of murder. Potatoes and a dash of blood. It's going to happen, I'm sure of it, but that doesn't mean I accept it. The thought of dying here, slaughtered in this miserable place, shreds me like the piece of paper I've gone to work on. I'm shaken by it. I don't want to die, not like this. I don't want him to win – but it all feels so hopeless.

'Mum, please calm down. It's going to be okay now.'

Slowly, I turn my head to look into the familiar eyes. Claire's bright blue eyes look back into mine. I see my own reflection in her pupils. I barely recognise myself, my haggard face and white hair relics of another life than the one I associate with myself. Who have I become?

I look at my daughter and say the words I don't want to but must. It's gone too far now. I should've never let it get this far. 'I can't stay here anymore, Claire. Take me home.'

Claire winces as if I've stabbed her. She cradles my hand to her cheek, kissing it again. Her lip quivers, and I instantly feel guilty for what I've asked. But I also feel something else – frustration, anger and helplessness. I'm so vulnerable here. I can't protect myself.

'Please,' I beg, hating the word that exits my lips.

'I'm sorry, Mum. I'm sorry. I can't take you out of here. I just can't. Do you understand? I'm sorry.' Tears fall from her eyes freely, cascading down. I can see the agony she's in. I hate myself for what I've done to her. But more than that, I hate him. I hate what he's done to me, to my life, to this place.

'Please. I can't stay here. I can't. I can't do it. He's going to get me. He's done it before,' I say, my words slow and methodical at first. As I continue, they crescendo until they become violent screams, my words blending together into a cacophony of rantings. My torrential sobs mix with ragged coughs, and my free hand yanks on my hair. I tug on it, my scalp burning. I can't stop. I rip on my hair, the tears flying, and the words spewing from my mouth. Round and round in the cycle I swirl, and I can feel the unravelling happening. Like the killer, like ageing, like Crawley's hellish grasp on me – I can't stop any of it. I'm at the mercy of it all.

'Mum, please, please,' Claire sobs. 'Please.'

'I killed my baby, and now he's going to kill me. I killed the baby. He wants revenge. He does, you have to believe me,' I shout, banging my skull against the headboard. 'I don't know how they're connected, but it must be because of the baby. He didn't want me to kill the baby, but I did anyway. I did. And because of him, I never saw them again. They burned, and it's all my fault. I should've been there.'

The guilt spews from my mouth, words flying uncontrollably. It's true. It's my fault. I made the decision. All of the steps in this cobblestoned path to hell began because of that decision. Mum and Dad would have never forgiven me. What if I had chosen differently? Would things have turned out better? I don't know. It was so long ago.

But I killed the baby. I killed it. And then Oliver wanted to kill me.

Here I am, decades later, still dealing with the fallout. Why am I still paying? Can't some sins, some choices, just stay in the past?

Tears fall and fall. I can't even speak, can't explain. Who can understand? Decades of guilt I've carried around, hidden and tucked away, float to the surface, but it's too late. It's too late to make anyone understand. And soon, it'll be too late for me.

'What's going on?' a voice shouts.

'Please help, I'm sorry, Mum. I'm sorry,' Claire says, backing away from me. I see her huddled in the corner, hugging herself. I see the agony on her face.

As the nurse shouts for backup, my head still banging off the headboard, I feel the needle slide into my arm, stabbing in over and over as the nurses try to hold me down. After several botched attempts, the sharp end finds its target, violently stabbing into my vein. A crisp pinch bites into my flesh, and I wince, my stomach flopping. I feel everything start to slip away, and for once, I think that maybe the woman who died before I got here didn't have it so terrible. Maybe drifting away into the darkness isn't such a dreadful thing sometimes. But, as I'm fading away, my eyelids painfully heavy, I manage to spot him across the way.

I love it when they stick 'em. His words echo in my brain, as the odd sensation spreads.

'No,' I murmur before I can't move anymore. The man in 300. I can't let this happen. I can't. It's not safe. He could ...

West Green Serial Killer Strikes Again!
West Green, Crawley, West Sussex
30 July 1959

The West Sussex Constabulary has reported the discovery of the body of Miss Gloria Carlton of Canterbury Avenue late last night. Miss Carlton's body was uncovered at 7.01 p.m., Saturday night at the edge of the property belonging to the Crawley Community Church. Police are currently investigating her death, which is presumed to be homicide.

Miss Gloria Carlton, 21, has been missing from her family's residence since 28 July 1959. She was last seen by her father and mother, Richard and June Carlton, at approximately 6.00 p.m. The couple left for a dinner in Brighton, leaving Miss Carlton behind due to an illness. Upon returning, Miss Carlton had disappeared. Detectives have been searching for clues to her disappearance. No valuables were removed from the property, but there were signs of a struggle.

Detectives believe the murder is related to the four previous murders in West Green due to the nature of the death and the characteristics of the victim.

The discovery of Miss Gloria Carlton's body by

a West Green resident who was walking his dog came as a startling find Saturday night. Police were immediately called in. Reports indicate that her body was stripped of all clothing and tossed underneath a hedgerow at the edge of the church property. Several lacerations on her chest and abdomen were discovered. Bite marks were also discovered on her left arm and the back of her neck, connecting her murder to those previous murders in West Green this summer, all of whom also had bite marks on their corpses. Flesh was found underneath Gloria's fingernails, just as it was under Caroline's, indicating a potential struggle with the killer. No other clues were detected, but investigators are still combing the scene, looking for potential leads.

'It's just terrible. Gloria was a lovely person. Her fiancé is destroyed by this,' a close friend of the victim stated about the jolly blonde who was noted as being godly, kind and beautiful by those who knew the deceased. No known enemies or motives have been uncovered at this time.

West Green residents are questioning the family's choice to leave Gloria alone with a killer on the loose.

'I don't understand why they would leave her alone. I won't let my grown daughter in a room alone at this point, not with everything going on.

I guess some people just assume bad things won't happen to them,' a source who wished to remain anonymous stated.

The residents of West Green continue to grow increasingly anxious and frustrated that there continue to be no new leads in the case. Several suspects questioned and investigated in the last few weeks have been released after evidence cleared them. Gloria's fiancé has been brought in for questioning, and detectives continue to gather dental records from persons of interest. However, residents are beginning to grow restless as it seems the killer remains on the loose.

Additionally, as word of the murders spreads, false leads are becoming a major hindrance to the case. The West Green Constabulary has reported that 548 letters have poured in, all signed by persons claiming to be the killer. Several were purportedly signed by Jack the Ripper. Numerous persons have also come forward to turn in neighbours and persons of interest, but these leads have led to multiple dead ends.

As detectives investigate false leads, it is becoming more difficult to sift through evidence that could lead to an actual arrest.

Residents of Crawley are asked to stay alert for any suspicious occurrences and to be cautious.

The feel of her sweet, soft skin ripping open as the blade slashed into her. Her screams that turned to whimpers and then faded to nothing. The terror, the recognition, the confusion in her eyes. I relish in the thoughts of what I've accomplished yet again.

She never expected it. A night out, away from her parents' watchful eyes, was all she was after. She knew the dangers, sure. But it wouldn't happen to her. Why did they always naively think they couldn't be next? When she left her house and wandered into the darkness, did she get a chill? Did she sense me lurking nearby, as I have been for days? Did she feel the life slipping away before I'd even grabbed her?

People convince themselves of anything they want. Gloria was no exception. Just like the others, she'd assured herself that the prickly feeling on her skin, that sensing of a presence – it was all nothing but a breeze or the sway of a tree. It was nothing.

But it was, in fact, something.

Somewhere, deep down, she knew. They always knew, even

if they didn't want to. And once they admitted to themselves that danger had been creeping too close, it was too late. I'd struck by then, made my mark. I'd won at exactly the right moment. I had my fun, enjoyed the pursuit. I lingered in the knowledge of what would be mine, like a lover seducing my sweetheart.

Lost boy. Stupid boy. I'd-never-love-you boy.

The crinkled note thrown back in my face, the one I'd painstakingly written for her. The smashed daisy, missing three petals, that she stomped into the dirt under her shiny, red shoe.

I'd tried to love her. I could've loved her. I wanted nothing more than to taste her sweet-smelling flesh, to kiss her neck, her cheek. I wanted her to love me back.

But they never loved me back.

It's okay. They don't have to love me now. I love them enough for the both of us. I was a naive teenage boy when that girl stomped my heart into the ground, when I swore I'd never be nice to a girl again. But I'm grown up now. I'm wiser. I know that you can't ask for love from a female.

You have to just take it.

You have to claim it.

Women like to be claimed. And I like the thrill of the chase. I like the struggle for power. I like to leave my mark. There's no returning it once I've sunken my teeth in. There's no denying the truth that I was there.

I was there for all of them. All five of them.

I run my teeth over the envelope one last time, the feel of the paper thin. Usually, I snatch the letter two or three weeks before I make my move. I peruse them, waiting for just the right letter. One that is personal, that captures who they are. But one that won't be missed. I don't know how I know when the letter is right. There's nothing special I'm looking for.

Just a letter that speaks to me, that captures a piece of the essence of who she is. A memento of her life, of the plans she thought she'd make. A reminder of what she was going to do – what I stopped her from doing.

The letter I took from Gloria? It came only two days before I made my move. I was getting worried there wouldn't be one that spoke to me, and I didn't want to rush things – but I was getting antsy. What did I take? A notice of her acceptance into a nursing school. Did her fiancé approve? A beautiful woman like that shouldn't be working. I'm glad I picked her. Foolish woman.

I can almost taste the words in the letter I've now memorised. A congratulations Gloria would never get. I let my teeth run over it once more before I pull it back down and glance at her name, her address.

Letter five is now to be tucked away with the others. Before putting it with my collection, I stare once more at the script on the front of the undelivered post. I trace the loops of Gloria's name and address. Did I pick the right letter? It doesn't matter. It's too late. Besides, it's never really about what the letter says. It's just the fact that I could take a piece of her with me. It's all I need, the only proof I require of what I've done. For memory's sake.

Five letters now.

Five articles reporting their bodies had been found.

Five victories in this intoxicating game.

Five, soon to be six.

And then, only then, can the final one be claimed. The one I'm anticipating, the one that most excites me.

Adeline Walker. It's almost your time, *I think as I click shut the door of my flat, whistling on my way to work.*

Chapter 31

West Green, Crawley, West Sussex
1 August 1959

'Andrew, don't be ridiculous. Of course I love this town. But are you telling me you're not the slightest bit worried about what's been occurring?'

'You know I am. But don't you trust that I'm keeping you safe? Haven't I been keeping a closer eye on the house? And the knife in the bedroom? I've barely slept a wink since all of these horrendous murders have been happening.' A fist slams on the table or the counter, and I jump even though I'm far away from the action, curled up on the hallway floor at the top of the stairs.

'But you can't be here all the time, Andrew. You're working. And when you're working, how are Addy and I supposed to stay safe? There's a lunatic on the prowl, and no one can catch him. Who's to say we're not next? Who's to say our only daughter, the girl we tried so hard to have, isn't going to be slain by some maniac? I couldn't take it, not after everything. I've lost five children, Andrew. Five. I won't lose another.'

'You think I don't realise that? They were my children, too. I was there through every single miscarriage. Through every single apology from the doctor. Through every heartbreak. How dare you claim I don't want to keep you safe.' Dad stomps across the room. I picture him staring out the window as he often does, deep in thought and rubbing his chin.

'Aren't we more important than some house, some neighbourhood then? Do something, Andrew. I won't lose another child. I won't.'

I pull my knees to my chest at the top of the stairs, my back against the wall in the corridor outside my room. It's late, much later than my parents usually stay up. Their hushed whispers in the kitchen, however, have quickly turned to a booming argument that's been going on for a half hour. It's never a good sign when Mum starts talking about the miscarriages. All those graves, all those flowers she leaves year after year.

Five miscarriages. Five reminders that she might never have a baby. I was their miracle child. I've heard it so many times, how I was a gift. A true gift. How babies are gifts to be worshipped, to be thankful for. I close my eyes, leaning my head against the wall, willing myself not to cry again.

How has it come to this?

When we moved to West Green, Mum was certain this would be a place to start over, to find that charming, suburban life we were missing. She insisted that it would be a fresh start for all of us, that we'd be able to reinvent ourselves, grow closer, and find that life we all wanted. And, I know in her mind, we'd be able to move past the not-so-glowing reputation I'd built in our last neighbourhood, the scarlet, stained reputation of being a girl with questionable morals. We'd move past that pregnancy scare from our last town, the one that incited tears and tirades of how to get pregnant before marriage was a mortal sin – and that to give a baby up or, the unmentionable, terminate its life, would damn me straight to hell. Moving to West Green and away from the boy who had stained my 'perfect' reputation, in Mum's eyes, was a way to save my soul. And, in truth, it was a way to save what she saw as our family's chance at a higher social status. Once news of my escapades with the Taylor boy spread to her inner circle of friends, Mum was certain a move was necessary, especially once we received affirmation that I was not pregnant. She convinced my father that picking up the family and moving us hours away to a place where I could start over, where I could regain my holy reputation, was a way to ensure I would find a suitable man and, in turn, an honourable life. Crawley, to Mum, was a sanctuary where she could put her daughter back on the path to a sanctimonious, domestic life with a man who could elevate the family's social standing.

If only she knew that moving here would only permanently damage all of her hopes and dreams.

Nonetheless, here we are, three years later, and things

aren't better. It's not the life we'd imagined with charming flower boxes, sunshine and sweet get-togethers with the neighbours.

I hate to admit it, but Mum's correct. It's dangerous here, and with every girl who turns up missing and then dead, I can't help shake the feeling that any of us could be next. *I* could be next. My heart races in fear at the prospect.

Mum's idea to pick up and leave this town is certainly unsettling to Dad, who wants things to just be back to normal. He wants to believe that the detectives will do their job, that all of this will go away. I suspect the prospect of picking up and leaving again isn't at the top of his to-do list.

Leaving would make a lot of these ugly truths disappear. I must admit I'd sleep better being out of reach of the West Green Killer. It would be refreshing not to have to sleep lightly, every noise a potential red flag that I'm next. It would be nice to be able to venture out again without Mum having a coronary that I'm going to be murdered. More than that, though, it would be nice not to have to tiptoe around West Green wondering when Oliver is going to show back up in my room, to spill my secret, and to ruin everything. To be away from Oliver would mean I could let go of the decision I made. I could move on.

However, leaving West Green with Mum and Dad would also mean leaving Charles. It would mean saying goodbye to a relationship that has stolen my heart in every way. That won't do either. Would we survive a long-distance relationship? More aptly, would we survive the possibility of Oliver being in Crawley with Charles, able to spill the secret whenever he chooses? Would Oliver keep the secret quiet, or, with me gone, would he be more than happy to spread around the vicious truths? Mulling it all over, only one question rises to the surface. When did life get so complicated?

'Nora, look. I know we're all on edge. I get it. But let the investigators do the job. I'm sure they're close to cracking the case. There's no sense in turning our lives upside down hastily when they could be moments away from solving the murders. The murderer is getting more brazen. Look, he's left the body of Gloria out in plain sight. He's going to make a mistake if he hasn't already. He's going to get caught. And then life will go back to normal.'

'And until then? What shall we do until then, Andrew?'

Silence and then footsteps across the kitchen floor. 'Until then? I look out for you, like I always do. No one's going to hurt us, Nora. I promise.'

'Don't make promises you can't keep,' Mum replies.

'I never do.'

I scurry back to my room, careful to avoid the creaky parts of the floor. I tiptoe to my bed, tucking myself under the covers. I squeeze my eyes shut, thinking about the killer on the loose, about my ex on the loose, and about my life on the loose. Opening my eyes, I stare into the darkness. My weary mind flutters back to the winter, when life completely changed for me and sealed in my fate.

*

I paced back and forth behind the church, wearing a path in the freshly fallen snow. The scarf Mum had knitted practically strangled me, but I didn't dare loosen it. I was too nervous, too terrified. Would this really make everything better? Or would it only solidify my soul's place in hell? I couldn't think about it. It was too late to think about it. This was what needed to be done. It was what was best. Wasn't it?

Life with Oliver had started out like a dream. That cold winter day when I'd seen him at the church festival, I'd been dazzled by his eyes, by his smile, by the way he nodded hello. It had been a whirlwind, one that Mum had highly approved of. After all, Oliver has been on the fast track to success his whole life. Top of his class, a well-positioned family. He's the boy that mothers dream of for their middle-class daughters. He was the boy I'd dreamt of over and over once he'd taken me to our secret meeting spot in the woods behind the church. He was the boy I dreamt of when I'd given myself to him completely after we started courting. After all, I was no stranger to intimacy, despite my mother's warnings against staining my reputation. It was why we had moved to West Green, after all – the town we had lived in knew I wasn't one to guard my heart, or my reputation.

In the past few months, though, things had changed. I'd seen a different side to Oliver that was hidden behind that charming smile. It started with a few rough moments during an escapade at his house when his parents were out for the night. Choking, a few slaps, a glint of something dark in his eyes.

At first, I convinced myself it was nothing. He was being playful. He was taking charge. A woman should like a man who takes charge. It was just part of his persona, of the strong man he was. I assured myself he was still the same Oliver I knew and that a future with him would be one of happiness. I imagined our life with an adorable house, cheery afternoon teas, and posh parties with the up-and-comers of London. I could see our family, our children, our beautiful, safe lives together.

Until it all took a darker turn. Until I saw the true side of Oliver emerging, the side he'd kept hidden long enough for me to grow smitten. The squeezing of wrists, the threats, the questions about my every move. There had been the bruises up and down my body and the horrific, threatening comments about my family. There had been the violent sexual acts too unspeakable to mention. He was power-hungry, and he wasn't afraid to assert himself in every way. His lust was for control, but also for blood. He wasn't afraid to hurt those he loved, and his temper often flared in violently dangerous ways.

The bruises, the tears and the fear had all helped me understand one thing: Oliver Parsons was a dangerous man. And someday, he would go too far if I let him. It was easy to see that life with Oliver, that the ring he promised was coming soon, would be a life sentence of powerlessness, of a lack of freedom. It would be a life of frigidness, one

I wasn't ready to commit to. Suddenly, the visions I had of our life together, of the life Mum pictured for us, exploded in my face. I became terrified that I would be the victim of a horrific, terrifying detonation.

I'd made up my mind that things were going to change, that Oliver wasn't the one for me. I was afraid of saying goodbye, but it seemed like the appropriate thing. I couldn't be with him anymore. I couldn't commit to that life. I wanted something much different. I had to escape him while I still could. It wasn't safe with Oliver, not like I'd imagined.

I'd planned on telling him the truth, on breaking it to him gently. I would walk away from our love story that had blackened into a harrowing tale. I would let him go, would move on, would find a new dream for my life. I was prepared to tell him, to shatter the final link between us.

Then the morning sickness had come. The tender chest, the missed period. The universe had other plans. Oliver and I would be linked forever. Forever connected by a baby I wasn't ready for. I knew I couldn't let that happen. I couldn't let Oliver get his hooks into me for good. I couldn't live that life, no matter the cost.

I also knew what Mum and Dad would say if they found out the truth. *Babies were gifts.* I would be locked into a life with Oliver if they found out – they'd make sure of it. I would have no choice, no freedom and no escape.

I paced some more. It was the time we had agreed on. I knew she would be there any second. As if on cue, footsteps in the snow alerted me to the presence of someone. I turned to see her.

'Hey,' she whispered, grabbing my hand. Phyllis was dressed in a black coat and a red scarf. Her scarf hung loosely about her neck, the ends flapping with every step. 'Are you ready?'

I exhaled. 'I don't know,' I murmured for the first time, doubts plaguing me.

It was what I had to do. I'd convinced myself of it. A life stuck with Oliver would be no life. But still – this was no small choice. This was the thing of hellfire and damnation, according to our pastor. This was the thing that Mum and Dad would never forgive me for.

This, according to them, would be one of the gravest of all my sins. My heart churned with trepidation over what I was about to do. Could I really kill my baby? Could I take a life just so I could be free of Oliver? Was it the right thing to do?

It settled heavily in my heart. The thoughts, the choice I had to make, kept me up night after night. Visions of my baby dying, screaming, crying swirled in my head. Tears fell as I pondered over the choice, over the consequences: could I truly go through with it?

'I don't know,' I said again. Phyllis stepped closer.

'I know you're scared. But you haven't got a choice. It has to be done. Otherwise, you'll be with him the rest of your life. And who knows what he's capable of. Addy, he's dangerous. Someday, he might not stop at bruises. Do you want to take that chance?'

Tears fell, and I wiped at them. 'But how can I do this? It's illegal, Phyllis. It's dangerous. And according to the church, it's wrong.'

'Don't think that way. Do what is necessary and move on. It'll be all right. You'll see. And someday, you'll find a good man. You'll start over with him. This will all just be a forgotten thing of the past. You mustn't think of it as anything but the past.'

My stomach dropped, and deep inside, I knew the truth. It wouldn't be something that would simply go away.

All those nights in our old town, all those nights with Oliver, I'd never thought it would come to this. I never thought it would be me, standing in the icy air, waiting to go and kill a baby inside of me. Why had I been so reckless? I shook my head. Mum had been right. I should've been more careful. I should've been a better girl. A smarter girl. A more pious girl.

Why did I always take it too far?

'Addy, come on. I'll be there for you. Now we must go. Do you have the address?'

'I do. But I don't know, perhaps there are other options I'm not considering.' My hands trembled as the moment of reality struck. Even in the icy blackness, it felt as if it were a pivotal point in life, a precipice I was glancing over. I felt vomit rise in my throat. There would be no turning back. What I was about to do was a crime, in the eyes of the church, in the eyes of my parents, and in the eyes of the law. I squeezed my eyes shut tightly, placing a hand on my stomach. This was no small thing, and the momentousness of the choice threatened to shatter me, even if I knew my reasoning for making the choice was rational.

Phyllis shook her head. 'Be strong, Addy. You must do this. Now come on, we should be going.' She grabbed my hand and pulled me on the path through the woods. We walked in silence, my feet aching as we trudged forward.

'Are you certain he's coming?' I asked.

'Yes. I gave him the half payment he requested. He'll be there. Do you have the rest of the money?'

I patted my coat pocket, feeling the envelope of cash that I'd managed to pilfer from Mum and Dad. Phyllis had also helped contribute. I was fortunate to have such a good friend on my side. Tears collected in my eyes as we stood underneath a tree by the side of the road, the selected street corner where Phyllis' older brother's friend was going to collect us to take us to the spot. I was terrified, my hands shaking. So much could go wrong. The truth was, I could die. Or I could be caught, everyone in town knowing what sort of girl I truly was. What would Mum and Dad think?

But perhaps Phyllis was right. Perhaps it was worth the risk. I couldn't be connected to him. I couldn't bring a child into the world knowing what Oliver was, knowing the life we would have. I wasn't ready for that.

On the way to the meeting point, I reassured myself, convinced myself over and over that I was doing what was necessary. I would worry about the consequences later. It had to be done. When the driver screeched to a stop in front of us and we climbed into the car, Phyllis still holding my hand, I squeezed my eyes shut.

God, please forgive me. I can't do this. I can't. You must understand. I chanted the demented prayer over and over in my mind, knowing it was a weak substitute for my actions. We sped off into the night, four silent souls about to become three – or maybe even two.

*

Tears fall down my cheek as I snap back to the present.

'I'm sorry,' I mouth into the blackness, a lacklustre confession to a child who never got to breathe the air. I *am* sorry for so many things.

I'm sorry I ever laid eyes on Oliver.

I'm sorry he turned out to be nothing like the man I thought he was.

I'm sorry for all those nights I climbed into bed, into his arms.

I'm sorry I wasn't strong enough to forge my own path for us without him.

I'm sorry that I murdered your life that grew inside of me.

I'm sorry that I felt like I had no other choice.

Most of all, I'm sorry that he knows the truth, and that it could completely ruin my entire life, my entire future, and any sense of happiness I thought I could claim.

Perhaps I don't deserve to find happiness in the world. All along, I've felt like Oliver is the monster – but perhaps I'm beastly in my own right. I don't know what to think anymore. I don't know if I made the right decision. The world is an evil place, and we're all pawns in the hellish game. No one gets out of here alive – but some of us leave with more regrets, questions and guilt than others.

I fall asleep that night dreaming about a nondescript alley, medical tools and a baby that never came to be. A baby I killed so I could escape to a new life.

What kind of selfish monster takes an innocent life to preserve an already tarnished one?

*

I'm staring into my tea the next morning at Molly's Café, a tiny place Mum insists on dragging me to from time to time – usually on days she's thinking about the miscarriages. 'Nothing a spot of tea can't fix,' she insists. But staring into my cup as I think about the nightmarish memories that kept me up half the night, I know there are many, many things in life too big for tea and biscuits.

'So, yes, after we're done here, we must be off to get that fabric. Adeline, are you listening? Hello?' Mum yammers from across the table, her voice grating. I don't want to talk about fabric and tea. I don't want to pretend everything's okay.

There's a murderer on the loose, Mum and Dad are

talking about leaving the town, and I can't get over the horrific choice I made. Life's, in short, a disaster.

'Mrs Walker? Is that you?' a voice echoes from across the café. I turn around, and my stomach drops. As if things can't get any worse.

'Iris, good to see you. How are you?' Mum asks, smiling chipperly as Oliver's mother meanders towards our table, her bright outfit blinding against the neutral decor of the café.

I try not to vomit, terrified of seeing her. I haven't talked to her since the breakup. She stares at me, a glare painted on her face as we make eye contact.

'Adeline.' My name darts off her tongue.

I nod simply, averting my eyes. I don't want to talk to her.

'How are you holding up with all of this craziness in town?' Mum asks, gesturing to a chair at our table. Mrs Parsons shakes her head, standing over me. I feel her stature looming like a foreboding omen. I steady my breathing. Certainly she doesn't know everything. She can't possibly know what happened to lead to my breakup with Oliver. Can she?

He mustn't have told her. He wouldn't. She can't possibly know what transpired. She must think that it was just two wandering, youthful hearts that were too wily to settle down.

'It's terrifying, isn't it? But we've stayed focused on the business. Did you hear that Oliver earned a promotion?

Following right in his father's footsteps. He'll be running that business someday. He's such a charmer, that boy. Just a matter of time until he finds someone worthy of wearing his ring.'

I stir my tea, fully aware her words are a pointed jab at me.

'Apologies, Adeline. I did not mean to offend you. I know things with you two just didn't work out. Perhaps it's for the best. After all, I'm not sure you two were a perfect match. I just mean you certainly have a bit of a, shall we say, *wandering* manner?' Her words are accompanied by a softened yet smug grin, as if to mask her bitterness.

I feel my cheeks flame red. I notice my mother clenches her jaw. Still, ever the socialite, she manages to force a pained smile and remain calm.

'Well, it is quite a shame. I did think our children were a truly lovely match. But the young are fickle, aren't they? Who can tell. Perhaps they'll come to their senses,' my mum says jovially. It makes me livid that she sounds so desperate. She can't even acknowledge that Mrs Parsons is being downright rude in her remarks.

I remain quiet, not wishing to discuss Oliver or the sordid details. His mother thinks he's a champion, a charmer, a gentlemen. She has no idea. Then again, does anyone really know their child? My mother doesn't know all of my secrets. She will never know.

'However, if I have my way,' Mum continues, 'we will be out of this town soon.'

'Is that so?' Mrs Parsons asks, still eyeing me from above.

'Yes. All this killer nonsense, it's too much. And the detectives don't appear to be any closer to solving it all. I don't want to take the risk. I'm hoping to convince Andrew to leave town, and soon.'

'Well, I'll be certain to let Oliver know so he can say his farewells. Such a shame to see such a cracking family leave,' Mrs Parsons says with a bite of sarcasm in her voice.

Mum and Mrs Parsons exchange pleasantries, but I don't hear a word. My mind is stuck on the fact that now Oliver will know we may be leaving town.

Will that lead to a new level of desperation? With the possibility I'll be out of his clutches, will he heighten his need for vengeance? Will he speed up his game of cat and mouse? I shudder at the thought, thinking of what he might do next.

West Green gets more and more dangerous by the minute, from every possible angle.

Chapter 32

Smith Creek Manor Nursing Home
2019

My skin feels itchy, and my eyes don't want to open. Slowly, excruciatingly, my eyelids flutter, breaking through a thick crust that's gluing them shut. I'm on my side in my bed, the sheets tangled around me. I'm so thirsty. Goodness, I'm so thirsty.

'Trust me,' a voice murmurs from outside of my room. A female voice. Youthful sounding. It's as though I'm hearing the phrase from the other end of a tunnel, the quality echoing and distorting in a way that makes me nauseous. 'She's safest here. So many people your age go through this guilt. But this happens, love. It's just the dementia taking control. Terrible disease, I know. My own mother suffered from it in her final year.'

'I just – it's so hard. It's so heart-wrenching to see her so unhappy,' a voice responds. A familiar female voice. Claire. Claire is here. What happened? Why am I so tired?

'You're doing the right thing. This is the best place for her. She gets the care she needs, and you don't have to worry.'

'But what about all of this nonsense? About someone trying to kill her? And a baby? I have no bloody idea what this could mean. Why would she be saying that?'

A sigh. 'The mind plays ugly tricks sometimes.'

'I suppose. I just, I don't know. Her eyes used to be so clear when she looked at me. So determined. But now it's like she's already gone.'

'This happens in old age. But if it makes you feel better, I'll keep a closer eye on her.'

'Okay. Has she woken up yet?'

'She slept through the night. She should be waking soon. The doctor was in to see her this morning. I do hate it when the sedative is the only option. But sometimes, it's the safest for them.'

Sedative. I look down at my arm, see the prominent bruises where they stuck the needle in. I remember. The needle piercing my skin, and the burning of the medicine. The heavy eyelids. Me begging Claire to believe me. I close my eyes. It's all so frustrating. No one trusts me. Why doesn't anyone believe me? How will I ever make them believe me?

'I'm going to sit with her until she wakes up,' Claire announces.

'If you need anything, you know where to find me,' the other voice replies.

Claire walks in, and I look at her from the bed once she's close enough.

'Mum, hello! How are you feeling?' She swipes at her eyes to cover the tears. Her smile is her generic smile, the one I've come to loathe. Her genuine smile is so much prettier.

'I'm fine,' I whisper, painting on my pretend smile as well. I know now to play the part. I *have* to play the part. If no one will believe me, the best thing I can do is solve the situation on my own. I must figure it out, but Claire isn't the one to help me. There's no one here to help me anymore, and that fact daunts me.

'Do you need anything?' Claire asks after she helps me get freshened up.

'No, I'm fine,' I lie again, because what else can I possibly say?

*

I rock back and forth, staring at the game show as the lady beside me cheers for the contestants. I don't have the heart to tell her that the contestant just lost. She celebrates the victory like she's just won a car and has somewhere to go in it. I stare on, the empty seat beside me underscoring the hopelessness.

'Church time. Let's go. Time to pray,' a booming voice shouts down the corridor. I ease my neck backwards to see Father Patrick shuffling towards the community room, a Bible in hand. He stops near me, staring at me. He shakes his head, and then marches on.

'Time to repent. Repent sinners, repent,' he chants, his voice booming and angry, like brimstone and fire speeches from my youth. I involuntarily shudder. *Repent*. He said *repent*.

No matter how much contrition I serve, I know it will never be enough when my time comes. Sure, time has softened the choices I made as a naive girl who felt cornered. Still, I know that time doesn't assuage the cold, hard facts.

I killed that baby in a back alley. I let my fears of Oliver, my own desires, and Phyllis convince me it was the right thing to do. But it's been decades, and my heart still knows the truth. Times have changed. I've changed. And maybe, looking back now, I can say I was justified in my actions. Still, the murky, indistinct face of the baby I never birthed haunts my nightmares. I can never forget what I've done, not completely. And sometimes I fear maybe I will never entirely forgive myself.

But the choice I made to kill my unborn baby isn't the only choice that haunts me. It started a chain reaction of events that would lead me to other sources of guilt, to other regrets. Because when I ended that baby's life before it began, when I incited the vile, raging side of Oliver I had only been privy to in small doses, I started out on a path that would lead me far away from West Green. It would lead me to a place that felt safer – but was never quite untouched by the troubles of my youth.

And it would lead me to a place where I thought I could

wipe away the past, pretend it didn't exist, and live a normal life. But the dark choices of our pasts are never left buried for long, and years and years after that decision, the hands of time would continually reach out and remind me that every choice has far-reaching consequences.

The abortion is only one of several black stains on my soul, if the church's teachings are to be believed. And now I can add Dorothy to the list. It was my fault. It *is* my fault. She's gone because of me. Who else will have to pay for the things I've done, for the wars I wage? How many lives will I destroy because of my choices? I stand from my seat and head for my chamber of hell instead of the chamber of prayer – for some of us, no amount of holy words can cleanse us. And no amount of time will be enough to figure out the gory truth.

We'll all die here. But some of us will go with more regrets, more pains, and more questions than others.

*

I'm flipping through a book in my room the next afternoon – the harsh-faced nurse agreed to bring me a novel from the reading room. Of course, she grabbed me some boring, drab historical fiction book.

With Philip Woman out at an appointment, I'm alone with my thoughts. This isn't a good thing as of late, the occurrences around me lead my mind down a twisted, malevolent path of possibilities. Who needs to read a horror story, after all? I glance out the window, staring over at 300. For once, there is no one peering back at me. Maybe that's a good sign. Maybe all has quieted down after all ... maybe ...

And then I hear it. Footsteps. Shuffling footsteps. A flapping paper. I look up from my book, turning my head to the door – and there he is.

He leans on the doorframe for a moment, a cherry red paper in his hand. He smiles at me without showing any teeth, a crooked smirk that unsettles me. But his leer isn't the most troublesome thing. It's in his eyes, always in his eyes. There's something so familiar in the way he looks at me, something thirsty in the way his eyes travel over my face, my hair, my hands.

I shudder, my hands pausing in the middle of a page flip. He methodically traipses into my room. There is no hesitancy like that first day so long ago – was it long ago? A month or two perhaps? Maybe even less? I can't be certain as the days have blended into one another. But it feels long ago.

Two hands on the paper, he walks towards the noticeboard, his body turned so he never takes his eyes off me. When he gets to the noticeboard, I notice how large he is. Not in an unhealthy way – no, in a powerful way. In a way that could do damage. His breathing is rapid. I squeeze the pages of the book tighter, never letting him out of my line of sight. There is a lingering pause, a space between us he doesn't quite fill but claims, nonetheless.

Finally, he opens his mouth and says the words that are so simple but so terrifying.

'I've missed you. Oh, how I've missed you,' he murmurs.

I grab at my chest, worried that I'm going to lose control. I can't let him get to me. But as he takes a step forward and smirks, staring at me, the familiar flash comes forward in my mind. So familiar. He's just so *familiar*. But why? Why is he recognisable? I don't understand. I don't know what's happening. My head thuds with pain and uncertainty. I grab my forehead, my thumb rubbing my head methodically between my eyebrows.

'I've missed you for a long time,' he hisses, so softly I think I must've misheard him.

And that's what does it. I know for sure I know him from somewhere. I know him in some way, in some form, from the past. But how? Where? I can't trace him in my memories.

Does it matter, though? I know he's dangerous. I know what he's capable of. Tears start to flow as I realise how easily he could end things. I'm at his mercy, the weak one at the end of the corridor. The forgotten one everyone thinks is crazy. No one will believe me. No one. He holds all the cards. As he violently flicks the pin into the board on the menu, stabbing it with impressive force that absolutely petrifies me, my hands wobble, still holding the book. He turns slowly, agonisingly slowly. Hands now in his pockets, he is cool and confident.

'What do you want?' I ask through the tears, through the shakes, through the fear. This needs to be settled.

His poker face gives nothing away, and other than my heaving breaths and his raspy ones, there is silence in the room. Somewhere on the floor, a resident shrieks and cries. Somewhere else, a telly blares. But here, in Room 316, silence. Bone-chilling silence. He leans closer and closer, rattling his teeth together a time or two in an absurd display. I don't move, afraid to look away. I'm petrified to the core. When he is so close that I can feel every exhale, when his face is just centimetres from mine, his toothy grin appears.

'You, Adeline. It's been you for so long. It's always been you.' He reaches out and grabs my wrist, squeezing it, his fingers finding my pulse. I try to pull back, but it's no use. He's got me. He's not breaking a sweat or looking stressed. It's so easy for him to control me. He looks right into my face, grinning and whistling. Oh, the whistling. It's some sad tune from long ago, and it pierces into me.

I've heard that song before.

'Please,' I beg, but with that one word, something dark and twisted happens to his eyes. They turn from a look of defiance to a look of need. They turn both hungry and angry, and my heart beats. It is that look in his eyes, a look I've only seen a few other times before, that verifies the truth. I know for sure this is no regular man I'm dealing with.

This is a beast. This is a vicious fiend who has survived well beyond his expiration date. I open my mouth to scream but he grabs my mouth. He shushes me with his finger. I look at him, shaking my head, trembling at the ludicrous nature of him, of what he's doing.

He pulls his hand away, still shushing me. My breathing is laboured, but I stare at him, incredulous, as he turns to head towards the door.

Just as I'm getting ready to breathe a sigh of relief as he leaves, I see him stop. One hand on the threshold, he turns around, glares at me, and licks his lips. And then, before he's gone, he bites his teeth together two times so I can see.

I am lost once more.

Brazen Killer Ups His Game, Terrifying Train Station
Northgate, Crawley, West Sussex
10 August 1959

At 7.00 p.m. on 9 August 1959, the dismembered body of Muriel Claubaugh was discovered in Northgate, Crawley, by a ticket attendant at the train station. Bite marks on the body have led investigators to believe that the murder is the work of the man now being dubbed the West Green Killer.

Muriel Claubaugh, 24, never returned to the flat she shares with her sister on Meadlowview Lane, West Green, on Monday evening after work. Muriel Claubaugh worked as an administrative assistant in Langley Green. Her employer notes that she left at the same time he did, but her sister, Sarah Claubaugh, told investigators she didn't return home.

Muriel's body was discovered in the train station in Northgate. A ticket attendant noticed several unclaimed, oversized, unmarked bags outside the ticket window. When they were opened, the dismembered body was discovered. Investigators later determined the body belonged to Muriel Claubaugh, the head having been discovered in a separate bag.

'The killer is getting sloppy. He's getting bold. It's giving us hope that he will make a mistake,' a detective told reporters early this morning.

The suitcase left in a public place is a more conspicuous move than the hiding places of the other bodies, which were at least partially concealed. Detectives have been questioning passengers at the station, hoping someone saw the owner of the nondescript bags. So far, several suspects have been questioned, but detectives note they have all been dead ends. Just last week, the prime suspect in the West Green murders, Denis Butler, was released after witnesses confirmed his alibi. Denis Butler was the fiancé of the late Gloria Carlton and was the prime suspect in the case after her death. Reports tell of a series of affairs Denis Butler was involved in, suggesting a motive for the murder of his fiancée. He was also loosely tied to the first victim, Elizabeth McKinley, as the two were once romantically involved. Initial dental record comparisons suggested Butler was a match to the killer. However, detectives released Butler this week after several other pieces of evidence cleared him.

Detectives appear to be starting from scratch as they move forward to solve the cases.

The residents of Crawley grow more uneasy as the weeks go on and no leads have been found.

Detectives assure the public they are working around the clock to bring justice for the now six women murdered over the summer, but many fear that the killing spree will continue.

'We're not safe here. My neighbours, my friends – we're all thinking about picking up our lives and moving. We just can't stay somewhere that isn't safe,' a resident noted. She wished to remain anonymous.

Investigators are looking for links between the victims. So far, all victims are females in their late teens to early twenties and residents of West Green, living within a few streets of each other. No other definite connections have been discovered.

All residents of Crawley, and especially of West Green, are asked to be on high alert. The extra police presence in the area has not seemed to deter the killer.

'We aren't dealing with an amateur, here,' one constable noted. 'This killer is cunning, calculating and very intelligent, which has made our job difficult. He works fast, cleanly, and doesn't make any mistakes. But that always changes. They always make a mistake, and when he does, we will catch him.'

The brutal dismemberment of Muriel's body has left many residents forlorn. 'It's disturbing enough that women are being murdered. But the brutality, the disrespect of the body – that's on another level,' Mrs Nora Walker stated when investigators interviewed her.

Anyone with information is asked to contact the West Green Constabulary. Residents are encouraged to lock their doors, to travel in groups, and to remain on high alert until the case is solved.

Sloppy?

Laughable, I think, shaking my head. Six women, and they have no leads. Sloppy isn't the word I would use.

No, I'm not sloppy. I am, if I do say so myself, quite brilliant. Brilliant indeed.

Brilliant boy. Wise boy. Careful boy. Finally, finally, I am something to admire.

Despite the jolly mood I'm in from my success six times over, it's not easy. In fact, it's getting harder for me to be patient now. I feel the weight of the ticking clock hammering into my head. The rush of watching them die, of claiming them – I'm getting more insatiable for that feeling. Especially now that Muriel's been finished. What a rush she was, truly. She had been particularly delightful. I am thankful I made her number six.

Catching her on the way home from work had been a breeze. So easy to learn their routines, all of them. People don't realise how accessible they are to me. To the people of West Green, I'm often overlooked. I'm just a face in the crowd who stops by. When they see me, they still see that weak, sickly boy they once knew. The one with dirt on his face. The one who just never quite became much, even when he tried. The boy in the corner while all the other kids played. The boy with the odd eyes and weird tics. The boy with the clicking teeth.

But I'm different now. Still, they're too bloody self-centred to see it. I'm a face they know to see but don't know enough to enquire about. I slip about my business, carrying on in the world without a second glance. No one would give me a second glance because why would they? I'm solid and trustworthy. Quite dull to the outsider, probably. Maybe even some of them look at me with pity, thinking about what a sad, pathetic life it's been. I'm capable at my job. Respectable even. They look at me and think, oh thank goodness, he's done quite well. Settled in quite nicely, despite it all. Thus, who would question me? I'm nothing to worry about.

But I am. Oh, I am. They are all talking about me now, in fact. I've got the whole town in an uproar, yet they don't even realise it's me.

I'm brazen. I'm terrifying. I'm brilliant. God, am I brilliant.

It felt good to put Muriel on a bit of display, to leave her in the open in a public place to be found. I was bubbling with excitement when I'd left the train station. I'd wanted to stick around, to watch the moment of discovery. But I'm not a fool. I'm patient. I knew I could wait to hear about it later.

The town fears me, and I bask in that feeling of power. I relish in this newfound, glorious feeling. It's good to be strong, to be a formidable force.

I hold Muriel's undelivered post now, running my fingers over the edges like I've done with the others. I count the sides over before holding it up to my face, the smell of paper and ink faint but engaging. Like I've done over and over with all the letters, I place Muriel's post between my teeth. Just a taste. Just a bite. Just once more before I stow it away. My teeth sink into the paper, my mind flashing back to the feel of something else of Muriel's between my lips and teeth.

Her flesh.

I inhale, intoxicated by the thought. And then, just like the others, I tuck the final piece of Muriel's life into my wooden box, the newspaper article on top.

Six trophies now.

Just one more to go.

One more and I'll be the best; I'll have earned the title of the West Green Killer. John Haigh had six definite kills to his name – although he claimed nine. But the bloody fool didn't kill nine. He didn't. He'd been caught, and he had only killed six.

I'm better, though. I'm smarter. I will achieve my goal.

I wonder sometimes if I'll be sad once the glow of the final kill wears off. It's been such a thrill to pursue the women in this vicious game they aren't quite privy to. It's been exhilarating. Will I want to stop after Adeline? Will I really be able to stop?

I sigh. Yes. Yes, indeed. She will be the last one. Her death will be perfect, breathtaking. I've always wanted her to be the last. The last one, the special one. It needs to be her.

There won't be another Adeline Walker. She will be my greatest kill yet. There simply will be no topping her. She must be the last.

My hands tremble. Muriel had been a satisfying kill, but not satisfying. Not completely. My thirst is wilder now, more volatile. I nod, knowing what I must do tonight. I need to prepare. Hers must be a spectacle. An unbeatable spectacle. A grand finish I will relish in for years. It will be a fine script, elegant and dazzling. She is my sign-off before the victory lap.

Adeline Walker will be perfect. She was always perfect, even before I realised it.

She is an enigma. I've heard about her reputation in the last town. She is no innocent. She is not one to be tamed.

She is, though, the perfect, beautiful disaster to conquer last.

Chapter 33

West Green, Crawley, West Sussex
14 August 1959

I groggily slink down the stairs, leaning heavily on the railing as my eyes blink away sleep. It's been a long week, the town in a frenzied craze since Muriel's body was uncovered at the train station. The killer is growing more bold, and a brazen killer is the thing of nightmares.

I've been edgier this past week, too. Every noise, every rustle, every movement sends me into a tailspin of fear. I could be next. I could be next at any moment. It's a fact that's usurped all possibility of sleep.

Rustling and jostling about in the kitchen impels me to walk in and see what's happening. When I do, I find Mum with a box on the worktop, carefully wrapping items and placing them inside. Her hair is pulled back, the dark circles under her eyes more prominent.

'What's happening?' I ask, approaching her.

She looks up, holding one of her prized vases and rolling

it in newspaper. 'We're leaving, Adeline. Now, help me get these things wrapped.'

I look at her, waiting to hear more, but she just stares back as if she's said all she needed to say.

'What?' I ask, stupefied.

'We're leaving. I've finally convinced your father. This town isn't safe, and I'm tired of tiptoeing about fearing the worst. Muriel's death was on a whole new level, and the detectives aren't any closer to solving the case. It's time we pack up and get far away from West Green.'

'Mum, no. We can't.' I shake my head, dumbfounded at this revelation.

I'd heard Mum and Dad arguing throughout the past few weeks about Mum's desire to get far away from here. Muriel's murder added more fuel to that fire, and I'd heard them in heated debates more than once this week. But I'd thought it was just fear talking. Certainly, just like with the other five, Mum would calm down after a time, and things would return to normal – or as normal as they could. Dad would never agree to uproot the family again, would he?

'We can, and we shall. Why risk your life, Addy? We can move away, find a new town to start over. And who knows, perhaps a change of scenery would be good for you.' She places the vase carefully into the box, delicately cradling it as she lowers it down.

'I'm not going. I'm not leaving Charles,' I spew, the words fiery and steadfast. I mean them. I'm not leaving Charles.

To move away now could spell disaster for us. I don't want to leave him.

'You are leaving, like it or not. Dad's already scouted out some housing in a few other locations. Until then, we're going to move into a flat near Bracknell.'

'I'm not going.' I shake my head, this new development enraging me. I am not a child. I cannot just be controlled by the whims of my mother. My life is not theirs to own anymore. I won't leave Charles, no matter the risk.

'It's not your choice.'

'It is my choice, Mum. I'm not leaving Charles.'

'So you'd rather risk life and limb for that impoverished man who can offer you nothing? You'd risk getting murdered to be near a man who isn't even worth your time?' she barks at me, stomping closer. Anger wells deep inside. I clench my fists, glaring at her and seeing her for who she really is.

'I'd rather risk it all to live a life with Charles than to stay with you,' I spit back, the words engulfing the gap between us in a conflagration too large to stop.

'I won't let you throw your life away,' she replies after a long, silent moment. 'You're moving with us. If Charles is truly the man you think he is, then he'll save up his money and make an honest woman out of you when the time is right. And if he really does love you, he'll understand the reason you need to leave. He'll want you to leave, to be safe.'

I shake my head, knowing it's no use. She doesn't

understand. She could never understand. I stomp towards the stairs, heading back up them.

'You know your father agrees with me. He's come to his senses. And so will you, Adeline Walker. So will you. We're doing what's best for you,' she yells from the kitchen as she continues her packing.

I know what's best for me. And she is right about one thing – I've come to my senses. I can't play this game anymore.

I spend the morning fuming in my room, pacing, considering the news. I think about all that's transpired here in West Green, how much life has changed. I think about all the complications and the traumas and how getting away would perhaps be a relief.

After a long while, I emerge from my room, jaunting outside to claim the post at its regular time. The postman wanders up, whistling as always. I stare at the jovial man, recalling his interaction with Oliver with a shudder. He digs through the stack in his hand, pulling out a letter for me. He hands it to me, and his fingers brush mine as he stares right at me.

And then, his rocky voice barely a hushed whisper, he murmurs, 'If that bloke is still upsetting you, I can take care of it. Just let me know.'

I stare back, thinking about his words. 'Cheers,' I reply, surprised by his words. I take the letter and head back towards the house as the postman walks away. I turn to look at him, and when I do, I realise he's done the same.

Shaking my head, I wander back inside and up to my room, studying the writing on the front of the envelope.

I want to sit in solitude and escape the realities of my life for a little while longer. I look back down at the envelope and glance at the front, my name in an elegant scrawl that sends a jolt of fear right through me. Once I'm at my desk, my hands flip it over and over as I wonder what it could hold.

I flip it to the back, the envelope already opened. Nothing unusual there. Our mail arrives in all varieties of wear and tear these days. I pull out the carefully creased page inside, my eyes dancing over the page.

My stomach clenches, my blood running cold. I study the thinly veiled threats, the angry words. I study the raging phrases about retribution and how it's time for me to pay. I look at the words over and over and then the signature.

Oliver Parsons.

He's not going away, and he's not calming down. In fact, it seems his anger is increasing tenfold. The supermarket, and now the letter. He's losing it. He's truly losing it – and only I know why. What will he do to unleash that anger? I shake my head, thinking back to those moments when he showed his true colours.

My fingers grip the paper as another thought slips into my mind. Has he already done something – or six somethings – to assuage his anger? Have I underestimated his temper, his craziness, his unstoppable thirst for power? I shake my head. The thought is too horrific. He's a monster, but he's not a killer. He's not. He wouldn't go that far.

But as I read the letter over and over, thinking about the secrets he houses, the anger he still obviously battles, and the danger lurking in every corner of West Green, I know without a doubt Mum's right. I need to get away. I need to be safe and happy – and I can't be either in Crawley. I need to act fast. I need to make a choice. And I need to escape from Oliver's clutches.

Adeline,

It's time for people to know who you really are. I'm sick of the mockery you've made of me, of us. I'm not enduring it any longer.

I'll be watching, Addy. I'm always, always, always watching, waiting for the moment to remind you that I make the choices. I am the one in charge, not you.

Consider this a gentlemanly warning. I'm a good man, after all. I am a patient man. I will have my time, and then you'll remember who I am.

Oliver Parsons

Chapter 34

West Green, Crawley, West Sussex
14 August 1959

'Addy, you need to tell the constables about this. Now,' Charles demands as his shaking hand grasps the letter. It's later that night, and Charles has stopped over to visit – Mother rarely lets me out of the house these days. We've managed to sneak outside for some privacy, the letter tucked away until this moment.

'Keep your voice down. I didn't tell Mum and Dad,' I whisper, looking hastily behind us to see if they've heard. Mercifully, they're listening to the radio with some tea. I readjust my yellow skirt, Charles still clutching the letter.

'Addy, this is serious. You need to turn this in. I won't have him threatening you. I knew he was barmy. I should just go and take care of it myself.'

I grab for Charles' free hand. 'Charles, you can't do that. Oliver comes from money. His family is revered in this town, in all of West Sussex. If you do anything, you'll just end up in jail.'

'Addy, he's threatening you. Why is he so angry? What is it that has him so livid?' Charles asks, holding the letter out.

I twirl a piece of hair as I try to hide my nerves. I'd debated showing Charles the letter. I'd debated showing it to anyone. If anyone knew about it, they'd go straight to Oliver – who clearly wouldn't be afraid to tell everything. And I can't have Charles knowing the whole truth, not when I've made my decision.

I'd thought about it hard all day, deciding Charles needed to see the letter. He needed to understand why moving away was the best choice for both of us. I knew that practical, rational Charles would want to wait, would tell me that being away from here would be a good thing. He'd try to convince me that we could make this work even long-distance. But I'm not willing to take that chance.

'Charles, I'm afraid of what he might do. He's power-hungry. He's clearly mad with jealousy.'

Charles clenches his fists. 'What does this line mean here? Where he says he wants people to know who you really are?'

I bite my lip, averting my eyes. It's the only comment pointing towards the truth.

I look at him, shrugging. 'He thinks I'm a bad person for leaving him,' I lie. The words hurt as they escape my lips. I despise lying to Charles, but I know it's the only way to protect him, to protect me from the whole truth. I can't let him know the whole truth.

'I'm going to mess him up. He can't get away with this. He's a lunatic.' Charles' jaw clenches with anger. I lean on his arm. 'And with everything going on in this town, how do we know it isn't Oliver? He clearly has anger issues. Maybe he's the one behind all of the murders here.'

I shake my head. 'He wouldn't do that.'

'How do you know, Addy? You clearly don't know him like you think you do.'

My head flashes back to those moments in my room, to that silver glinting in his hand and the terror in my chest. 'I know him. He's a terrible person. He is. But he isn't a killer. He's not that mad.' I say the words with a certainty that isn't quite real.

'He can't get away with this,' Charles argues.

'I know. I know. But I don't want to tell anyone about this. It'll just make things worse. And it doesn't matter anyway.'

Charles pulls back from me. 'Of course, it matters. I won't have him harassing you, Addy. And besides—'

I cut him off. 'Charles, listen. West Green isn't what I thought it was. It isn't safe. With the murders and with Oliver, it's not the place I want to be anymore. And neither do my parents.' I look up into Charles' eyes before I continue. 'My parents are moving. They're leaving West Green.'

Charles runs his free hand through his hair. 'Maybe that's good. I don't want to worry about you being safe.'

'But I don't want to leave you, to leave this,' I protest, squeezing his arm. 'I can't leave you,' I whisper, leaning on his shoulder. I feel his muscles soften, his lips finding their way to my forehead. 'I love you, Charles. I don't want to be apart.'

'Me neither, Addy. But your safety is more important. We'll make it work until I can get out of here, come to where you are.'

I pull back, looking into his eyes now. 'I love you. I don't want to spend a minute without you. Charles, marry me. Take me away from here. We can escape all this madness, all this danger. We can be away from my parents and be together. I want to start a life with you.' I smile at the words because they're true. They're completely true.

I love him. He's the one for me, and I don't want to be away from him for a single moment. Nothing can tear us apart. But it's more than just my heart speaking. I also don't want him here without me. I don't want Oliver to have the chance to tell him the words I can't.

'Addy, I love you, too. And I want to marry you. I want to give you the life you deserve. But I need time. I need to save money, to work out the details. And in the interim, it's not safe here for you. You need to get away. We can tell your parents. Tell them the plan.'

'No,' I reply, firmly. 'They won't understand. And Charles, they don't understand this between us. They'll never give their approval for us to be wed.'

Charles sighs, looking away. I can tell I've hurt him, and

I feel terribly about that. It's never a good feeling to believe you're not good enough.

'Maybe they're right, Addy,' he says, turning back to me. 'I'm no perfect man. Not at all. Maybe this isn't the life you want.'

I squeeze his hand again, firm now. 'Charles, I love you. I've loved you from the moment I saw you. You're it for me. Whatever life we have or don't have, it doesn't matter. I just want you. All of you, every day, from here on out. Please. Please, don't make us be apart.'

He sighs, but his eyes soften. I know I'm reaching him. 'So, what's your plan?'

'We leave. We leave this place in the morning. We get on the train, and we leave. We go anywhere. Near London. I don't know. Wherever you think there will be work. Wherever you want to start a life.'

'It's not that simple, Addy.'

'It can be. We'll be all right. I've managed to set some money aside,' I reassure.

'I won't live off money you've nicked,' he says, and for once, I wish Charles wasn't so principled.

'It's fine, Charles. Please. Please just trust me.'

He shakes his head, a smirk forming. 'You do realise that you're impossible to say no to, don't you?'

I smile back. 'Good. Then it's settled. We leave tomorrow. We can leave in the middle of the night, grab the first train in the morning. I'll have a bag packed.'

'What about your parents? I don't want them to worry.'

'I'll leave a note explaining everything.'

'And won't you feel terrible leaving? Won't you miss them?'

I consider the question. There have been good moments growing up, it's true. But looking at Charles, I know these moments are nothing compared to what we could have if I can just escape the clutches of West Green, of my past, of my choices. I need to start over. I need to start somewhere safe.

I think, too, about Phyllis. About leaving her here to fend for herself, with Oliver and the killer on the loose. My stomach sinks with guilt, but it can't be helped. I have to do what's best for me and believe she'll be all right.

'I will and I won't. I know they'll be fine without me. They'll be just fine.'

'And what about the time until we leave? Addy, who knows what Oliver's capable of. There's also the West Green Killer to think about. Who knows what could happen to us. I still think we should warn your parents.'

I stare out into the street, feeling a sudden shiver at the thought I could be making a choice that will seal my death. What if this is a mistake? What if Charles is correct? Should we tell my parents?

'You'll keep an eye out, and we'll be careful. That's all,' I reassure.

'This is insane,' Charles whispers, kissing my forehead.

I smile. 'Isn't love always a bit insane? It will be fine, Charles. You'll see. Just trust me.'

He rests his chin on my shoulder, his nose brushing my cheek. 'I'm going to keep watch, then. I'm going to be parked out here tonight to make sure nothing happens.'

'I can live with that,' I murmur.

I lean into Charles now, who gives the letter back. I shudder at the thought that I might be making the wrong choice. I chill at the thought he could come tonight or tomorrow, could strike before I can get away.

I count to three in my mind. It'll all be fine. Just a few more hours. Just a few more hours to survive – the killer, Oliver, my secret, and the goodbyes my family doesn't even know are coming.

*

I don't sleep that night. Not a wink. I spend the night staring out my bedroom window, watching the street, and waiting for a killer or Oliver, neither of which comes. I rock in the chair by my window, thinking about all that's happened, and thinking about the future. Am I making the right choice? It's crazy that life has come to this.

But it isn't just this threatening letter that's made the choice for me. No, I made *that* choice months ago. Because in truth, as insane as it sounds, it isn't just the letter that has sent me out of town. It's the fear of the truth coming out, of all being lost. It's the realisation that I'll never be free of Oliver if I stay here. I'll never be free to live the life

I want, to be with Charles, and to be faithful to the man who means everything to me.

Sometimes a woman must do the unspeakable to salvage a life worth living. My mind flashes back to the moment I realised how dangerous Oliver Parsons was. Life in West Green didn't become dangerous with the murder of Elizabeth. Life in West Green became dangerous for me before that – it became dangerous when I learned that the man I once loved was an unpredictable villain lying in wait.

*

'What have you done?' his voice snarled from the doorway to my room. I lay in bed, staring at the ceiling and wishing I could die.

I'd known the termination would be risky. The man in the back room had warned me before we started that things could go wrong, but he also implied that he was more skilled than most. Phyllis had held my hand during the entire, agonising procedure. She'd clutched me as I screamed in pain, both physical and mental, as the life of the baby was snuffed out – and, in my young mind, my soul with it.

I'd returned home barely conscious, barely functioning. Phyllis had offered to 'have me over for a visit' the next day, her parents mercifully out of town. I'd obliged, and I'd managed to paint on a faux smile convincing enough to ensure Mum I was okay. I was not. The healing process had taken weeks. I was a lucky one, though. I'd made it. Nevertheless, the pains came and went. The emotional agony, however, never left.

I'd killed it. I'd murdered the baby I'd never hold. I was a beast, it was true. And although I was thankful to cut the tie to Oliver, there was a piece of me that was drowning in guilt. I feared I always would. I was afraid that I'd never piece together a life beyond that defining moment. What had I done? What had I done to the baby, to my own life? I hated Oliver for the decision I made – but more than that, I despised myself.

I sat up in bed, my muscles aching from the movement. It had been several weeks since the procedure – and it had been several weeks since I'd seen Oliver, breaking up with him the night before I carried out my choice. His veiled threats and scorned face told me all I needed to know – there was no backing out. It had to be done. I had to sever any ties to the man who would destroy every piece of happiness I ever had.

I strained to stand now, to face whatever he was here for, but he stormed across the room, shoving me back down. I whimpered in pain.

'How fucking dare you,' he bellowed, seething. I saw something in his eyes that I had seen all too many times before.

'What are you talking about?' I asked, trying to steady my voice while not meeting his eyes. I was shaking, though, petrified of what he would do. With Mum and Dad out to dinner, I was alone and at his mercy. This was not somewhere I wanted to be.

He leaned closer, his face red, his mouth sneering. 'I know what you did, you slag. You think I don't have eyes everywhere? It took some digging because you covered your tracks, but when you have enough money, well, you can find out anything you desire.'

I shook my head. It couldn't be Phyllis. It wouldn't be Phyllis. Regardless, I cowered as I realised the truth. He knew. And he was never going to be okay with it.

'I-I don't know what you're talking a-about,' I stuttered, trying to cover the truth.

'Don't fucking lie to me! I fucking know you killed our baby. How dare you? You don't make that decision. I do. I make the decisions.'

I blinked at him, staring into his face, wondering how it all was uncovered and wondering how many people he'd told. My life, which was already on a downward spiral, was spinning out of control.

'How did you find out?' I whispered.

'I have my ways. Your friend Phyllis wouldn't talk, but her brother's friend did. Oh, did he give me the details. I figured out the rest, traced down the place. You slag. You selfish slag,' he spewed at me. In the middle of my quaking fear, though, I found it oddly comforting to know it wasn't Phyllis. Nevertheless, I knew it wouldn't matter in the end who had told him. The bottom line was that Oliver knew. He knew every single, sordid detail.

Strength surged in me, as did my resolve to stand up for myself.

'Oliver, you're a monster. I can't handle a life with you.'

'Me a monster? You fucking killed the baby. You didn't have the right.' He paced in my room now, anger dripping from his every movement.

'We weren't ready for a baby. I couldn't support a baby. I couldn't.'

'You wouldn't have had to. What, do you think I would let my child, my heir, be uncared for? I would have provided financially, and you know that. Don't even try to excuse your disgusting behaviour. I was going to marry you. Do you know what you've done? You ruined your chance to be married to me. Your station would've been better than you could've dreamt. You would've had the life. The perfect life. And now it's all gone to bloody hell. You've blown it all to hell.' He chided me like I'm a scolded child, a wayward dog. Even now, the condescension simmered beneath his words.

'And what? Had your mistresses on the side? Dictated my every move? Abused me? Is that how you would've provided for us?' I snapped, and then my cheek burned with the sting of his slap.

'Don't talk to me like that. Don't you ever talk to me like that, you trollop.' He shook with rage.

I looked up into his simmering eyes and recognised the

life I left behind. I hated that it took the choice I made to get away, but I did get away.

I smiled up at him. 'This is why I chose not to have the baby,' I replied coolly. I gestured to his quaking body.

His anger cooled as he unclenched his jaw and unfurled his constricting fists. Something else filled in where the anger had been residing – something exponentially more frightening.

'So,' he said now, smirking, sitting on the side of the bed. He tapped his chin. I shuddered at his sudden calmness. 'You think because you killed our child, you're free now? You think you can just leave me behind? What you did changes nothing.'

'Oliver, please. It's done. No one needs to know. We can go our separate ways.'

'You're right. It would be painful to admit to the world that you were in my bed, a woman way beneath me.'

I shook my head, tears falling. What did I ever see in him? How did I ever think I loved him?

'But, on the other hand, oh wouldn't everyone be so interested to hear about Addy Walker and her escapades? Wouldn't it be great for them to know the real you?' he murmured.

I shook uncontrollably. 'Oliver, please,' I replied. I hated that I had stooped to begging. He always loved when I grovelled. He had always liked to be reminded of my weakness and his own strength.

He stood now from the bed, and I trembled, wondering

what was next. I couldn't let this get out. I couldn't have the world knowing my shame, knowing what I did. What would it do to Mum and Dad? What would it do to me, to my reputation? And what would happen to the man who helped me in that alley when no one would? Most of all, what would happen when, every single day, I had to face the piteous or seething glares in the street? It was a small town. People would talk. I'd never escape what I'd done. I'd never be able to stop living in that nightmarish choice, in those whirls of regret. I'd be swallowed up by guilt, by the faceless baby that I'd killed.

Oliver rushed over to me in several quick, large strides. My chest heaved as he grabbed my face, his hands squeezing my chin as his other hand wielded a knife. Where did the knife come from? He held the blade to my neck.

'You're never leaving. Do you understand me? You're mine. You're mine to control. You don't get a say in anything you do. You belong to me. You will always be mine. No matter where you are or how far you think you stray from me, just know. You're mine if I want you to be. Always mine.'

I trembled, my hands clutching the quilt as tears blurred my vision. He held the knife in my face for a long moment, his teeth gritted as he heaved in air.

And then, without warning, he tossed me back on the bed, his hand releasing my chin. Before I could process all that had happened, he'd turned and left. His footsteps echoed in the corridor and then down the stairs as he stormed off, leaving me crumpled on my bed in a whirl of confusion and terror. My lips trembled, and tears crashed onto the quilt.

I spent the next hour choking on sobs and sorrows, wondering what I should do or how to escape the mess. And wondering how long I'd be at Oliver's mercy, enduring his reign of terror.

*

For days after, I remained in a shaken state of fear, wondering when he'd return. Flashes of Oliver with the knife at my throat kept me checking out the window and jumping at every noise. Was this really the man I'd fallen for? What had happened to him? I'd always known he was controlling, a bit cocky – but violent? I'd never thought him capable of what I'd seen in my room.

I awaited his return, trembling at the thought of him reappearing with his knife. Would the anger over what I'd done stew and boil? How far would the rage push him? I waited and waited – but Oliver didn't return. I'd passed him in town, the sight of him causing me to avert my eyes. But there wasn't an overt sign that what had happened in my room was real. To see Oliver in public, one would think I'd imagined it, that I was the lunatic.

Still, as the months passed, it was clear Oliver was just keeping me waiting. It was, after all, the waiting, the anticipating, the knowing what he was capable of that was perhaps worse than the knife at my throat. So many times, I thought about telling someone the truth. I thought over and over about telling Charles once he was in my life.

But I didn't. I couldn't. It wasn't just me I was protecting. It was Phyllis. It was the man who helped me that dark night. And, in a twisted way in my mind, I suppose it was the baby, too. The baby's life shouldn't be tainted by the ugly words that would come. I didn't want to hear my Mum talk about how I'd sent the baby to hell, unbaptised. I didn't want to hear people picturing my baby burning in the hellfire. I wanted to preserve its unlived life for myself.

I trace out my name on the fog on the window now, smiling with the thought that I'm getting away. Charles will take me away, and I'll leave this horrid place behind. All the mistakes. All the murders. All the terrors I've faced. West Green has never been kind to me, it's true. But no more. No more Oliver. No more threats. Oliver can say whatever he wants after I leave. He can tell the entire gory truth if he so chooses. He can tell everyone what a horrible woman I am and what a terrible thing I've done – because I'll be gone, long gone, a new life started. It simply can't come soon enough.

Chapter 35

West Green, Crawley, West Sussex
15 August 1959

I steady my hands as I set the note on the kitchen table. I glance around in the darkness, my bag on my back. I absorb the familiar sights of the kitchen, the living area once more. This is it, the finale to my time here. There's no returning after this. I'm sealing my fate.

A part of me is jittery at the prospect. Charles and I are taking so many risks. What if we can't make it? What if this is a huge mistake? We're both walking away from everything for this. Still, I know that the risk of staying behind is even greater. There is really no choice – not if I love Charles. Not if I want a new life with him. Not if I want to escape Oliver, the guilt, and my parents' judging gazes.

The house is so dark, too dark to fully appreciate it. Will I miss the kitchen where we baked tarts? Will I think about this house, about the moments we had here? I don't know. I don't have time to consider it all. We need to get going if we're going to leave this place behind.

It's a risk leaving now. Dad will be getting up in a few hours, catching the train at the same station we're leaving from. But our plan is to be there early, to be first on the train and out of town before he has a chance to board his. And then we'll leave and never, ever look back.

I tuck the note on the table, using the salt shaker as an anchor. I glance over the words one last time.

Dear Mum and Dad,

I know this may come as a shock to you, but perhaps it won't. Perhaps you've always known I've been ready to get away from this place. But I can't do it without Charles. It's our time to start something new together, and I'm ready to explore our life beyond the limits of West Green. I want to start our life together now.

Charles and I have decided to elope. I know he isn't the man you thought I should be with, but I love him. I think we can have a happy life together, and I want that life to start now. I want to get away from this town and all it holds for me. I want to start over.

I'm sorry to leave you this way, but if I move with you, I can't be with him. I'm happy, and I'll be safe. Once we're married and settled, I'll try to write to you. And maybe someday after everything has calmed down, we can visit. But for now, just know I'm out there seeing the world and living my life.

I want you to take care and to be safe. West Green is no longer the place we thought it was. I love you. Take care.
Addy

I hold the second letter, the one from Oliver, for a long moment. Should I leave it behind? Or perhaps I should just take it with me. It won't do to have Mum and Dad snooping around will it? Then again, once I leave, it will be Oliver who is left to paint the picture. I don't like that idea.

With a trembling hand, I make the decision to leave Oliver's note behind. It may not make sense, but at least Mum will understand that Oliver isn't the man he claims to be. Perhaps if Oliver decides to tell the town about my transgressions, Mum will have a glimpse into the real kind of man he is.

I set Oliver's note under the shaker, alongside my letter to my parents, studying it once more. With an air of assurance, I turn and glance at my home that is no longer a home one last time before silently opening the door, my bag on my back, and walking out into the darkness to meet Charles.

*

'I need to make one more stop,' I murmur, gripping Charles' hand. He is pale, quieter than usual. I know this is terrifying for him, too.

'Addy, we need to be at the train station. We need to be on that first train or everything will fall apart.'

'I know. I know that. But I want to make one stop,' I implore, pausing at the church.

'There's no way the pastor is leaving it open with everything going on,' Charles argues.

'The back door to the basement is open. It's always open,' I reply, knowing from experience that the pastor doesn't take the time to lock it.

'If we get caught here, it's going to ruin everything,' Charles replies.

'We won't. Trust me. I need to do this,' I assure.

'Okay. You know I can't say no to you.' He kisses my forehead, following me around the church. Once we're to the back, at the basement door, I look back at him.

'I need to do this alone.' He raises an eyebrow, and I register the hurt and confusion on his face. I pat his arm. 'It's just something I need to do. Trust me.'

'I'll be right here. If you're not back in five minutes, I'm coming in,' he replies, but he makes no move to follow me. I love that he trusts me, but then the guilt bubbles up. He shouldn't. He really shouldn't. I don't deserve him.

I enter the basement door, tiptoeing inside. I wander up the familiar stairs, finding my way to the front of the altar. Candles flicker in their spot, the hopes and prayers of so many lighting the dim church. Tears form in my eyes as I reach for the matchstick and light an empty candle in the front of the pack. I stare at the glowing light for a long moment, thinking about the baby, thinking about the life I snuffed out.

'God, forgive me. I'm sorry. I'm sorry. I hope someday to make up for my actions, if you'll let me.' I say a prayer for the baby and for the life I'm leaving behind. Then, I pivot on my foot, head back down the stairs and out the door.

I won't think of it again, I tell myself. I'm starting over. I need to give myself that chance. And so, with the last candle lit to commemorate the choice I made and the life lost, I march onward with Charles, towards the train station that will take me away for good.

But as we're walking, I feel a shiver down my spine, goose bumps across my arms. I pause, turning to look over my shoulder. There is nothing, just an empty street behind us, and bone-chilling silence. I shake my head. Clearly my nerves are shot. It's just me and Charles, after all, heading to a new life.

*

'All aboard,' a voice cries out, and Charles and I step forward quickly, rushing onto the train to claim our seat. My heart beats wildly as we prepare to head to our new life. What awaits us? What will we do?

Charles has an idea to head towards a distant cousin's home in Hemel Hempstead for a while until we can get situated. He assures me that the cousin will be welcoming, but with no notice, I can't be certain. There are no guarantees we won't end up on the street.

'We're off,' Charles murmurs into my hair as I claim the window seat. 'Are you ready to start this life?'

'Yes,' I say, looking into those eyes that make me feel like anything is possible.

'I left a note for my mum and dad,' Charles whispers. 'Hopefully they'll understand.'

I lean into him, silent now, trying not to think about all the logistics of what we're doing. I try not to think about Phyllis and my parents, about everyone I've ever known who will remain behind to talk about us, to wonder what drove us to the decision. I try not to think about what Oliver will say or do once I'm gone.

The train begins to move towards our new life and I shove the thought aside, focusing on the future that lies ahead instead of the dark past I'm leaving behind.

Rage bubbles in my chest as I pace about my flat, flying through the stages of grief. Mostly, I've been stuck on the anger bit, fists clenched and jaw working.

How could I be so fucking stupid? How could I have let this happen? I shouldn't have waited. Dammit, why did I wait? I lingered in the pleasure of the game for too long, and now my plan's fucked. Bloody fucked.

I was a fool. More than a fool. And now my chance is completely gone.

Rubbish boy. Dumb boy. Dirty boy. I-hate-you boy.

I'd read that bastard's note. The imbecile of a bloke, that Oliver Parsons. Who did he think he was, assuming he owned Addy? Thinking he was so sneaky, so malicious. He was nothing. That weak little boy was nothing, pampered and protected by daddy's money.

That twit wasn't a man. He wasn't brilliant. He wasn't capable of the great things I am. But the letter Oliver wrote to Addy had made me more excited to finish the work, to claim Adeline Walker as my own. I felt a need to show that annoying bloke how to claim a woman. I'd show him who Adeline really belonged to.

But I'd been distracted. The letter had thrown off my focus. I should've kept Oliver's menacing letter instead of the one I did. Why hadn't I kept it? Stupid, stupid, stupid.

But I didn't. I had been an imbecile. And now it is too late.

I'd heard the rumours. The town was abuzz with word. I'd been too stunned to believe it. I'd gone to work, hands shaking, praying it wasn't true. Not when I was so close to finishing. Not when it was almost done. I'd made my way to her street. I'd forced on the smile, whistling my favourite tune, trying to calm myself.

Tear-stained cheeks and hair a mess, Nora Walker had answered the door in a state that told the tale.

'Sorry to bother you, Mrs Walker. I just, well, I wanted to see if you're okay. I heard a terrible rumour about Adeline. Such a sweet girl. I was hoping it wasn't true.'

She sniffled. 'I don't know why she would do this.' Her words quaked with grief, and it was all I could do to stay standing after the confirmation of my greatest fear.

I'd wrapped up, painting on the condolences I felt only for myself but pretended to have for the Walkers. Taking off my hat and rubbing the scar that burned on my head, I'd walked away in a daze, abandoning my work for the first time since I started the job. I returned to my flat in a stupor.

I plop into my single chair now, staring out into the day.

She's gone. I missed my chance. That Langley Green bloke has stolen her. I'd been so focused on Oliver's games, I'd overlooked the other one, Charles. In the end, I was a twenty-two-year-old-man who lost to a fucking boy.

My heart burns, singed by disappointment. My fingers, my lips tingle with a craving I can no longer satisfy.

She is gone. *Three words that sear my life's greatest sorrow into my heart.*

I try to salvage something, my mind alight. My eyes dance around the room, unfocused, as my thoughts travel down a new path. I am brilliant. I'm no quitter. Yes, I could track her down. It might take time, but I could do it. I'm patient. I stand up again, pacing. My fingers trace the jagged scar as if seeking to touch inspiration itself.

Could it work? Could I really find her? Could I still win at my own game?

I walk to and fro, thinking, pondering, scratching, thinking some more.

But as the minutes pass by and my thoughts tire, my pacing slows. The energy drains from me bit by bit. Five steps become four, then three, then none.

Frozen, I accept the truth.

It won't count. It isn't how it's supposed to be. It needs to be here. It just won't count any other way. I am a rule follower. I'm no beast, after all. I win fair and square. I don't cheat.

Fuck.

Fuck.

'Fuck!' I shout, slamming my fist on the table as I sink to the floor now.

She is no longer going to be my final signature. There won't be one. She will forever be just the one who got away. I will forever be nothing but a failure, the man in a flat in West Green whose legacy was never quite completed.

Bloody boy. Bloody fucked boy.

Bloody useless man.

Chapter 36

Smith Creek Manor Nursing Home
2019

I've gathered my strength, and I don't care what the nurses say. I'm not staying in this room, in this bed or in this wheelchair any longer. I don't have the time to waste sitting around. I can't afford to be weak.

I get myself out of bed, my eyes heavy with exhaustion. I didn't sleep a wink, my eyes trained on the window and on my doorway, wondering if last night would be the night. Wondering what I could do about it.

I thought about calling the police – but would that do any good? Would they believe some woman from Smith Creek Manor? Certainly not, especially with my medical history. *Certainly not.* It all feels so useless. I am trapped here, body and mind, and he knows it.

Dorothy is gone. Claire is not going to be able to help me. There's only one person left – and in my time of desperation, I realise that it's a long shot. After all we've been through, after all I've done to him, and after all that's happened between us, will he even believe me? Will he even want to help me? And can I trust him after all he's done? It's doubtful, I realise. My mind might falter sometimes, but it's strong enough to know this isn't going to work. Still, I must try. I don't have a choice now. I'm out of options, and I'm frantic – frantic enough to consider turning to the beastly man who tortured me all those years ago.

I trudge down the corridor, taking a pause every few steps to lean on the wall. My legs scream in my pain. I limp onward, stopping at 313. I peek in, but he's not there. Where could he be?

I investigate in the television area, where Philip Lady sits in her spot. A few women crochet, and a man sleeps in his chair. But Oliver isn't there. I keep a wary lookout, watching for the man from 300, praying he's not on the loose. I march forward, checking the reading room, the dining room, the corridors. At each stop, I come up empty, and panic starts to set in. What if it's too late? What if Oliver's gone too?

After what feels like forever, I stop in the empty community room. He sits in the front of the area, staring at a painting hanging on the wall. He's alone, no one in the room. I lean on the chairs in each row, making my way to the front.

'Oliver?' I ask gently. He turns to look at me.

'What do you want?' he asks gruffly. He looks at me

with a hatred that has been boiling for decades, and I realise this is probably a mistake. But it's too late to turn back, and I really don't have any other options. He's the only one who could possibly understand, who might believe me. I don't sit down, standing beside him even though I'm so tired.

'I need your help.' The murmured plea feels even more solemn once the words escape my lips.

He scowls, shaking his head. 'You've got to be joking? After all you've done? You want my help now?'

My lip quivers, but I try to hold it together. 'I'm desperate. Please.'

'I'll say,' he replies, standing shakily from the chair now. He turns to me. 'You always were desperate for something, weren't you, Addy?'

'I'm sorry.' I choke out the words.

'You mean sorry for how you murdered our child? How you killed our baby without even asking me? You didn't give me a choice, Addy. You didn't give me a choice.' He steps forward now, anger seething. I tremble, taking a step back.

'You didn't give *me* a choice, Oliver. You weren't the man I thought you were. You were dangerous.'

'And you weren't the woman I thought you were,' he roars. His hands shake, balled into fists. 'It was my child. You didn't have that right. You didn't have the right to murder my only child. You went on to have other children. I didn't get that chance. I never got a chance to have another, not after everything. My father's business was the only thing I had to keep me company after you left. Do you know what that's like, to live your life alone? You stripped me of that chance.'

Visions of Claire come to mind, the miracle baby I thought would never happen. I saw her birth as a sign that I was forgiven. But apparently, Oliver didn't have such luck.

'You're unbelievable, you know? You're a monster,' he chokes out, tears falling down his cheeks now. 'You killed our baby, and then moved on with some other bastard like it was nothing. I was left cleaning up the pieces. Did you know I'd told my family I was going to marry you? A couple of weeks before you broke up with me and then killed our baby, I'd told them. My mum had already given me her ring for you. I was a bloody fool. A bloody fucking fool. And then to find out that on top of it, my child, my heir was murdered by you? It was too much. It's all still too much.'

'I'm sorry,' I murmur, and I am. In many ways I am. 'But I didn't have a choice.'

'It's just like you, to claim you didn't have a choice. Is that what you told yourself when you left Crawley? When you up and left, no explanation? Is that what you told yourself when you found out about your parents? Did you even think about what that was like for me? Do you know how many years I struggled to get rid of that blemish from my name? I never got rid of that stain, even when I was cleared. I never had a chance, Addy.'

Tears flow now as he brings up the event I'd been trying so hard to block out. I shove aside images of my parents, choking on smoke, of the house in flames. Of how it was my fault. It's my fault they were there. It's my fault they didn't leave West Green in time. It's all my fault.

'I'm sorry.' The words keep coming out of my lips like a record on repeat, but this time, the words aren't just to Oliver. They're for the baby I killed, for the parents I left behind, and for the chain of life-altering events I set off that night I let Phyllis talk me into that choice.

'Sorry? Sorry for leaving that note behind for your parents to find? Sorry that I was bloody accused of arson? And how you did nothing to stop them from pursuing me? Do you even know how long I was under scrutiny? How I almost went to jail? How that ruined my reputation? For God's sake, Adeline, you destroyed everything ... and then bloody destroyed it again. No one believed me. Everyone thought I was a maniac. Some even thought I was the murderer. And what could I say? That you bloody aborted our baby? It only made me look more guilty. So there you were, the innocent victim escaping from the beastly monster. I never fucking recovered. Never.'

He stands from his seat now, and I see for the first time what a toll it all played on him. I realise the true source of his anger. I'd usurped control from him all those years. I'd unknowingly led him down a path that proved to him he wasn't in charge, that he wasn't the powerful Oliver he thought he was.

For a moment, just a moment, a pang of guilt for Oliver weighs on me. He was a hellish fiend in his younger days – but did he deserve what I left him? Did he deserve the tarnished reputation? He did horrible things, but did he deserve to have the shadow of something he didn't do hanging over his head?

Did my parents deserve to die as they did, wondering where their only daughter was? I don't know anymore. I don't know anything at all.

'Yes,' I admit softly, my own tears falling. 'Yes. But Oliver, listen to me. Listen. You've got to believe me. I'm in danger here. Someone's after me. The man in 300 wants to kill me, and I don't know, I think he looks familiar. I can't figure out why.'

He stares at me as if waiting for more before uproarious laughter emerges from his mouth. He shakes his head, squeezing the bridge of his nose with his thumb and forefinger. 'Are you kidding me right now? You're madder than I thought. The whole floor's been talking about how you're losing your marbles, and I know they're right. Come on, Addy. Are you hearing yourself? Certainly, you must be mentally sound enough to understand how ridiculous this sounds. The man in 300, the one with a limp, wants to kill you? Is that what you're telling me?'

'I'm serious. I'm *serious*,' I say, watching my last tiny swatch of hope fade to nothing. Tears run down my cheeks, landing on my chest, on my hands. My arm shakes as I struggle to stay standing. My last glimmer of hope is being snuffed out before my eyes, and even though I expected as much, the reality hits hard.

'It's a funny thing, really,' he replies, staring straight into my eyes. His are icy cold. 'Nothing bad really happened on Floor Three until you showed up. It was calm, peaceful even. Sure, there was a few bad things, but nothing extreme. Nothing like there's been lately. There weren't any of the crazy, odd occurrences until you came along. I wonder if that's a coincidence.'

'It isn't, Oliver. It isn't. He was waiting for me. I'm telling you. The man in 300. He was waiting for me. It's him.' I stare into Oliver's eyes, waiting for a hint of recognition, waiting for a sign that someone is on my side. It doesn't come.

'When you first came to this floor, Addy, I couldn't believe it. After all this time, here you were, like you never left. It brought back all those memories. You got away from here. You may have let yourself forget what you did, but I didn't. I stayed behind. I lived my life here, took over the business. I never got to leave. Do you know what that's been like, staying here? Do you know what it was like coming to Smith Creek, stuck here to reflect on the life I never really got to live? I've been here, drowning in that sin of yours, thinking about all you took from me. When I learned you were here, I told Father Patrick about it. I told him everything you did. I thought maybe it would be my chance to make you atone for what you did, for killing our baby.'

I blink at Oliver. 'You told Father Patrick?' All the notes, all the warnings to repent. It all makes sense now.

'Yes. Yes, I did. I wanted him to see you for what you were. I wanted someone to finally understand.'

'Is that why he left all those notes?'

'Yes, Addy. He knows what you are. A fraud. A sinner. A trollop.'

I shudder at his words. 'Oliver, listen, I'm telling you. There's a killer here. There's been more than just the Bible verses.'

Oliver shakes his head, looking up at the ceiling for a moment before turning back to me. 'You know, Addy. I feel sorry for you. I do. You think everything is about you. In that warped head of yours, you think the whole world rotates around you. And everyone thinks it's your old age and your fading mind. But I know better. You're nothing but a selfish slag. You've always been one. It's just that now others can see it too. Others know the whole truth.'

My hand flies up, and I slap Oliver's cheek, the gesture stunning even me. When it's done, my hand flies to my mouth, knowing I've gone too far to go back now.

Oliver stands, stoic and cold, and I back up, afraid of retaliation. He doesn't touch me, though. He stares for a moment, seemingly gaining his senses. And then, he kicks at the chair I'm leaning on. It's a swift kick with power behind it and decades' worth of rage. The chair slides out from under me, and I'm thudding to the ground, my head burning with pain as I land.

'Stay the fuck away from me,' Oliver commands, looming over me for a long, vicious moment. He kicks me in the ribs, a hearty kick that makes me cough and sputter. Then, he turns on his heel and stomps out of the room. I cry in pain, my hip hurting and my ribs throbbing. Everything hurts. I think that he's going to come back, to help me, but he doesn't. I'm alone, staring at the empty room, wondering how long I'll be there on my side. Maybe this is where it all ends. Maybe this is where he gets me.

After a long while, I realise no one is coming for me. I must help myself. I've always had to look out for myself. I slowly, agonisingly get myself up, first pulling myself to the chair and then to my feet. My head throbs and my heart races, but I plug on, dragging myself down the corridor to my room, one hand cradling my ribs. I walk on, past 312's closed door, past Babbling Barbara who is sitting on the floor in the hallway with a doll. Its head is turned backwards, and if I didn't have my own problems, I would be taken aback by it. Instead, I walk on, ignoring her comments about the Black Plague. I pass Oliver's room, where he sits in a chair at the window. I glance at him, but he doesn't look back. I trudge forward to my room, to my lonely cell, and think about all that's been lost.

'Philip was here. He was here,' my roommate announces once I'm inside. I glance around, but nothing has been moved. Nothing new is tacked to the board. There is nothing alarming.

'I saw him. I saw Philip, I did. I promise I did,' she

yammers on, adding to my already intense migraine. I limp over to my bed, and that's when I see it.

A single daisy, flat on my pillow. I pluck it from my bed and set it on the bedside table beside the photograph Claire brought me, sobbing until my head feels like it might explode. I wipe at my tears, the Philip Lady still chanting on her side of the room. I pull out my Bible, and flip to the front cover. There, I write a note that I hope Claire will see once I'm gone. I hope she'll get the answers that no one else can find. My script is shaky, but it's legible. It will do the trick. It might not save me, but it will at least save someone else.

I close the Bible, the note waiting for the right time to emerge. And then, I sit myself into the chair and I wait – for the end, for the finale, for all to be revealed. After all, at Smith Creek Manor, there's nothing else we can do but wait for our time to die.

Potential Arson Case and Missing Girl Perplexes West Green Residents and Police Alike
West Green, Crawley, West Sussex
28 August 1959

A new development in the West Green community has residents and police alike confused as they try to ascertain connections in several cases. On the evening of 25 August, a fire at the Walker residence on 18 Deerswood Road, West Green destroyed the entire home. This development came shortly after the youngest resident of the home, Adeline Walker, 19, was reported as missing.

Police were called to 18 Deerswood Road earlier in the month after Mr and Mrs Andrew Walker called investigators to report their daughter as missing. Adeline Walker left a note of her plans to leave West Green. However, a troubling note was also left, signed by Oliver Parsons. Parsons had been questioned about the missing girl but claimed not to know any details about her disappearance.

Despite the notes, the Walkers were concerned that Adeline's disappearance was related to foul play; detectives were investigating whether or not the West Green Killer could have been involved in her disappearance.

However, Charles Evans of Langley Green, Crawley, West Sussex, also disappeared on the same night. The two were said to be courting, and detectives believe at this time that Adeline Walker left by choice, her disappearance unrelated to the West Green Killer.

Nonetheless, this case took a peculiar turn the night of 25 August when a fire broke out at the residence of the Walkers. Despite emergency personnel's swift reaction, Mr and Mrs Walker were pronounced dead at the scene, the home a total loss. Investigators believe the Walkers were asleep in the upper rooms of the house when the fire broke out. Their cause of death was ruled as smoke inhalation.

The discovery of several empty gas cans at a nearby property has led investigators to believe the fire could be the result of arson. It is too early in the investigation to determine whether or not the West Green Killer could be involved.

Oliver Parsons is currently a suspect in the case. After Adeline's disappearance, he was seen having several heated conversations with the Walkers, one of which turned physical with Andrew Walker, according to witnesses. Parsons is currently under thorough investigation. Authorities are searching for Adeline Walker to question her about her parents' deaths and the notes left behind. In the meantime, West Green is mourning the loss of two more of the community's residents in what is being deemed a summer of death.

'We can't take much more, truly,' a neighbour noted about the deaths. 'There is too much suffering in this community. We need answers, and we need them now. How many more will have to die before we solve this?'

Anyone with information is asked to contact the West Green Constabulary.

Chapter 37

Hemel Hempstead, UK
8 September 1959

'Addy, thank God. I've been so worried. Are you okay?' Phyllis' voice is edgy and distraught when I ring her. My heart beats wildly at the sound of her voice.

'I'm fine, Phyllis. I wanted to check in on you and make sure everything was okay. I tried to ring my parents and tell them I'm settled and fine, but I couldn't seem to connect. I'm fine, Charles and I—'

'Addy, listen. You need to come back.' Phyllis' words cut me off. I startle, playing with the phone cord.

'What?'

'There's been ... oh, Addy, I don't know how to tell you. There's been an incident, and ... well ... you need to come back.'

'Phyllis, you're scaring me. What's wrong?'

The news she tells me causes me to crumple to the ground as vomit rises in my throat.

Even as I struggle to process the news, my mind wraps around one thought: it's all my fault.

I've done this. My misguided, selfish choices have done this. And there's no going back now.

I hear Phyllis' tearful words as she walks me through the events of the past few weeks. I hear her begging me to come home, to take care of things. She tells me how the detectives want to talk to me, how Oliver has been questioned. I hear it all, yet I don't.

Because all I can hear is my pounding heart and the realisation that my choices have led to this. It's all my fault. Absolutely all my fault.

I sob on the floor, squeezing my eyes shut.

I'm so sorry, Mum and Dad. I'm sorry.

Chapter 38

20 November 1959

The rain splatters against the window, heavy drops plummeting from the sky and assaulting all below. The children in the street don't mind, the drops stabbing into them as they continue their game of catch. A weak grin spreads to my face as I stare through the wet glass, watching and wondering what they're thinking about. Wishing I could be in the midst of simple, childhood naivety.

But we can't go back in time. We can't change our choices or relive the past. We can only deal with the present. At least that's what I've been reminding myself over and over.

'You okay, dear?' Charles has been worried about me ever since I got home. The doctors told him to keep a close eye on me.

I look up and paint on the faux smile. Everything about me is fake these days. 'Yes, dear. Just watching the neighbourhood children in the street.'

He hands me a cup of tea carefully, gently, as if at any second, it will slosh over the cup and onto the ground, sending me over the edge. The edge has been painfully close, as we all know.

It's been a complicated couple of months. I think back to that day in September sometimes, the day I called Phyllis to tell her all was well only to find out it was far from it.

How do you process that? How do you handle the fact that your choices led to the death of those you loved? How do you even begin?

I didn't. I crumpled under the weight of it, to the point that there was no choice but for Charles to seek help. I spent time in hospital, under careful watch.

But they didn't know. How could they know? Because even now, with all that's happened, I haven't been honest. The secret start of all of this – the abortion – remains a dark secret in my heart, looming just below the surface. Killing my baby led me down this path, and no matter what anyone tells me, I know the reality of it – it's my fault. I made the choice. I left West Green. If I hadn't left, my parents wouldn't have died. They would've been moved out of the house. Or I could've woken them up if I had been there. It's my fault. They spent their last days, their last moments, searching, worrying about the selfish girl they once called a daughter. They spent their last moments wondering, questioning, seeking answers. I did that to them. How could I do that?

I take a deep breath, Charles' hand on my shoulder as

I try to let the dark thoughts fade away like my doctors have told me. But it's no use. There's no getting over this. And there's still so much guilt swirling – like how I missed the funeral service.

I was in hospital when I should've gone home.

The police did track us down thanks to Phyllis. She sent them our way. Charles handled most of the questioning, as I wasn't in a good state to deal with it. Questions were answered, and we were cleared of any wrongdoing. From what I've heard, Oliver, too was eventually cleared – but not without damages to his reputation, to his life, and to any hope of a normal future. Rumours are endless about his role in the murders of the summer, in the death of my parents. What will become of him now? My head throbs. Despite all he's done, I can't help but feel like he, too, is a victim of circumstance and of my choices.

Or is he truly the victim? Around and around, the questions whir.

It was an accident, the police have told us. A freak accident in the midst of a terrible summer. I don't know if I believe that. I don't know what to believe anymore.

There were more questions, too, last week. The killings in West Green have stopped since we've left. Which is a blessing – but also strange. And it led to suspicion around Charles. It seems, in many ways, that West Green won't stop haunting us. We can't escape its grasp. Sometimes I wonder if we ever will.

But still, we haven't been back. I feel like a bad daughter, like I should pay my respects and see things through. I owe them that much. But I just can't bring myself to go back. A part of me thinks it's because of everything bad that happened there. The honest part of me, though, knows it's something else.

Oliver.

Our secret.

The fact I don't want Charles to know the truth about what I've done.

It is a secret, I realise, I must take to the grave. It pains me to lie to him. But I can't risk pushing him away now. What would he think of me? I don't know. I can't take the risk.

'Addy, we need to talk.' The words I don't want to hear from Charles. The words that mean something heavy is coming. Nothing surprises me anymore, though.

I make a noncommittal noise, urging him to continue, as I raise the cup to my lips and continue to stare out into the grey day.

'Things have been hard, Addy. Really hard. I know that what happened in West Green, well, it's something that's never going away. I know you'll carry that pain with you forever. But I think we need to move forward. We need to start our new life here, start looking to the future. The doctors said it would do you good to plan, to start over. I want to do that. So if you need to talk about what happened and West Green and the whole lot, I'll listen. But otherwise,

I think we should diligently focus on us, on the future. Let's put it all behind us, as much as we can. Let's attempt to find a life together, a happy life, and see if we can't find some new sense of joy. I know it's going to take time. I do. And I'll be here for you the whole way. But Addy, I don't want to lose you. I want you to find joy again. I want that more than anything.' He squeezes my shoulder, and I look up at him.

I look into Charles' soft, reassuring eyes. Such a good man. Nothing like Oliver. Nothing like me. A genuine, good person. Do I deserve him?

I don't. But right now, looking up at him, I know I need him. I so selfishly need him. And I need exactly what he's just said – a new start. I look back out the window, putting a hand on his that's still on my shoulder. I take a breath and nod.

'Let's put the past behind us,' I say shakily, trying to mean it.

He's right. I need to try to move on. What happened in West Green may always be a part of me – but maybe there's hope. With Charles, maybe I can move on. Maybe someday I can heal, forgive. We look out into the rainy day, and for the first time in months, I see something I didn't think possible.

A tiny ray of hope.

Chapter 39

Smith Creek Manor Nursing Home
2019

I stare at the ceiling, my brain trained on the past. Perhaps it's the conversation with Oliver, or maybe it's just that it feels like my whole life is a circling, whirling cacophony of chaos and disaster. I pick at the edge of my pillowcase, thinking about flashes and memories and moments. I think about those hellish months after the horrific news, tears welling as I silently whisper the millionth apology to the parents who have been dead for years.

Even after the day I told myself I'd found hope, that Charles and I could be happy, things weren't easy. The guilt racked me for months, threatening to derail my progress.

If I'd just told the truth about it all. If I'd have just been honest, maybe things would've been different. Maybe I wouldn't have been so desperate to flee West Green. Maybe if I hadn't left when I did, they'd still be alive. The baby, my parents – I'd had a hand in the loss of so many.

In some ways, I wonder if this is all some form of twisted karma for the choice I'd made. I'd spent so many Sundays in our church hearing about how abortion was a sin – but I hadn't believed it. Had this been the universe's way of getting retribution? I don't know anymore. Life is complicated, and it's more complex than my nineteen-year-old self could ever have processed. Life went a very different way than I thought it would that summer. I had no idea that I would have to live with three deaths on my conscience forever. But even now, life is still a mess. Guilt still racks me. There's truly no expiration date on guilt, on revenge, and on how the past can hurt us.

Why had I come back here? I'd known it was a mistake all along. *Charles, why did you make us come back? Why?*

I shake my head. It's all felt like a twisted game, and I'm just a pawn. When will I regain control of my own life? Have I ever had it? My head spins with questions, with guilt, with memories.

I turn in my bed, trying to settle my wayward mind. I listen to the muted moans from Floor Three. The footsteps in the corridor I've come to expect echo down the corridor. But mixed with Philip Lady's snoring, I hear something distinct that I haven't heard before. What's clicking? Is something clicking?

Click. Click. Click, click, click.

Two soft clicks, then three fast and hard.

I blink open my eyes, my brain groggy and my eyes

blurry. I glance around without moving my head, trying to pinpoint the noise. Nothing seems out of the ordinary. There are raindrops tinkling against the glass of the window, but it's not the click I hear. I reach up and rub my forehead, my fingers smoothing over the hard, dry lines.

Click, click, click.

It's coming from behind me I realise as a sinking feeling usurps my ability to reason. My palms begin to sweat as I carefully roll over in bed, praying there will be nothing behind me. For once, I'm crossing my fingers that it's just my own mind playing tricks. But when I roll over, holding my breath, my eyes land on the cold, hard truth.

It's him, standing over me, stooped and deranged. Even in the blackness of the room, I can see the familiar glow in his eyes as he towers over me. I sit up, trying to scurry away from him in bed, my feet tangling in the sheets. He doesn't move, though, just standing over me, his eyes studying me intently.

Click, click, click.

He clicks his teeth slowly, steadfastly, his lips held at an angle that allows me to see them. It stirs my innermost fear and chills me. I feel about for the call button, but it isn't where it usually is. He creeps forward.

'Don't take another step,' I command in a hushed voice. 'One more step and I scream.'

He chitters faster, his teeth still clicking, but he doesn't move.

'I'm serious. Don't,' I demand a bit louder. Philip Lady

stirs. Maybe I should scream. Maybe I should let them all see what I've seen.

He chatters faster and faster, coming at me now like a rabid animal. What's wrong with him? For a moment, I'm stunned by the oddness of his behaviour, by his blazing eyes. He keeps lurking, keeps coming closer, his movement unpredictable and jarring. I tremble, and he stops centimetres from my face.

'If you scream, I'll kill you,' he murmurs, his eyes lasering into my face. My stomach drops at his words, an affirmation of the evil in his intent. But just as I'm contemplating searching for the call button once more, he's gone, turning on his heel and leaving.

The room is quiet, the man from 300 gone. I shake my head. What is this madness? What is this game? In some ways, I wish he'd just carry out whatever he's planning already. I wish I could just be done with this all. I must work it out. This uncertainty is driving my mind to a place I'd rather not go. Every waking moment is torture as my mind dances around the questions, the facts, and the fear of what's coming next. He's trapped me in a living hell.

I peel myself from the bed, unwrapping the blanket from around my feet. I wander into the loo, quietly clicking the door shut and turning on the light. I glance into the mirror, the bags under my eyes more pronounced than usual, my skin ghastly pale. I'm a walking corpse, unearthed from an untimely grave. I'm a bag of bones waiting to be returned to ash.

Who have I become? The woman who came to Smith Creek Manor isn't the same woman I am now. I am tired. I am worn. I am defeated. I pull on my hair, tears falling as I swallow hard. I want to go home. I want to escape. I want Charles to be here, to make it all better. Most of all, I want to know – why does the man in 300 want to kill me? I saunter to my chair, sitting up all night. I don't sleep. I just rock, back and forth, thinking about everything as I stare at the man in 300, who stares back.

Why does he look so familiar? Why does something in the recesses of my mind scream every time he comes near that I know him, that I've known him all along?

But if Smith Creek Manor's taught me anything, it's that you can never know for sure what's right around the corner.

Chapter 40

My eyes pop open at the sound of a crashing down the corridor. My heart races as I glance around the room. The Philip Lady's already gone, presumably to breakfast. The sunlight streams in through the window, but the warming rays do nothing to jostle my soul.

I look over to the noticeboard, weary and anxious. I prop myself up on my elbows, willing myself not to cry. In the middle of the noticeboard on an unassuming piece of white paper, a message is scrawled. The letters are so big and bold, I can read them from my position in bed.

It's time.

Two words that incite so much terror. To an outsider, they wouldn't seem like much. To me, they say everything. They're the message I've been avoiding in my time here at Smith Creek. They're the words I've been racing against. But now, they're the words I just don't know if I can fight anymore. For the first time, I'm certain of my mind's analysis of the situation. I know I'm not crazy or imagining it. A calming yet petrifying sense of clarity settles over my typically foggy mind.

This. Is. Real. It's all real, and now it's come to this.

It's all real.

A lonely tear cascades down my rough, weathered cheek. I bat it away with my aching fingers, my eyes still studying the words scribbled in red. My head spins, and I feel woozy. I consider my options but know that it's useless. I have no options. I am imprisoned, just like I've always been.

I drag myself from bed, the whole exercise feeling pointless but also necessary. I force myself to go through the morning routine, to trudge to breakfast, to get out of the room and away from the reality slapping me in the face.

I sit alone as I so often do these days, the empty table a reminder of all that's changed. No one seems to notice. In a place surrounded by death and demise, empty chairs cause no stir. A few tables over, Father Patrick loudly proclaims Bible verses, but everyone ignores him. I turn away, not wanting to think about any of it. I chew on the toast in front of me without really tasting it and wash it back with the weak tea my taste buds have adapted to.

The thought of the foreboding note tacked on the noticeboard doesn't encourage me to return to my room quickly. Thus, after breakfast is cleared, I decide to rest in the community room for a bit. I sit alone there as well, always alone now. It feels like a lifetime ago when I first came up that rickety lift, sat with Dorothy. I'm just so tired now. *Charles, I'm so tired now.* And I'm afraid. I'm so afraid.

Still, I know I must stay strong. I can't go out without knowing what this whole mess is all about. I owe it to those women to figure it out. I owe it to myself. Strumming up the fortitude to chase after this nightmare is getting harder and harder, though. I'm not ready for the battle that is certainly coming soon.

After a while, the frenzied game-show music pounds into my skull in a way that threatens to drive me bonkers. I'm not ready to go back to 316, to face the harrowing truth. I decide to wander into the community loo off the main room, to splash some water on my face. It seems like the only thing I can do.

I'm standing at the basin washing my hands, leaning on the porcelain as I stare into the mirror. I'm stretching the skin on my face, feeling the paltry, sagging cheeks when the door to the loo opens.

And then, before I can do a thing, I'm pinned against the tiled wall, my back aching at the angle. She is impressively strong when she wants to be, and I flail and fight to get away, my feet losing traction on the shiny tile as my heart pounds wildly.

She comes at me, the three shiny prongs stabbing towards me with a ferocity that makes me cry out. My arms shake with tension as I try to shove her away, to escape the merciless chamber – but I can't get past her. The fork darts at me, clinking against my cheek, poking into my sagging skin. I feel the sickly burn of blood oozing from my flesh, and I wonder if this is where I die – with no answers.

Chapter 41

'The red rain's coming for you. He told me. You're the reason he's here. He told me,' she screams and squeals, stabbing at my eye with the fork. I fight Babbling Barbara off for what seems like an eternity. I slap at her and shove at her, my arms trembling with the effort as I also try to shield my face.

She claws at me ferociously like a dog in heat, the prongs of the fork piercing into me. It chases after my eye, darting towards it with every thrust of Barbara's hand. Her eyes glossed over and crusty, she works purely out of passion. Her free hand feels my face as if she's aiming for the target. I scream and shriek, praying for help to come. I huff in air, my lungs starving for it as I gasp in between sobs. My muscles ache, straining to keep her back, to protect myself from the bludgeoning, bloody battle of the fork that threatens to pierce through my eye.

The door opens again, heavy footsteps pounding the

floor. A yell ricochets off the tiled walls as Barbara is pulled back, snarling and shrieking repeatedly.

'You're the reason. You're the *reason*,' she wails. I clutch at my aching chest, cringing. The edges of my vision blur as an arm lifts me up, the fork clattering to the floor like an abandoned treasure.

'You're the reason,' she screams as they drag her from the bathroom and a nurse helps lift me from the ground, asking if I'm all right.

I'm not all right. How could I be? My head feels fuzzy as the nurse calls for more help, as my legs first tense up and then lose their strength. I slip down, down, the arms of the nurse trying desperately to hold me up but failing.

And then all is dark, Barbara's shrieks about the red rain and the man in 300 going silent as I think about Charles, his soft face blurring the frightening edges of reality in my mind.

Chapter 42

I sit on my bed, my feet planted on the ground as I stare out into the courtyard. Evening settles in, and the note from earlier settles in too.

It's time.

I'm not ready to give in, to give up. However, I've learned in these past weeks that you can never truly know what terrors await you. It's better, perhaps, to be prepared. With that thought, I reach for the phone, my shaking hands dialling the familiar digits. I listen to the ringing, turning around to glance at the doorway as I wait to hear the soft voice.

She doesn't answer. I get the voicemail and think about hanging up. Maybe I can ring her tomorrow. But I don't want to risk that. I fiddle with my hands, unsure of how to proceed but knowing what needs to be said.

'Claire, it's me. Mum. I just ... I'm all right. I don't want you to worry. I was just sitting here thinking about some things, and I, well, I want you to know this. You were my miracle, Claire. You were the baby your father and I didn't think we could have. You were the life I always wanted, and being your mother, watching you grow – it was the greatest gift of my life. So much happened, and there were so many mistakes I made. But raising you, watching you chase your own dreams, that was the greatest accomplishment of my life. I will always, always love you. I want you to go out there and live life with no regrets, to chase whatever makes you happy. Live this life now, Claire, because it goes fast. Goodness, it goes so fast. I love you forever. I love you so much. Goodbye, Claire. I just wanted to say goodbye.'

When I click the phone down, I choke back sobs that burn in my throat. Won't do to wallow too much in the sadness now. It won't do any good at all. I've said what I needed to say.

I've told her what was most important – she was my miracle. I got a second chance with Claire. I got the opportunity to do one thing right. Not everyone gets that kind of opportunity.

Saying goodbye to her is perhaps the hardest part of all this. I just hope that if there is any sense of mercy in this world, any sense of justice, she won't know how I suffered. She will not contemplate the true terror of these final days. At this point, that's the best I can hope for.

I slide backwards in bed, sitting fully clothed on top of the quilt as I stare at the words on the noticeboard once more. It's not fair. None of this is fair.

But then again, nothing in life is. Not everything works out, and karma doesn't even the score. Not every villain pays his dues, after all, and not every hero gets to save the day.

Chapter 43

It's dark out when my eyes flutter open. I'm on my side, facing the window, and my head spins. What am I doing? I don't remember crawling into bed. What time is it? And is he – an arm pulls me in, tighter and tighter, a strong body nestled against me. I lean into him, his warm breath tickling my neck. I close my eyes again. Charles. He's here. It's all going to be okay. I lean back into him, his lips kissing my neck, the blanket pulled around both of us. It's been so long since he's held me like this, and my heart swells with the feeling of his strong arms squeezing me tightly. I can't move, but I don't want to. I could stay like this forever, I realise, breathing a sigh of relief for the first time in months.

'Move, and I'll kill you,' Charles' voice whispers into my ear.

Why would he say that? What's happened to Charles? I'm scared. *Charles, why are you doing this? It hurts.*

But it isn't Charles' voice, I realise with a shudder as awareness peaks. Terror grips my stomach, my heart, my mind. It isn't Charles at all. Suddenly, I want to crawl out of my skin, to slither out of the grasp of the arms that suffocate me.

I cringe, the sharp point of something scratching my neck. He moves the sharp object to the front of my throat. I feel it press against me, and I picture the delicate skin on my throat slicing open, my blood spilling out.

The sharp object in place, he kisses my neck again. 'Oh, how I've missed you,' he murmurs, sniffing my hair, my neck. I stare out the window, tears slowly floating. And then a sharp pain on the back of my neck, teeth pressing against it. I whimper, but the sharp object digs into the front of my throat, reminding me to hold it all in.

'It's been so long. Too long. I'd given up, Adeline. I'd thought this would never happen. But here we are, and oh, is it delicious. It's madly delicious. The wait has only made you better.' His words echo in my head, bouncing around. I want to scream. I want to cry out for help.

I want him to be finished with it all. But I also want so desperately to know why.

'Don't worry, darling. All will be taken care of. You'll get what you need. After all, I've got to finish my job right, you know? I'm not sloppy. No, not me. I'm careful. Cunning. Brilliant, actually. How do you think I got away with it all these years? You don't get away with it all if you're sloppy. That's why I took my time. I had to make this just right. And now, here we are, darling. It's finally your time.'

I shake now, my body trembling, the jerking of my body causing the sharp object to dig in. I think about the searing pain it will cause biting into my flesh. I can almost imagine the burning sensation as my blood boils out, as life exits with a final exhale. Will Charles be waiting for me? Will I land in his arms? Or will this maniac cling to my body and soul, holding me back from whatever waits for me?

'Why?' I croak out, needing answers and willing to risk a sliced throat to get them.

'You know why,' he spews through clenched teeth. 'You're the one who got away. But let's not get ahead of ourselves. I have something of yours. See it? Right there? It's your final one. I've kept it all this time.'

Confusion whirls, as my eyes land on the letter on the bedside table. I see the script, my name in bold letters on the front. Adeline Walker. In my right ear, then, he begins to whistle. The tune from long ago. The tune from decades ago, when life was so different.

And suddenly, it all clicks, my mind wrapping around the right moments, the right images, the right sensations.

'You,' I murmur, tears flowing freely as I realise my imminent doom is here.

10 years after West Green Killer, Still No answers

18 August 1969

West Green, Crawley, West Sussex

Ten years after the West Green Killer went silent, investigators are no closer to answers than they were when the murders began.

The 'summer of slaughter', as it is now dubbed, began on 12 June 1959 when Elizabeth McKinley's body was discovered in the Crawley Community Hospital skip, dismembered and covered in bite marks. McKinley had been missing for several days.

In the following summer months, five more female bodies would turn up, many of which were dismembered and showed signs of corpse abuse. These victims were: Helen Deeley, Doreen Thompson, Caroline Young, Gloria Carlton and Muriel Claubaugh. All women were residents of West Green and lived in close proximity to each other.

After the brutal death of Muriel Claubaugh, however, the neighbourhood of West Green returned to seemingly normal. No more women turned up missing, and no more murders happened in the neighbourhood that appeared to be related to the work of the mass killer. Investigators continued to search for a suspect and a motive, but none were uncovered.

'We haven't abandoned the case. We won't rest until we find justice for the six women,' the chief constable told reporters last Friday. 'Anyone with information is asked to come forward. It's not too late to bring justice for these families.'

'It's despicable, if you ask me,' a West Green resident who wished to remain anonymous, told reporters. 'After all this time, the detectives can't find anything? What have they been doing all these years? You're telling me a killer can murder six women, and no one can find any clues? It really makes me lose faith in our system.'

'Sometimes, bad people get away with horrible crimes. It's not a fact we like to face,' a constable said of the case. 'It's not something I'm happy about, and it doesn't happen often. But occasionally, a criminal gets lucky or is very, very smart. The person we're dealing with here knew how to cover his or her tracks and did it well. They had intimate knowledge of the families he or she preyed on and used it wisely to go undetected. Over the years of studying this case, I've come to believe the suspect was someone close to each family in some way – he or she would've known their schedules, known intimate details of their lives. Otherwise, how would he or she have pulled it off so perfectly?'

Detectives have worked over the years to piece together a profile of the suspected criminal. Detectives believe the suspect is a male between the ages of 20 and 35 who perhaps hails from Crawley or a surrounding area. Police have also gathered that the suspect has some connection to the train station due to Muriel's body. It is believed the suspect has a history of stalking or potentially abuse of women, due to the violent nature of the crimes. It is believed that the killer had preselected his victims, but no further connections between them have been drawn other than their locations.

While the fear of the West Green Killer has faded in Crawley, detectives are still desperate to solve the case. Some residents still hold out hope that he or she will be caught, citing John Haigh as an example. After all, the similarities are haunting – both killers claimed six definite victims. Regardless, residents are sure to remember the terror of the summer of 1959 for years if not decades to come – whether the killer is ever caught or not.

The filthy, ignorant son-of-a-bitch. Comparing me to John Haigh? John bloody Haigh?

That fool had been caught.

I haven't.

There's no comparison.

But I also haven't finished. I haven't had Adeline Walker. She would've completed the collection. Instead, her unopened letter sits in the box, taunting me.

This isn't the newspaper article I wanted to stow away with it. It should have read completely different. I should've finished the job. I should've finished her.

But she got away.

When the fire happened weeks after her disappearance, I'd been so excited. A stroke of good luck! Karma at work! Or perhaps that other crazy bloke in town. It didn't matter how it started, in truth. She would be back. She'd have to come back.

And I'd get my chance.

I waited. Day after day. Week after week. I waited and

watched, my letter opener at the ready. I would have her. I'd have my chance to finish her.

But she never came. She never bloody came. What sort of despicable daughter didn't return after her parents' death? What kind of person didn't attend the funeral service for their own parents? What kind of person was she?

A bloody reprehensible one. Sometimes, in those early months, I hated her. I was livid. I wanted nothing more than to make her pay. Mostly, though, I was livid that I'd been a fool. If only I'd have taken her when I had the chance.

Stupid boy. Poor boy. Disgusting boy.

I've tried to come to terms with it, but the hunger hasn't ceased. No other flesh will do. It was her. It will always be her. She was always supposed to be the finale. Out of all the gorgeous women on my route, she'd been the one who excited me most. But instead of an article about the awe-inspiring death I'd have given her, I am left with this rubbish – an article commemorating the failure of it all.

I was and always will be a failure.

Stupid boy. Foolish boy. Failure of a man.

And it is all her fault. It is her *fault.*

Chapter 44

Smith Creek Manor Nursing Home
2019

I've heard that tune before. He used to whistle it when he'd hand us the post, his notes always slightly off-key. I think back to all those moments he dropped off the letters, his cap perched perfectly on his head, his eyes dancing up and down my body. He was the harmless postman, a quiet but efficient man only a few years older than me. He was the odd boy who grew up to be a quiet man, the one we sometimes whispered about. We'd heard the stories about his flat, about his mother, about everything. But we never paid attention. Why would we? He was the one we so often overlooked. He was the perfect criminal, it seems now.

I remember that day when the final letter came, the terrifying message from Oliver that made me escape – I remember him whistling the tune. It all comes whirling about, the greatest mystery of my life and of the past few weeks ending.

The letter 'P' in the letters, the postman's signature – P for postman. The song. The words he whispered to me in his room that day with Dorothy, the words that made me faint.

'*You're the one*,' he'd murmured nonchalantly to me. '*You're the one who got away. I killed your friend because she found out too much.*'

Had Dorothy seen the letter of mine? Had she pieced together that he was dangerous? What had she seen? What had she figured out?

It doesn't matter now. It's too late. The object stabbing into my throat, the final letter on the table. It all has come together.

The West Green Killer. The postman was the West Green Killer all along.

And I was, apparently, his final victim. I was the one who got away. I'm the reason he stopped his spree in West Green. My mother was right – it wasn't safe. I got away from him. I was the next on his list, I must've been – and by some twist of fate, by the universe, or by karma for a sin I haven't yet repented, he caught up to me. I was delivered to him, meat on a platter, by the daughter I let live. I'm the finale in his twisted, murderous game.

'I dreamt of this for so long. For so, so long. All those days, I'd drop those letters in, wondering when it would be my chance. Wondering when I'd get to crawl through that door, up those steps and to your room. I thought about it over and over how I'd do it. You were going to be my grand finale, you know. I had such big plans for you. You were going to be a magnificent display, the truly perfect end. I was so hungry for it, starving to see your lifeless body. I was laced with joy over the mere thought of what that close-minded, backwards town would think. They would know my power, my glory, my intelligence. It was brilliant, really.'

I squeeze my eyes shut, praying for an end to this suffering. I have the answers now, but I realise they aren't what I really wanted. This isn't where I thought my life would go. This isn't what I imagined all these terrors would lead to.

'But then, the plan was foiled all too soon when you escaped. Why did you leave me? Why did you have to do it? Why couldn't you have waited? It would have been so much better then. I had so many grand plans. But then you were gone. You left. You ruined it all, Adeline. You fucking ruined it.' The object cuts into my flesh, and I feel the stickiness of a dribble of blood. My breathing increases, but every breath aches now. Tears mix with my blood, my head resting on the pillow. I hate that I'm in his arms right now. I hate the intimacy of it all.

'I spent my life wondering if it would ever be all right again. I chased those dreams, but it wasn't the same. It wasn't you. You were the missing piece to my achievement. You were the one. No one else would do. I tried. I really did try. But whenever I tried to kill again, I couldn't go through with it. I knew they would just leave me hungry for more because they weren't you. It had to be you. Dammit, why did it have to be you?'

'Please,' I beg, but he just chuckles. I feel him kiss the back of my neck, and I tremble. This can't be how it ends. This can't be the answer to the mystery I've been searching for.

My mind thinks of all those other women. I think about all those women from so long ago. Is this how they felt in those final moments? Are these the words he spoke to them? What raced through their minds at the end – and how much did they suffer? I shake at the thought. I shake at the realisation that he was right under our noses the whole time – the unsuspected, unassuming postman, who had so much access to our lives. Who had so many ways to get close to us.

What would the finale have looked like? Each murder was bolder than the last, each display of the body more brazen. What would he have done to me? If we hadn't left when we did, what would've happened? What end would I have faced?

'I came to Smith Creek years ago, thinking I would die a failure. I hadn't succeeded. I had lost. You were off my route. You were gone. I hadn't got you in time,' he continues, bringing me back to the reality at hand. I've escaped him for so many years, but there's no escaping now. There's no escaping the end. Barbara was right. I'll die here.

'Did ... you ... t-try to find me?' I choke out, wheezing out the words.

'You left me,' he spews, gripping me tighter. 'No one knew where you went. Your parents didn't know. The police didn't know. And when the fire happened, you didn't come back. Why didn't you come back? It doesn't matter, though. Even if I could've found you, it didn't matter. I needed you here, in West Green, just like it was supposed to be. You were the most beautiful in West Green. I wanted you from the time you moved into that house. I knew you would be in the plan even before I knew what the plan was. But after you left, something about it wasn't right. I wanted you here, on my route, like it was meant to be. It wouldn't have counted anywhere else. I needed to beat his record here, fair and square.'

'Whose?' I ask, confused and terrified. Who is he talking about?

'John, of course. He had six. Six confirmed, anyways. I needed seven. Everyone lauds him as the most notorious killer here. Are you kidding me? He had six. The fucking fool. And he got caught. He didn't have a plan like I did. I had a brilliant plan.'

My mind chases the name John, but I can't remember. What is he talking about? This really is all a game to him, I understand now. A sick, twisted game of wits. And I'm the final checkmate.

'The universe delivered you to me like a dream. It was a dream, Adeline. I thought it was a fever dream at first. It was too perfect. You, wrapped up like a damn gift. Coming back here, on my floor. On my route, nevertheless.

You were back on my route. I could die achieving my goal.'

My heart beats wildly, and I try to clutch at my chest, but he squeezes me so tight, I can't move. I'm at his mercy, and I don't think he has any left to give.

'It's not the same of course. It's not as beautiful. It's not as magical. I'm too frail now, and you're not as wily of a fight. But it still counts. I still get to strip that life out of you, watch your embers burn out. I still get the seventh. The one who got away has come back. I get to slither your life out of you, snuff it out. I win, Adeline. I'm the winner now.' I can feel his lips curve up into a wicked smile. I look out the window into the courtyard, the rain pattering against it. Fitting that it's raining. Fitting that it all ends here, in this room with a view. Because it will be the last view I'll see. I won't go out saying goodbye to the sweet, chubby faces of grandchildren. I don't get to lay my eyes on my daughter one last time or go out peacefully clutching a picture of Charles.

I will go out in bed with a serial killer, with the maniacal man who has lusted after my death for decades. I will die cold and suffering in my own bed, the terrors of my past skulking close by. There is no time to repent or to beg forgiveness. There is no peace of mind.

'Get up,' he orders. For a split second, I think maybe this is all going to end differently. He's changed his mind. There's still a glimmer of hope.

With a swift move, he yanks me backwards and pulls me to my feet. His arms are still wrapped around me as I shuffle and struggle, trying to gain my balance and my bearings.

'Scream and I'll slit your throat, splatter your blood all about.'

I inhale deeply, my eyes adjusted to the darkness. The sharp object stabs harder into my throat. I think about screaming, about taking my chances. I wonder if I can make enough noise to wake the Philip Woman. She snores in her bed, unaware of the peril prowling nearby.

He drags me backwards, the sharp object to my neck. Where is he taking me? Fear settles into my chest, and my heart races. I pray for relief from this. I pray that he comes to his senses – although there are clearly few senses there.

Backwards, backwards, he drags me, his breathing on my neck causing me to shudder. The corridor is empty, and his movements are swift. When we stop at the stairwell, I sigh in relief. He's trapped. He's made a mistake. I will be—

But then, he leans over and punches in the code. I hear the four buttons beep, echoing down the corridor yet drowned out by the groans and moans characteristic of the floor. Where is the nurse? Where is Jones? Please, anyone—

The door shoves open, and I stand, hovering above the steps in the stairwell I wanted to see all along. How did he get the code?

'Sometimes, Adeline, it's all about being observant. I was always observant. It's paid off so many times. People aren't observant anymore. People are helpless, caught up in what they mistakenly think is important. I see what's important.'

The sharp object still stabbing into my throat, I stare at the steps, wondering if the banging, if all those noises in the stairwell were a coincidence or something much more sinister. I wish I'd been more observant, more dedicated to figuring it out. Why couldn't I figure it out?

'This isn't what I planned for you,' he whispers. 'But it'll have to do.' He trudges towards the top of the stairs, and I think about crying out. But who will hear me? There is no one to hear me. There is no one to save me.

There is just sharp pain and the horrors of knowing he'll hold me close as I say goodbye to this world. I think about Charles, tears falling, as the postman creeps me towards the top of the stairs. The steps loom below me, a deadly long fall to the next floor making my achy, weary bones shake. It's all over now. This is where it ends. And there will be no one to tell my story, to tell them how the one who got away didn't. There will be no one to tell them all that I'm not crazy. I will die a lonely, old, batty woman, forgotten by many. Remembered by Claire, but not as I should be. He will win. In the end, don't they always? Don't the mad or the evil always win? They like to tell us otherwise, but here we are. Sometimes, there really is no escaping the horrors we're destined for.

'Goodnight, Adeline, dear. Goodnight, sweet girl. I told you that you would be mine, after all,' he whispers.

I open my mouth to plead with him, to implore him to

think again. I'm so tired, but life is always worth fighting for. No one willingly fades into that darkness. I struggle against his arms, managing to turn slightly. I claw at his arms, no longer worried about the sharp object at my throat.

I want to live. The need to survive is stronger than the grip of his arm. I claw and kick, screaming and flailing about with every bit of strength I have in me. But it's not substantial enough, and he's too strong. I am a dying carcass in the jaws of a predator.

My clawing and pawing at him does nothing but expedite his plans. With an unmatchable strength, he shoves me down the steps, and I have no time to react. I roll, my head burning as it clunks on the steps, as I tumble, as the scorching, searing pain silences me. I feel the shattering of my body, and the air I claw for does not come. He whistles from up above as everything blurs, as the pain becomes too much, as the reality sinks in. I'm dying here, in Smith Creek Manor, in the sight of the postman, under the wrath and careful plotting of the man on Floor Three, the West Green Killer.

When the blackness swallows me and my lungs drown in the thirst for oxygen, my last thoughts aren't of Claire or Charles or the life I've lived. My last thoughts are the stark realisation that all the questions, the torture, and the events of the last months were all for naught. Evil trumps all in the real world, even if we don't realise it.

Evil always wins.

Death of Resident at Smith Creek Manor Under Investigation
West Green, Crawley, West Sussex
9 July 2019

The death of Mrs Adeline (Walker) Evans, 79, at Smith Creek Manor in Crawley, West Sussex, has been labelled as questionable by investigators. Mrs Evans' death has incited an investigation into the nursing home's alleged abuse and neglect of its patients and has stirred protests from family members and the public, underlining concerns with care facilities across the nation.

On 1 July 2019, the body of Mrs Adeline Evans was discovered in the stairwell near her room, 316, in the Smith Creek Manor Nursing Home at approximately 5.02 a.m. The coroner declared the cause of death to be a deadly fall. However, injuries on the neck of the victim and several bite marks were also noted, leading to suspicions about her death. The time of death is approximated to be around 2.02 a.m.

A nurse who works on the second floor discovered the body. Staff members are labelling the death as a terrible accident. However, investigators question how the resident obtained the code for the locked stairwell and why the victim's neck revealed cuts and bite marks.

The roommate of the deceased was described to have been in hysterics and removed from the home. Her current whereabouts are unknown.

Mrs Adeline Evans, born 17 May 1940, is survived by a daughter, Claire Evans. Claire is working with investigators to determine the cause of death and potential perpetrator of this suspected crime.

The death of Mrs Evans has led many to question the ethical treatment of residents in the particular home but also across the nation and has prompted investigations into other deaths labelled natural at Smith Creek Manor. The deaths of several other patients are now being examined as some discrepancies in records and reports have been uncovered. Investigators are determining potential suspects as well as questioning the staff's potential negligence, considering Mrs Evans was deceased for several hours before her body was discovered.

Many family members have removed their relatives from the home after Mrs Evans' death, citing gross negligence on behalf of the nursing staff.

'It's an outrage that a patient died in the establishment in that manner. I don't care what they say. She was murdered. We entrust them with the lives of our loved ones, yet gross injustices and violent crimes are happening there. Someone has to be held responsible,' a resident's son told reporters last week.

Evidence is still being gathered, but no eyewitnesses have been named. Reports indicate that cameras in the nursing home facility are not available due to technical difficulties, leaving surveillance of the corridor out of the possible sources of evidence. It has been discovered that several other policies are consistently ignored regarding care of the elderly at the facility.

Epilogue

I trudge down the hallway, passing Father Patrick from 310 on my way back to my room. He holds open a Bible, flipping through and repeating verses from the Book of Revelation, giving me a slight nod as he ambles towards 316, which is still cordoned off. Something tells me, though, that the priest will find a way around it. There really is no stopping him when he sets his mind to something, after all. He needs to spread the good word, and he won't let a little tape get in the way.

Which Bible verse will Father Patrick pick for Adeline? I wonder if he'll use one of the ones he used for the others, or if he'll pick a new one. I shake my head as I plod along. I used to get angry when Father Patrick wandered into Adeline's room. I felt like the man was prying on my business, was claiming what belonged to me. But Father Patrick was harmless enough, leaving a few verses here and there. Coupled with that Oliver bloke's senseless tampering, it had all worked quite well. I still hate that bastard, hate what he stands for. Still, Oliver's manipulative, transparent ways paid off. All of them worked almost like a perfect ballet, concocting clues in an elegant dance that led Adeline's suspicions away from me. They led Adeline astray, and that made the game last longer. I'm thankful for that.

Which verse would be befitting of a magnificent beauty like her, of my number seven? It's a hard question. I'm glad I don't have to decide. After all, she's always been my favourite, the wild one with gorgeous features. She had some kick to her, always, even in her older age. That was why I'd originally saved her for last. She was going to be the challenge, and I was crafty enough for a test like this one. The last one, after all, had to be splendid in every way. It would be the finale. It had to be perfect.

I smirk, clicking my teeth as I march into my room. I need a rest. There's been so much excitement this past week. The fools are pathetic. They're so oblivious. It saddens me sometimes to think how moronic they all are. Some things don't change, even with technology and time.

After parking myself on the edge of my bed, I sigh in relief. It is done. The raving lunatics of the place made it easy. There were so many to blame. There were so many distractions. From Babbling Barbara to Oliver, it had been so simple to fly under the radar. It had been easy to torture her without getting caught. Add to the whole scenario Jones and his volatile personality, the staff's incompetent nature, and Adeline's declining mental state, and I had the perfect recipe for my game. Smith Creek Manor is a microcosm of insanity, which made it effortless to toy with my prey. The blood on the wall, the daisy, the mice, the notes. All those nights watching – they had all been relatively simple to pull off thanks to all the other chaos. I'd almost gotten angry at her for taking so long to figure it out. But I'm patient, so I simply waited and watched.

There were so many oversights on her part. It had been child's play, really. People generally aren't smart. They aren't observant. I would feel bad if it didn't feel so good. I, after all, am brilliant. I was always smart. Smart boy, the teachers had told me. Smart, smart boy.

But oh, to see that life snuff out of her, to watch whatever was left of Adeline Evans' soul leave her body – wow, had it been satisfying. Satisfying indeed. I'm not hungry for the first time in decades. I am finally content.

Of course, it had almost been foiled by one person. That blasted friend of hers, Dorothy, who had caught me emerging from the stairwell that night and who had clearly snooped in my room. Had she seen the box? Had she seen the letters? I couldn't risk it all. I couldn't let the game get ruined again. How had I been so careless? Still, I'd known she'd have to pay. I'd been patient with her, too, had been careful. I'd waited until the exact moment to strike. After all, I know a thing or two about getting away with murder – and I wasn't about to let some moronic, ugly woman with a big mouth get in the way of my master plan. I'd waited too long. So I took care of it – even that had been so easy for me. I hadn't lost my touch, even after all those years. Even after I'd been discounted as nothing but a loner on Floor Three. They had no idea. They still don't. But once I flexed my killing muscles on Dorothy, I realised I was still brilliant. I was still more than capable. It had given me hope, the hope I needed to finish the task.

'They're all dead. They're all dead now,' I mutter, rocking back and forth, back and forth. I shake my head, beaming in disbelief. They are all *dead*. All dead, indeed! I never thought I could accomplish it, but dreams could come true. Dreams could finally come true if you were cunning and persevering. And, I admit, if you have some strokes of good fortune.

I stretch my legs out, leaning back and staring at the ceiling, wondering if they'll figure it out. Will they pin it on me this time? True, it seems the police have better systems now. But still, it's been over a week since I held her tight and felt her tremble. She's long gone, deep in a hole that her daughter had wept over. I wish I could've been there. Funerals were always a glorious moment for me, a shining trophy of the accomplishment that I shared with so many others, even though they didn't realise it. I close my eyes, almost tasting the glory of being in that church, watching the townsfolk in West Green pray for the return of the missing girls. It was hilarious, in ways, to watch them think they could pray hard enough to make the girls come back, like the church was some wish-granting fountain. It was dramatic irony at its finest – I'd known the truth, that the girls were long gone. But that was also part of the thrill of it. Watching, waiting for everyone to realise what had been done. Sure, it wasn't as good as the kill. Nothing could equate to that climactic satisfaction, for sure.

Thinking on it, I know I'll get away with it, I always do. It feels like I've been born again. I'll get to live out the rest of my life basking in the glory of my accomplishment. I am finally at peace.

I had been brilliant, after all. No one had ever known. I've lived my life, have managed to get away with it all. Every bloody, orgasmic detail. From the kidnappings to the burglaries to the slashing of throats to the dismemberment of the bodies. I got to watch their terror close, right under their condescending noses. I got to read the articles. I could bask in their fear – all as a free man, though. It was splendid, really.

I shouldn't be surprised that they haven't figured it out. The police get everything wrong. They'd been so easy to outmanoeuvre, to outsmart. The bobbies had assured West Green they were safe. Six murders in, though, and I was able to fly under the radar.

After Adeline left West Green, I'd mistakenly thought that maybe I could find solace in the killing of another. I tried stalking new subjects, but it just never felt right. It wasn't the same. They weren't her. They weren't the one on my list. They didn't count, I realised. And even as I examined new possibilities on my route in Crawley, I knew there never would be another one. I'd failed. I hadn't carried through my plan. My thirst for death was strong, but my thirst for victory was stronger. After all, I wasn't a quitter.

No, I'm not a fucking quitter. I spent most of my life hungry and unsatisfied, thanks to Adeline Walker's escape. It was all her fault.

I often think of those plans I'd made on that day in 1959 when I finally realised my destiny. I finally realised what would give life meaning, would satisfy me. I understood what I was meant to use my brilliance for, what would make me worth something in the town. I wanted everyone to know my name.

And I wanted to make her proud.

The stupid, foolish, broken, dirty boy inside of me needed to make her proud.

I'd laid out the seven girls, had selected them in a meticulous fashion from my postal route. It all had to be just right. I would outdo that Haigh bloke everyone was so quick to mention when they talked of West Green. That man was a blasted fool, gave a bad name to killers. He made them all seem incompetent and foolish.

But *I* wasn't a pillock. I was, quite the contrary, an intellect. I was smart, even if people couldn't see it. On that day in May, nonetheless, when I'd made the official plan, I knew they'd see it eventually. I would leave behind a legacy, a true legacy, of brilliance, of patience, of strength.

Her death was going to be glorious. I'd known from the start she'd be the greatest achievement, the most beautiful killing. I wasn't going to hide it. I was going to put her on display for all to see. I would drag her lifeless body, intact, to the station, let everyone see her in her shining glory.

And then she left me.

My fists clench as I think about those moments when all was lost. But it's different now, I realise with a smile. I didn't fail after all. Finally, all these years later, I succeeded. I finished what I started, had snuffed out the last one. The body hadn't been hidden this time, after all. It was there for everyone to see. Even if they didn't figure out she was murdered, it didn't matter. She'd met her end just like the others, just like she was supposed to. I murdered seven women, seven beautiful women.

But I didn't set the fire. It pissed me off royally when the initial articles in West Green had accused the West Green Killer of the fire. Arson is for lazy assholes like that Oliver Parsons bloke. Arson is the kind of revenge someone takes who wasn't committed, who isn't smart enough to do anything else. I'm still certain that it had been that Oliver bloke who started the blaze, probably pissed at her for leaving. The detectives had ruled it an accident, but they were so often wrong. No, I'm certain that Oliver had something to do with the fire, no matter how innocent he seems.

Sure, I'm not one to talk, with all of the anger I have inside of me but still, that Oliver Parsons isn't a man to be respected. That one is too hostile, too haughty and too arrogant. He doesn't appreciate the beauty of women like I do. He didn't see Adeline for how magnificent she really was.

Even though I didn't set the fire, watching Adeline's house burn, hearing the screams, and seeing the charred remains had been exhilarating. They'd deserved to die in pain, after all, the Walkers. They'd pushed Adeline out of town. They'd been fucking stupid, letting her get away. When I watched the blaze that night, I was in a dark place. She'd just gotten away, and I felt like my grand plans were forever foiled. I seriously considered tossing myself into that fire, letting all of the disappointment of my failure be singed away.

But that wasn't who I was, I'd reminded myself. I wasn't a quitter, after all. I would roil and sulk in my failure and see it through.

And then, as if some sign from God telling me I had to finish, Adeline had wandered into Smith Creek Manor. What were the chances? After all those years! There she was, mine for the claiming. And claim her I did.

I reach under my bed to pull out the familiar, worn box. I open the tiny pine box, feeling the stack of letters underneath my rusty letter opener. A speck of blood rests on it. Adeline's blood from that night, that beautiful night.

Seven total letters rest underneath the opener, seven pieces of undelivered post. Letters from friends, from cousins, from acquaintances. Letters that had mysteriously disappeared thanks to my careful watch. I take out the letter addressed to Adeline Walker of West Green. I sniff the letter, the scent of aged paper and glue mixing into a riotously delicious cacophony. I savour the moment, raising the letter to my nose so slowly, so perfectly, that I wish someone were here to witness it.

Opening my lips, I put the letter in my mouth, clamping my teeth shut. My tongue tickles the edge of the envelope as my teeth firmly chomp down. My job is done. Adeline has met her end. I've succeeded on my mission.

All is well now. All is well.

I tuck the letter back into the box with the six others and the newspaper articles. I slide the box back under the bed.

Staring out the window on Floor Three of Smith Creek Manor Nursing Home, the sun beaming in spite of the strangling vines, I repeat my new mantra once more with a stoic reverence.

'They're all dead now.'

They are all dead, indeed. A crooked finger on my weathered hand raises to my forehead, finding the scar with a masterful precision. I trace the jagged, raised line back and forth, back and forth.

'Are you proud of me, Mum?' I whisper into the empty room, my voice cracking with the warped nostalgia of too much time passed and too much of life lived.

My finger traces over it one more time before I drop my hand to my side, place it in my pocket, and shuffle out to the corridor to live out what days remain. Whistling a haunting tune from long ago, I amble down the corridor, alone but satisfied for the very first time.

Brilliant boy. Brave boy. Victorious boy.

All is well indeed.

Acknowledgements

First and foremost, I want to thank the entire team at One More Chapter/HarperCollins for working tirelessly to make the publishing of this story a reality. I especially want to thank Katie for believing in my stories and for helping me achieve my dreams of introducing my characters to the world. I am so blessed that my books have such a wonderful place to call home. Thank you to the entire team for making *The One Who Got Away* the best version it could be. A huge thanks goes out to Laura for giving such amazing suggestions during the structural edit and really helping me finetune the plot. Thank you to Hannah for guiding *The One Who Got Away* into readers' hands and putting in so much hard work that happens behind-the-scenes; I am so lucky to work with you.

Thank you to my husband, Chad, for being my best friend and my biggest cheerleader through this entire process. You encouraged me to step out of my writing box and tell the stories that haunted me most. I am forever grateful for your love, support and your ability to make me laugh even on the toughest days.

I am also grateful to my parents, Ken and Lori, for fostering a love for literature and writing in me from a very early age. Your encouragement taught me to dream big and to work tirelessly to achieve those dreams. Thanks for all your love and support through the years.

Thank you to my in-laws, Tom and Diane, for always encouraging me and supporting me. I am blessed to be a part of your family.

A writer's journey is never travelled in solitude. There are so many people who have supported me along the way. A special thanks goes to Jenny for being my beta reader for both of my thrillers and for being my listening ear when I need a second opinion. You have given me the confidence I need to pursue my goals, and I am forever grateful for all that you do. Thanks also goes to my fabulous co-workers who support me in so many ways, especially Christie, Kelly, Lynette, Alicia and Maureen. Thank you to Kristin and Ronice for always checking in along the way and for encouraging me to keep writing. A special thank-you goes out to Leah for helping me with my questions about all things British.

Thanks also to Jamie for being the best friend a girl could have, and to Kay for being such a huge support from the very first book. I would also like to thank my grandma for being at every event and tirelessly promoting my works.

Additionally, I am so thankful for my local bookstores who support the big dreams of a small-town, local girl. Thanks especially to Jennifer for always being so welcoming to me for book events.

I want to thank every reader and blogger who has taken a chance on my works and read my stories. I couldn't do this without all of you, and I am forever grateful to all of you for welcoming my characters' stories onto your bookshelves.

Thank you to my mastiff, Henry, for being my moral support and best friend. Whether it's eating celebratory cupcakes or snuggling on the sofa on a tough day, you are so important to the entire writing process.

Finally, I want to acknowledge my grandfather, Paul Frederick, for his role in *The Home* becoming a story. A World War II veteran who was married to the love of his life, Dorothy, for over fifty years, my grandfather has quite a history of stories to share. It was a visit with him last summer that sparked the idea for this entire book.

Let me clarify that the nursing home he lives in is nothing like Smith Creek Manor, fortunately for us all. However, visiting with him one summer day and talking about all the friends and family he had lost over the years incited the idea for a book set in a nursing home. He made me think about how at the end of our lives, there are so many vulnerabilities, regrets and emotions swirling. It also made me realise how many fears could play out in such an unexpected yet potentially chilling setting. As many writers will tell you, stories often come from a place of mixing reality with a "What if?" question, and that's exactly what happened with this book.